We Are Them

The Apocalypse Syndrome

L.K. Samuels

Freeland Press   Carmel, CA   2021

Contents

Chapter 1

We Are Them:
The Apocalypse Syndrome

L. K. Samuels

When I swung open the door, I knew something was wrong. I could almost smell the faint whiffs of trouble in the air.

I can still remember that day so clearly. I peered inside the dimly lit room and swallowed. It was time to endure another torturous session. I had no choice but to endure a time-freeze, a place where time almost stood still. At least it seemed that way.

Even worse, I had to play the chump. I had to sit quietly and listen to the endless hours of psychobabble drivel. Sure, my life had faded into a never-ending circle of joyless reality. Such agony would soon be the least of my problems. I would soon star into my own special "Twilight Zone" episode. That role would take me on a madcap roller-coaster ride where I would never stop clenching my stomach muscles. If only I had the common sense to know when to jump off the cliff. That was my dilemma. Like most idiots, I had waited too long.

But back to the beginning. Back to where I decided that my marital problems were too big to handle. I had arrived at a stark conclusion: marriage was not a spectator sport. With that realization, I declared my marriage dead because, for all practical purposes, my wife was dead, metaphorically speaking. No matter how many marriage-counseling sessions I attended, nothing was going to change. I knew that they would not solve my problem. Yet, I found myself stuck in limbo-land. If I wanted to be released from my marital bondage, I had to endure the stinging nettles of therapy. I had to become the proverbial pincushion to my wife's grievance. I had to deflate, unpack, and reveal my alleged dirty laundry to a doofus thera-pist. I would rather die first. As it turned out, that was remarkably prophetic.

When I stepped inside the building, I peered across the room and spotted the thorniest idiocy of my life. The woman was sitting in a folding chair next to a half-bald psychologist hastily scribbling something in his notebook. There she was in all of her reptilian glory, a plain, cold-blooded creature who needed the warmth of the sun to keep alive. I had tried to spark the warmth of friendly conversation. Instead, she ignored me and shifted to a wish-you-were-dead frown. She was not just my estranged wife. No, she was a predator, inclined to flick her forked tongue with indifference or strike with deadly force. That might be an unfair assessment, but divorce is war from the get-go, and I was determined to win.

I started to breathe in deeply and sighed. For a time, it seemed like life could not possibly get worse. I was dead wrong. My misery scale would soon zoom off the charts and surprisingly it had nothing to do with my divorce proceeding against Sarah. No, the subject of divorce would soon fade away, like a mirage in the desert.

I shook my head and said nothing. Similar to past sessions, I decided to sit down right next to her, almost arms-length away from her motionless body. I could see what she was doing. She always did the same annoying antics. She would hang her head low and stared blankly at the carpeted floor, probably counting the loops in the Berber carpet. She was good at that—counting things that did not really matter. She always had a talent for taking lunacy to new heights. In my mind, Sarah did not belong to the human race. She belonged somewhere else, to some sluggish species that never amounted to anything.

I tried to look at her without looking at her. From the corner of my eyes, I watched her finally move. She lifted her right arm and began to fuss with her tangled hair. That spirt of activity lasted a split second. She soon returned to her comatose state, now more engaged in her carpet staring. I knew what she was doing. She had withdrawn into her own special imaginary world, a land that was never opened to me. Despite her obsession to escape reality, I felt compelled to watch her antics with a somewhat amused expression, as if I were an anthropologist examining the ancient ruins of long-dead people. I was never sure why I felt that way. She was never going to let me unearth her secret hideaways. She was never going to invite me inside and show me her hidden artifacts. Her lips were sealed shut.

Naturally, I felt that I had to reciprocate and return the favor. I had to keep my own distance. I had to conceal my own insecurities and inner fears. I guess we were all guilty of trying to conceal our dark secrets and purposeless lives. Unfortunately, this had become our pathetic routine. But at least she was not one of those freakish crazies. She was civil, not like those sourpusses that I began to refer to as "THEM."

I leaned back in my chair and rubbed my neck. My wife was many things, but she did not want to control every single atom in the universe. Sure, she had some bossy genes that bubbled up from time to time. Who doesn't? Who could resist the opportunity to scream a few obscenities when the shit hits the spinning fan blades? Yet, Sarah was not a connoisseur of finely crafted devilry. She had no burning urge to drive through landmines for the pure pleasure of killing innocent bystanders. She found no pleasure from tossing people into whirling wood chippers. No, that took a dedicated maniac with a diabolical scheme to conquer the world.

By the time, I had gotten all comfy in my flimsy metal chair, I stared down and slouched as the therapist began to drone over my tardiness. I would ignore his passé and trite words. Why get upset? At that time, I felt blindly blissful. I just wanted to wait out the clock, and completely ignore any suggestions. I had no urgent need of professional help. I could stare up at the wall clock for hours, hum a silent tone, and watch time tick away while dreaming about the

Dodgers finally winning the World Series this year. I could do that all day.

"Spencer!" Dr. Everett von Hagen began to speak louder with his heavy German accent. I ignored him. He began to drum his fingers on his chair. "Are you even listening to me?"

"Sure!" I replied. The doctor's forehead furrowed into ridges and grooves. I pretended to be interested in his wisdom, just as he pretended to be interested in my mental well-being instead of his exorbitant fee.

"If you don't listen, you will not be able to change. Why are you still avoiding your wife's concerns? This must be a two-way street. Otherwise, you're an avoider. Right, Mr. Crane?"

My response was always the same. With a big cheesy grin, I nodded like a bobblehead on my car's dashboard. I had my reasons for caring little about much of anything. I knew how to detach my emotions from my body. I could do that all day long without any professional help.

"Well, Mr. Crane?"

I shrugged my shoulders and gave a blank stare, pretending not to understand. All I wanted was a quick divorce. Nothing complicated. Just send her back to Venus so that I could live alone on Mars. Naturally, the authorities would not grant my wish without first attending countless hours of counseling, which only hastened the doom of our marriage.

"You know," Dr. Hagen said, "a new millennium is almost upon us. This is your chance for a new beginning. Or perhaps time to rekindle old commitments."

"Well, I'm always behind schedule. Anyway, the Y2K bug will probably kill us all."

"That's not an answer. You know, making up excuses can only prolong the pain and cause more damage in the future." The doctor peered forward, looking over his eye-glasses. "Right?"

I tried to downplay my response but his astute insight had caught me by surprise. With my typical knee-jerk angst, I blurted out my old pathetic shtick. "But that is the best excuse I have."

That did it. Our overpaid headshrinker groaned with an exhausted sigh. He next rolled his eyes and then flashed a disapproving glare. We were all miserable, as always.

Of course, this was when my wife would usually enter the fray. She knew I had spent most of my ammo and excuses. Now she came in for the kill. It was not a pretty sight. She stared at me with her sad puppy eyes. Next, she rubbed the back of her neck and droned with a perfect monotone voice, "I'm not a dead herring. You act as if I'm not here. You are always zoning out. Dead to the world and me."

"Now, now." Dr. Hagen focused his attention on my wife, mumbled something in German, and then finally adjusted his wire glasses. "Don't take the role of validator, Mrs. Crane."

That stopped her outburst, but only for a brief moment. She would bow her head, frown and clench her hands into little fists. "I'm trying to be more social. I know that is important."

That reply excited the doctor. He turned and looked at me, his face sparking with smug satisfaction. "And how do you feel about that?"

I hated that expression. I leaned back and simply put my hands behind my head. As he kept staring at me, I simply shrugged again. No point in encouraging him. My marriage was on life support, and all I wanted to do was pull the plug.

Naturally, my aloof response caused Sarah to go ballistic. She stood straight up and peered down at me from her moral high ground. "How dare you ignore me! You sit in that easy chair all day long and just vegetate." Next, she locked and loaded her index finger and pointed it at me as if I were a naughty child. "My God! You're just not there. You never say anything, do anything or go anywhere."

"You're wrong," I bust out with a self-satisfied grin. "I get up during commercial breaks."

Like always, Sarah shook her head, folded her arms, and glared at me with her dark, beady eyes.

"I believe you have a point, Mrs. Crane," Dr. Hagen broke in and took a quick glance at his watch. This was the moment when he would clear his throat, stand up, and wear a fustian face of disapproval. "What do you really think? Or is that too much to ask?"

"Well…" I usually paused. I knew that the doctor did not want to know my real thoughts. He had heard them countless times before and ignored them with a cold disposition. What I really wanted was to be left alone. Was that so terrible?

"Why are you so determined to dismiss these problems so… readily?" Dr. Hagen inevitably asked in a frustrating tone. "You cannot hide from your feelings forever."

Sure, I could, I silently murmured to myself. The real question was more troubling. Did I want to put any effort into trying? Sarah was a plain and unassertive woman without much education or good paying job skills.

"Well," Dr. Hagen asked, "Do you actually want to abandon her?"

I stared at him for a moment. Sure, I mumbled to myself. The thought of leaving her felt intoxicating. That was all I wanted. But every time that happy notion entered my brain, my therapist would sabotage it with more silly questions like, "You still have feelings for Sarah?"

The obvious questions were always the worst ones. The doctor and I knew it was a rhetorical question. Sarah had nothing in common with me. Never did. We were from different political planets—as if that really mattered these days. Anything I favored, she was always against. I was Catholic and she was one of these serious-faced Lutherans from Minnesota. I admired big monster trucks; she adored little fuel-efficient cars that could barely climb over a gopher mound. I worshiped sloppy Joes, and she despised red meat. I owned a Chevy; she had one of those fix-or-repair-daily Fords. In fact, the little message above my license plate said it all: "Driven over a Ford lately?" We could not even agree on what music to play. She listened to caterwauling Italian operas that lasted six hours, while I embraced the soothing beat of Led Zeppelin with two huge subwoofers hanging from the ceiling. Nothing matched.

"Why don›t you take a walk and see the lights of the city?" the doctor suggested near the end of every session. "They are very lovely from up here."

Usually, I just got up, displayed a disingenuous smile and walked out the door without any word or goodbye. Yet this time, for some unknown reason I agreed to take a short stroll. I am not sure what came over me or why it happened that night. Never before had I taken any interest in taking a moonlit stroll along a mountain ridge overlooking the city. I had no visions of romantic bliss. I had no plans to mend any crumbling fences or rebuild any broken bridges. The walk by itself would have been fine, except that I had to be in close proximity to my wife. To Sarah, fun meant a wild night at the church bingo parlor or singing in the choir on Sunday mornings. When I tried to engage her in some lascivious behavior in bed, she became the proverbial sack of potatoes, unemotional, unmoving, and yawning at every intimate moment. Most nights were not fanfares of romantic ecstasy; rather they were re-enactments of the night of the living dead.

We stood up, walked to the door, and wandered outside into the cool air. She said she wanted to talk about something important. Very important. She indicated that she had finally reached a final decision. Her only problem was that she still needed a little more time to phrase exactly what she wanted to say. I could wait.

We took a short, mostly silent walk past a few small resort motels and rustic cabins on the outskirts of Idyllwild. We just kept looking at each other in silence. I kept thinking how crazy all of this was. A reticent walk was not going to solve anything. We both knew that the counseling sessions were just delaying the inevitable. The "divorce" word was surely inscribed on our lips. We were destined to travel alone on separate highways.

Sarah did try to get me to chat. She started to reminisce about camping at a lake near Garner Valley. We did have fun with one broken-down pup tent, two ancient sleeping bags, and a jug of red wine. But that was when we were footloose and fancy-free, minus obligations, mortgage payments, and responsibilities.

We decided to stop at the edge of a jagged rock outcropping that overlooked Hemet over four thousand feet below. I remember thinking that the city seemed so small from up here. I had turned my face upwards, catching a glimpse of a shooting star. Then I stared back at Hemet. "The lights of the city are beautify tonight."

Sarah faced me and displayed a weak smile. Then she offered her typical divisive commentary, complaining that there were too many city lights and that someone ought to prevent any new development in the city.

I tried to ignore her grumbling and continued to gaze at the cold dark sky, wishing that somehow things might get better. Just after I kicked a rock down the hillside, Sarah turned to me and finally said something I was waiting to hear for over a year. I can still recall her exact words: "What's the point? We both want out. Why don't we just forget the counseling? Let's just go our separate ways. Isn't that what you want?"

Praise the Lord and pass the divorce papers! My face immediately lit up like never before. I told her that it sounded like a good plan. She said she would sign the papers. I smiled. She nodded. Finally, it seemed that things were starting to go my way. The world was now in perfect harmony; the ocean tides flowed in accord with the moon, and the movement of the stars followed their universal rhythms. Everything was splendid.

At almost that exact moment, Sarah lifted her arm and pointed at a fast-moving object in the eastern sky. The fiery ball was streaking almost straight towards us. Before it could hit a nearby mountain, the fireball suddenly stopped, hovered high overhead, and spun like a wooden top. It began to drift slowly towards the city lights. In a blinding flash of light, the object exploded like a 3,000-ton rocket. Long strands of silvery sparkles floated down and spread across the entire town, engulfing it in a dense cloud of purple gases.

I looked up and watched some of the colorful gas floated above us. The cloud eventually morphed into a purplish mist that cast a faint glow. As it lowered, Sarah reached up to touch it, but by then the vapors had quickly dissipated. I told Sarah that it was both insanely beautiful and mysteriously freakish. We oohed and aahed for a good couple of minutes. I speculated that the object must have been an old satellite that had fallen from space and exploded.

Surprisingly, Sarah agreed and turned to me. She reached for my hand and held it in a loving fashion. That was weird. The most bizarre part was that I did not mind. I began to feel a softness in my heart for Sarah. How was that possible? Maybe it was just a bad case of heartburn.

Sarah began to open up. She began to share her fear of living alone, without me. I felt compelled to sympathize with her plight. The thought was unnerving and uneasy. Nobody likes growing old alone. I acknowledged that simple fact, and she seemed pleased for once. She drew me closer as if she wanted to kiss me. I moved a little closer. This turn of events was totally messed up. I could not believe that I was somehow changing my negative attitudes towards the Wicked Witch of Northern Hemet. Amazing what a little strange gas could do.

Suddenly, I could not stop thinking that perhaps the counseling had actually been worth the money. What an amazing thought. This was truly a night to remember on so many levels. If only it had not been the night destined to mark the beginning of the end.

Chapter 2

It all started on a Monday, naturally. I had always detested Mondays more than any other day of the week. It was obvious. Mondays always heralded the first workday of the week. Perhaps if they just called Monday a Friday, everything would be tolerable. Of course, then Tuesday would take over that dreaded slot. No matter which way one shuffled the cards, nobody ever won.

"How was Idyllwild?" Tommy asked as he popped an organic bagel into the microwave in the employee's kitchen.

"As always, sheer pleasure."

"Oh, you must have been hanging out with your marriage counselor and wife again. Sorry, man. Real bummer."

Tommy Kramer was a good friend, as well as an immense source of amusement. He was thin, tall, and often bleary-eyed. He spent half his time listening to the Grateful Dead, basking in pure transcendent bliss. His scruffy goatee and stringy black hair gave him the glow of an anointed holy man instead of a dysfunctional bureaucrat.

Tommy always seemed out of place and ill-equipped to handle life's little challenges. Someone once referred to him as a starving squirrel who kept forgetting where he buried his food stash. Sure, Tommy's memory was impeccable, but his focus was narrow, blurry and often wavered somewhere else. And when his imagination stared to run wild, he became obsessed with taking center stage and basking in the limelight of attention.

Once I watched Tommy dig into his fat wallet looking for something of value. I had to ask. Apparently, he said he was searching for an old expired receipt for stereo equipment. Then with his bright face and gentle eyes, he explained Einstein's theory that time would someday end and everything would snap backward. You heard me right. He contended that time would someday go in reverse order back until it reached the Big Bang. He just wanted to make sure he had his old receipt because he wanted to know what he would buy before he had bought it. That was Tommy in a padded nutshell with psychedelic lights hanging from the ceiling. One rumor claimed that he was a permanent resident of the Twilight Zone. I just assumed he had lost contact with his home planet and decided to sit it out on earth. Anyway, since he had such a cheerful demeanor, nobody had the heart to call the local mental hospital and have him committed.

"See that fireball the other night, Tommy?" I asked.

"How big was it?" Tommy often answered a question with a question.

"Big. Exploded right over Hemet."

"Exactly when?"

"I guess, somewhere around 10 PM. You could not have missed it."

"Wasn't there, man. Sorry. Didn't I tell you I was going to West LA?"

"No."

"Another great Deadhead tribute for all of eternity. You keep missing all the fun. You need to get out. Life's not for amateurs."

"So, you did not see it?"

"See what?"

I slapped my hand across my forehead. I was getting nowhere with my zoned-out spaceman. "The big explosion in the sky. The other night. Lit up like an exploding sun."

"Boy, that would be something to see," Tommy's eyes blazed with excitement. "No, but I bet it was like the one in Russia in 1908. You know, the Tunguska Event. They said it was a massive 40-megaton blast. So extremely rad. I heard that people melted as if they were standing at ground zero in downtown Hiroshima."

"Well," I mumbled and stepped back a few feet. That was not what I had heard. I remembered a supermarket tabloid article exposing the truth about the incident. The Siberian remoteness prevented any human casualties. Then again, whom can you trust?

"They say that trees and plants were affected genetically. Some scientists believe it was an antimatter explosion. You know, a mass of antimatter shooting out from our galaxy core. Then it formed a plasma shield that burst when it contacted our denser air. I wish I had been there to see it firsthand."

"Yeah," I rolled my eyes. "I would like that too."

"Totally."

I was not going to argue about standing at ground zero in anticipation of a good and glorious time. That ship had passed under that bridge long ago.

"So, what did you see, oh, Captain?"

"Not much... really. There was this big flash and then a circular explosion. Saw it from the mountains in Idyllwild. The gas that floated down had a sort of purple haze to it. Probably up too high in the sky to cause much damage to the town."

"Still, it must have been tight. Wow! Wow!"

It took something special to get a double "wow" from Tommy. He was into so much strange reading material and ideas that even the FBI once felt an obligation to arrange short chitchat with him. That was a day to remember. I could see the agents across the office from my cubicle and I immediately knew that they were not selling accounting software. No. These agents were the best-dressed men I had ever seen. Not a single wrinkle in their black suits. They were no Fox Mulder or Dana Scully chasing bug-eyed aliens under haunted houses or through the sewer pipes of Washington, DC. These men looked almost pretty.

Well, they were investigating some crazy man from Palm Springs who had threatened a federal judge in Ohio. This half-baked loony said he was going to fire a laser beam two thousand miles away at the courtroom and kill the judge right in his judicial seat. Of course, I listened in and discovered that the FBI agents admitted that our own military could not perform such a technological feat. What did does Tommy have to do with this farce? He was on the crackpot's mailing list. It seemed as if FBI was wasting its time, but what did I know? I only paid the tab for the good suits.

"Have you heard about the 'second moon of the Earth?'" Tommy was just warming up.

I nodded. "Again?"

"No, no. They call this heavenly object Cruithne. Comes around every 700 years. Actually, it's an asteroid, but everyone calls it Earth's second moon. But believe me, there is more. Some people think it might emit some type of bio-field magnetism. Others argue that it has something to do with paranormal stimuli since strange things happened on Earth the last time it came around. We'll see it again in…"

"Tommy." I had to stop him or he would have gone on for hours. "I've got to get back to work. The people upstairs insist that I do something after I punch the clock."

"Sure, man. Rope in those little buckaroonies."

"Yeah." I turned and looked around for my special "I Hate Mondays" coffee mug. It was hiding somewhere beyond my reach, probably upset that I had failed to wash it again.

I actually hated to interrupt Tommy's gig. He was full of fascinating ideas, facts, and gibberish. I supposed some of it might even be true. But the truth did not matter. I enjoyed every sizzling cup of Tommy's gossip. It was entertaining as hell compared to work. In fact, if it were not for Tommy's anecdotal stories and oddball humor, I would have jumped in front of a garbage truck years ago.

After I located my mug, I moved it next to the coffee maker and proceeded to pour in the last dregs of luck-warm coffee. Before I could overwhelm it with heaps of sugar, Brian McNally from Accounting entered the kitchen. Tommy went for him like a hyena chasing after raw meat. Poor Brian.

"Found that ozone air purifier," Tommy smiled at Brian.

"Yes," he rubbed his chin. "It better work this time."

"No problemo."

As Tommy and Brian left, another infamous character sauntered in for coffee. It was Big Al Pugsley, one of the planning commissioners for the city of Hemet. He took the job more seriously than I ever had when I graced the board. For various reasons, I represented the board's bleeding heart, too soft on citizens who violated setback restrictions, easements, and zoning. The other commissioners called me "Citizen Crane" because I was often the lone holdout who was overly sympathetic to the plight of disappointed citizens. I did not mind the nickname. It was a far better moniker than what many outraged citizens called the other commissioners behind their backs.

"I heard you were in Idyllwild?" Big Al chomped on his cigar with vigor. Nobody could now smoke in City Hall, but the law said nothing about mouthing an unlit cigar until it became soggy and limp.

"Yeah."

"What route did you take after Hwy. 74?"

"Cedar Avenue to East Washington."

"Ramona Expressway would have been more efficient."

"Well, I didn't feel like taking it."

"Why not?"

"I don't know. I just didn't."

"See!" Big Al moved closer and prepared to pontificate. "What a waste of time and energy. There must be a way to make motorists chose more efficient routes. We must do something about this crisis."

It never took Big Al much time to get him all riled up over tiny nuisances and recommend a slew of half-baked policies. He had a whole notebook of impending crises stashed in his desk, and fortunately, that was where most of them were buried. We all hoped that none of his hare-brained schemes would ever see the light of day.

It was not that Big Al had a few missing light bulbs up in the attic. *Au contraire*, he was a pretentious Ivy Leaguer who had accumulated a lot of knowledge, but could not locate it when the need arose. In other words, as they say in Indiana, he was an educated fool. That fact alone guaranteed him a position of power, which put him within earshot range of Mayor Jessie Quinn's office.

Still, I must admit that Big Al had a point. I hardly ever took the most efficient route to the office or home or to the store. I knew there were shortcuts, but I was too lazy to find them. I guess I just detested rolling up one of those so-called easy-to-roll-up maps.

"The mayor and the council should be informed of this problem," Big Al said, "and as problems go, this is a really big one."

"Well, it's not quite up there with global hunger or nuclear winter." I loved to tease Big Al.

"I'm serious. We need more controls. When I look out onto the streets, all I see is anarchy. Anybody can drive anywhere, at any time, in any direction. Noon or midnight, people are out there driving without proper planning or knowledge of cartography. They have unfettered discretion and access. That is just plain nuts. Something is wrong. How do we know if drivers are doing the right thing?"

"But!" Tommy had come back into the room. "How do we know they're doing the wrong thing? You're assuming every motorist is in error? How do we know? Man... that is rather provincial."

Big Al eyed Tommy with disapproval; his frown flickered across his broad face, big mouth, and sea-green eyes. "Who are you to say I'm wrong?"

"Who are you to say that I'm wrong?"

"Well, someone must be wrong," Big Al huffed. "Anyway, don't you have some work to do?"

"Yeah, I suppose," Tommy lowered his eyes and looked at the ground without refocusing on Big Al. He turned and reached for his now-cold bagel and departed in haste.

As I watched everyone leave the kitchen, I wondered who was wrong and who was right. I mean, somebody had to make the right decision. Then again, maybe this illustrated the fact that nobody could make decisions for another. Perhaps each individual had to make such choices for themselves. Of course, that assumed that the general population was on the intelligent species list. That was a laugh. After years of dealing with Mr. Public, I had concluded that most citizens were clumsy, self-centered, and rather dim-witted. Most of my co-workers espoused this same notion. They saw citizens as idiots who just happened to pay our salaries.

Chapter 3

Whoever said that your home is your castle? Certainly not I. After working in the City Planning Department for years with a brief stint on the Planning Commission, I knew that nobody's home was safe from City Hall. Such land grabs were so pervasive that most considered it an acceptable way to do business, except for those who lost their land. These residents were surprisingly vocal. They argued that city officials ran Hemet as their own personal fiefdom. Others dubbed such takings "plain stealing." I tried to avoid such controversies. That was difficult. Even I had backed a number of eminent domain projects, which riled many of our abject serfs.

Almost everyone wanted our city to grow and prosper and to do that we needed land for bigger roads, schools, and government buildings. I could see that clearly, but when the city began to confiscate land for Q-Mart, sushi restaurants, and church parking lots, I was wary. We would uproot any family and bulldoze any home so long as it increased Hemet's retail tax revenues. Our power to destroy and create like a godlike entity was frightening. We felt invincible. Nobody messed with our Planning Department. Why, if Joe Stalin had been alive, he would have pinned red ribbons on our chests for outstanding nationalization of the community-at-large.

Luckily, I did not live in a redevelopment zone. In addition, my abode was almost historical, built back in the 1920s. It was a rather large bungalow with a broad front porch and double-hung windows—the type that is often painted shut because they would never open in the first place. Because of my job, I was confident that City

Hall would leave my little hovel alone and not rezone my little plot of land. It was sort of an unwritten rule that nobody in the bureaucracy disturbed another bureaucrat's territory. As for everyone else, let them eat chipped paint and old plaster.

I usually arrived home before Sarah. I would first feed Natasha, Tommy's cat, throw on some old grubby clothes, and read the newspaper in the kitchen. In some ways, I resented the routine feeding of Natasha. It was not really my cat. Tommy had rescued the abandoned feline from the animal shelter. She was supposed to stay for only a few days. Tommy promised me he would find a good owner. It has now been four years and counting. I guess he did as promised. I just did not know it was going to be me.

Before I could remove some food from the refrigerator, the witching hour had arrive. This was a sacred time when our relatives and neighbors would dishonor us with their presence. Rant was always the first trespasser. She was Sarah's half-sister, the baby of the family, but they were completely different. Sarah was meek and demure, but Ms. Elisa Rant had a fervent, forceful, and loud personality. Sarah took a flower-arranging class; Rant practiced Kung Fu. They were like day and night.

I just assumed that Rant had lived too long in war-torn Israel and came back with a nasty shrapnel scar on her thigh and a giant chip on her shoulder. Actually, her real surname was Rantburg, but she refused to be identified by her surname or first name. She went by one simple word—Rant.

She was always looking over her shoulders. I would too if I had her athletic body. Rant was quite stunning in her tight Gothic suit of black leather armor, metal studs, and dark glasses. I have often thought that she resembled Carrie-Anne Moss in the *Matrix* movies, oozing a raw badness from every pore, just daring anyone to mess with her.

Actually, Rant's paranoia was justified. Sarah explained that her sister feared a late-night attack by some revengeful skin-headed neo-Nazis. That happened on one occasion in Los Angeles, but she was the one who carved swastikas across their white foreheads.

"Spencer!" Rant shouted, pounding on the door. She was a part-time typesetter for the local newspaper, and worked odd hours, which seemed to encourage her erratic behavior.

"Just come in. It's unlocked." It was always unlocked, and she had a key, but she always had to make a grand entrance.

"Spencer!" Rant rushed inside, shut the door and leaned against it as if an angry mob was ready to ram it down with a telephone pole.

"Sarah is not home yet," I said without paying much attention to her.

"Someone is following me." Rant quickly whipped off her fashionable sunglasses. "They're spying on me."

"Again?"

"I'm almost sure of it. The man had no hair and no neck." She drew a pistol from under her jacket, lifted it up, and pressed it next to her cheek.

"An admirer, I'm sure."

In a flash, Rant's eyes narrowed to beady points and stared at me. The wrath in them could torch the entire room.

"Do you always have to show off your Glock?"

"Do you know that the Jews in the Warsaw Ghetto uprising had only five handguns? Only five! And they held off two German divisions."

"Did I mention that Sarah is not home?"

"Your lack of concern is appalling."

Rant had some reasons to be worried. There was gossip that a new skinhead group had come into town. It was more than a rumor. The city police had investigated and determined that the newcomers spent most of their time dancing to hate-rock and drinking beer out of dog bowls. At least, that was how one local newspaper columnist described it.

"By the way," I asked. "Did you see that fireball in the sky the other night?"

"No!" Rant snarled with a smirk plastered across her face. "I was in Los Angeles at a Defense League meeting. Where were you?"

"Well, I was..."

"I know," Rant interrupted. "Wandering Hemet's empty streets with a can of flat beer and Mr. Dead Head."

"No. You're wrong," I retorted. "I made a fortune at Billy's Bingo Parlor. I made enough money to buy a Rolls-Royce—you know, the itty-bitty matchbox version."

"You're a pig!" Rant huffed. "Sarah should have canceled your marriage years ago."

"Everything in its own good time," I smiled.

"Your time is up. You're way past your expiration date. You know why?"

I shook my head, curious about what she meant.

"Because you're like this town—dead and listless. They could film a zombie movie here and nobody would be able to tell the difference between the morbid residents and the brain-eating stiffs."

I had to grin. There was a lot of truth to Rant's statement. I did feel the sheer boredom. Life in Hemet was tedious, lifeless and meaningless. There was little to do or experience in Hemet with no real excitement. We simply loiter around and wait for our inevitable demise. At some point, we keel over in an abandoned parking lot, are loaded into an ambulance, deposited at a funeral home, embalmed with a formaldehyde solution, shoved into a crematorium, and finally poured into an urn. It is not glamorous, but at least it is something to do.

Hemet often resembled a cemetery. Hardly anybody graced the streets of Hemet on the weekends. Who could blame them? Downtown on Saturday night was quieter than a one-horse ghost town. Most residents rolled their wheelchairs to mobile home parks with a cup of pea soup in one hand and a bingo board in the other. Visitors often describe Hemet as the "Black Hole of Southern California," except our town pushed you out instead of sucking you in.

"Well, actually," I said, "there was some excitement the other night. A massive explosion sent flames shooting across the sky. Very beautiful."

"Sure!" Rant spat out her reply with the venom of a cobra. "Stop badgering me!"

"You would have enjoyed it. Very eerie and disturbing. It felt as if something had changed. Something important."

Rant looked away and raised her right eyebrow, appearing deep in thought. "I did sense something last night." She walked a few steps, stopped, and tilted her head to one side. "It was a strange sensation. Like something had taken hold of the world, and wouldn't let go. That something terrible was coming our way." She shook her head. "I must have drunk too much Slivovitz."

"Well, it was not that crazy." I felt like laughing but dared not. She did not take kindly to criticism. Besides, Rant's past predictions were rarely indicative of future events. A 90-day weather report was more accurate.

Not long after Rant holstered her Glock, Tommy came beckoning at my door. He did not knock. He never knocked. He swung open the door with gusto, as if he just concluded an impressive magic show, and now demanded a round of applause. In no time, Tommy rushed past Rant, entered the kitchen, and plopped down in a wooden chair right next to me. "What's up?"

"The usual."

"No, Bro!" Tommy quickly radiated the room with his infectious smile. "Anything can happen. Nothing is ever constant in the universe. You have it all wrong. You need to open yourself to a universe brimming with infinite possibilities. You must expand your brain by immersing yourself in creativity."

I shook my head. Tommy probably had just read another strange science fiction novel. There was no reason to try to counter his fantasies. He has been that way since I befriended him at Mt. San Jacinto Community College. Tommy's sheer idiocy proved that college night classes bring out the strangest bat-crazy people. Then again, Tommy had taken several pre-med courses and passed with flying colors.

"Okay, what do you need now?" I asked with a straight face.

"Oh, the usual. I have ten more banana boxes to store."

"Not here!"

"Just ten small, tiny weeny ones. Mostly engine parts."

"For your vehicles?"

"No, they're for a Mercedes-Benz."

"But you don't have a Mercedes-Benz."

"Well, yeah, but someday I might."

I took a deep breath and held it, waiting for a sigh of relief to calm me down. I should have never allowed the camel's nose into my tent. Now his entire bulky body laid claim to my abode. Maybe I should post a sign outside advertising a few storage spaces still available. Sometimes I wondered if he wanted a good friend or just a good place to store his stash of worthless junk. He still had 60 big banana boxes stacked against the wall in the garage.

"You have so many already. Just let me add a few more and..."

I thrust my hand in front of his face to stop him from talking. "No more. That's it."

"I could make a list of all the boxes and their contents."

"Really? How long would that take?"

"Well...ah..." Tommy struggled to find the right words. "Not too long." He shrugged his shoulders and uttered in a weak, broken voice. "Maybe three or four weeks."

This was sheer madness. Last year Tommy had secretly stuffed an uncountable number of banana boxes in my attic, which almost collapsed the living room ceiling. Luckily, I saw the ceiling cracks before they could cause a mass extinction of the Crane family. I had temporarily installed 4x4 beams in the living room to prop up the ceiling.

He had also secretly stacked his cardboard boxes in the third bedroom. For a time, I could not even open up the door to experience the horror in living color. Finally, I had to rent a self-storage unit for most of his rubbish. I guess you could say that Tommy was the junkman's best friend. Yet, in spite of his huge, unending collection of stuff, he still dumpster dived behind the commercial buildings late at night. If I had rented the massive storage unit he had first requested, there would be no need for any city garbage trucks.

Tommy was not just Hemet's most famous hoarder par excellence. He also collected old Volkswagen bugs jam-packed with highly valued rubble of questionable worth. His mobile storage units were scattered across the city, usually parked in outlying public streets. His mostly non-operative vehicles did not go unnoticed. The police regularly impounded them. Sometimes when Tommy was low on funds, I would bail out his hobby. I felt more like a banker than a loyal friend, but it only took a few minutes before I would give in to his dire pleas for help.

I stared at Tommy. "I desperately need a beer."

Without hesitation, Tommy pulled out a six-pack from his large knapsack. They were usually some strange-but-cheap foreign beer from Trader Joe's. He pulled open the beer can tab, reached over and handed me a cold one.

"So, what's also up?" Tommy asked.

I turned to Tommy and spoke softly. "Well, like always, Rant predicts doom for Hemet because of last night's fireball."

Frowning, Rant stared at me with a cold, icy look. She turned and started to rummage through the refrigerator searching for something edible. Find nothing appealing, she leaned against the wall and pulled out a small paperback book from the bookcase. She began to read.

"Wow! Really! Awesome, man!"

Tommy opened his beer can and lifted it up to celebrate. We toasted to limitless money and more storage space.

I wanted to up the ante on celebrating the future. "How about toasting to the new millennium?"

"You want to welcome the new millennium?" Tommy's face soured. "No, that's not appropriate."

"Why not?"

"It's so disappointing. Our future is not futurist."

I lowered my jaw. "And what is that supposed to mean?"

"By now, we should have had a large space station established on the moon. Hey, remember the *2001* movie? I mean, we're very far away from that destiny. We don't even have regularly scheduled flights to the lunar surface. How can we study the mysterious monolith? And where is the spaceship that was supposed to orbit Jupiter? No flying cars, no space fleet. What future? Very disappointing, man."

"Well, then let's instead toast to surviving the Y2K bug."

Tommy suddenly cheered up. "Yeah, that's something to look forward to. But we're still all going to die."

I patted Tommy on the shoulder. "Don't worry, that's almost a haft a year away. Who needs computers, TVs, or electronics? All that is required for life is an ample supply of cold liquor. Right?" Of course, that loony proposal called for another round of crashing our beer cans together and spilling some on my checkerboard linoleum floor. "Besides, Rant thinks that the strange explosion in the sky foretells another streak of bad luck."

Rant could not help but listen to our idiotic gabfest. She strolled in front of us, stopped, and peered down. "You are the biggest losers in the universe."

I raised my hand to object. "Hey, maybe the galaxy, but not the whole universe." I was starting to feel the effects of the beer.

"Why?" Rant tapped her fingers on her thigh.

"Well, I've never been to the universe. I think we'll stay with something local." Tommy just loved my joke line, but Rant was losing her patience.

Rant sniped in her usual irritated tone, "It was just a feeling. That's all. Grow up and get over it!" She eyed Tommy with open disdain. She often chided my drinking buddy as an aging hippie who never grew up. . I had to smile. I considered Tommy as my secret weapon against Rant, sort of my Kryptonite to Rant's paranoia and anxiety.

"There's a rumor," Tommy said, eyeing Rant, "that the fireball could be seen from as far as Utah. Utah! Boy, that's really far, I mean farther than any universe. Right?" His nonsensical assertion was an attempt to incite the wrath of Rant. It fizzed. Rant refused to play along.

Now it was my turn to stir the pot. "You want to hear about a really potential disaster in Hemet!" I said in an effort to keep the conversation from drifting back to the holocaust or freaky skinheads. "Big Al at work wants to make commuters take the Ramona Expressway. All for efficiency's sake. Now is that crazy or what?"

"You're not serious?" Rant looked down at me, appalled.

"Hey, it's Big Al. He'll forget all about it by tomorrow. Anyway, we should all take a more efficient shortcut to our destination. You know, save a little money on gas."

"He's totally a control freak." Tommy grabbed another beer, leaned back, and chugged it in one long gulp. "They're dangerous hombres."

"Yeah," I added, "If you want to control people just sow fear and anxiety. Works every time. And if an obsessive-compulsive jerk takes charge, well, he can convince almost anyone to do a swan dive over a 60-foot cliff."

"Yeah, like in Western movies," Tommy said. "Just shoot some guns in the air. Cows will trample people, knock over chuck wagon, or terrorize a town. I think I saw that in an old John Wayne movie."

"He's not serious?" Rant interrupted Tommy's overview of Western movie lore. "Come on! Big Al was just bluffing."

"Oh, I think he is just looking for something to do," I said as I reached into Tommy's knapsack to retrieve another beer. "Big Al is mostly wind and whine."

"Hasn't he done enough?" Rant almost shouted. "I mean I heard him advocate for more eminent domain seizures. And more disarm-the-victim laws. We have a right to defend ourselves."

Listening to Rant, one might think that Hemet was a high crime area, comparable to East Los Angeles. In truth, crime was not much of a problem. It is difficult to rob a 7-11 and flee the crime scene in a two-wheel walker. Still, the Hemet police were rather slow in making their appearance.

With a sober face, Tommy stood and stretched out his arms. "Rant is right. This is serious. You cannot control where people travel on the public street. We have a right to go where we want to go. Right?" Tommy looked at me with his big puppy eyes.

I decided to take a different approach. "Well, if it is for public safety, I suppose you could, with enough state and federal funds. I mean, with enough hard cash, you could construct a bridge to the Australia. But it is a stretch to use police power to enforce who travels where. That kind of talk is utter lunacy."

"They have the power to do anything," Rant raised her voice. "Haven't they empowered armies to oppress minorities?" Rant was curt. She always got back to the subject of anti-Semitism and Nazi atrocities. She acted as if we were still fighting World War II. Maybe that was why she had enrolled in self-defense courses at the local community college. She was ready to fight any oppressor. Now she just had to find one.

"I mean the city could provide maps and advice to people to find the more efficient driving routes," I said. "We could start up an educational program with workshops and seminars and put out press releases. Create community awareness. No big deal."

"Wouldn't that create more jobs for city workers?" Tommy asked.

"Sure," I replied.

"Where's the money going to come from?" Tommy asked. "Like, I mean, they never give me a raise."

I had to hold in a laugh. Tommy's performance was not good enough to command any salary. Of course, I held an extremely biased opinion about his work skills; I was his good friend.

"I thought the city was strapped for funds," Rant said. "They keep saying they have no money. Where will it come from?"

I had the perfect answer. "It's simple. We get city officials to go around and steal anything not bolted into the ground—you know, trash receptacles, kids swing sets, inflatable pools. All the expensive stuff."

"Don't they do that already?" Tommy's grin widened.

"You should know," I said.

"Like, for sure!" Tommy started his little comedy act. "I see them at midnight; they're the 'Morlocks of Hemet' Creatures of the night. They steal dogs and campfire pits. Beware of the dumpster divers! They will take your banana boxes."

It was not very funny, but Tommy's childlike charm compensated for his lack of timing and humor.

Actually, it was pathetic, considering that he worked for the government, too. Of course, for Tommy, "work" was too strong a word to describe what he actually did at City Hall. He was in my Planning Department, but spent his time at the front desk trying to explain zoning and building codes. Everyone, even the old-timers, had to struggle to decipher our unintelligible codes that accumulated more pages than the Bible.

Tommy was no exception; he could become as befuddled and confused over the simplest questions from the public. When frustrated, he would drag a real city planner to the counter to explain our outdated, contradictory, and complicated rules.

"You tell Big Al." Rant finally reached for a beer. "Tell him that I will never follow his road advice."

"Even if it is a better route?" I asked.

"I don't care. I do what I want. And as long as I don't harm anyone, what's wrong with that?"

Rant's philosophy always seemed plausible until the particulars came into play. She hated taxes and governmental agencies, calling them coercive. She would almost growl when anybody had a kind word for a politician or bureaucrat, which had me softly tiptoeing around her hard-core ideals. Usually, her anger was reserved for the system of rulership, not the people caught in the middle, like me. Still, I had a feeling she would have loved to funnel all the government people into the nose of a rocket bound for Mars.

Before we could delve deeper into crazy talk, Sarah walked through the door and briefly interrupted our intense debate. Like always, she would say her customary "hello" to everyone and retire to another room. For some strange reason, I felt an urge to follow her into the living room. Usually, I reigned over a kitchen inhabited by intoxicated multitudes. But this time I sought out the meek and sober.

"How was your day?" I asked.

"You're asking me about my day?" Sarah stared at me.

"Why not?" I asked.

"You have never shown any concern before. Never."

"Never say never," I paused. "So, how are you?"

Sarah stood there for a moment. She looked perplexed, unable to figure out what to say next.

"Oh… I guess I am fine. Yes,… doing well, I suppose."

"Want to do something?"

"Just us?"

"Sure. We've done that before. Gee, I think we have at least once or twice." Now I was beginning to question my own memory. I could not recall the last time I asked her out.

"We could go to a movie," I volunteered.

Sarah looked down and softly bit her lower lip. "Ah… You know I don't really care for movies."

I nodded. "Right. Well, what about dinner at some nice restaurant?"

Sarah sneered. "You know that I'm allergic to most foods."

I felt like I was talking to some old, crippled woman in a nursing home—no alcohol, no high-calorie foods, no sudden movement, and no fun. She might as well live in a plastic bubble so that our world would not contaminate her small, sterile environment.

At first, she frowned, but soon nodded in agreement. "I suppose I could find something to eat at a restaurant."

"Great!" I was finally going out on a date with my wife. She had decided to leave the Bat Cave for a little food and excitement. I did not know if I could contain my excitement.

"But only if I pick the restaurant," she stipulated.

"Sure," I said knowing full well that she had no idea where to eat. She always made her own lunch and dinner and generally hid from the consuming masses.

I kicked out little Ms. Rant and crazy Tommy. Of course, I did it with diplomatic finesse by asking them if they wanted to come along. I already knew the outcome beforehand. Rant avoided public places like the plague, unless surrounded by her band of close and armed friends. As for Tommy, he hated refined "dead foods" found at most eating establishments. Of course, I had to take a little dig and offer to buy him a big bag of French fries. That got him out the back door fast.

We finally agreed on an Italian restaurant—the Butterfly Café—which I had frequented when I attended San Jacinto College. After arriving at the restaurant, Sarah took considerable time choosing something to eat and settled on a Cobb salad. I went for the lasagna. The evening was surprisingly enjoyable.

"So, how is it going at work?" Sarah asked, actually showing a good deal of interest.

I glowed with a smile. "Not much. Same old bull crap. Except for one strange curiosity. Big Al wants to tell residents which streets to drive to get to their destinations. Now,... how crazy is that?"

Sarah laughed. "You're kidding."

"No, it's true. Of course, nobody is going to listen to such drivel."

"Are you so sure?"

"Trust me, Al's big idea will be gone like the wind in a flash.

"You mean the big windbag will soon be deflated?"

"Precisely!" In sheer delight, I reached out and cupped my hand over Sarah's forearm. She reciprocated, leaning over to plant a sweet kiss on my cheek. What a great evening. We talked late into the night. Her eyes twinkled and my spirits lifted to new heights. It was magical; it was stimulating. What was happening to us?

I began to wonder if all those sessions with Dr. Hagen were paying dividends. And yet it was more than that. Ever since that weekend in Idyllwild, I had felt different. I was more relaxed, and plagued by less anxiety about work, life in general, and about Sarah. It reminded me of some offbeat science fiction movie where paradoxical worlds collided, and nobody knew who they were. It was a strange sensation that I could not shake.

The dinner was delightful. I actually discovered a few things that I never knew about Sarah. Imagine, married for almost 10 years. I never knew she liked to watch baseball when she was a child. Who would have guessed?

Maybe we did have something in common after all.

Chapter 4

I have rarely sat through a meeting that accomplished anything of importance. They were usually a sheer waste of time and energy. In a sense, such meetings resembled musical chairs. Everyone had one sole purpose, to keep from losing a chair. If they lost their chair, it meant late-night work assignments without extra pay. So, when Mayor Jessie Quinn announced a meeting with most of his city workers, I knew I was about to become a chairless volunteer. I was going to be assigned longer hours, get less sleep, and become burdened with more responsibility.

Standing behind an impressive solid wood podium, the mayor cleared his throat and spoke in a loud, commanding voice. He thanked everyone for coming, pointed out the important people in his staff. Then he began a long-winded rant about an imminent crisis threatening Hemet. To solve this catastrophe, he urged city officials and staff to immediately introduce a new program to address this impending calamity.

All of this talk about doom and gloom sounded serious, except that the mayor had failed to explain the exact nature of this impending storm. He was resorting to political hype designed to scare the public—to panic people into doing things they did not want to do. I had seen such political schemes go awry in the past, where public officials offered bowls of hogwash for empty sugarcoated promises. The public got nothing. To my way of thinking, nothing was not an awful lot.

My first reaction to anything new was to question its validity. In fact, I questioned everything. Someone once accused me of being skeptical of skepticism. I took that as a badge of honor. Devoted to old habits, I felt compelled to doubt every possible thing in the world. Of course, I often paid a dear price for my saucy insolence. So, without much hesitation, I foolishly rushed in where angels feared to tread. I stood, raised my hand, and let it rip.

"Mr. Mayor, so—what is this crisis?"

"Well, Spencer," Mayor Quinn's beady eyes trained their burning glare directly on me. "We all know how serious this crisis has become. It is our duty to prepare ourselves to defend our city and our way of life. We must see this as our responsibility to future generations. This will someday be seen as our finest hour."

I stood there, arms folded, and waited for a real reply. He had not answered my question. I had expected that.

The mayor swallowed and struggled for a deep breath. He tried to maintain a pretense of calm, waiting for someone to come to his rescue. Nobody did. Apparently, few city officials had read Quinn's lengthy proposal. "Okay." The mayor finally resumed eye contact with me. "So... you want some particulars? Right?"

I simply nodded.

The mayor turned to his left and then to his right, expecting someone in his staff to help him with the question. Again, he was disappointed.

"Fine," the mayor exploded. He tightly clenched the podium with his big hands and leaned forward. "Well, if you had been listening, Spencer, you would know that answer."

"Well, I'm just in a low-level staff position, but I would appreciate it if you could restate the crisis and our plans to solve it?"

Now I had done it. The mayor seemed speechless, approaching the moment where he was ready to push the panic button. I was really enjoying this opportunity to embarrass a public official. It did not last long.

One of the first things you learn about politics is that if you cannot answer a question from the public, you give it to a subordinate.

Almost on cue, Mayor Quinn turned to his side and eyed Colonel Jack Bellamy, the city manager, who seemed delighted to take over.

Jack's speech was brief and almost cryptic. "It's all about the lack of directions for people in motorized vehicles. This is because there is little social cohesion in America. This injustice must change."

I sat back down and turned silent. To Jack's way of thinking, you were either with him or against him. His eyes would pop out at the least hint of disapproval or criticism, causing low-level staff to nickname him "Old Fish-Eyed Jack." One moment he could be having a scary temper tantrum, while minutes later he could display a delightful sense of humor, depending on how the day was going. He was an elected councilmember until the city manager position suddenly became available.

Next, with a flick of the wrist, the mayor motioned for Joe Maffini to take center stage. Tall and slender, Joe was one of the more memorable city council members. When he became angry, his veins would swell across his temples. He was a harsh taskmaster who complained about everyone and worried about nothing unless it personally affected him. With his five-o'clock shadow, he looked like an old-style political boss from Chicago who could miraculously raise the dead so they could vote in an election.

Next came Leonid Sergeevich Mikhailovsky. With a slight push, Big Al nudged Lenny into the center light. He slowly stepped towards the podium, appearing to fear the limelight. Lenny was a Russian immigrant who arrived in America not long after the Berlin Wall fell. His only passion seemed to be chocolate and admiration for strongman dictators. But chocolate was his true vice. No matter where he roamed, he carried a half-eaten chocolate bar in his hand.

Lenny was in his mid-fifties, plumpish, gray-haired, and wove in and out of the meeting like a friendly squirrel begging for food. He was constantly rearranging his eyeglasses. Few people wanted to talk or share information with a foreigner who was involved in union activities and rumored to be a former KGB agent.

Lenny stuffed his candy bar in his pocket and wiped the sweat from his head with his palm. He looked over the podium, paused and cleared his throat. "Great to see all here today. I think Mayor has good idea. Very durable. We need much public dedication to make Hemet better city." He bowed his head and rushed out of the room.

Gene Holiday came next, our Vice Mayor. He did not even bother to approach the podium. With a sudden spurt of awareness that almost caused him to stumble over his words, Gene proclaimed everything peachy-keen. He gushed with a short litany of well-worn platitudes that had very little to do with the mayor's new initiative. Gene had the habit of trying to be the shadow hiding behind some else's shadow. Invisibility was his strength; he was a wanderer without any sense of direction. The rumor was that he was saddled with loads of credit card debt and lived with his mother. He was Hemet's most notorious "povertarian."

After Gene's meandering statements, all eyes turned back to Mayor Quinn at the podium. With a weak grin, the mayor finally picked up an official document, leafed through it, and began to read. "The time has come to make our city's motorists more efficient. Our fine citizens are not using the public streets properly. Therefore, the City Council has decided to establish a new program and department to inform citizens about the best possible routes in their daily travels."

The mayor paused, cleared his throat, and glared directly at me, as if I had committed some unforgivable hate crime. I began to feel like dead meat until I realized that our tight city budget had no additional funds available for such an ambiguous program. In fact, most departments were growing much more slowly than in previous years. One city accountant secretly acknowledged that our city was essentially bankrupt.

I stood up again and raised my hand. "What about our budgetary problems? I thought we were trying to save money?" Of course, Mayor Quinn had already anticipated my next move. It is hard to outguess career politicians.

"That's not a problem," Mayor Quinn declared with a wave of his hand. "I know we have some budgetary problems. But which city doesn't? Every mayor deals with tight budgets. Nothing unusual. We'll simply submit a plan to increase our tax revenues in the coming months. In the meantime, we can save money by borrowing a few people from each department and create a new agency, which we have named the Driving Efficiency Department. Big Al has graciously agreed to be the first director of DED. He will notify each employee who is being transferred to his department. That's all."

Mayor Quinn turned to the city manager and invited Jack to say a few parting words. Jack stood there in a fixed position while smiling with his big teeth showing.

"Alas, we all have to make sacrifices," Jack assured in an insincere tone. "I want everyone to understand our priorities. I want you to know that we consider DED a breakthrough program. It will make Hemet dazzle like a progressive city with a yearning desire to provide every service possible for our dear citizens; a city that is not afraid to challenge conventional governance; a city that will usher in a new dawn of government relations. This will be a landmark program. We will be the vanguard of a new day. Thank you for coming."

I shook my head. I could see this was going to be a first-class disaster. I prided myself on having a few superpowers. I had the X-ray power to detect pure bunk, along with projecting rays of skepticism. I was proud of my talents, except that nobody took a particular note. I guess I needed a red cape and an eye mask.

That was my good side. But I also suffered recurrent bouts of weakness. Like Superman, I was vulnerable to a type of kryptonite that compelled me to care little about my fellow man. And why should I? They were always a disappointment. Let humanity stew in its own juices. I was no hero. I would often cower when I heard strange or loud noises. Who was I to inform the public about the pitfalls of DED? I was only endangering my career and wasting my time. Let the public be damned. Besides, I was far too busy in the Planning Department to devote any time to uncover corruption at City Hall. I was sure that DED would simply die a natural death. It was nothing but a money sink that would fade away in a few months.

As my pessimism battled my opportunism, I noticed something moving towards me. Out of the corner of my eye, I saw a big shadow lumbering directly at me. I assumed it was Big Al; he was also good at turning light into darkness.

"Spencer. Come over here." Big Al waved an enticing finger at me.

I wandered over and stood in his big shadow, expecting to have a long, unpleasant chitchat that would blur the line between fantasy and reality. I felt trapped. My boss had the superpower of intimating people while boring them to death. All with the flick of his forked tongue.

"You know," Big Al inched closer. "I have a need for an expert like you. Any interest in signing up for my new department? You can be my right arm, my second-in-command. And get a good paycheck to boot."

I guess my mouth must have unhinged wider than the Grand Canyon. Big Al seemed to have taken a keen interest in my silver fillings in my back molars.

"Well, come on? What do you say?"

I mumbled for a moment. Finally, I stared directly at Big Al. "Sorry, but I'm kind of booked up with City Planning projects. We have that new condo development on State Street and…"

"I know you have a heavy workload, but I can partition it out to the other planners. And I can promise you a big sweet pile of money for your assistance."

"Who will take my position in Planning?"

"No problem. I can promote Tommy to an official, but temporary, city planner."

"Tommy? Tommy Kramer who still gets lost between the mailroom and the cafeteria?"

"Sure, but as a temp. We can get him on the cheap."

I have told many people that you get what you pay for. Perhaps Tommy would do a splendid job in planning—screwing up zoning codes, wreaking havoc during on-site inspections, and misinforming future developers. I was feeling better already.

"What do you say?" Big Al chomped on his soggy cigar.

"I suppose I could try something new," I responded while viciously scratching my forearms. They would get itchy every time stress reared its strained head.

"Good. We need a man with your ability to plan and control. Why… with your skill we could organize the future all the way up to Armageddon! And, oh yes, did I mention that you'll be my main man?" He did, but I was not going to correct him. I did not want to interrupt Big Al's pageant of self-congratulatory joy.

Without saying goodbye, Big Al turned and rushed off to shake everyone's hand. I wished I could be that delighted. Only one word could describe my feelings—"drudgery."

Eventually, Big Al ran fresh out of hands to shake. He made his way back to me. He smiled at me and shrugged his shoulder. I felt compelled to say something nice.

I smiled back and nervously rubbed my neck, "Ah… I guess I should thank you for thinking of me." I reluctantly replied.

"Hey, I came up with this project. Somebody had to."

"And I am sure that your department will provide a vital service for the public," I said, stretching the truth to its breaking point.

"You bet your sweet ass. And I made it all possible," Big Al cajoled.

Of course, I had an endless fountain of doubts and fears. There was a theory that Tommy loved to banter about late at night after a few beers. It was dubbed the "boomerang effect." It stated that any time a government agency attempted to do some great service for the community, the exact opposite resulted. It sounded nuts enough to be true. I guessed I would soon find out if the theory held water or not.

"What you think, Spencer?" Lenny sidled next to us. Lenny was the recently elected shop steward, and wandered City Hall to keep an eye on management. He was usually cheery, but in an artificial, disingenuous way. He said he was looking out for the workers' best interests, but I suspected he was interested more in his own well-being. And still, there was something disturbing about this Russian immigrant who spoke English like Japanese-written stereo instructions. With his dark, stubbly beard framed by wire-rim glasses, he embodied the ragtag look of a revolutionary Bolshevik. I could see that image in winter, when Lenny dressed in his long black trench coat and a fur cap embroidered with a red star. He bore a frightening likeness to a fat Vladimir Lenin.

"Well, I'm sure it will help someone," I said.

"We'll need plenty workers. That's what I do see." Lenny grinned.

"Of course, you realize we don't have any budget for this program." I was just going back to my practical side. I had taken some economic courses in college. Money was one of those items that economists call limited resources. There was only so much of it hanging around in Hemet at any particular moment in time. But like magic, if the city council voted for a project, money would seemingly appear out of nowhere. If only I could find some of that invisible money.

"They will find good funds. Raise taxes, no?"

"We just did that."

Lenny cocked his head to the left. "No problem. They've got ways to pluck geese again without geese knowing."

It was a revealing metaphor. Historically, I suppose Russians were experts at fleecing unsuspecting fowl. I just hoped that Americans were smarter birds.

"Wow." Tommy finally came over to me and joined our merry band of bureaucrats. "Sounds like a big project, man. I hope they did not bite off more than they can chew. Gluttony is a big health problem."

"Who cares about healthy food?" Big Al said as he muscled his way into our conversation.

"Really big shoo," Big Al boasted, trying to imitate Ed Sullivan›s voice. "And, of course it was my idea. You know, it's so damn good that I'm sure the city will someday commission a bronze statue in my honor. I can see it now. Hey, maybe they'll turn it into a holiday. 'Big Al's Day.' You know, close the banks, schools, and post office. Why, I bet they'll close down everything."

"Yeah," I said with a straight face. "It might turn into a regular going-out–of-business shut-down holiday."

"Will be magnificent. Good goose for everyone," Lenny grinned. "Make big union."

Tommy turned to me with a puzzled look. "What about the side effects?" Tommy had a habit of publicly disagreeing with people who embraced rosy pictures of the future. "What if the new department develops a life of its own?"

"What in the blue blazes are you talking about?" Big Al›s wide smile trickled back to a puny snicker.

"You see," Tommy started to explain, "we can only assist drivers up to a certain point. They need to figure out how to get around the planet on their own. Otherwise, they will become dependent on us.

You know, calling us all the time. They will become disoriented and helpless."

"We want them dependent on us," Big Al roared. "Hey, we're supposed to take care of our citizens. What are you—a subversive?"

"It's all about not feeding the bears." Tommy boldly stated without further explanation.

We looked at Tommy with blank stares. There did not seem to be any logical connection between feeding bears and a government program to help drivers find their way.

"Like man, don't you see? The forest rangers always warn tourists not to feed the bears, so they don't get too dependent on handouts. They will lose their natural ability to forage on their own, and destroy their self-reliance. If the handouts stop, the bears will starve."

"What gobbledygook!" Big Al huffed. "Feeding bears? Someone should feed Tommy to a grizzly bear."

"You make good Russian bear, no?" Lenny beamed and patted Tommy on the shoulder. "Try get some certified health care. People need much help and we can do it." Lenny turned and watched a group of workers near the water cooler. "Must go. Union work."

Appearing bored with Tommy's nonsense, Big Al followed Lenny to the crowded water cooler, eager to toot his horn to a larger audience.

I glared at Tommy. "Ever wonder why you never get promoted?"

"Sure, but Big Al's scheme could spiral and flush everyone down a gnarly sinkhole. Not pretty."

"Unlikely. It's just a little program and it's voluntary. Nobody has to pay any attention to it. So why the hostility?"

Tommy shrugged. "Not sure, man. I just have this bad vibe. Something does not seem right. I sense peril at the visceral level. As if the earth will be swallowed up when our galaxy collides with another galaxy. And then it will resemble..."

"Tommy," I interrupted. "You're just imagining this because of what Rant said. You need to refocus. Don't go off half-cocked."

"How about fully-cocked?" Tommy said with a childish tone that seemed too cute to resist.

"Sure, why not?" Poor Tommy. He just could not focus on anything important. Yet I was starting to understand his reference to his "don't feed the bear" analogy. Actually, if he had expressed it more coherently, it might have been rather profound. It might have been brilliant. But Tommy was never going to get any attention with such crazy notions.

"This is why," I said with a heart-felt sincerity, "you're always going to be a rider and never a driver. Understand?"

Tommy lowered his head.

And with that said, I was sure that someday Tommy would face his hungry bear and discover the truth that he had been avoiding for so long.

Chapter 5

Within several weeks, our DED office had finally opened down the street from city hall. Everybody had settled in with big offices, computer equipment, and a desire to serve the helpless public. As I walked near the front entrance, I stopped and watched a distant man rushing towards me. He swung the front glass door open and darted inside.

At first glance, he looked like a government official who was investigating an important case. But as he drew close, I could see that he was sporting a stain on his rumpled tie. He appeared to have stayed awake all night, his hair unkempt, face unshaven, and exhausted. Whoever he was, his rough appearance was more befitting of a homeless transient bereft of shelter or income.

The man was middle-aged with strands of gray hair and a scraggly mustache. He stopped in front of my desk and tapped his shoe impatiently. He peered down at me as if I were a stuffed monkey. I simply stared back at him with a thin, determined smirk. Frankly, his politeness was so damn charming that I had to return the favor. With a blast of cold air and narrow-slit eyes, I asked, "May I help you?"

"So, you're the head honcho of the DED?" The man huffed with an unamused tone.

"Second-in-charge."

He bowed sarcastically. "Please accept my condolences."

"So, our reputation has proceeded us. Don't take rumors as fact. You might regret it later."

The man waved his hand in a sign of disapproval. "I'm not here to discuss formalities," the man scoffed. "Frankly; I don't care about your piddly-diddly department. I need to talk with Spencer Crane."

I immediately stiffened my back. "How about that. You're a lucky man. You've just found your piddly-diddly man."

"You?" he snapped.

"Yeah, who would have thought? I only do this part-time. On my days off, I substitute for the mayor."

"Fine! I'm James Montgomery." He reached out with his long right hand to shake mine. "I come from an agency that I cannot name."

"Well, that's okay," I ignored his hand gesture. "I'm accustomed to working with nameless and clueless government agencies. In fact, most of the people here can barely spell their own names."

"Really?" James squinted his eyes with a glare of suspicion. "Which agency did you say you were with?"

"I didn't."

"Well, you pass my cognitive screening test. Did you know that most idiots can never keep a secret?"

"It wouldn't matter," James boomed. "Nobody has ever heard of my agency. Nobody!" His hand slowly reached down to caress his hip holster. "But if you had, I would have to shoot you."

"Okay," I raised my hands. "I surrender. You won this pissing contest and the Golden Urine Award."

James shot out his hand and ring-wearing finger. "Good. Now kiss my championship ring."

"Whoa!" I quickly jerked back in my chair. I thought I had become accustomed to such emotional outbursts by Big Al. But this mystery man had a flair to scare the heebie-jeebies out of anyone. Without moving my face, I averted my eyes to search for a guard, but they were never around when you needed one.

James stepped back, grinned and soon displayed a warm, but faint, smile. "I was just fooling. My associates tell me that I should have been a comedian. Especially one who employs self-parody, dark humor. You see, I like my humor dark, without any cream or sugar. What do you think?"

I nodded with a sense of nervous urgency. I had no idea whom I was dealing with. For all I knew, he was a homeless man with delusions of self-importance. Then again, perhaps he was working for a super-secret agency that even the U.S. President didn't know of.

"You really should talk to our director. Big Al should be back from lunch soon." Actually, Big Al took two or three-hour lunches, but who was counting. Nobody cared if Big Al was out to lunch for the whole day.

"No, I want to talk to you."

"Why?"

"Listen tight. I'm investigating a mysterious explosion in the sky two weeks ago. My job is to interview anyone who has firsthand information. I understand you witnessed the event?" He pulled out a small notebook and a pen. He opened it and started writing. "Go on."

"Not much to tell. I was in the mountains near Idyllwild. A bright object flew overhead and disintegrated over the city. It seemed to have first hovered over the city and then exploded with the intensity of 100 suns. Kooky. Right?"

"Sure. You can say that without any top-level clearance."

"But why are you interested in an astronomical oddity?"

James hesitated and carefully looked over his shoulder. Next, he scanned the entire large office room, which was sparsely populated. Most of the office workers were still out to lunch. Before I could regain my composure, he suddenly flopped into a nearby office chair. With a beaming smile, he wheeled his chair next to mine. This was getting a little too personal.

"Why the curiosity? Well, there are a number of good reasons," James inched closer and whispered into my ear. "First, the object has been described as rather large, and should have hit Earth's surface and knocked down everything within a 60-mile radius."

"Like the Tunguska Event in Siberia in 1908?"

"Precisely!" James backed away. "You know your astronomical history. And secondly, it seems that nobody saw the explosion except those on the outer perimeter of the city."

"You mean nobody in Hemet saw it?"

"Correct."

I began to think of freakishly crazy science fiction stories that had no meaningful links with reality. There had to be a logical reason. Good reasoning or not, Tommy was going to love this enigma. Wild speculation and crackpot conspiracy theories were his forte. He had a knack for chasing down a nonexistent wild goose.

"I know it's hard to believe, but the guys above my pay scale conjecture that the object should have lit up the sky like a dozen atomic bombs over Hiroshima! Anyway, we have a crack team running all over Hemet interviewing citizens. We have another team of geologists and meteoricists searching for the impact area. So far we have found no trace of any meteorite or comet."

"There must have been some debris."

"None."

"Why would the Pentagon be interested in fireballs?"

"I'm not with the Pentagon."

"Oh,… Right."

"We need to solve this oddity. There is something more to this story."

"Yeah, but wouldn't NASA be more equipped to handle an astronomical anomaly?"

"I'm not so sure," James said. "This phenomenon doesn't seem to be a routine investigation. Normally, we refrain from chasing inanimate objects that fall from the sky. Actually, that would be a job for a team of geologists and geochemistry graduate students with experience in meteorite falls. However, we speculate that it was something more. That's my guess."

"Then you have experience in astronomy or astrogeology?"

James cocked his head to one side and brandished a wagging finger. "What planet did you come from? I am not a scientist; I'm an investigator. Let the eggheads do geochemistry testing and analysis. Like I said, I investigate."

All of a sudden, I found this man refreshingly honest for someone in an unnamed agency that had a non-military capacity. Maybe not everyone from the top echelons of government was a screwed-up moron. Perhaps it was just the city of Hemet.

"You want to know the real reason I took this job?" James leaned forward.

I nodded with a serious look on my face.

"Because this case resembles an X-file case. It is a real humdinger of a mystery, begging to be solved. Besides, I once had an uncle in

Roswell, New Mexico, in 1947. He said that the authorities came to his house and told him the object that fell from the sky was just a plain old weather balloon. They told him not to say anything, which was easy since he never saw anything. But, in my mind, if it had been a weather balloon, they would not have threatened my uncle. The mere fact that the U.S. Army was jumping all over Roswell indicates something extraordinary had happened."

"Like what?"

"I don't know. But it wasn't a weather balloon. That's for sure."

"Well, but shouldn't someone at the Pentagon know the answer?"

James smirked. "Give me a break! The Pentagon is so large that the right arm doesn't even know it has a left arm. I have heard that they have secrets so hush-hush that it is a secret to know that it is a secret. And you better believe that Roswell has one of those nobody-knows classifications."

"Well, I wish I had more information."

"If you hear or see anything more about the fireball, call." James handed me his card. "I just love solving a good mystery. I should have been a Sherlock Holmes detective, or a comedian."

With those few parting words, he stood, shook my hand again, and rushed back to the front entrance.

I settled back in my chair and exhaled. Now that was a whirlwind meeting. I did not know what to think, except that James probably knew more than he could officially reveal.

Within minutes, my world ratcheted down. Big Al had finally come back from his extended lunch hour. Now I could relax. At least that was what I thought. It seemed that someone had already informed Big Al about my mysterious visitor. With little decorum, he darted to my desk and towered over me with a stupid smug grin that would make the Cheshire Cat jealous.

"So, what is the scuttlebutt?" Big Al asked in a flash. "I mean, did anything happened when I was away? Anything?" His inquiry seemed more like a demand than a question.

"Not really." I settled into my chair, all comfy again, and crossed my arms behind my head.

"I heard we had an unusual guest."

"You mean that investigator from the Pentagon?" I said. "Yeah, well, he wanted special information from me."

"I assume he wanted to talk to me. Right?"

"He wanted to talk with anyone who had seen that fireball a few weeks ago."

"He wanted to see just you?" Big Al had two personal traits that made him rather unpopular with the public. First, he was nosy about everything. Secondly, he had a *bona fide* craving to be the center of attention. He pried into everyone's business, especially office romances and any indiscretions pumped out of the rumor mill. In fact, I often felt he was snooping on me just to see if I had any deviant sexual practices like cross-dressing, sadomasochism, or public nudity. Of course, I had no sexual anything, not even with my wife.

"Didn›t you see the fireball?" I asked.

"What fireball?" Big Al eyed me with suspicion.

"A meteorite exploded over the city. It occurred on a Saturday night two weeks ago," I said. "I'm sure you heard about it."

Big Al rubbed his neck. "That's a lot of hooey-blooey. I was outside that night cooking on my new gas-turbo BBQ. Made some marvelous ribs. Anyway, I did not see a thing. I think the Pentagon man is just making it up to find a fall guy. That's what they're good for, blaming the innocent, and spying on rivals. I do not want you or anyone talking to those meddling people. They're just trying to cause trouble for my department."

This was strange. Big Al was egotistical, wrong-headed, and mule-stubborn, but he had never shown any outward signs of paranoia. Now I got the feeling that he was hiding something from me. He usually loved to suck-up to bigtime governmental officials in hopes of climbing higher up the chain of command.

* * * * *

After arriving home that night, I found Sarah in the living room reading a book, which in itself was unprecedented.

"Want to hear something crazy?"

Sarah quick put down her book and looked at me with a penetrating gaze. "Sure. I would love to."

I almost did a double take, uncertain to whether I had walked into the right house. "Well, I had a wacky episode at work with an agent from the Pentagon. At least it seemed that way."

"Pentagon? How do you know?

"I don't. That was crazy part about his visit. He would not say where he came from. Very hush, hush."

Sarah laughed. "You mean a secret agent."

"As secret as they get."

"But why?"

"Something to do with the big explosion over Hemet."

"Finally, someone is showing interest."

"Yeah, but they don't seem to know any more than we do."

"Well," Sarah said, "what do you expect?"

"Yeah, that what I thought, too."

Sarah sat there and found everything I said astounding. We had a meeting of the minds. She listened to my every word, and I did the same. I could not figure out why she would engage in light conversation with me. Normally, she barely acknowledged my presence when I came home from work. What had gotten into her? It felt like I had come home to a strange woman.

After our delightful exchange, I started to drift into my predetermined routine. After microwaving a TV dinner, I dined on a wooden TV tray in front of my living room television. I would watch unrealistic crime shows, stale sitcoms, and uninspiring sports. If everything on the boob tube was really bad, I could go to my wall-to-wall collection of videotapes and DVDs. I was set for life.

Sarah considered my obsession with Hollywood films an addiction not worthy of any great social value. That was fair. Then again, who needed a nagging wife when a guy could experience the whole world and galaxy in the comfort of an easy chair? Realty was painful, full of responsibilities and sacrifices. I was determine to escape from the gravity of reality and embrace the fantasy worlds of Steven Spielberg. That was my long-term goal, but for some inexplicable reason, I started to find the virtual world empty and devoid of life.

Instead, I felt a pulling force, as if I were being drawn towards Sarah for some reason. That was crazy, but I was actually enjoying my conversation with her, sharing stories, experiences and a bit of humor. That seemed more satisfying than any science fiction fantasy.

"So, what do you think about the Pentagon man," I asked as she ate her TV dinner. "Don't you think he is hiding something?"

"Of course. There is far more to this story."

"Agreed," I replied.

"Have you filed the divorce papers yet?" Sarah changed the subject.

"I'll get to it."

"I suppose we still have plenty of time."

"Sure," I said. "All the time in the world." I could see that Sarah was wavering on the divorce. There was no real rush. We could get divorced at any time. Las Vegas was only a four-hour drive.

"So, your Pentagon man saw aliens crash at Roswell?" Sarah inquired. "Little green people?"

"Oh, he never mentioned anything about seeing aliens. He just speculated on why our military would try to cover up an incident that was merely a broken weather balloon.

"That's not what I meant," Sarah replied.

"Oh."

I waited for a hostile reply that would discredit my memory, logic, or racial heritage. She would often interrogate me like a well-seasoned attorney from Hell or worse—Los Angles. Except for this time, Sarah had nothing disparaging to utter from her normally derogatory lips. She just sat there waiting for me to correct her misinterpretation. I leaned closer. "Are you all right? Do you have a fever?"

"I'm fine. I just thought that the Pentagon man might have gone deeper into the Roswell incident. That's all."

"No, but he did tell me that nobody in Hemet saw the exploding object. Nobody!"

"That is impossible." Sarah blinked her eyes and looked puzzled. "How could anyone have missed it?"

I shook my head in agreement. "You think the Pentagon man simply lied?"

"No, he's just not telling the truth."

"Why would he do that?"

Sarah paused and seemed to move in and out of heavy concentration, something that I had never seen. She was actually taking her time weighing the pros and cons. It was either that or she had fallen asleep or the pod people had duplicated her body.

"He must have been ordered to hide information or spread disinformation. He might be a spy."

"That's a disturbing thought," I said, nodding.

"But the big question is why would anyone seek you out in the first place? You said he had a horde of grunts to do his mundane bidding."

"I only saw one person," I replied. "But I am sure there are more in his team."

"But why?" Sarah reiterated.

I stepped back, paused, and began to rethink my opinion. Amazingly, Sarah was right. She had a good and valid question. Why me? Until today, Tommy and Rant were the only people I had told about seeing the fireball in the sky. Something was not right. In fact, nothing seemed as it should. I mean, Sarah was acting like a different person. She was showing signs of intelligent life. I could no longer put her in the category of a hopeless airhead. How was that possible?

"You need to be careful. Someone is playing tricks," Sarah said in a tone of friendly concern. "Maybe the world of science fiction has taken over our minds."

Then I did something stupid. I stood up and moved toward Sarah as if some magnetic attraction had taken hold of me. I tried to resist. I stopped at the bookcases and pretended to inspect my videotape collection. I pulled one tape and tried to read the title, but instead stared at it blankly. The power became stronger, and I found myself drifting toward the light that enshrined Sarah. Like some puppet on a string, I plopped down next to her on our nice brocade sofa. She was startled. So was I.

"I see Mohammed has come to the mountain." Sarah›s wit was improving by the minute.

"I just thought that this was easier than shouting across the room."

"You don't have any ulterior motives?" Sarah asked with a thin smile.

"Me? I thought I was the inert king of the easy chair. I am just an impotent species addicted to my sterile addictions."

"Oh, but you are so much more," Sarah hummed with an exaggerated gaiety in her voice.

I was starting to get creeped out by Sarah's change of attitude. She never had any ambition to do anything. Once she discovered her inability to have children, she crept further in the dismal direction of avoiding risks, people, and confrontations. All too often, I had seen her saddled with profound sadness. Life for her had become a boring routine without bearings or desires. By all reasonable standards, most days she was deader than a zombie, which was of course redundant, but to her life appeared redundant. But right now she perked with the caffeine of animated life.

"We need to do this more," I said as I reached for her hand and caressed it.

"What are you doing?"

I decided to ignore the question. Anyone could see what I was doing. Finally, she admitted that she enjoyed our little informal talk.

"You're good at small talk," Sarah said. "I think I will hire you."

That was it. I began to suspect that she was on heavy drugs or that she was someone other than my wife. Two witty sarcastic remarks in one evening were just too coincidental.

"Are you all right?" I asked.

"Have I done something wrong?"

I started to ask her little things that nobody else could ever know, like the time we traveled to Fresno and ran into a taxi cab driver who knew a friend of ours in Hemet. Then there was the time we found ourselves hopelessly lost in the Mojave Desert on an unmarked dirt road. She had wanted to see a remote desert tortoise reserve, which turned out to be nothing more than a small sign and a few rabbit burrows. She remembered all of that. Of course, a clever alien replica of Sarah would know all of that too. Had some extraterrestrial body snatchers taken her over?

Oddly, she found my little drive down memory lane intoxicating. She put her thin arm around my neck and started to kiss me on the lips. I responded in kind. I could not believe that she had initiated physical contact on her own volition. She started to lick my lips with her tongue, teasing them. It was exciting and shocking. This proved what I suspected; she had been taken over by aliens. But I was not going to protest.

Chapter 6

I was amazed that only a handful of citizens had voiced their displeasure with Hemet's new program to increase driving efficiency. The scanty few who did protest were an aging gang of tightwads who begrudged any government expansion whatsoever. We christened these rigorous bean counters "The Usual Suspects."

I had numerous encounters with this motley crew. They would regularly invade city council meetings and yap about our wasteful habits and restrictive zoning codes. Nothing could ever appease them. They envisioned themselves as the spitting image of the late U.S. Senator Everett Dirksen, who had the audacity to question the cost of the eternal flame over President Kennedy's grave. Like Dirksen, these aging relics of bygone days were so frugal that they would risk back surgery to pick up an abandoned penny.

I knew most of the malcontents by name. Bert Wallace was their ringleader. He seemed to be everywhere, attending every civic meeting that had ever been held in the history of mankind. If any meeting were open to the public, Bert would be there, even if it was scheduled for midnight. It made me wonder if he had anything resembling a real life.

There were many occasions where I watched Bert and his crew of anti-tax cadre overwhelm city council meetings. They would sit up front in their checkered short-sleeved shirts and wave copies of the U.S. Constitution as if that little book had any effect on corruption or misconduct. Many considered Bert as Hemet's equivalent of Howard Jarvis in a quixotic quest to cut spending and red tape. Luckily, his shiny armor had started to rust. He had suffered a stroke and found it necessary to navigate life on new terms. I guess it was too difficult to round up and corral agitated taxpayers from a wheelchair.

I can still remember engaging these zealots in the hallways after city council meetings last year. My approach was to be brutally honest. I explained that it did not matter if our city kept overspending tax revenues. That was just a minor problem for the politically adept. That was because the city leaders would shake down citizens by using scare tactics. In fact, it seemed the more we scared the populace, the more money they would toss into our city coffers. When I would get a little cocky, I would taunt these penny-pinching relics. I would openly declare that the city could spend like a drunken sailor because the public was almost eager to pay the overpriced tab, no matter the price.

When I mouthed these words after the city council meeting, Bert and his cynical rabble-rousers became unglued. At the time, they were pushing hard to get the city council to slash city spending. They were having little success. I approached Bert and tried to reason with him. "Come on, our city just needs a little more funding to operate efficiently. Just a wee bit more. Besides, you have little power to stop them."

Bert cleared his throat. "You can give every dime you own to the tax goons, but it won't be enough. It will never be enough."

"Well," I backed away. "But we're in such desperate need of funds."

"So, taxpayers aren't?"

"Come on, they're not that poor."

"That's a crock of manure!"

"Oh," I folded my arms, "Then how come we're running a big deficit?"

Bert stood there with a crooked grin spread across his face. "Okay, how about this? Why can't our city fathers simply spend money more carefully. This is really a spending problem, not a revenue problem."

There was no use talking to a headstrong tightwad. Everybody knew that Bert was an unreasonable man who persisted in trying to change the world one tax cut at a time. That was never going to happen.

Bert shook his head and departed. That did not stop the churl-ish mob. One got into my face. She was a skinny woman with men-acing glare. She had taken an offense to my assertion that politicians could easily play the public like a fiddle. In her mind, such political shenanigans were impossible under a democracy. I was sanguine.

"Oh," I quickly responded. "You would think that would be the case, but you're wrong."

I then preceded to describe what city leaders needed to do to trick the citizenry to open up their fat wallets. City officials only had to conjure up a full-blown crisis, create a sense of urgency, and then publicize the horrible and dire consequences of the city going bankrupt. To get their message across, they would run advertisements warning that people would die if voters failed to pass another big tax increase. They would make thinly-veiled threats that without more revenues, the city would be forced to impose deep cuts to public services. These cuts always focused on defunding police, fire depart-ments, public hospitals or popular parks. Such claims held little truth. Truth and politics are rarely synonymous. But the citizenry were weak-minded and made of mostly spineless sheep, gullible, and easy to manipulate.

You could have heard a pin drop. I enjoyed watching their faces fall into ridges of despair after I finished my little sermon. I had a feeling that they really did not understand what I was trying to say. I guess it did not matter anymore. Ever since Bert's medical problems, the mob was now leaderless and fading fast. There was no reason to worry about being frugal. The revenue floodgates were thrown wide-open, allowing taxpayers' cash to flush down sinkholes. I was hoping that some of this generosity would trickle down my way, considering that DED would require a big cash lifeline. Lucky me.

* * * * *

Getting involved with DED was heaven-sent. I began receiv-ing a number of generous benefits. Big Al had presented me with a spacious office, a mahogany desk, large picture windows, and fancy white blinds to shut out the world. Life was good.

The best part was that our project was very successful. It was working marvelously, except for its higher cost overruns. The public also seemed happy, or at least unaware, of the mounting costs. We had placed advertisements on city busses, newspapers, radio stations, and other media campaigns. It was working. Citizens were calling in and receiving valuable information on how to plan their driving routes. The whole concept seemed noble. People always required a lot of assistance, and it felt good lending a friendly hand to disoriented and confused drivers.

My old job as a city planner had been mostly unrewarding. It was stressful to try to pin the blame on someone or something when bad situations arise. It happened almost every time I informed residents that they could not add a new bedroom or family room due to their undersized lot. I had to deflect their anger and cite outdated building codes, instead of indifferent officials who approved them. I was not the guilty party. I was not involved in adopting such restrictive housing codes; I was just following orders. Of course, most agitated citizens never saw it that way.

It took less than a month for our new department to organize into a well-run operation. Every phone call was processed and routed to DED, where our staff took the information and calculated the most efficient route. The system worked, but the process was time-consuming, sometimes taking over ten minutes or more per call. Some callers became frustrated and aggravated and hung up on us. Other times they would call back and asked us to recalculate their driving route. We discovered that these drivers were either lost or had changed their destinations. I began to wonder if they were just fickle or were somewhat impatient for the correct answer. I knew that something was wrong, but my pay scale did not entitle me to come up with solutions. That was Big Al's primary job. As for me, I just assumed that we were a big success.

The best part of the job was that I had little supervision. Al spent most of his time at three-hour-long martini lunches and at supposedly important private meetings. A least he came in most afternoons to keep up with the latest expanding workloads. At the end of most days, he would drag his half-liquored body into my office and quickly study the daily chart. He would rub his fat chin, hum a queer little tune, and declared that we were in line with expectations.

However, today was different. Big Al almost ran up the stairs and rushed into the office lobby. I could see him through my glass door. I checked my watch. It was still early in the morning. Something was wrong. I shook my wristwatch. No, it was still working. Someone was in trouble. Naturally, he made a beeline to my office, opened my door, and slammed it shut. Almost out of breath, he stopped in front of my desk, peered down, and displayed a funny look. It might have been the evil eye or just gas leaking from indigestion. Whatever it was, I wanted no part of it. I closed my eyes.

"Spencer," he barked out, "I'm disappointed. Really disappointed."

"Well..." I hesitated. "Could you be more specific? I mean, I'm good at many things, but disappointing people is not one of my strengths."

Al leaned over my desk. "Quit fooling around. Do you know the population of Hemet?"

"Hemet?"

"What other city do we work for?"

"Right. Ah... I have the figures right here somewhere." I went through a stack of paper and pulled out one sheet. "Yes. Here it is. I just did a study on that exact question." I looked down and quickly scanned the page. "Here it is. The most updated version is that Hemet has almost 60,000 inhabitants in the incorporated areas and around another 14,000 in the outer unincorporated areas, mostly in East Hemet."

"Wow, that many. That's great detective work." Big Al reached over and grabbed my datasheet. He took a few minutes to read its details. "The question is, how many calls are we getting daily?"

"I put the new numbers on your desk each afternoon. Haven't you been..."

"That's not important. What are the numbers now?"

"Okay, as recorded yesterday, the number is now averaging at least 200 calls a day."

"That bad?"

"No, we had less than 50 calls per day a few weeks ago. That's a big dramatic increase."

"Not good enough!" Al roared. "What's wrong with this picture?"

"It's out of focus." I shrugged.

"You're not looking at the bigger picture, Spencer. The bigger picture."

"Okay, it's out of focus and not big enough."

"Do I have to do the thinking for everybody here?"

"Well... that's your job description."

"Oh, yeah, well..." Al broke out in a rueful smile.

I sat there confused, trying to understand his train of thought, if there was any. I struggled to access more of my limited gray matter. That hurt. All I got was a headache. But at least I was starting to see some correlation between Hemet's population and the number of calls coming into the DED. "Well, I suppose more people should be calling us."

"Bingo! We should be receiving thousands of calls each day. The motorist desperately needs our help but for some reason, they are forgetting to call us. We must do more."

I did not like the way his train of thought was heading. A sudden thought pierced my brain. We could not even handle a few hundred calls a day. Was it possible to explain this concept to a man who thought he was bigger than life? I had to find some way to bring my boss back to his terra firma senses, some surefire method to both avoid and solve the problem. I lied. "I'll start working on it right away."

"Fine. But I'm no fool."

I sat there speechless. The silence was embarrassing. I was not sure what he wanted me to say. A comedy routine came to mind, but I was positive he was not searching for a humorous climax to his stupid question.

"I know what you're thinking, Spencer."

I truly hoped not, I shuddered in quiet thought. The DED was not my project. My pay was not nearly enough to solve unsolvable problems and come up with a brilliant and workable plan. That was why we had upper management. They get the big bucks for coming up with harebrained ideas that could bankrupt the city treasury. Then again, a failed project would likely lead to larger departmental funding. At least that is how it usually worked out for government work. I remembered an adage from an astute accountant who assured us that "government succeeded by failing." That seemed so true. I could achieve success by failing miserably and yet fulfill our mission. They might even give an award for an outstanding work record.

"Spencer. Come on, I know you know."

"I suppose we sort of underestimated our potential and need more staff." I murmured in a soft and hesitant tone.

"That's it! You're a genius. A sheer genius. That's the perfect solution to our problem. We must enlarge our staff and funding to better serve the public." Big Al paused, closed his eyes, and concentrated for a moment. "But on second thought, we should do even more. We should make all call-ins mandatory." Al bowed his head slightly to me. "You're another Einstein."

"Sure… I mean why wouldn't that work like magic?" I looked away, trying to hide my shocked expression. We were starting to sound like some fascist-communist comrades from World War II. What was next—the Hemet's police force shipped to Europe to invade Poland?

"I like the sound of all of this," Al raised his hand and twirled his index finger in a tight circle. "It has panache written all over it."

"But will the people dutifully obey?" I tried to backtrack. This whole line of thinking was getting out of hand. "Doesn't the public have a right to make their own decisions?" I smiled with a weak mixture of guilt and shame. "I think I read that somewhere in the Constitution."

Big Al started to stroke his fat face with his stubby fingertips. "That's right. But we have to protect the public first. It is our duty to provide health and safety support."

"They might find our program somewhat odious. You know, they might just ignore us."

"Not in my city. We will have to make sure every motorist gets proper authorization and a special driver's card."

"You mean a driver's license?"

"Spencer, get with the program. We need a special card and ID for everyone. If we don't, they might feel tempted to cheat. We need to make everyone use our services. Besides, the public should not have the option to drive anywhere they want. We own the roads. We can do what we want. Besides, nobody wants chaos in the streets. Nobody!"

"But we don't have the means to enforce it."

Big Al looked straight at me. "Boy, you're right again, Spencer. What would I do without you?"

I sighed with a mixture of relief and elation. Finally, Big Al was coming to his senses.

"You know what this means?

I shook my head, assuming that Big Al had seen the lunacy of his ways.

"We'll have to arrest, prosecute, and imprison lawbreaking motorists. Of course, we will require some serious muscle. People need to respect the law. We need to enlist the entire police department, maybe the whole National Guard. They can handle any bad-ass drivers."

I almost fell out of my chair. "Isn't that a tad bit drastic?"

I could not believe Big Al was actually suggesting a prison sentence for driving somewhere without prior approval. Big Al was definitely off his meds.

"Why," Big Al said with a serious face, "state law already forces our citizens to buckle their seat belts and to wear motorcycle helmets. It is mandatory to have auto insurance, although I understand more people today are uninsured. Still stiffer laws will solve that problem. You see, the law is there to facilitate better humans."

My eyes shifted away from Big Al's power-hungry gaze. Why listen to a buffoon who could talk for hours about useless stuff? I knew he could never get his new pet project off the ground. Nobody would listen to him, at least nobody who was sane. In fact, it was my unofficial job to diffuse his crazy ideas by distracting him. Anything would do it. Last week a copy of an old *Playboy* magazine kept him occupied for days. Of course, he said he only read the articles. On other occasions, the whole office chipped in money to buy him boxes of creamy donuts. That could keep him locked up in his office for hours, zoned out in a sugar trance.

"You know," I said calmly. "The council will probably give us a bigger staff to increase our numbers. But not for policing power to enforce our rules."

"Oh, I can get that done. I'm the king of political potentiality," Big Al boasted. "I heard someone whisper that message to one of the councilmembers the other day."

"But why?" I asked.

Big Al stretched out his fat sagging arms and almost sang an operatic aria in a dozen verses. "You see, Spencer, human beings are totally flawed. They act like the bumbling albatross in the South Pacific. We have a duty to fix that problem. We have to revise our ordinances to re-shape and reform human behavior to our way of thinking. That's because we know best. Otherwise, we would live in sheer chaos."

Just when it seemed that Big Al would never stop, Lenny walked by and joined the conversation.

"We need more than little itchy-bitchy control," Lenny interjected. "Very bourgeois. We must strive for greater perfection. Make people less selfish. You know, make 'em share everything. Give much to others. Real purpose of ruling plebs."

"Well," Big Al took his time to think. "We're not trying to achieve perfection, just efficiency."

"We could do both. Don't you see?" Lenny insisted as he pulled out a candy bar and gulped up half of it in one bite.

"Nobody's perfect and that will never change." Big Al gnawed on his sagging cigar. "At least not yet."

"We must try plenty," Lenny pitched his voice higher and pointed his candy bar at Big Al's face. "If we don't do anything, we get nothing nowhere."

"So," I sliced in between the two before the debate could prolong my boredom. "What do you want me to do?"

Big Al turned to me. "Take a poll of the citizenry and see if they will support a mandatory program. You know, make it sound good. Say it's for the children or something like that. People eat those things up."

"For the children? I don't think they can drive yet." I pointed this fact out as gently as possible.

"Talk to some of our advertising consultants. They will find a way. They always do."

"What if most drivers polled are opposed to it?" I persisted. "They can be very stubborn."

"Then we must be asking the wrong questions." Big Al frowned at the thought that his precious program might be unpopular with the public. "Just tweak the survey. Do a push poll. You know, slant the questions so that any answer appears supportive. We cannot allow our project to be torpedoed by a bunch of losers."

"Good policy," Lenny said. "Did that in Soviet Russia much times."

"Have it completed in a few days." Big Al turned, opened the door, and almost pushed me out of my own office. Lenny followed while trying to continue his silly conversation.

I always thought it was bad karma to deceive the public. Sooner or later, the truth would be discovered and an enraged public would demand our heads on a platter. They would chase us down like dirty dogs, wielding pitchforks and flaming torches. We would be exposed and brought to justice or the guillotine. I started to rub my neck.

I had no desire to rely on the tools of deception to alter public opinion. It was so wrong, but it seemed that public officials and pollsters were willing to keep doing it. They thought they could fix everything with cooked polls. It reminded me of an old saying that my mother loved to tell: "If you are a hammer, everything begins to look like a nail." I never really understood that aphorism until I started to work for the city. I soon found such mindsets flawed beyond measure. All I could do was hope that nobody would mistake me for a nail.

Chapter 7

I arrived home later than usual. I walked into the house and found Sarah reigning supreme in the kitchen, without the customary crowd of relatives and weirdoes. It was eerie, just the two of us staring at each other. I wanted to say something about what we did a week ago to assure that we had indeed performed some form of contact sport resembling body-grinding acrobatics. Of course, bringing up the topic would have embarrassed her to no end. I decided to take another step towards extending a peace offering and suggested another fun event. "How about a movie tonight?"

"A movie? Is that all you are interested in doing?"

"No, but it takes less energy than what we did last week."

"It's more expensive."

"I know, but it's worth it if you want to do it."

"Any suggestions? You know I don't like violent films."

"There must be something out there. How about the one where an operatic diva kills a time-traveling vampire with kryptonite?"

"You're making that up."

I was, but after looking at the entertainment section in the newspaper, I found something remarkably similar. I have discovered that Hollywood movies can be broken into two distinct classifications—somewhat plagiarized movies and completely plagiarized movies.

"How about a romantic one?"

She smiled with a seductive grin. "Only if it's X-rated."

I felt a jolt. Was my soon-to-be-former wife turning into a genuine sexpot? I searched through the movie pages with a greater sense of urgency. "Well, if we cannot find one with enough fleshy moments, I suppose we can make up the difference."

Sarah grinned. "If you bring the Crisco."

"Sure!" I immediately agreed. Of course, I was not quite sure if she was joking or not. I was only half-serious, but her sudden attitude shift regarding erotic feelings was mind-boggling puzzle. She had always been prudish, finding nudity offensive, even behind locked doors on a moonless night. Now she had transformed into a Lady Godiva, appearing eager to ride through town wearing just a smile.

As we drove to the theater, it struck me that I had not called DED in advance for directions. And who would? The whole idea was batty. If the project was somehow approved, the rules would add another chore to my already overburdened schedule. If it became too odious to go anywhere, people would simply stay home and sulk. The local economy would take a dive. That would ding the business community in the pocketbook, and lower tax revenues in general. Surely, most people would raise a ruckus and put a quick end to the madness. At that point, City Hall officials would be put under great press to slash expenses. That grisly scenario might drive a silver stake through the heart of DED. That meant that my possibility to negotiate a higher salary would likely die with DED. I hated worrying. Pessimism was not for the fainthearted.

"How have things been going lately?" Sarah asked as we neared the theater.

I stared at her with a dumbfounded glare, almost causing me to swerve into a telephone pole. She never asked me about my life, and I never asked about hers. In fact, I was not sure where she worked. Maybe she was still employed at Target or Marshalls' as a store clerk. Then again, she might have gone back to styling hair at a salon. Just not sure. We rarely discussed what we did at work in any substantial way.

"Same old stupid stuff. Nothing too exciting." That was not true. Sarah deserved more than empty words. "Actually, it is starting to get a bit strange working for City Hall."

"Oh, you still work there?"

It was a dry joke. Sarah knew that I had always worked for the city in some capacity. However, it was a noteworthy stab at humor.

"Are you having problems with your boss?" Sarah asked.

I nodded. "You could say that."

"My boss is a big bully," Sarah confessed. "She refuses to listen to most of my suggestions to improve customer service. I just wish she would shrivel up and blow away."

"If that happened to my boss, well, it would cause a dust storm large enough to blot out the sun for weeks."

Then something happened that I could not remember ever witnessing. She giggled. It was a short, sweet hiccup of a laugh that she quickly suppressed. Life was getting wild. Then the laughter grew more pronounced. She exploded into a belly laugh that any stand-up comedian would have surrendered his best rubber chicken to experience. I was gratified to hear her enjoy herself so entirely, even for a split moment.

"You should have your own comedy show!" Sarah said.

"I would hate to put Jay Leno out of a job."

Sarah nodded. "I see we do have something in common: a bloated, egotistical boss."

She was very observant about the miracle of mutual hate; it brings people together in so many ways.

"My boss is toying with the idea of forcing all drivers to check with City Hall before they can go anywhere."

"You're joking." Sarah's face resumed its usual gravity-drooping frown.

"Unfortunately, not."

"You mean I'll have to call the city in order to drive somewhere? If they think that, they must be smoking something awful strong at City Hall."

"Well, to be honest, my boss has a point. Most drivers are failing to call us to get instructions. And if they do, they seem to be ignoring our advice. We are just trying to help."

Sarah's voice stiffened. "I won't call. I have better things to do. People have a right to go where they want."

"I know, but I am second in command. It's my duty to obey my superiors. Right?"

She thought about this for a while before answering, and slipped into a deep state of concentration and focused attention. "Fine," she finally spoke up, "but what if your superiors are wrong?"

"Wrong?" I almost doubled up with laughter. "My boss is usually wrong about everything."

"That's my point. You're the one who explained to me the significance of the Nuremberg trails. The Nazis kept blaming their actions on orders that came from their superiors."

"Right. They pleaded that they were just following orders."

"Well, it appears that you're trapped in the same quagmire. You know you're under no obligation to follow an unlawful command. You can question or disobey any order you consider unethical or criminal."

My head was spinning. I vaguely remembered discussing the Nuremberg Trails with her after watching the old black-and-white *Judgment at Nuremberg* movie. Still, I was shocked that such a complex issue was flowing from Sarah's own vibrant lips. I began to wonder if she had turned into a woman of letters. Rather impressive.

* * * * *

As we entered the parking lot, I realized that Sarah had taken a political stance. She never found politics worthy of discussion and hardly ever gave an opinion. It was taboo, something not nice to discuss in public or private. Once Tommy had confronted Sarah over her lack of interest in politics. He explained to her that just because she had no interest in politics did not mean that politics had no interest in her. Apparently, politics had finally invaded her private sphere of life.

In pleading my case, I felt I had to defend the indefensible. "Fine, but the City just wants rogue drivers to learn a better way to get from point A to point B."

"But why force us?" Sarah turned and stared at me. "We're not vegetables."

I had to laugh. Sarah often compared people to inanimate objects, rocks, animals, and food. She must have gotten that trait from her hayseed parents.

"It's just a little phone call."

"But what's next?"

She was right. I often worried about things going too far, the so-called "slippery slope" argument. Yet, in my humble opinion, Big Al's project had gone as far as it could ever go. What else was left to recommend? Was Big Al going to urge an invasion of nearby cities because they were not following our example? Of course not. However, on second thought, knowing Big Al's appetite for public assistance, I might be proven wrong.

Our conversation stopped as we drove into the 12-plex theater parking lot. The place was brightly lit, huge, and brand new. I had forgotten all about this controversial development. Nevertheless, it was still a sore spot with my co-workers and me. Initially, the Planning Department had denied a remodeling permit, arguing that it had a 25-space parking lot shortfall. In my mind, the project had been declared dead, never to be resurrected. There was no extra space for parking or funds to build a public parking structure. Our updated General Plan was quite specific about too few parking spaces, increased traffic, and bright lights. Of course, that never stopped a Big Project with Deep Pocketbooks. The City Council simply ignored the General Plan, the Planning Department, and common sense. They voted unanimously for the development anyway. It made me wonder why we had spent so much money and time developing a General Plan if nobody was going to follow it. Go figure.

As we got out of our car seats and walked to the theater, we were not surprised to find a few friends loitering in front of the ticket booth. Some of them were completely out of place. I saw Tommy and Rant in close proximity. Amazingly, they were almost touching each other.

Still, I was somewhat wary of hobnobbing with people who had bolts in their noses and silver marbles stuck to their tongues. I eased into the young crowd and waved to Tommy. At least he was not into self-mutilation. He moved closer to me.

"Which flick?" Tommy asked.

"Oh, the one where a reporter writes about a woman who always breaks off her engagements right at the altar. Another Julia Roberts and Richard Gere love film."

"Dude, I saw that one! It rocks!"

Next to Tommy stood one of his close friends, Rudy Dillon, a young half-black Jamaican who lived out of his van. Rudy's good sense contrasted with Tommy's imaginary world, except for his curious interest in psychic readings, astrology, and channeling. Nobody is perfect. Still, Rudy's affability was infectious. He was bright, and I particularly enjoyed listening to someone endowed with a slight British accent. He was studying to become an electrical engineer, with some Java programming flung in just in case. I would see him out in the van reading technology books half the night and practicing New Age spiritualism during the day. He was going places that I could not imagine.

To show my support for his scholastic aspirations, I let him keep his van on my driveway overnight and showered him with food, an electrical cord, cold beer, and an open invitation to the bathroom.

Rudy loved to sweet talk and crack jokes, always asking me how I was doing. His jokes were silly, but innocent. Every time I asked him how he was doing in his circuit board designing class, he would exuberantly roar "Electrifying!" That was his trademark line.

This chance meeting was different. After Rudy extended his hand and gripped mine with the strength of a professional wrestler, he stepped aside to show off his cute, brunette companion, Candy Clarke. His girlfriend, also Jamaican, was energetic, barely able to hold her unbound energy in check. Her ink-blue eyes glistened across her tan skin as she rearranged her rainbow Reggae cap. She too desired to work in the computer industry.

After a few more moments of chitchatting, Sarah and I meandered over to the ticket booth. It was a particularly lovely night, with a warm breeze that wafted the sweet smell of night-blooming jasmine in our direction. The teenagers took advantage of the warm weather, vying to show how little clothes they could wear without fearing jail time for exhibitionism. Tommy was no exception. He wore a sleeveless mesh top, tight pants, and not much else. He did not bring his knapsack that usually held more tools and electrical equipment than the average garage. Of course, he was banned from bringing it into the theater; just too many hiding places for a refrigerator and a pantry.

The girls were just as immodest, prancing around in see-through blouses that displayed their belly buttons. At that moment, I discovered Tommy holding an unopened can of cherry Coke.

"You're not taking that inside?" I said incredulously.

"Duh!" Tommy exhibited his usual child-like response.

"But how are you going to hide it?" This was a challenge that all young moviegoers faced. In my opinion, it was impossible for men to conceal a can of cold soda on a warm summer night. The girls at least had purses to evade the snack police.

"Hey, I just put it down the front of my pants."

"What will you say if they see it?" Sarah asked.

Tommy's tremendous grin said it all. "I'll just say I'm hung like a horse."

That was Tommy. Original to the last drop of flavored soda, at least until I heard the same joke from an old movie or a *Saturday Night Live* rerun.

"That's not right," Sarah was first to protest.

"She's correct!" Rant stood nearby and began to criticize Tommy's behavior, arguing that he should obey the rules. She had an entire ethical system worked out concerning self-responsibility and insisted people ought to pay attention to other people's rights. Although she could be abrasive at times, she did practice what she preached. I tried to give her some pirated software once and she refused, saying it was intellectual property theft. Rant acted pretentious and dogmatic, but she had well-defined boundaries for conduct. And that was always comforting.

"It's private property and the owner does not want you to take it inside," Rant clearly stated with firm conviction.

"I suppose." Tommy backed away.

"Just drink it here." Rant put her hand on Tommy's hand. "Or give it to someone else. Someone not going inside."

Tommy and Rant were not meant for each other. It was unnatural. They were at opposite ends of the emotional spectrum. Rant was a green-blooded Vulcan, cold, logical, and rational; Tommy was a hippy-dippy butterfly, fluttering in twenty directions at the same time. They were similar to Sarah and me, just not very compatible.

Tommy shrugged, opened the soda and shared it with the whole group of wannabe hippies.

"The movie is about to start," Sarah grabbed my hand and pulled. "We don't want to be late."

The movie started out great, but not nearly as good as a strong dose of authentic human drama. During a slow part, Sarah stretched her arm across the back of my seat and stroked my neck. She rubbed my shoulder in just the right place, kneading the sore muscle strings that cried out for attention. It must have been unconscious. She rarely instigated affection. She had rarely put her hands on my shoulder or initiated an affectionate hug.

As we drove home, I had a feeling that we were not going to sleep in separate bedrooms. What had come over us? Could have that strange fireball caused this anomaly, sprinkling us with a magical fairy dust that made us better, more loving people? That seemed too wild to be considered possible.

Chapter 8

Mondays were not the only dread of my life. Office meetings ranked nearly as high on my misery scale. When combined, the two were a living hell. It was like being strapped to a cancer bed, spoon-fed, and kept alive on a ventilator while nurses struggled to clear blockages from my lower intestines. It was the preverbal dental surgery without Novocain. Actually, any of these scenarios were more enjoyable than listening to a political figure drone with insincerity.

The mayor's office had just announced an emergency meeting. Everybody was required to attend. The topic of the meeting was not immediately clear. As witnessed by past performances, emergency meetings often became omens of worse things to come, but I still retained an optimistic outlook. This meeting could only mean one thing: the city council had convened over the weekend to consider Big Al's ridiculous proposal. Of course, I was nearly sure they were going to shoot it down. That was the only sensible course of action. Nobody could be so stupid to think that such a half-baked plan could do anything but set fire to the kitchen and roast the cooks alive, good intentions or not.

Mayor Jessie Quinn walked into the room and waved to the excited crowd. Some chanted his name as he posed for photographs for the local newspaper. I turned from left to right, wondering why anyone would cheer a second-rate politician before he had had the chance to say one meaningless word. Something was terribly wrong. My fears were quickly validated by an unsettling incident. A dozen armed police officers marched into the back area of the room.

Parading in military formation, they lined up against the wall and stood at attention.

The mayor gripped the podium and glanced out to the assembled hordes of city workers, staff, and managers. Puffing up like a bullfrog, he spoke in a very loud, offhand way.

"Good morning," the mayor finally greeted the audience, taking time to clear his throat. "It is my extreme pleasure to announce an expansion of DED. Our esteemed City Council has decided to make a bold statement by introducing a new program to guide disoriented drivers. To enhance the quality of life, we have decided to institute a revolutionary program to save taxpayers time and money. We have passed new ordinances making it mandatory for all citizens to participate in our DED program. I have ordered the hiring of more staff workers. We are in negotiations to rent a large office building down the street. Operation 'Mandatory Advisory Directions' or MAD, as we like to call it, will be launched in a few days. I want everyone to work closely with Big Al and make this project an absolute success."

The mayor paused, stood back, and smiled proudly, waiting for a reaction from the crowd. Thundering applause soon erupted from the audience. With a greasy smile and a bit more grandstanding, Mayor Quinn continued. "I dare say this is a momentous occasion. We will boldly go where no city has gone before. We will help those who need our service most. In all humility, I can proudly state that never before have so few given so much to so many deserving citizens. I can assure you; we shall make history with this new and exciting program."

Of course, everyone clapped even louder after Mayor Quinn's speech. Half of the audience rushed to the podium, clamoring to shake his hand and give him compliments.

I froze in place, almost paralyzed, as if suddenly time had stopped and I had turned to hard stone. In fact, it felt as if the future of Hemet or even the world hung in balance. This was sheer madness. What was happening?

I had to think this through. I knew that the City Council had no authority to approve any measures without weeks of hearings from residents, business owners, civil rights attorneys, and Bert's howling Hemet Watchdogs. There were a number of statutory laws prohibiting such fast-track laws without public input. I suspected that such limits on city power were buried under mounds of dust in the basement archives. I could guarantee that nobody was searching for them.

Worse than being illegal, MAD would be a failure at an unheard-of scale. If Phase One had failed due to non-compliance, then Phase Two would likely reproduce the same results. History does repeat itself, usually at the expense of the foolish. I began to sweat and felt nauseated and hot. I had difficulty breathing and wondered if I needed medication. I knew that when all of this was over, someone had to be the fall guy. I began to worry that I was recruited as the possible sacrificial lamb to appease an angry mob or god.

The evidence was all around me. I had observed that every time a city project failed, the knee-jerk reaction was to throw more money at the problem as if that would actually correct a flawed system. There was no end to the spending cycle. More money meant more failure. The system was rewarding failure and penalizing success. I wondered what they would do if their program ever succeeded—abandon it altogether? That thought unleashed a pounding headache.

The agonizing part was that Big Al had never received my finished polling data. In fact, I was still working on the final questionnaire. I had neither printed nor handed out any survey results to the public. How could the City Council members know if the citizenry would support such a strange endeavor?

A sudden chuckle burst crossed my lips. My somewhat analytical mind was starting to kick into gear. This might be an opportunity. I knew how Americans hate inconvenience. Once they understood the implications of MAD, they would storm City Hall and lynch the mayor and Big Al. I wished I could stop this madness. I could become a savior of Hemet. If only I could stop dreaming about getting a bigger pay paycheck for supervising more people.

As I stood there envisioning a life of wealth and happiness, Tommy grabbed my arms and shook me. He was disrupting my fantasies of swimming in mounds of newly-minted cash. Tommy kept shaking. I kept resisting. With one final shove against a wall, I was thrust back to reality, though kicking and screaming.

"What?" I growled at my old friend. My eyes narrowed down to slits of rage and hatred. I wanted to stab my dream-destroyer with a Bowie knife. Spear him right through his heartless body. How dare he steal away my precious illusions. "Stop it!" I barked. "Stop harassing me!"

"Come out of it, man!" Tommy shouted. "Don't you see what is happening? The freakin' tards are taking over the city. It's like the Invasion of the Body Snatchers. Everybody is acting like mindless drones."

"No way!" I pushed Tommy away.

"The fruit loopers are taking over the city." Tommy elbowed me from the side. "We've got to flee before it is too late."

"What do you mean?" I asked, still contemplating my soon-to-be- enhanced salary and wondering if I should buy a Lexus or a Mercedes Benz. I was partial to silver-blue cars with white racing stripes.

"Nobody's going to comply!" Tommy grabbed me and started to shake me again. "Come out of it, man. This is so Nazi retro."

"Who cares?" I said, my mind still oozing with thoughts of riches. I want a luxury car. Tommy was going to have to pry my dead fingers from my new car keys. I could almost feel my hair flying freely from a fast-driving convertible. Who was going to stop my dreams?

With a sudden swung of his hand, Tommy slapped me across the face. It was hard. It hurt like hell.

"Spencer! Spencer! Earth to Spencer!"

"What? What's going on?"

"You are under somebody's influence."

"Me?"

"Yeah…. I don't know where you have been, but you have to come back."

I shook my head and rubbed my sore face. I must have been deep in thought, so deep that I almost got lost. How could that have happened? My dreams never took me for such a long, unscheduled ride.

"Something has abducted the mayor and all the councilmen," Tommy said with an alarming tone. "You know, put them under some trance and mind-control drug. Some type of bipolar illness caused by Vivo immunological experiments must have infected them. Abductees have testified to that. They say they were manipulated and hypno-programmed to act in a particular way. That's what must be happening here."

"What are you talking about?"

"You know, aliens from other worlds."

I stepped back. Tommy was always talking about anal-probing aliens. "They're just control freaks," I said. "Nothing alien about that. My own mother would put these yo-yos to shame. She's an expert on controlling people, especially with food. She's a certified food pusher."

"Whatever!" Tommy's voice rose. "I won't do it. I will never call the DED phone line! That's that."

"You know that you're exempt since you work for the city."

Tommy shrugged his shoulders. "Well, that's even less fair."

He was right. Why should city employees be exempt? This was beginning to sound like the old Soviet Union model where the communist bosses were the only ones allowed to patronize well-stocked luxury shops. The peasants got squat. They had to wait for hours to enter state stores with a limited selection of poor-quality goods. Still, my paycheck would be riding high up there with the rest of middle management. I could take that trip to the Caribbean, sweep Natasha off her four feet and leave Sarah behind. It would just be me. I would get a great suntan on the beach, a warm purring cat for my lap, and a cold beer for my thirst. Who could ask for more?

"No," I said shaking my head. I had to snap out of my get-rich-quick dreams. This was all wrong. I needed a serious discussion with the pillars of the community. I had to talk to someone about this approaching shitstorm. I needed to know if the mayor's plan had any community support. If not, we all would be targets of hot tar, cold feathers, and a free ride out of town. "You're right. This will not work. Come with me."

Tommy followed, but seemed perplexed. "You mentioned something about higher pay. Will that include me? And what about retirement benefits? Some city employees get 90% of their salary after they retire. Boy, that's really a sweet deal!"

"Forget it," I said. "We will be lucky to escape the city limits with our scalps."

Tommy stopped me. "What do you mean?"

"When the citizens discover the city's scheme, they will be after our heads, too. It will be like Bastille Day. The hordes will storm the City Hall and put us before the guillotine. Won't be pretty."

"We'll just call in the police," Tommy replied.

"Not a good idea. The police might ally with the angry mob. They might just shoot us as City Hall sympathizers. If I'm correct, French troops eventually joined the angry mobs that beheaded Louis and Antoinette."

"I see." Tommy rubbed his neck. "Like nobody uses guillotines anymore. Right?"

"No, they use bullets and tear gas."

Tommy swallowed. "Like real bullets?"

"Duh!"

* * * * *

Tommy and I decided to track down Bert Wallace from Hemet Watchdogs. Grapevine rumors spoke of Bert's return to attending public meetings, despite his debilitating stroke. If he were still wheeling his chair about, he would be attending some obscure city meeting about the sewer system and road maintenance. He would have a good take on what regular citizens were thinking, and yet, I knew his answer beforehand. He and his old geezers would be spitting balls of fire when they learned of the city's MAD plan of action. They were so tightfisted that they barely spent money on food and clothing for themselves. I knew this because I saw Bert in the same Hawaiian shirt for weeks at a time.

I flipped through the master calendar and found a sub-committee hearing on storm drains. We rushed over to one of the conference rooms and found him in the back of the room, next to a row of folding chairs and writing something in his frayed notebook.

I called out his name, but he failed to look up and see who was standing next to him. He did not have to, though; he seemed to know everyone at City Hall by their voice.

"What do you want, Spencer?" he said without glancing up.

"Bert!" I sat next to him. "So, you do remember me?"

"Sure, you're Spencer from the DED. I know all about you. You're that kid who flies off the handle and runs around with that goofy hippy."

I ignored his remarks. "We've learned something important that you should know about."

"Like the world is falling apart?"

"Isn't it always?" Tommy inserted himself.

"If we let it," Bert responded, still engrossed in his scribbling.

"Listen, Bert." I tried to get his undivided attention. "The City Council just passed a measure requiring drivers to call in before they select their destination. No hearings or public participation. Blatantly against state law."

"I've heard about it." Bert continued to write down figures on the costs of upgrading Hemet's storm drains.

I waited for a reaction. There was none.

I continued. "Beyond its questionable legality, it will cost a fortune. We'll have to hire hundreds of more city workers to handle the load. Violators might be imprisoned."

Finally, Bert looked up with a straight face. "So? It's an important project. We need it."

Tommy chugged a few deep breaths, recoiled, and lightly slapped his own face. "Wow. That's a cold blast from reality." He moved closer to me and whispered in my ear. "He's defected to the other side."

Bert overheard the remark. "I have not." He stopped writing and stared up with a scowl. "They came to me to discuss the particulars. I agree with Mayor Quinn and the others. We should start immediately."

"Bert, didn't you tell me that you once met Howard Jarvis?"

"Yeah."

"Well, he certainly would not approve of this—I mean if he were alive today."

Bert thought for a moment. "Well, sometimes even Howard Jarvis went too far. Look at it this way. All of these years, I have opposed tax increases on everything from water treatment to school bonds. But what if I was wrong? These agencies actually have a need for more funding to serve and protect the public interest. Why should a rickety old man get in the way?"

"Shall I smack him?" Tommy asked. "Man, the dude has lost his grip on reality."

"Bert. What happened to you?"

"I have been a thorn in their side for too many years. I need to let them help the multitudes of unfortunate people. Who else can do it? You should understand that; you work for the city."

"But taxes will skyrocket," I tried to reason. "Someone has to pay for all of this."

"Let them increase taxes. Give them what they want. Let them take every dime. It is out of my hands. Nobody cares if society turns into poor and homeless peasants. Nobody cares."

"Come on, Bert," I said. "If they get it, they will spend it. You know that."

"If the city took every cent we made," Tommy replied, "it would still not be enough."

I turned to Tommy. "Yeah, but you hardly make anything anyway."

"Listen, boys," Bert put down his pen and notebook. "I know government spending is a black hole. I'm sure you've heard me say that countless times. The government is like a gigantic vacuum cleaner that sucks in every penny not nailed down. So what? The predator must eat the prey. There is nothing we can do."

I could not believe what I had heard. How could Bert surrender? It was against his nature. He was the premier skinflint in town. "You've changed," I said.

Bert picked up his pen and started to write again, ignoring me.

He must be getting something from the city, I said to myself. They must have paid him off—money, power, or prestige. It had to be something. Tightwads don't come cheap. Whatever it was, it reminded me of a quote from George Bernard Shaw—"A government which robs Peter to pay Paul can always depend on the support of Paul." Bert must have befriended Paul big time.

Tommy and I left the meeting and wondered what to do.

"When this hits the papers tomorrow, we better keep a good eye on the exit doors."

"Yeah, but I can run faster than you," Tommy joked. "I'm so much younger."

"Not if I tie a massive bag of French fries to your desk."

"Hey, that's cheating."

"I know. I just hope we have somewhere to work tomorrow." The words were light-hearted, but the meaning was dark

Chapter 9

The next morning, I picked up the local newspaper and prepared for some fireworks. As I walked to City Hall, my eyes focused on the front page. There was a big headline and a story about the new Mandatory Advisory Directions—MAD—with a photograph of Mayor Quinn and the other City Council members. They were smirking as if they had just stolen an important historical artifact from the Hemet Museum.

As I began to read deeper into the article, I discovered something odd. The newspaper story was not neutral, not even close. It had many digs and sarcastic remarks about a few naysayers who denounced the Mayor's MAD decision. They characterized these loners as goofy oddballs who had no idea of what they are saying. The paper had marginalized these critics as idiots without minds of their own. The problem was, none of this happened. There was no opposition at the meeting. Nobody jumped up and spoke one bad word. Bizarre.

The newspaper used considerable space to lampoon these bellyachers as "losers who would complain about the sun rising in the morning." It was a hostile editorial disguised as a news story. The article was completely one-sided and fixated on fabricated dialogue by phantom protesters. It was great fiction, but just that.

I hurriedly flipped through the rest of the paper. There was nothing but an overload of dazzling stories about the Mayor's new initiative. They lavished praise on his insight while offering grateful homage to his bold new plan. He was the man of the hour and could do no wrong. Every page was heavy on photos but rather light and vague on what MAD would do. None of the stories mentioned that drivers were required by law to arrange their drivers route beforehand. Nor any word about big fines that were in store for lawbreakers. Those important details were somehow missing. I had a feeling that divers would soon be in for a shocking surprise. It was almost as if the newspaper writers wanted drivers to be stopped, detained, and arrested. Incredible.

When I reached City Hall, I perched myself near the front door. I was expecting an angry group to swarm to the building with pitchforks, nooses, and torches. Gazing over the landscape, I saw only a mail carrier and a stray dog. That was it. City Hall was safe for another day.

Well, if nobody cared, neither would I. There was no time to think about the rights or wrongs of the new directive. I had a job to perform. I went back to my office. My new assignment was to organize MAD as fast as possible. Of course, I had to hold my nose. I knew the problem. My conscience was eating away at my soul. Sure, I knew that my actions reeked of hypocrisy, but at least I could ignore my conscience. I'd done that before. What was harder to do was finding a way to hide the stench.

At least my long hours of work forced me to forget any loyalty to principles. In quick succession, I arranged furnishings for the new three-story DED office, interviewed a swath of young workers, hired the most qualified personnel, and signed computer contracts. Luckily, the new government building was just a few blocks away from City Hall. I could walk back and forth, organize, and find time for a leisurely lunch.

The workload was overwhelming my senses to the breaking point. I could not find enough qualified help. New workers streamed in like an army of busy ants devouring a dead animal. I had to keep purchasing truckloads of desks, crates of telephones, and stacks of large wall maps. I arranged for training and instruction manuals. Next, we had to update our software and memory to provide faster information to commuters. One of the biggest problems was gathering competitive bids. It took forever. I wanted the best deal. Big Al had a better idea regarding my dilemma: "Just buy it and forget about the cost."

Sure, I could do that. I could do that all day long. I loved buying new expensive things, especially when I could spend other people's money without shopping for the best price. That helped to unjam the logjam. In a flash, both Big Al and Mayor Quinn were impressed with my organizational skills. I was sure to win a commendation from City Hall as one of their best managers. I considered myself the Man of the Hour, the Hot Property of Hemet, the Big Kahuna. I was now driving an expensive new city car. Life was good.

To inform the public, I initiated a citywide mailer on the official City of Hemet letterhead, notifying citizens in incorporated areas that they must call us first to have their driving plans authorized. At first, we had a massive response from good citizens attempting to obey the new ordinance to the letter. However, our system became over-extended and increasingly overloaded as more citizens participated. I estimated that it was taking 10 to 20 minutes to get hold of a DED operator. I kept adding more people and more lines, but I could not catch up with the demand. By the time we had reached a crescendo of sorts, we still found ourselves plagued by long waiting periods.

People got impatient. We were getting hate messages and a few death threats. Our flow of phone calls had flatlined in the third week. The chart was showing a steady decline in the number of requests for travel routes. I had predicted that scenario secretly to myself from the start. Nevertheless, I tried to pretend that 1,500 to 2,500 calls a day was a tremendous success, and I was proud of my staff of operators for accomplishing the impossible. I knew that euphoria would not last long.

"Spencer." Big Al finally beckoned me to his richly decorated office on a Monday morning. I had a feeling this was more than a pep talk about planning my own office party to celebrate my success. I entered his massive office with thick Berber carpet. The room was the size of an Olympic pool that could have had its own zip code. I walked next to a wall and swore that the Rembrandt oil paintings were originals. He even had an engraved portrait of Niccolò Machiavelli.

"I'm disappointed." Big Al sank deeper into his custom leather chair. Right in the middle of his desk sat an undisturbed box of creamy donuts and a large soda. Sure, he was officially on a diet, like almost everyone else, but I knew he planned to eat every single donut. He always did. When I eyed the donuts with a disapproving frown, he lifted up the soda and apologetically said, "It's diet."

As I looked out the window, I wondered what the problem was now. I could tell that he was restless, that something was not right. I suspected that he thought I was probably not doing all I could. I inched a little closer to his desk and flung my flat-palmed hands forward in a gesture of doubt. I pleaded, "You don't think we are running on all cylinders? Correct?"

"Bingo!" Big Al exploded with delight. "However, that is only part of the problem." Big Al stopped to swallow a donut in one bite. "Do you realize that we have no way to enforce our new law? That's what we have to solve next."

"I never thought about it. Just don't have the time."

"I understand. You're not being paid to think about the big picture. That's why I'm in charge. I'm the real brains in this organization."

"I guess if you want to enforce our program, the police might be useful," I said.

"You're right, Spencer. The police must be part of this operation. Boy, you're slicker than green fried snot. Thanks for the advice."

With that disgusting image etched in my head, I backed away. No wonder Big Al could never land a job in the private sector. Nobody was going to pay someone teeming with such unsavory language.

Big Al sucked down another donut and swiveled around in his chair. He reached for the phone and started to dial, but stopped and turned back to me. "Oh yes, there is one more thing. We need to find a way to get tourists and the people outside our city limits involved in our program. Under state and city law, they are required to obey the laws of our city whether they know about them or not."

"I see." I never did like that idea of obeying laws that nobody knew about. I could not think of any means to get outsiders to obey our local ordinances. Tourists and occasional visitors were rather elusive. We never knew their itineraries in advance. So how could we control their traveling plans and patterns?

"Spencer, we need to get them aboard. Find a way to do it." And with that, Big Al grabbed his box of donuts, struggled to stand up, and slowly walked to the door. I stood, lower my head and felt ashamed. What had I done? I slowly retreated to my office.

I kept feeling I was responsible for all of these headaches. I was the one who supplied Big Al with new, exciting ways to impose his screwed-up agenda. I was sure I was going to get a whopping dose of bad karma for all of eternity. I had given Big Al a do-or-die mission. He was going to get our law enforcement department involved in something that was out of their jurisdiction. The city police had a tighter budget than most other departments. They were not going to spend time going after misbehaving drivers. They were preoccupied with felonies, not traffic misdemeanors. At least I hoped so. But what did it matter? I was destined to be reborn as a yellow-bellied banana slug.

As I entered my office, Tommy quickly rushed inside. He closed the door and fiddled with the doorknob, determined to lock it. There was no door lock, but that did not deter Tommy.

"Man, you have no security," Tommy said in frustration.

"It's an office door; there is no lock."

Tommy leaned down, fingered and rattled the doorknob, and then shrugged.

"What do you want?"

Tommy wasn't paying attention to me. He was watching Big Al's every movement instead. It was not difficult. I could plainly see my bosses' antics through my office door window. I knew his routine. When he felt restless, Big Al would lumber around the third floor, searching for a bowl of treats on employees' desks. After catching his sugary prey, he would wolf down handfuls of chocolate M&M's or jelly beans. After appeasing his sweet tooth, he would stroll between long rows of cubicles. As Big Al passed by each workstation, he waved his hand at the workers, acting like a victorious Caesar crossing the

Rubicon River. After reviewing his troops, he would make a quick dash for the stairwell and disappear.

"What is our big dude going?"

"Lunch."

"At 10:30 in the morning?"

"Yes, and never complain about that to anyone. Never!"

Tommy smiled and put his hands forward, flashing a thumbs-up gesture. "Oh… when the cat's away. I get it."

I looked up and rolled my eyes. "What do you want?"

"Things are getting spooky. I mean crazy spooky. You know, it's not easy navigating unchartered waters. Have you tried it?"

"Tell me something I don't know."

"Okay. So, what is Big Al up to? I sort of like to know what he is going to do before he does it."

"Wouldn't we all?"

"You must know something."

"Believe me. You are talking to the wrong man. You need to consult a very good psychic."

"Come on, man," Tommy pleaded with a note of exasperation. "You're almost his mentor."

"No, I am not!" I took offense to that. "I'm just second-in-command."

"*Au contraire*, O Capitan," Tommy almost sang. "Big Al said you're the big man who comes up with all the big ideas."

I leaned back in my chair, feeling dizzy. I had simply told myself that I was just following orders, that it was my job to assist Big Al in any endeavor. I was a public servant who was trying his best to help others. Except maybe, my conflicted sense of duty to either my government or to my fellow man. I was not sure which one was more important. It was getting fuzzy.

"So, what's the big dude planning to do?" Tommy interrupted my inner battle. I had trapped myself in a hellscape of remorse. I turned to Tommy to pull me out of despair. He soon rescued me with the aid of diversions. "So, what do you know?" Tommy kept asking.

"Well," I paused to regain a sense of clarity. "Not much. Big Al is still working it out. He's mostly kept me in the dark."

"But has he found another nefarious means to force the numbers higher, to get more drivers to call us?" Tommy continued to pester me with harder questions. I began to appreciate his ability to distract me with trivial matters. I was starting to feel better.

"Nobody really knows," I responded. "Big Al is like a large railroad train that has run off its tracks. You cannot predict where it will crash. You only know that it will continue to steam ahead until it hits something."

I stared at Tommy. "Don't you have somewhere to crash and burn?" I was the one who signed the paperwork to let Tommy transfer to my department. The office manager at city planning signed the transfer papers in record-breaking time. I was not privy to the office manager's reasons, but I suspected that Tommy had screwed up big time and the whole staff wanted to dump him. Actually, it was my good fortune. I needed him around.

Tommy stared at me. "Hey, man. This is my job. You told me to help you corral Big Al's ambitions. Remember?"

I nodded. I vaguely remembered saying that after downing a 6-pack of beer in my kitchen. Beer is a really good lubricant to push a babbling mouth into gear.

"I'm your little helper." Tommy pulled out a small roll of duct tape from his knapsack. He cut off a few small strips and slapped them down on his hands and wrist.

I scratched my head and looked at him in a state of puzzlement. "What in the hell are you doing?"

Tommy looked up apologetically. "I'm trying to get rid of some warts. I heard that duct tape makes them go away."

"You can't believe everything people tell you." I began to lecture a 25-year-old on the merits of modern medicine.

"No, it works, really. I read about it in a medical journal. It dissolves anything you don't want."

I began to envision Big Al all wrapped up in duck tap from head to toe. I wanted to hold that thought. I settled back in my chair, pushed away from my desk, and propped up my feet. Modern medicine or voodoo, Tommy's disrespect for conventional wisdom did wonders for my mental stability.

I studied Tommy. He didn't come across as an intelligential heavyweight, but he was equipped with a quick wit. If only he could concentrate on one thing at a time, he would go far, even in our little Podunk town of Hemet.

* * * * *

The trouble with leaving my door open—my general policy—is that it gives the impression that I am an open house to any riffraff who happens to be passing nearby. An hour later, Lenny was next to invade my sanctuary.

Naturally, Lenny had overheard Big Al's booming voice. He wanted to spend my time rehashing what our leader had suggested.

"You know," Lenny said as he stood next to Tommy, "Big Al has good idea. People have nasty bad habits. Ignore this, ignore that. Most not knowing what's good for them. So,... we force them. How you say? Put screws to thumb. Tighten down real hard. Make them scream like little girl."

"What's wrong with you?" Tommy chided Lenny. "Why can't we just leave people alone?"

"They're too stupid!" Lenny said nonchalantly.

"So, we're all too stupid." Tommy exploded in an angry outburst, discharging sharp shards of outrage across the continent.

I almost felt an impulse to duck behind my desk. It looked like the Cold War had returned in full force. I started to search for a sandbagged trench to endure the bombardment. Tommy's hostility was not really about Lenny per se. It dealt with past Russian atrocities against Ukrainian farmers in the early 1930s. Many of Tommy's ancestors were Ukrainians. After the collapse of the Soviet Union, documents were found proving a deliberate policy to starve millions of Ukrainians. Some of those victims belonged to Tommy's Ukrainian lineage. To Tommy, Russia was a synonym for injustice. He even refused to eat beef stroganoff because of its Russian origins.

Lenny's reaction to Tommy's accusations was predictable. He simply grinned with a bright glimmer of self-satisfaction and uttered something in guttural Russia.

"If we're all stupid," Tommy responded, "then that includes you."

Lenny folded his arms and scowled. "Not us, of course. We smart ones."

"Naturally," Tommy huffed.

"Don't you know?" Lenny started to wave his hands in the air. "World is big mess. Riots, civil war, starvation. All very bad. Because nobody knows what they doing."

"Maybe that's due to a lack of human rights." Tommy's face was turning to an alarming shade of red. A vein in his forehead looked ready to burst.

"No. Attitude rather bourgeois. Never working. Know why?"

Tommy shook his head.

"Because bread more important than freedom."

Tommy almost blew a gasket. "But you can't grow bread without the right to grow it. The Ruskies tried that crap. Failed every time. Ask the Ukrainians. The people starved because there were more Soviet *apparatchiks* controlling farming than farmers."

"Oh, those bad crop years," Lenny shot back. "Besides, you cannot eat freedom."

"Well, you can't eat bread if nobody is allowed to make it."

"Ridiculous." Lenny moved closer and pointed his finger at Tommy's chest. "You're just anarchist. You want no society, no controls. Very bad."

"So, this is why you don't want drivers to control their own destinations? They want the freedom of movement, and you want to control their movement. Right?"

I suddenly stood up and stretched my hands out in an offer of peace. The bloodletting had to stop. Tommy had held his own, but I felt I had to stop it before it turned into another Stalingrad. Anyway, I had little time to listen to a debate that had already been settled with the fall of the Berlin Wall.

Tommy folded his hands and gave his parting shot. "So, if control is so great, why did the Soviet Union collapse?"

Lenny's eyes narrowed. "I don't want play game no more. No more talking. Besides, I came to see if workers have mailed their union dues. Is mandatory. Like most things."

I could see that Lenny had retrained his gunsight on me.

"Spencer," he turned and impatiently gestured for him to move closer. "I must tell something to you."

I walked over to him and stopped an arm's length away. Lenny was a man of political muscle and union power. When he told you to "jump," you had better say "how high?" He had such a scary way of saying things that a few angry words could cause a person to pee down both legs.

"I hate to say this," Lenny murmured with a pale smile, "but your future not so bright as you think."

"Well, the lights in here are low voltage. Saves money."

Lenny struggled to hold back a grin. "Okay, funny man. Listen to me good. I don't want to,… what you call 'bitch,' but you're not doing job right."

I gave a little nervous little laugh. I could see that Lenny was not amused, his brow wrinkling with a scowl of disapproval. "I'm working on it, Lenny. We just hired another 100 new people. It takes time to train, equip, and get them to fill out all the paperwork."

"Is vital they pay up soon," Lenny said slowly and coldly. "We need to know who to charge. We need them pay union dues."

I was doing the best I could. I was trying to follow the letter of the law. The lack of time was the culprit, not me.

"I expect report," he ordered. "I want names. I want names of everyone. By tomorrow." Lenny turned around almost in military-style and stomped away in his black boots.

Tommy eyed me with a sense of relief. "Can you believe that blowhard sourpuss?"

I shook my head. I could just envision Lenny taking charge of our newly mandated MAD, arresting violators, imposing long jail sentences, or simply shooting the guilty parties against a stone wall. It seemed like an eerie scene right out of *Dr. Zhivago*.

"He's got a butt load of problems," Tommy grumbled.

"I'm sure he has the same cheerful thoughts about you."

Tommy shook his head with disgust. "The problem is, my ideas may be wrong. I admit that is a possibility. But I believe I have no right to ram my precepts down another person's throat. I mean, like we decide our own fate, our own future. But I don't think Lenny would give me the same consideration."

Chapter 10

I hated dealing with a bad itch, especially at the office. For the next several days, I sensed a tingling throb that provided little relief no matter how much one scratched. Big Al had was the likely source of that incurable irritation, demanding more and more from his department while we worked with fewer and fewer resources to do his bidding.

Any first-year economics student could have predicted our problem. DED had overspent its operating budget. The city treasurer sent us threatening letters of financial doom. They warned that Hemet would soon file for bankruptcy if we kept burning cash like there was no tomorrow. I held the same feeling. I feared that I would be unable to pay off my five-year luxury car loan without my city job. Something had to be done.

Our department had to go on a strict no-spending diet. But that was never going to happen in my lifetime. Big Al would simply ignore any financial restraints. He might think he was a social visionary, but his starry-eyed expectations reflected a skewed worldview. He could not see what he was doing wrong. His vision was impaired; a blind man was better at seeing the future. I had no idea how he would attempt to accomplish his quixotic tasks. I was afraid to know.

As I understood it, the citizens of Hemet had two choices; they could either call DED or ignore our mandates. If they disobeyed, we were powerless to force compliance. We still were unable to discover a forceful means to guarantee compliance or generate revenues for our invaluable services. We simply had no teeth. Moreover, we could not easily identify most lawbreakers. I racked my brain to unearth some technological way to discover who had driven around without authorization. It was maddening. Many drivers told us that they would obey, but somehow, they kept forgetting or neglecting their duty. Others, the more silent and subtle ones, seemed to be sabotaging our effort, determined to stop us from bringing positive change to Hemet.

Big Al was furious over the high numbers of disloyal drivers. I tried to reason with him and point out the spontaneous nature of humanity. We were a weak and disorganized species. People were absent-minded and hasty, and always forgetting to buy a gallon of milk to feed their hungry children. Big Al had another take, arguing that neglectful drivers were actually going on unauthorized trips to liquor stores. I chuckled. I had to plead guilty to that behavior. I was infamous for my late-night beer runs.

* * * * *

As I was updating the work schedules for my senior people, a murky shadow blocked my light. I looked up. Immediately, I felt inadequate to resist its odious presence. It was Big Al. He was acting a bit strange. He almost appeared happy and elated. Something was wrong.

"Spencer!" Big Al boomed as he stuffed his loose white shirttail into his pants. "I've figured it out. It's brilliant if I may say so."

"What's brilliant?" I was almost afraid to ask.

"My plan to solve our financial challenges."

"You found a way to get more money?"

"Was as easy as crossing an empty street. Some days my intelligence just knows no bounds."

"Okay," I leaned back in my chair, folded my arms, and stared up. "Let it rip."

"Here it is. The mayor and I have decided to impose a fine on any driver who fails to inform DED." Big Al fished in his pocket, pulled out a wad of paper, unwrapped it, and read. "The fine for the first violation is $250. The second violation is $1,000. After that, it's $5,000." Big Al paused and eyed me. "That should make our lazy citizens sit up and take notice."

"Is there a fourth violation?" I asked with a smirk, knowing that the fine could not be any higher. I was wrong.

"Sure. That is the beautiful part. We can charge them with a serious felony. That allows us to use civil forfeiture asset laws and seize their home, boat, and car. In fact, we can use a loophole. The law says that we don't even have to charge someone with a crime. We can take what we want. No expensive trials or lawyers. It's like a free smorgasbord of monetary delights." Big Al glowed. "Boy, we'll be back in the money."

I swallowed with great difficulty. I had to talk some common sense into him.

"So," I asked innocently, "we get to take citizen's property without any criminal charge or jury trial?"

Big Al nodded in agreement.

"Don't you think the public might find that a bit improper?"

Big Al pursed his lips in thought. He tilted his head slightly and gazed up at the ceiling. "Okay, I guess we should charge offenders with a crime. I mean, we'll win in court anyway. The judges know we need more revenue to afford our judicial branches' higher salaries."

"What's the penalty?" I asked.

"We have not settled on the mandatory and minimum sentencing yet. However, I am pushing for ten years of hard labor, minimum. But that's being worked out as we speak."

"Aren't we going a bit too far? I mean, many murderers and rapists spend less time behind bars. The violators are simply drivers who failed to call DED."

Big Al's eyes flashed like cannon fire. "What's your problem, Spencer? You're always complaining, always trying to belittle my achievements. Do you want me to transfer you to another department? Is that what you want?"

I recoiled with horror at his suggestion. I was not going to tell him the truth. My thoughts on accepting a demotion were a closely guarded secret. Even I was not privy to them. I just wanted to stay the course. Keep my job and prevent Big Al from diving off the deep end.

Then again, he was always swimming over the Mariana Trench.

I stared hard at Big Al and fumbled for words. "Well, ahh... I just want to make sure everything is perfectly legal."

"Hey," Big Al said in a jovial tone, "the City Council voted to approve the ordinance. It's legal as anything can be."

"I mean the bigger picture. You know, on the state or federal level?"

"Don't worry about those federal clodhoppers. They don't have that much jurisdiction over our local municipality. We control the local area. They won't interfere with us unless there is an earthquake, flood or foreign invasion. And when those emergencies do arise, we always make out like bandits. Never let a crisis go to waste."

I found this a little disheartening. We were supposed to have local autonomy, not local monarchy.

"So how do we enforce it?" I asked.

"Well, we have made arrangements with the police department. Every time they pull over a driver, citizens will be asked whether they called us to schedule their driving destination."

"And what if they lie?"

"That's the beauty of the system." Big Al stroked his chin. "The police will call the DED and confirm their claim. We can get them on perjury as well as failure to follow the law. Well, I mean we could if they were in a court of law. Anyway, we're planning to record their response and, if they lie, we can sock them with massive fines and years in jail. What a great way to fund the DED! Our financial woes are behind us."

"Yeah." I gulped, struggling to stop a rising sense of dread. "Sounds like a great way to increase our funding. Especially since I will need more people and equipment to communicate with the police."

Big Al beamed. "That's the spirit, Spencer! I'll get you everything you need. Remember, this is almost like a war! It is us versus them. Right? And, boy, we will soon have the enemy on the run."

I had a sick feeling in the pit of my stomach. In fact, I felt ill on too many levels to describe. We were sinking fast and deep, and I could only guess where the bottom lay.

"Have everything ready in two days. That's when the police will start calling us."

"Ahh... Okay." I took a deep breath. I knew our entire staff of software engineers would have to stay up for over 48 hours. Even that would not be enough time to finish the job. I began scratching my forearms.

"That's what I like to hear." Big Al almost did a little jig. "Get the system up and running. I want something that will quickly identify every criminal cheater. I want everybody's name available for the police, except, of course, city officials. We have important things to do, and we cannot be bothered calling up every time we have to go to the dry cleaners. Got that?"

"I will need the list of those exemptions," I said, wondering if I was destined to be on the VIP list. I was like everyone else. I liked to travel without any restrictions. "Will I be on that list?"

Big Al gaped at me as if I was a side of beef hanging in a slaughterhouse. "You?"

"I need the exemption," I pushed him. "You know, official city business."

"It's only for top management."

"I'm almost top management." I felt a sense of helplessness washing over me. Nothing was more humiliating than begging for rights you should already have.

"I suppose so," Big Al said with condescending tone. "But I expect close cooperation with the police department, especially when the first few violators are caught. You see, we plan to come down hard on these lawbreakers. You know, make them an example to the community. Shame them until they start obeying us. And to make sure that they will never betray us again, we will print their driver's license photo in the newspaper. That will humiliate them. If we are lucky, maybe a mob will drag these betrayers out into the street and make an example of them."

"Well, that's one way to encourage compliance," I said sheepishly.

"Hmm." Big Al bit his lips and looked around slyly. He turned to his left and then to his right. Soon, his attention shifted back to me, staring directly with a wild fervor in his eyes. "I wonder if some-one could entice good people to stop wicked ones."

I was not sure what he meant. Did he want me to arrange some questionable activity? Was he encouraging me to mobilize our work-ers to engage in illegal activities? That was a frightening thought. I stared back at my boss and pointed to myself with a puzzled look. "You mean,… you want me to be more pro-active, more direct and forceful?"

Big Al nodded his head with great satisfaction, seemingly to convey his secret and expected wishes.

My heart shuddered, skipping a beat as if it had jumped into my throat. "Well," I mumbled with a quivering voice, "Ahh… I mean… are such acts necessary to help our department? I mean, don't we have better things to do?"

"Why forgo all of the fun? No, we must make sure these law-breakers look as guilty as hell in the newspapers. You know, dredge up some personal dirt—past convictions, bankruptcies, late payments for child support, debt, rumors, anything that will make them reek of depravity. That should scare the willy-nilly out of everyone. Nobody will ever challenge us again. It will make people think twice before ignoring us." Big Al smiled with a satisfying grin on his face. He pulled out a new cigar, popped it into his mouth, and rushed out the door.

I felt victimized. My boss gave me no chance to reply to his ter-rible and probably illegal proposal. I was not going to organize mobs to shame opponents and manipulate public opinion against others. This was one bridge too far to cross.

I just sat in my chair and looked out the window in disbelief. What was next? Were we going to shoot protesters and hang them from lampposts? Had we come to that? When was someone in the community going to start protesting our deplorable city government? Someone had to stop us. But who?

"What's wrong?" Tommy asked as he leaned against my door-frame, munching on wheatgrass.

"This world is getting too complicated," I said. "I think we have lost our sense of balance. No," I paused, "we have lost our sense of decency."

"Is that all?" Tommy laughed. "I thought it was something serious."

I jumped up and rushed to Tommy. I grabbed hold of his forearm, slammed the door, and dragged him into my office. "My God, this is serious. I'm not sure where to begin. We must now use the police force to enforce DED's new laws. It will be a disaster."

"Sure!" Tommy smirked. "I'd like to see them try that. Nobody's going to obey that."

At that moment, Lenny barged in without knocking.

"Heard about new enforcement rules." Lenny slowly shut the door and walked to my desk, looking worried. "Well, well, looks like shit has nick the fan."

"*Hit* the fan." Tommy corrected him.

"Oh, yes, and more than that. Top City officials are exempt from new rules. Know what that means?"

"No, what?" Tommy's voice soured.

"Means special treatment. No equal treatment. Not fair."

I stared at him. "Does this mean you're not exempt?"

"How you know?"

"Just a hunch," I said.

"Well, that is wrong, very wrong. Everyone at City Hall should be exempt. Not right. Everyone should have equal treatment."

I nodded. This was the first time I had ever concurred with Lenny. "You're right. It's definitely unfair."

Even Tommy nodded in agreement.

"What can we do?" I asked, hoping that he had some ideas.

"Don't know what we can do." Lenny moved closer to me and whispered, "But something is wrong here. Everyone acting queer. Hard to put fingernail on it."

"Were you in Hemet when the fireball hit?" I asked.

Lenny stepped back. "What you talk about?"

"The meteorite last month."

"Oh, that. Big explosion in sky. I was at a union seminar in Los Angeles. Why?"

I began to see an emerging pattern so large that it could easily overtake the suspicions about the infamous Illuminati conspiracy. Something had happened to Hemet that night. It was beyond spooky.

Everyone who was in the city during the explosion had been altered in some way. It sent a chill down my spine. It was like something out of the "Invasion of the Body Snatchers"—both movie versions. They had all transformed into frigging control freaks with a Dirty Harry "make-my-day" death wish.

"Why..." I almost shouted, "Because over half of the city residents have gone bonkers."

"Oh," Lenny shrugged. "So, big bang in sky is culprit."

"Well, it seems that way," I said.

"Very good." Lenny seemed overjoyed. "I thought was me. Nice to know I'm not going *psikh.*"

"No, you're not," I said, trying to sound as confident as possible. "Something has gone wrong. It seems that only the people who were in Hemet that night have become zombie-like followers. Somehow, the purple gas from the fireball must have changed them."

"They eat human flesh," Lenny had a fearful expression on his face. "Not good. Never liked zombies."

"No," I assured him. "No zombie apocalypses. I was just making an analogy."

"Oh." Lenny pulled back his shoulders and stuck out his chin like a pouting child. "Don't be funny. Strange things happen all time."

With a skeptical eye, Tommy turned and directly faced Lenny. "This nightmare had to come out of somewhere."

"Sure," Lenny agreed. "But purple gas?"

I confronted Lenny. "So, what is the cause? If not the gas."

"I don't know," Lenny said with a puzzled face, his hands held out, palms up. "First noticed when union gone crazy. They want promote workers on merit, not on seniority, special favors, or privileges. Boy, cannot make this shit up."

I stared at Lenny. I also felt we had entered some weird parallel universe.

"So what?" Tommy shot back, looking confused.

"Another bad thing," Lenny said. "They plan raising union dues 300%. Maybe more. Way too much. I guess city running out of greenbacks."

"That's interesting," I remarked. Of course, with all of the logic-defying spending, the lack of funds had to rear its ugly head. Money had to come from somewhere other than trees.

"It's all phony baloney," Lenny said. "I say we're all hell going. Tell me. Makes no sense."

"Anything else?" I asked, wondering if this day could get any worse.

"Let's see," Lenny paused, glanced up, and squinted his eyes. "Oh, yeah. One other tiny thing. They want to brand Social Security numbers on forehead. Said it reduces paperwork. Little strange. No?"

I almost fell backward. "Yeah, I think that one qualifies for weirder than weird."

"Wow!" Tommy›s eyes widened. "This is like a Stephen King movie. But without all the gory special effects."

"Surely you're joking?" I asked Lenny.

"*Nyet!...*" Lenny replied, shaking his head. His face furrowed into a fog of worry and confusion. "Funny thing you ask that."

"Why?" Tommy asked.

"That's what I asked them," Lenny said. "Were they doing comedian skit?"

"And then what?" I asked.

"Said nonsense. They said I should go to guy who would shrink my head. You know what that means?"

I turned to Tommy. "We must do something. This is getting completely out of hand."

"Let's go to KGB," Lenny proposed. "They know what to do."

"You mean the FBI," I corrected him.

"That's what I said."

I had to laugh at Lenny's many quirks. His most annoying one was his refusal to admit any error. I wish I could figure out if it was a Lenny thing or a Russian thing.

"So, we go to FBI. *Nyet?*" Lenin asked.

"Maybe?" I replied. "But we have nothing to show. There is no proof of any strange or alien presence. We have no hard evidence. Just a City Hall running amuck; nothing out of the ordinary." I paused and started to scratch my arms.

"But they're treading on our rights," Tommy argued. "That's totally unacceptable."

"You don't understand," I turned to Tommy. "We're a municipality. We have strong local control. City Hall has the power to suspend the First Amendment or anything they please, at least until someone sues the City." I had attended enough city-sponsored seminars to know how tough local ordinances could be. One speaker had told us about a case where a Denver gun nut decided to protest a city's ordinances prohibiting concealed handguns. To prove his point, the man pulled out a handgun in front of City Hall. The police swiftly handcuffed and arrested him. During the trial, the judge explicitly disallowed any mention of the Second Amendment, ruling that it had no material effect on a local case. Tommy was incorrect—city governments had the ability to tread on long-established rights.

"We need to meet," Lenny said. "Sooner much better."

I suggested my place. Tommy and Lenny agreed.

"I'll bring my combat boots and bear hat," Lenny suggested with a sly smirk. He was obviously joking.

"This is not a war," I insisted. "We just need to figure out what's happening."

"War is better." Lenny continued with his questionable remarks. "Gets blood to boil with excitement."

"Let's just talk over pizza," I said. "Nothing formal. We don't have to take over the world quite yet."

"I'll bring the wheatgrass." Tommy held up a small container of the green substance.

"I have vodka." Lenny grinned, pulling a flask from his hip pocket.

And that was that.

Chapter 11

I was sure that our clandestine meeting was going to be anything but normal. I looked around my living room and eyed every one of our comrades. It was not a pretty sight. We had enough people to start a six-player musical band if now we only knew how to perform in harmony.

The problem was our lack of experience. None of us had training in leadership skills. Most of my co-conspirators were not just nobodies; they were on the kooky fringe. With paper and pencil in hand, I began to make a list of my team›s strong and weak points.

I examined my profile first. I saw myself as an ordinary bureaucrat who could not make definite decisions. My strength was hiding from my boss during crises, and when an unsolvable problem reared its ugly head, I was prepared to play dead like a possum. My strength was to redirect blame to others for my shortcomings. My power was to bring together a bunch of losers and make them actually think they could succeed at something.

My sidekick, Tommy, was neither dependable nor predictable, but at least intelligent and thoughtful. His mettle was not cast of solid bronze, maybe soft butter, but not hard metal. Nobody would ever commemorate his deeds as heroic; he was scared of his own thoughts. Instead, his genetic makeup matched a geeky nerd who worshiped computer games and silicon chips more than life itself. His strength was playing video games all night and ignoring his basic needs like food and bathroom breaks. He had the power of concentration.

Lenny was a spooky union official with a serious demeanor. He roamed the shadowy world of primal politics and remained distant for fear of exposing his darker side. I was afraid that he was not suitable for our group. He could be blunt but also assertive. Of course, he had strengths. His bulky and hairy Russkie body and bad attitude made him the perfect troglodyte brute. He had the power to put fear in the hearts of men.

Take Rant, for instance, and I wished someone would. Her bleak anti-social outlook of life precluded her from ever agreeing with anyone. She was terse, overconfident, and bossy. Most people avoided her, and no wonder; she usually packed heat in an obvious shoulder holster. She was our warrior princess and loony bin all rolled up in one formidable *Xena*. She had the power of arrogance, paranoia, and the willingness to shoot someone, hopefully not us.

On the other hand, Rudy was amiable, good-natured, and currently parked in my driveway. He added a sort of New Age pseudo-spiritualism that had more substance than Lenny could ever muster. Still, his infectious enthusiasm could bring people together despite their abnormal differences. He was popular with the younger crowd, and people naturally gathered around him like ducks swarming after moldy breadcrumbs in a murky lake. I admired his dedication to well-groomed dreadlocks. Very cool. His strengths were minor, but his power to convince people to try dangerous things was impressive.

Rudy's on-and-off girlfriend, Candy Clarke, was a different story. I labeled her an airhead beautician with a temper. She once decked a football player with a heavy hair drier for pinching her butt. Go, girl. She definitely had the credentials for the Valley Girl of Hemet, considering that I had to explain what "meteorite" meant. Unfortunately, her moods swung back and forth to the rhythm of Dr. Jekyll and Mr. Hyde. I could never tell which personally she currently occupied. Her strength was unpredictability and possessed the power of creeping behind big men and whacking them with electrical gadgets.

The real reason I invited Candy was that she could not remember if she had been in Hemet during the fireball explosion. That was why I let her attend our little secret gathering. I wanted to watch her reaction and see what she would say.

Lastly, I came to Sarah. She had been a hairdresser, but now occupied a store cashier position at a grocery store. She never got involved in anything of importance. I thought about Sarah for just a nanosecond but considered the time ill-spent. She was definitely out of the picture. She had never shown any interest in political or controversial matters. She even refused to vote during elections, quibbling that to do so would make her partisan. I marked her off my list.

I stared at my list, feeling slightly queasy. I closed my eyes briefly and swallowed with some difficulty. I knew our future was not very promising. I scanned everyone in the room. They sat in a half-circle in the center of my living room. I tried to calm myself. My co-conspirators were not some revolutionary army from the jungles of Colombia; it was more like a menagerie of socially maladjusted dingbats at a Star Trek convention. But then again, prosecutors would only need to disclose the strange mental deficiencies of my accomplices to get a guilty conviction. They would be convicted in a heartbeat.

I tossed my notebook on the coffee table. I stood and decided that it was time to get the rabble roused up. My malcontents were waiting for my signal to stir up some type of action. With a heavy sigh, I walked to the center of the room and glanced at Sarah standing near the hallway entrance. She flashed a warm smile as I passed by. It seemed like she was looking at me with approving eyes.

"Thanks for coming out," I said nervously. "I want to make it clear that we're only here to discover what's happening. You know, compare notes and talk things over. Nothing revolutionary, just some inquiries. That is why I asked Tommy to bring his computer. We can search for other towns that might be experiencing similar behavior."

Tommy perched his bulky laptop on top of my coffee table, knelt, and proceeded to engage a search engine. A fast typist, Tommy moved in and out of official city websites, offbeat organizations, and news articles.

"We won't find much of anything," Lenny said. "Every time I find a strange incident occurring in in other parts of the country, the data suddenly disappears."

"So, somebody is hiding stuff?" I asked.

"Control freaks," Rant barked out. "They conspire to control and hide everything. Knowledge is power."

"It's more than that," I suggested.

"More than what?" Lenny asked with a confusing scowl.

I turned to Tommy. "Have you found anything yet?"

"Nothing," Tommy replied without looking up, still clicking away on his laptop keyboard. "You realize that the internet has limited content. It has not been around that long."

"Fine," I said, "but we still need to know what is happening. And whether the fireball caused this insanity."

"Maybe it's not a cause, but a sign." Rudy volunteered his New Age opinion. "There are ungodly forces at work here, and they might be warning us of future events. We could possibly be witnessing the birth of a new world, a new paradigm shift, or a distorted reality. Maybe two worlds have come together to occupy the same space. Maybe we have lost our existence."

"That's bullshit," Rant suddenly exploded over Rudy's speculation. "A is A. Nothing transcends existence. A leaf cannot freeze and burn at the same time."

Tommy stopped typing and looked up at me. "Rudy and Rant both have taken that out of context. We are dealing with a linear system that is dedicated to secrecy and controlling the narrative. That is what the statecraft paradigm does. They believe nothing can be left to itself. They know that under fear people will demand the imposition of countless measures to solve endless problems. I mean, everybody wants a piece of control over other peoples' lives. That's why they need to enact controls over body and mind."

"What bunch of *musor!* Nothing is wrong with controls," Lenny ventured to make a bold statement. "Soviet Union fell because of bad leaders, not bad controls."

Rant shot up out of her chair and stared down at Lenny. "Bad people can only make bad policies. Duh!" She snapped, "Why are we listening to his sheer nonsense?"

"Not nonsense." Lenny sneered. "We had great country."

"Who's the Commie pig?" Rant wagged her finger at him with an air of mock severity.

Lenny shot up out of his chair and glared at Rant. "Who's the anarchist whore?"

I thought World War III had just broken out in my living room.

The two locked eyes as if they were preparing to duel in a Western standoff, ready to do battle to the death. Lenny clenched his fist. Rand bit down on her bottom lip and let her fingers drift towards her gun holster.

I wedged myself between the two hotheads. "We're not here to reenact the Cold War. Right?"

"She started it," Lenny huffed, peppering his remarks with a few Russian expletives.

Before I could say anything, Tommy found a way to defuse the situation. He reached over and handed Rant a cold beer.

"You know," Tommy said, "make beer suds, not war, or something like that." He smiled profusely.

To her credit, Rant turned away and retreated to her chair, mumbling a few inaudible words.

Lenny took longer, but finally sat down, arms folded, fuming like a red-eyed bull.

"What about the new fines?" Sarah said timidly during an awkward moment of silence. "Tell them, Honey. Tell them what you heard."

All eyes instead trained on Sarah.

"Yes, the new fines," I said, looking somewhat warily at my wife. I had just realized that Sarah had called me "Honey." That never happened before, at least in living memory. To her, I was just "Spencer this" or "Spencer that." At other times, her cute nicknames for me were laced with far more descriptive nouns.

"The new fines are very stiff," I continued until Candy interrupted me with a big gasp that jolted everyone to an upright seated position.

"What's wrong with you people?" Candy shrieked, her hands outstretched, groping at the air. "You act like the world is ending. If someone breaks the law, of course, they must pay a hefty fine, or go to jail!"

"But what if the law is wrong?" I asked. "What if it is a bad law?"

"How can you say that?" In a burst of outrage, Candy grabbed her Reggae cap and threw it at me. She missed. "Come on!" she pleaded. "Elected officials enacted our laws. They wouldn't mislead or abuse us. You're just conspiracy wackos. I mean, shouldn't we trust our politicians?!"

"Well…" I groped for an answer. I was not prepared to get into a deep philosophical debate far more suitable for a political scientist. I had no clear-cut answer to Candy's question. I stared at Rant and waited for her to reply. She was politically adept and had a better grasp over such matters. However, it appeared she was still fuming over Lenny's unpleasant outburst. She spurned my nudges to get her to participate. Like a stubborn mule, she refused to move on to greener pastures. I poked Tommy, hoping to get a definitive reply. That was risky. Tommy could be extremely loquacious. If someone asked him the time of day, he might feel compelled to explain how to build a clock.

"Well," Tommy thought for a while and spoke rather elegantly. "Elected officials cannot arbitrarily make life-or-death choices for their citizens. They cannot abridge our consensual rights. Otherwise, they could lynch anybody anytime by a mere council vote. We're more important than then a crowd-pleasing vote."

I was amazed. Tommy actually had been concise and relevant, and did not try to explain the origins of the universe for two hours.

"You people are disloyal." Candy grew more agitated. "You're supposed to obey our leaders, not belittle them. Traitors!"

My head shot backward so fast from the blast that I might have suffered whiplash. So did everyone else. Nobody seemed capable of replying quickly to Candy's accusation due to shell shock. I lead the first wave of responses. "We're not traitors, Candy. That's ridiculous."

"Not from where I stand."

"I only wanted to that talk about the fact that some laws are not soundly based." I felt like I was tiptoeing through a virgin minefield.

"Do you believe that no matter what the law says, we must obey it blindly?" I asked with an innocent face.

"Sure!" Candy retorted. "We must obey it to the letter. We are their citizens. They are our leaders. Who are you to say it should be different?"

For a moment, I pictured Candy in a stylish brown shirt, goose-stepping with thousands of soldiers in military formation. I could see her carrying a tall red banner painted with a white swastika, parading in her fashionable black jackboots. The thought sent chills down my back.

"You cannot be serious?" I said in a volume so low that I could barely hear it myself. I started to think back to my studies of history. What if a reincarnated Hitler came back from hell and took a position as our mayor, governor, or president? Would Candy parade in lockstep with him across Europe with Panzer tanks and armored personnel carriers at her side? And what about the air war? What about the invincible Luftwaffe strafing innocent civilians in bombed-out cities? I tried to stop thinking. Of course, I had watched too many classical World War II flicks, but I knew a National Socialist evildoer when I saw one. I knew my patriotic duty to help our desperate allies fight for justice, freedom, and the American way. I had to sit down before I caught myself singing "The Star-Spangled Banner."

Settling into my chair, I attempted to refocus everyone's attention back to the matters at hand. I decided to delve into particulars. I dutifully noted Candy's objections and moved on. "As I was saying, the city has decided to start fining drivers for a large sum of money after the third infraction."

"How much? Candy asked, still smarting over our obvious traitorous ways.

"To the tune of $5,000," I said.

"My God!" Candy's voice burst open like an overflowing floodgate. "They cannot do that. I don't have that kind of money to waste on a stupid traffic fine. Why those greedy bastards! I hope they all rot in Hell!" With a quick motion, Candy jumped up, spat out an array of cusswords in Jamaican Creole, and ran outside.

I was stunned. "What happened?"

"Maybe she has too many overdue parking tickets," Tommy said with a touch of humor. "You should see the penalties they charge if you forget to pay on time."

"Funny," Rudy said. "I have never seen her so angry."

Candy had gone berserk over a minor incident. It made no sense.

I continued the meeting and mentioned that violations beyond the third would encompass jail time and even higher fines. No one else jumped up and screamed. I had hoped a few of them would flare with a burning sense hostility, belt out a few befitting swear words, or utter a sincere growl of injustice. If anything can pull a group or cause together, it is mutual hate for a common enemy.

"I will not pay the fine," Sarah spoke calmly. "They have no right to punish us like that. We should vote them out of office."

I was amazed again. Sarah had never voted in her life. Nor did she take hard-core positions or absolute stands on anything. She considered herself one of the blessed peacemakers who would use any passive means to prevent a confrontation or conflict. Now she sounded like one of the Founding Fathers after signing the Declaration of Independence—that she would give her life, honor, and fortune for the cause. Quite sexy in my opinion.

"So, are we talking about some type of Gandhi civil disobedience here?" I asked.

"Like what?" Lenny asked sarcastically. "You want stop buying salt and textiles? Like Gandhi did?"

"Spencer." Sarah stared directly at me. "You can do something about this madness. You're an insider."

I leaned back. "Me? I have no special powers."

"You're second-in-charge of DED," Tommy reassured me. "You could be more assertive."

"I've been ignored on every occasion." I became defensive. I felt justified in defending my inactivity. I had lodged several milquetoast protests with Big Al. Then again, every time he shot me down, I simply backed down like a spineless old whimpering dog. I was no Lassie.

"There must be something you can do. Stop it or slow it down," Tommy said.

I just swallowed. I had never thought of myself as a heroic figure. I was a government employee who just happened to be living in a screwed-up city that had gone berserk. I had very little authority to do anything. The mayor and the city council ran the show and the next election was almost two years away.

"Use monkey wrench," Lenny suggested with a mischievous grin. "Throw something in big machinery. Old Russian trick."

"You mean sabotage?" I asked, a little horrified at the thought.

"What about slowing down the computers?" Tommy proposed. "That would cause drivers to get discouraged and stop calling us."

"We're already backlogged," I stated with a lopsided grin.

Tommy shrugged. "We have to fight back somehow."

"This is not a war," I tried to explain. "We're not even sure who is the enemy."

"Maybe, the real enemy comes from within," Rudy spoke up with a chilling notion. "Something is making our elected officials overextend their authority. I mean, they're risking their political careers over petty road directions. How stupid is that?"

"I see the enemy clearly," Rant said. "Those in authority are our adversaries. They're the ones who seek to overstep boundaries. You know, the camel nosing its way into the tent. To them, we are mere cockroaches, suitable to be squished when convenient. That's why there have been so many genocides. They see us as disposable."

"It's not that simple," Tommy said and looked up from his typing, glancing at Rant. "We all have cravings to control our neighbor. It's an ancient, primal response. We're pre-wired to take control of others before they can control you. Today, that urge is mostly dormant. And yet, something has to provoke this reactionary instinct to bubble to the surface. Think about it. Something or someone is pushing the gas pedal. Someone has rev up this human trait to full throttle."

"Phooey." Lenny made a sour face. "Could be strange virus accidentally released from biological lab?"

"You mean on purpose?" Tommy asked.

"We don't do things like that no more," Lenny's lips slowly parted into a thin grin. "We civilized now. The Russian Federation plays nice. Besides, who wants worldwide pandemic? Not good for anyone."

I lowered my head. We were getting off course again. But what if it was some type of toxic organism that had been released to harm humanity? This was a serious issue. I paused and thought about the problem knowing that there was no clear answer.

"Well," Tommy turned to me and asked impatiently. "What do you think?"

I bit down on my lips, looked up, and stared at everyone with a scared look. "If some compound, chemical, or biological weapon had fallen from the sky, it would eventually wear off. The effect would diminish with time. But the opposite is occurring. Everything is getting worse."

"A time-released weapon, maybe?" Tommy stopped typing. "Sorry, but I've found nothing so far."

"It could have been a missile," Sarah said, drifting to the middle of the living room. She found a chair, sat, and looked eager to participate. "Why do we assume it was just a rock from space?"

Tommy closed up his laptop computer. "There is so much we do not know about the vast universe. I mean, our galaxy rotates once every 220 million years. And man, we have no idea what type of new space we're entering each day. Or what unknown materials might enter our atmosphere and infect us. Real bummer."

Tommy was right, unfortunately. I had seen reports that in a few hundred years we would be entering space clogged with significantly more debris of unknown origins. Some scientists believe that this space dust and gases might cause another Ice Age. Nobody really knew for sure.

"Then what is our plan?" Sarah asked.

"There is nothing we can do," Tommy said. "We're still totally in the dark. I suppose we just have to eat what nature dishes out. Always been that way, because of the magnetic pull of the planets..."

"Fine!" I interrupted Tommy in mid-sentence. I knew he could talk until everyone had died from boredom. And yet he had avoided most of his normal ramblings for days.

"So, what can we do?" Sarah asked again.

"I'm not sure," I said. "We need more facts to figure out some type of strategy." This was exactly why I hated meetings. They were just one long talkfest that often provided more questions than answers. I could see that we could not agree on anything, except to meet again sometime in the future. What a waste of time.

Chapter 12

The next morning, as I sat in my office chair and sipping coffee, I kept looking over my shoulder. As I worked on work schedules, I kept pondering over Candy's quick changing reaction. One minute she herald City Hall leaders as virtuous and wise. In the next instant, she had switched over to the other side. In the span of a nanosecond, she had dumped what I thought were her long-held and deeply cherished values. Curious.

Candy's statement about the citizen's duty to always obey city laws seemed excessive. Our public office holders were chosen to govern the citizenry, not to rule like tyrants. They were usually seasoned in democratic sauces of limited potency and obstinacy. They were our head chef of fine politicking, and yet, our current crop of political culinarians often left a sour taste on many palates.

What I did not find illuminating was my predicament as the ringleader of a secret society. I knew it was just an innocent discussion group, but as fear morphed into full-blown paranoia, my nerves found little solace. It was just a matter of time before my activities made the front-page headlines. I would not last long in solitary confinement.

My fears of spending time in jail had to take a pause. From down the hallway, I could see a walking hippo destined to alter my career path at a moment's notice. Like a good weatherman, I knew that my future was going to be stormy with an occasional tornado.

"Where's Spencer?" Big Al shouted as he lumbered from the hallway into my office.

I wished I could ponder weighty issues in peace and tranquility. We lived in a world of so many fascinating mysteries. I could be happy in studying a diverse range of fascinating fields and disciplines. But no. I found myself caught in a trap of my own making. As Big Al approached, I knew I was only going to get a crash-course in how to survive inside of a prison-holding tank.

"We caught our first violator." Big Al sailed into my office with an air of supremacy.

I closed my eyes.

"What's wrong, Spencer?"

"I just have something in my eye."

"Both of them?"

"It all depends."

"On what?"

"On circumstances."

Big Al laughed. "Quick fooling around. I have big news."

"Okay, I will bite. What news?"

"Like I said, we apprehended our first violator under the new rules."

My eyes shot wide open. "Really?"

"Yes," Big Al said. "Gee, you almost act as if it were you."

"No, I'm just too busy working to pay close attention to the enforcement branch."

"Well, it's a big one."

"So, you caught a big fish. Why don't you take a photo of your prized catch and hang it on the wall?"

Suddenly, Big Al exploded with excitement. "What a wonderful idea. I guess I could put it next to one of my wall paintings."

I could understand his wild enthusiasm if he had actually apprehended a violent criminal from the FBI's Most-Wanted List. But I bet his net entrapped a poor stupid sucker who forgot to call the authorities before going to the laundromat.

"Oh, it gets better," Big Al almost attempted a little Scottish jig. "A lot better. You see, the driver refused to accept the ticket. She tore it up in front of a pissed police captain. Right in his face. Boy, the squad of officers took her down. Handcuffed her and threw her in the back of the police vehicle. This will make great copy on the evening news."

The way Big Al acted, it seemed that he was not telling me the whole story. I got the distinct feeling that I might be acquainted with the victim. Maybe it was Mayor Quinn's wife. Now that would be asking for too much.

"Guess who it was?" Big Al taunted as he slipped a new cigar into his mouth. "I understand she's a real terror."

I shook my head. "No, who?"

"Your soon-to-be-ex, Sarah!" Big Al bellowed ecstatically.

My head drooped. Just great. I had explicitly told Sarah to call the DED in the morning, just to play it safe. She resisted at first, but after I supplied her with an earful of negative consequences, she agreed to call and get approval to drive to her workplace, about the only place she ever went. Now it appeared she had ignored my warnings without considering the harsh outcome.

Poor Sarah. My first response was to find a way to quickly rescue her. I could be her knight in shining armor, ready to slay the dragons of injustice and provide comfort to a wrongly imprisoned jailbird. Of course, I could also hire a good lawyer and post bail.

"She's over at the police station. I think you might want to have a little chat with her."

Luckily, Big Al was mainly amused and not angry with me. I supposed that was because he had gone through a messy divorce and detested sassy women. Luckily, I had not told him that Sarah and I were getting along much better.

* * * * *

I gained swift access to Sarah because of my political connections. Still, I was not sure what to expect. In the past, Sarah did not take self-made errors well. Her habit was to pin blame on others at any cost. She was always the innocent one, playing the victim of someone else's fault. I had to be careful not to get caught in her web of victimhood.

As I entered the crowded holding tank, I saw her in a corner sitting on a bench all by herself, looking disheveled and scared. When she saw me, she rushed up and smothered me with a big hug.

"Spencer, I'm so happy to see you."

"Are you okay?"

"No, but I will survive. Besides, it was my own damn fault."

I leaned back, surprised by her honestly. Her response was a breath of fresh air and made me wonder if she had suffered a head injury. This was not like her.

"I hope this will not cause any problems for you at work."

I smiled. Sure, there would be some repercussions at work, but her little act of defiance was not going to jeopardize my position at DED. I was simply too valuable. I was actually proud of her for finally taking a stand. I was almost jealous. She was outshining me. My attempts to revolt against the Man was pathetic.

Sarah sniffled, trying to hold back her tears. "I tried calling. I could not get a line. I was on the phone for over thirty minutes. I had to get to work. They depend on me. I had to take a chance. I had to disobey."

"Well, you did the right thing."

"Are you sure?"

"Of course. That is not what is troubling me," I said. "The real problem is why it took my people thirty minutes to answer your call. That's not possible."

"You don't believe me?"

"No, I don't believe my staff. They are purposely misleading me. I've been assured that waiting time is no longer than ten minutes max."

"There's more," Sarah continued. "I hate to tell you this, but the police now have roadblocks. The traffic is simply horrible."

"Roadblocks? Are you sure?" The only time I had seen roadblocks were on New Year's Eve, and that was late at night in an effort to catch drunk drivers who might kill innocent people.

"You doubt me?"

"Sorry. I didn't know." I could not believe that the city police had resorted to such strong-arm tactics. In fact, I was almost sure that the Supreme Court had ruled random roadblocks unconstitutional, citing that it was an affront to civil rights.

"I understand."

"No, this is my fault," I said shaking my head. "I should have known that my staff was falsifying data."

"You couldn't have known."

I nodded to Sarah as if I was in total agreement with her. I was not. I was definitely the person to blame. I should have known better. My trust was misplaced.

Sarah put her head against my shoulder and sighed. I enjoyed the feeling of closeness and trust and wondered if this was what true love was supposed to feel like.

I paid Sarah's bail. The police had impounded her car, and it was going to take a day or two to work out the paperwork, especially since they caught dozens of other violators that day and impounded their cars as well. I drove her back to work and arranged to have her picked up later in the evening.

The real pain was filling out the mountains of paperwork and understanding all of the conditions for Sarah's court date. The police department handed us a twenty-page packet with information, warnings, and forms. I had to schedule a psychological test for Sarah and get her to sign up for six months of sessions on anger management. Next, they required a history of any drug use, past sexual abuse by friends and relatives, if she ever had had an abortion, a medical examination by a doctor, information on our insurance, who we banked with, our investments and IRA accounts, what organizations we belonged to, and so forth. It was a total invasion of privacy, but the penalties for failure to report were high.

Returning to work, I sought out Tommy in his cubical behind a wall of filing cabinets and boxes of records. His office qualified as a pint-size closet, filled with dusty shelves, and cluttered with overflowing wastepaper baskets. When I found him, he was being rather intimate with a bag of French fries. I frowned. He grinned, and quickly justified his fatty diet by lifting up a bowl of old alfalfa sprouts.

"Tommy, I have something important for you to find out. What is our average waiting time on the phone?"

Tommy shrugged. "The daily stats say six minutes average."

"I've heard someone say that it actually takes almost 30 minutes. Could you mosey around the office and chitchat with some of the more friendly operators? And forget the daily stats." I knew that anyone could manipulate statistics to prove any point of view. I wanted information from the horse's mouth, not Big Al's windpipe.

"I heard they caught Sarah," Tommy said in a low, wistful voice. "Like, man, that's a real bad career move."

"Just get me the information."

"Sure, what am I looking for?" Tommy was stalling. He wanted to do something first. That is how he flaunted his independence, and I usually allowed it. "It's time to check my wart project."

Tommy still wore at least five patches of duct tape on his hands. He peeked under one and remarked that it had diminished a little.

"Can't you do this later?"

"You cannot rush science. Besides, I've got to record the results." Tommy pulled out a little spiral pad of paper and wrote down a few figures. I supposed it was the scientific thing to do, but not on company time. I could see that I was excessively lenient with him. A few of my now 150 workers resented the preferential treatment Tommy received from me. Some complained bitterly, but they were crazy. They acted as if I was substituting Tommy for a son. How could anyone believe that hogwash?

"How about another $20 until payday?" Tommy asked as he played with his duct tape.

I quickly handed over a bill. "But don't buy any more fries. They're terrible. They'll clog your arteries."

"They're tasty."

"You won't get any more money."

"That blows." Tommy made a disgusted face. "I'm not a child, you know. Like I should be able to buy anything I want."

"Shall I take the $20 back?"

"Fine! No fries."

I shook my head. Tommy was incorrigible but entertaining. He would make a fine gypsy, a wandering free spirit disconnected from realty. I should have fired him long ago, but then the world would be a dark hellhole.

Ignoring Tommy's childish response, I made a hasty retreat back to my office. Surprisingly, he dutifully obeyed my instructions. Like a bumblebee, he flew from workstation to workstation to pollinate egos and gather information. I watched as he became chummy and congenial with everyone in his path, tossing his thin arms above his head, as he got excited over some subject that probably had nothing to do with his mission. Within an hour, he had gathered a sense of what was happening to our system.

"It's a mess," Tommy said matter-of-factly. "Everyone is telling me that they cannot handle all of the calls. The wait is up to 30 or more minutes during the morning peak hours. Demand levels off in the afternoon. The reports only show averages, not the spikes."

"So, you are saying that when people need to call most, they can't reach us."

"Yeah, how do you like them apples?" Tommy grabbed a handful of cold fries and soggy sprouts from his pocket. "Want some?"

I turned away in disgust. It was so unfair. If I ate just one fry, I would gain 20 pounds before I stopped chewing. Tommy was the opposite; he was impervious to the ravages of fat. He could devour dozens of cream puffs and lose weight in his sleep. Life was unfair.

Tommy's information was both bad and good news. The long wait was obviously bad, but the implications of hiring more staff and equipment meant a salary of even higher proportions for me. If this growth continued, I would be able to retire handsomely in Beverly Hills with several Rolls-Royces. The thought was both satisfying and heartbreaking. It was all an artificial growth, not based on filling the demand for a product or service, but on controlling and punishing normally good people. That was what made it so ludicrous. These jailed drivers were not committing some violent act, robbing a neighbor or perpetrating fraud. They were just minding their own business. And yet, a few altercations with the DED might ruin their whole life. Then there was a problem with getting the police involved. You would think that they would have something better to do than to spend precious time going after forgetful drivers. What about burglars, rapists, and murderers? Were those now on the back burner?

"Spencer," Big Al returned, still in his cheery mood. "Do you know that we caught over 50 violators just this morning? That is not…"

"Listen!" I interrupted Big Al's train of thought. "I've discovered our problem. Our waiting time is too long."

"I saw the averages; they are not that bad."

"But they peak during rush hour traffic in the morning. There can be as high as a 30-minute wait."

"Is that what your wife said? You know you cannot trust women. I'm surprised she fooled you. You're so naive."

"I've done some research on the matter. I definitely need more staff and equipment for peak hours."

Big Al chomped on his cigar with a worried look. "I was meaning to talk to you about that. We're starting to experience a negative cash flow again. But it's nothing serious."

That was not difficult to believe. I saw some of the numbers from accounting. We were not a revenue-generating machine. It was mostly red-ink expenses and not enough green-ink income. And then there was our unreliable accounting system that would make a crooked car salesman blush. City money was fungible; our funds might end up anywhere, depending on how the city council voted.

"So, what about more people and equipment to fix this problem?" I felt confident pressuring Big Al. I knew the lingo of big-budget spenders. I knew he wanted to make our department grow larger than any business in Hemet, or California for that matter.

"The city treasurer said we need to cut back on spending. How about this—just hire more people but hold back on extra equipment?"

"We already have far more people than stations."

Big Al stepped back and rubbed his chin. He seemed to be unable to figure out the problem.

I just folded my arms and waited. I knew he would come up with some harebrained idea. He always did.

"Ahh…well, I will find some way to get more equipment and personnel. Don't I always find a way?"

With those few encouraging words, Big Al left for his extended lunch hour that was becoming longer than the weekend. I knew he would come up with something. His pay increased as more workers came aboard our money-leaking ship, but maybe that was how the system worked. If drivers could not call in, they had two choices, stay home and lose their job, or risk getting caught and paying a heftier fine. And with each additional fine, the city would get a little richer. I wondered if Mayor Quinn and the City Council knew about this rip-off. Maybe it was really their idea.

* * * * *

I had worked late that night and arrived home exhausted. Sarah had already cooked dinner and left me a hearty dish of leftovers in the refrigerator, which was a newly-instituted ritual. After I started eating, I noticed Natasha hiding under a chair, all scratched up and bloody. Usually, she avoided catfights as much as she shunned baths. But this time, after getting antiseptic and a little loving care, she was eager to go outside for another round. When I heard growling and hissing coming from the backyard, I decided never to let her out again. I held her in my arms and rocked her back and forth. If I liked it or not, she had become my baby.

"Listen to the cats screaming." Sarah came into the kitchen wearing her thin nightgown. "Coming to bed?"

"Yeah," I said distracted by Sarah's almost see-through sleepwear. "Sounds like a battle out there."

"Cats will be cats," Sarah almost purred herself.

"I suppose so."

Sarah moved closer to me. "I just wanted to say I was sorry. You know, about not calling the DED."

I nodded and stared down at Natasha. "I should keep her inside tonight. Something is not right."

"Oh, she'll be fine." Sarah leaned over Natasha and tried to pet her, but I stopped her. "You're not supposed to do that. Remember? You're allergic to cat hair."

"I know," Sarah said as she backed away. "I just forgot."

Before I could figure out how Sarah could ever forget her cat allergies, Natasha acted up. She started to struggle and roll to get away from me. When I released her, she ran to the locked cat door and pawed frantically. She wanted out. I was positive she wanted to join the others and socialize. Yet, Natasha was mostly a house cat. She rarely ventured out at night.

"Let her out," Sarah said, not understanding the problem

"She might hurt herself," I replied. I somehow knew that if I opened the door, I would not see Natasha for days.

"Don't be silly. She just wants some exercise," Sarah insisted.

"No. She doesn't get along with other cats."

"Spencer, you're anthropomorphizing. She's just an ordinary cat. She is probably in heat. Just like me." Sarah kissed my ear, walked a short distance, and wiggled her butt. "Females have to do something to get the attention of males."

That was the best invitation I had had all day and I followed Sarah into our bedroom despite Natasha's cries for freedom. Talk about being in heat. Sarah had turned into a wild pussycat in her own right, wanting every sexual gratification that I could ever fantasize.

Natasha continued to meow most of the night until the cat noise outside finally stopped. I had never seen her so resolved to go outside. Maybe it was just over mating. Maybe there was nothing wrong at all. And yet, I had this strange premonition that her odd behavior had something to do with our human problem. As I slowly fell into an exhausted sleep, I attributed it to my over-active sci-fi imagination.

Chapter 13

Sparks jumped around the office like a bursting star. Anger ignited the air with enough negative energy to collapse the office into a black hole. Nobody was happy. My day was speeding towards a broken bridge, and it seemed hopeless to stop the carnage. Our shiny new IBM System/390 mainframe was down. Our world had ended.

Our computer and its networking system had crashed for over two hours. To make matters worse, over a dozen workers failed to show up, and the phone lines were humming with a crackling noise. Then there was Big Al. He did not take this downtime lying down. His short fuse was burning bright, and I was looking for cover. I knew that the next explosive Big Bang was going to rock our office.

"Spencer!" Big Al barked from across the large room of dark computer screens and grumbling computer operators. I could hear his distinctively loud and raspy voice. As he searched for me in my vacant office, I had just reached the technicians assigned to fix the problem. I was actually doing something important; Big Al, meanwhile, was simply looking for a scapegoat.

As I peered from behind a technician's shoulders, I discovered that a software glitch had spawned a nasty nest of ugly bugs. I was informed that our team of programmers had written dozens of sub-routines that not only failed to solve the original problem, but they had created a few additional ones. The prognosis wasn't good.

"Too many quick fixes. The entire software program needs to be rewritten," my best programmer, Howard Benson, carped.

"Just get it up. Downtime is killing us," I carped back.

119

"If we fix it too quickly, it will just be another patchwork job," Howard warned.

"Just so it works for a little bit longer."

"How long?" Howard snapped. Normally, my best programmer manifested a polite and docile demeanor. Except today. He was evincing a defiant computer engineer with the means to settle scores.

"We'll worry about that tomorrow," I bellowed. I only cared about what worked this exact minute. Who cared about two hours from now? My first priority was real-time, not the distant future. I had to get the system running or a host of motorists might be subject to arrest, fines, or incarceration.

"So, we are fine here?" I asked cautiously.

"Yeah, if you don't ever switch on the power," Howard cracked. He turned away, peered down at his ancient monochrome monitor, and started to write more coding. For some reason, Howard loved his out-of-date green screen monitor. He simply lugged it to work like it was his child. Strange. Then again, his bedside manner was decent compared to the younger uber-dorks, geeks, and code monkeys. They had no patience with middle or upper management.

"You know," he said, "trying to solve problems in these systems often creates worse problems. Nobody takes the time to figure out what is really causing these nonstop errors. We just have to rewrite new routines, compile them, and hope for the best."

"Sounds messy," I said, trying to placate him. Actually, I did not want to hear how or why software problems were so prevalent. I wanted results. Nor did I want to be told that programmers often blundered their way through the complexity. It was unsettling. It was alarming to think that nobody could handle all that might go wrong with computers. As I stared at my wristwatch impatiently, the system finally came back online. I closed my eyes and thanked the Big Kahuna of computers.

"You know what the old-timers call this problem?" Howard took off his thick-lensed eyeglasses and glanced up.

I shook my head. I really did not care.

"Spaghetti Loop. That's when coders try to chart all the subroutines on a blackboard to understand the big picture. The drawling resembles a thrown bowl of wet noodles plastered across a wall. You know, all contorted and jumbled. Cute term, Hah?"

I began to scratch my forearms. It was mildly humorous but in a sick, distorted way. Suddenly, it made me question the bigger picture. You know, how the world operates on a day-to-day basis. Maybe this Spaghetti Loop concept had bigger ramifications after all. Maybe our city had cooked up a hot pot of spaghetti and did not know how to handle it.

"I wouldn't celebrate yet," Howard said. "There's just too many incompatible sub-routines. It's bound to crash again. Real soon." He shrugged as he started to wipe his dirty glasses on his sleeve. "And yet, solving such disparities keeps coders in business."

Suddenly, an epiphany slapped me across the face. I look around the office, especially at the busy phone operators and computer-entry clerks. So many people spending so much energy to solve little problems. And yet nobody factored in the fact that humans and their decision-making capabilities are often faulty and imprecise. Complexity was a bitch. With so many people creating faulty computer sub-routines, inputting mountains of raw data, decreeing a host of inflexible controls, and then finally analyzing information of questionable accuracy, the results had to be less than spectacular. This scenario gave me a cold chill. Our local government could probably never isolate the real problem in order to mitigate it. They could only hope that what they threw at the problem might stick.

I trudged back to my office and slammed the door. I felt like hiding in a corner or some deep basement. Instead, I sat under my desk. I wanted to escape from the helter-skelter swirling around in a vortex of chaos. It was sucking all the oxygen like a firestorm. It seemed unstoppable, and yet I knew that all things must end; at some point, the critical mass would be reached and everything would implode. I sighed and rubbed my throbbing temples.

I began to appreciate the beauty of simplicity. Let natural systems do the work instead of foisting some artificial and arbitrary mandates. But how could anyone control things without resorting to brute force? Maybe that was the real problem, trying to control everything and everybody. Maybe the lesson of Spaghetti Loop was that control was fleeting.

"Where's Spencer?" Big Al's voice thundered throughout the office. I knew my time of pondering deep thoughts had ended. I quickly hid under my office's desk.

I would have been safe except that I accidentally bumped my head. That caught Tommy's attention. He came over and stared down, perplexed to find me on the floor. I immediately lied with a silly grin, explaining that I had dropped my best pen. Tommy seemed satisfied and relayed Big Al's urgent message. My time was up.

I took my time to walk over to Big Al's office. I was in no hurry to be chewed out.

"Where have you been?" Big Al clamored as I entered his office.

"Oh, you're looking for me?" I asked.

He frowned and thumped his big fingers on his cluttered desktop. "Are you trying to avoid me?"

"You!" I scoffed.

"That's right. I may run a taut ship but it's an even-handed ship."

"Amen."

"Okay, so, where were you?"

"Software problems."

"That's all I keep hearing. Trouble this and low memory problems that. What is it now?"

"It's technological. Even I'm not sure what is causing the system to crash and freeze up."

"Well, just fix it! Besides, I have something more important to discuss. Did you notice the checkpoints across town?"

"Some." I paused, remembering a memo saying that checkpoints would be rare and infrequent. "There can't be many, though? Right?"

"You got it wrong again." Big Al shook his head. "We plan to have roadblocks on every major street."

"But our city doesn't have the manpower."

"Sure, we do. The local National Guard is assisting us."

"But is that wise or even ethical?"

"Spencer, do you know that you're a stick in the mud? Get with the program. We're bringing in gobs of money from fines. But that is not our real problem."

"Not our... real problem?" I almost slurred my speech. My mouth drooped into a bewildered frown.

"That's right, we're still dealing with a populace that refuses to listen to us. They are not following our instructions."

"But they cannot get hold of us." I was feeling sick. I moved next to the wall and leaned against it. "Because of our problems, we cannot provide drivers with proper information and authorization."

"No, I don't mean that. That's not what I am talking about. I'm talking about solving our initial problem of honesty. We just conducted some serious research and the results were shocking. Shocking." Big Al eyed the last yellow Twinkie cake on his desk. His fingers began to slowly inch towards his sweet, vanilla-filled prize. He looked up at my disapproving face. He backed off.

"Go on."

"Well, we instructed our police to follow dozens of vehicles in unmarked cars. We knew their destination beforehand. And guess what we found?"

"Well, maybe they got off track a little?"

"Boy, did they!" Big Al pounded the desk with his big hand. "Over 40% did not follow their own pre-approved destinations. They flouted the law like Machine Gun Kelly."

"I see."

"Put on your thinking hat. We need something better." He looked down at the desktop, reached for the Twinkie, ripped off the wrappers, and stuffed some inside his mouth. "I know you're good at that, very good," he mumbled.

I was afraid to suggest anything. I remembered taking a brief seminar on brainstorming. We were told to say whatever came to our beady little minds on a particular subject, no matter how stupid or insane it might sound. Just let it all hang out. No gems of wisdom ever crossed my lips, but the others often had a few workable ideas. Well, I was not going to do any brainstorming session with Big Al. No way. My ideas were probably crazier than the average idiot's, but he would still try to implement them.

"Ever heard of brainstorming?" Big Al hinted.

"I'm no good at that," I said quickly. "Actually, I must get back to our software problem. The system's been up and down for most of the morning."

"Don't worry about it. The city only makes more money when it's down."

"Isn't that slightly...unfair?" I asked.

"Not if nobody knows about it."

"Well, I still have my duties."

"Fine. Go ahead. The morning rush hour has already peaked anyway."

That was so big of Big Al. I was sure the citizenry would have appreciated his loving concern about their well-being. He had few worries when he traveled—he had an exemption permit like all of the city's big honchos. In fact, all city workers had secured exemptions, right down to the part-time janitors, so why should we really care about the less fortunate? Let the public eat fines and ferment in jail cells.

"By the way," Big Al said. "We have an outstanding plan to solve this problem."

"Shoot! But keep it short." I leaned forward, ready for another spasm of outrage.

"We're thinking about making the decisions for them."

I squinted my eyes and bit down on my tongue. I did not want to say anything that would sound negative. "Go on," I said, trying to act civil.

"We'll tell the drivers where and when to drive. Of course, they will give us some initial feedback, but we will be the ones to plan their destination and timelines. No-fuss, no muss." Big Al slowly reclined in his chair. "It was Joe Maffini's suggestion."

"His suggestion?"

"Okay, it was my idea." He grinned modestly. "It goes into effect tomorrow."

"What are the fines?"

"This time they will be colossal. We upped it at $10,000. It will be a felony on the second violation, and a possible sentence up to fifteen years at the county or state prison. That ought to solve this problem in no time. Nobody will show contempt for the law again."

"Yeah, that should solve something."

"What else can we do? The death penalty seems a mite too stiff." Big Al laughed and shoved the entire Twinkie into his mouth.

"Have you considered the unintended consequences?" I asked, looking straight at him.

Big Al eyed me with a confusing scowl. He wanted to reply, but one-half of the yellow cake still protruded from his mouth.

"I mean, what about our revenue stream?" I asked innocently. I enjoyed watching him struggle to talk. It seemed so unnatural to find Big Al constrained from mouthing his nonsense. Normally, If only I could find a warehouse large enough to supply Big Al's appetite for his precious fat yellow pillows of heavenly delight.

Big Al rubbed his chin. "What do you mean?"

"If most violators end up in prison, who will pay the fines? And without increasing revenues, our budget will shrink."

"By George!" Big Al almost choked. "You're right. We will have less money available. That will cramp our style." He paused and looked up. "Hmm... I'm sure I'll figure this out. I always do. Just give me a day or two." Big Al slapped me on the back. "You're just too good for us, Spencer. How about a Twinkie?"

Big Al pulled open a desk draw filled with wrapped Twinkies. He grabbed a handful and threw them on his desk. "Boy, you deserve a great treat."

I was not sure whether I deserved a congratulation, a treat, or the hangman's noose.

* * * * *

Late that afternoon, I received a call from the city manager's office. A secretary from City Hall informed me that Jack Bellamy, the city manager, wanted to see me. That had to be bad news. I tried to get out of the meeting, but I was told that I had little choice. I grumbled, moaned, and slammed down the phone in frustration.

As I walked over to City Hall, I began to sweat. They must have uncovered my little covey of provocateurs. I slowed down my pace; why hurry to my own execution?

I tried to assure myself that we had done nothing wrong. We were simply discussing the strange behavior of some Hemet citizens. We did not belong to any militant group sworn to overthrow Washington D.C.—just an informal group looking for answers. We had the First Amendment behind us. Then again, free speech and assembly were barely lawful in Hemet anymore.

I entered City Hall, meandered down a long corridor, and entered the city manager's office. To the left was a side door with an emergency "exit" sign above. It was so inviting. This was an emergency of epic proportions. All I had to do was mosey over to the exit door and slip the surly bonds of Hemet. I could easily vanish.

"Sit right down here, Spencer," Jack walked up to me and shook my hand. He gleamed with a pleasant smile. That was my first good sign. He was not Mr. Hyde today. But then again, I had another grim reminder staring at me from a dim corner—Jack's evil sidekick, Joe Maffini, one of the more churlish councilmembers. I never did like Joe. He dressed like a Chicago gangster with baggy clothes and an unshaven face. I was always expecting him to start flipping a coin in the air like gangsters from the old black-and-white flicks. I began to perspire. They must have heard about my little meeting. They were going to fire me or maybe something worse.

"We called you in here to discuss a delicate matter," Jack announced, turning serious.

"It was not my fault," I blurted out.

Jack stared at me for a moment, fingered his tie, and started up again. "This is a serious matter, Spencer."

I tried to smile confidently.

Jack pulled closer to his desk. "We have a problem. We have discovered that some of our fine citizens are not too supportive of your department."

"Well, that can happen," I said. "There're always a few complainers who detest government officials."

Jack slammed his hand on the desk. "You're damn right! But not in my town!"

"You see, Spencer," Joe moved into the limelight and spoke in a raspy undertone. "We have discovered certain elements, criminal elements who are dissatisfied with our administration. They have made ugly threats."

"Yes, well, I'm sure the police department will handle it."

"They will," Jack asserted, "but they are undermanned. What I need is a sub-division at the DED that will survey those who oppose our program. All I want is to have someone to take down their names and watch them. You know, make a list and note any antisocial or rebellious activities. Nothing nefarious."

"They're probably just some crackpots who live in their mother's basement," I said, trying to downplay their fears.

"Their phone calls were rather explicit, Spencer," Joe said. "They threatened to bomb City Hall unless we dismantled DED."

"Bomb us?"

"Yes, that is exactly right," Jack said. "Here we are trying to help our dear citizens and instead we have become innocent targets. We cannot permit such barbarity."

"How can you be sure they're really serious? Most hotheads are usually harmless. Their bark is worse than their bite," I said trying to bring in a sense of humor and perspective.

Jack frowned with heavy white brows. He pulled out a shoebox, lifted it up and pulled out a metal pipe wrapped in wire. "We found this pipe bomb near City Hall this morning. Rather crude. Our explosive experts said it was so primitive that only the explosion of another bomb would set it off. Still, they will figure out how to build a better bomb. You had better believe they will. They will learn. They always do."

I wanted to say something to Jack about how crazy our whole program had become; that we were the ones responsible for inflaming citizens' wrath. We were the ones interfering with people's personal lifestyles. We drew the first blood.

Instead, I asked, "Shouldn't Big Al set this up?"

"He's too busy. Besides, he's going to be working on a number of out-of-town projects," Joe said. "He knows about it. He said you were the organizing backbone of his operation."

"But I'm busy too," I said.

"No problem," Joe said. "Just appoint a head of surveillance and have him report to us each morning with a new list of suspects. I am sure this will help us all. So, get on it. We want to start this new project immediately."

"You can count on me," I said as I got up, bowed slightly, and backed away.

"And one more thing, Spencer," Jack murmured as he glanced around to see if anyone was listening. "Let's keep this very low-profile. No need to discuss this with anyone except Joe, your new appointee, and me. Right?"

"Sure," I said. "I assume Big Al is in the loop."

Jack glared at me. "Nobody except the people I mentioned. Like I said before, Big Al is far too busy to be bothered with such details. You understand me?"

I nodded, turned, and walked out the front door in record time. Almost falling down the steps of City Hall, I was elated to get outside of the place and feel the fresh air. It was at this moment that I noticed something peculiarly odd. Every entrance to building was teeming with guards dressed in black military uniforms, armed with wicked-looking guns. As I continued on my way, I heard more noise from City Hall. I turned back and focused my attention on the roof. Heavily armed men ran across the rooftop, taking sniping positions. The sight was so disturbing that I accidentally walked into the street. That was a mistake.

Before I could gather my thoughts, a new, more frightening scene confronted me. Two rows of military drummers led a parade of hundreds of heavily outfitted soldiers, decked out in green camo-clad combat uniforms. Wearing helmets and goggles, they shouldered assault rifles, all heading my way. Twenty yards behind them, rumbled dozens of armor personnel carriers, sporting .50-caliber machine guns. Thirty U.S. army trucks and umpteen jeeps soon followed.

From across the road, I also spotted a squad of soldiers setting up dozens of large green tents in a parking lot, while military helicopters hovered overhead.

All of this fuss over one fake pipe bomb?

I could understand the need for a few security guards at our buildings. That was reasonable. A number of our buildings already had some type of security system. I could not blame the councilmember for upgrading our security policies. After all, it was not every day that a lunatic insisted on remodeling City Hall to a war-torn, bloodied lands architectural style. But this show of military force was off the charts.

When I finally got to the front door of the DED building, I waved at the two men now guarding us. I did feel a little safer. However, I began to question the safety of the ordinary citizens of our town. What about them? They had no city-funded protection for their homes and offices.

But then again, nobody was threatening them with pipe bombs.

"This sucks way too much," Tommy said after he rushed into my office and slammed the door. "You can't do this!"

"Do what?"

"I heard that you were with Jack and Joe at City Hall. That you have been given special and secret instructions."

"Oh, secret instructions? Really?"

"Well," Tommy backtracked. "They must have given you something crazy to do. That's why they demanded an immediate audience with you. Right?"

"Maybe."

"Come on! Everyone saw you rush out with dread in your eyes."

"Fine," I said. This was what I got every time I left my door open. I never learned.

"So?"

"Okay. I did get an assignment. It's rather mundane."

"Nothing's mundane anymore," Tommy said.

"It's just a stupid order," I said.

"I bet it's wrong, really dead-ass wrong, man."

"There are lots of things wrong with the world. Why should I care about this particular one? I'm getting well-paid for doing this job, and so are you."

"Yeah, but money isn't everything. I mean, I know that money makes the world go around, but who wants to live on an out-of-control spinning ball?"

"If it's that bad, why don't you quit?" I stared at Tommy directly for several seconds.

He moved back. "Because I've got to keep an eye on you."

I laughed. "Listen, I'm just following orders."

"Like, that's what the Nazis said at the Nuremberg trial."

My laughing stopped. "That's not a fair comparison."

"Well?" Tommy looked at me impatiently.

"They only hanged the leaders."

"So, you're not a hangable leader?"

I swallowed. "Ahh... I hope not."

"So, what's going to happen?" Tommy peeked out through the blinds at the street below.

"I wish I knew," I said at first, almost forgetting about my orders to keep everything about my new mission a secret. I had told too much to Tommy or too little, I was not sure of which. I guess I had to tell someone. I still could not believe what was happening. Freud proved long ago that our subconscious mind has some type of self-protecting mechanism to hide unpleasant memories. I wished I could use it more often.

Tommy pulled up the blinds and stared down. "Wow! A parade! That's tight."

"You're completely wrong," I said, almost growling. "It's an invasion. We're becoming an armed camp."

Tommy's mouth became unhinged. "Like a gulag? You're not serious?"

I nodded with a straight face.

Tommy sat and rubbed his neck. "No Veteran's Day parade?"

"There's no parade. No confetti. No happy marching bands. No smile faces. No waving flags. It's not even Veteran's Day. Someone planted a fake bomb at City Hall last night. The city has gone berserk."

"And they need an army for that?" Tommy leaned his head back and started to breathe deeply.

"Listen, I still need someone to head my surveillance sub-division."

"Man, I need an aspirin. This really blows."

"Any suggestions?"

"Yeah, how about Brian McNally?" Tommy said sarcastically. "Like he hates having his privacy invaded. Totally hates any infraction of his rights."

"Was he in town during the, you-know-what?"

Tommy looked up at me. "You don't get it, man. He'll never take the job."

"Was he here or not?"

"No, he was somewhere in the High Sierras at a Rainbow Gathering. I would have been there, but I could not get the time off. You said you needed me. Remember? Real bummer."

"Oh, right." I walked over to the window and peeked from the blinds. I pondered what to do. I always had this crazy theory that the best man for any job was the one who would never take the position. It was an outrageous notion. Still, I had read that Alan Greenspan wrote many articles attacking the Federal Reserve in his youth, almost arguing for its abolishment. Later he became the FED chairman of the very same institution, and so far, he seemed to have done a half-way decent job.

Brian was one of my better managers on the second floor. He got things done on time and within budget. His people worshiped him and showered the DED with great call-in and recovery times. I was proud of that floor's accomplishment. Still, Brian was rather crude in his personality. He could be disagreeable, arrogantly boastful, and full of blunt language when he got up his Irish dander.

"He'll make a poor spymaster," Tommy remarked.

"I was assured that the new spy sub-division would just keep tabs on the opponents of the DED. No policy creep. Nothing more beyond what was originally specified."

"Like what happened to us?"

I rolled my eyes and sighed. I knew that our original project description had crashed and burned like the gas-filled carcass of the Hindenburg. Nothing I could do about that now. But if I had to set up an illegal sub-division to locate and catalog disloyal citizens, I might be able to stop it. Otherwise, I might be later known as the leading offender and spend a lifetime of regret behind bars. The big question was whether I could find someone to join my doomed rebel alliance. Then again, more importantly for me, would I do more good than bad? What a horrible life.

"Well," Tommy asked. "Are you going to appoint him?"

"Maybe." I did not see many good choices. Nearly everybody in my office had been in Hemet when that rock exploded, or whatever the thing was. Brian was apparently the only exception. He would have to do, but I wished he were not such an obsessive-compulsive perfectionist. He was a fanatical organizer and planner and excelled at nitpicking down to the last molecule. As a manager, he was supposed to delegate authority and let others worry about minor details. I had once caught him working late one night finishing a project that a subordinate failed to finish. Sure, he had missed the effects of the meteorite, but sometimes he sure acted like one of THEM.

* * * * *

Tommy arranged the meeting. Within an hour, Brian was knocking at my office door. I still had not decided how much information I should divulge to him. I wanted him loyal only to me, not to the crazies at City Hall. I would somehow have to let him know that I had my doubts about this new surveillance project and that we were violating the right of privacy and equal protection. However, such an acknowledgement could easily boomerang. If I dished out too much information, I might wind up at the top of his surveillance suspects list.

"You wanted to see me?" Brian asked with a slight Irish brogue. He had lived in Ireland for several decades before settling in Hemet.

I hesitated. I could not compose my thoughts into any meaningful order. He became impatient. I could see he was eager to get back to work.

"I'm not sure how to say this, but the City Hall wants me to develop a new sub-division. They want someone to compile a list of anybody who fails to support our DED program."

"Christ! You've got to be jacking me off. You mean spy on citizens without their knowledge?" Brian began to move about restlessly and impatiently. "The public won't stand for it."

I stared at Brian for a moment. He was far crasser than Tommy had led me to believe. "Well, yeah. But if they didn't know about it, they wouldn't protest. Right?" I almost felt like slapping myself. That did not come out right.

"That's my point! Someday they will."

"I know. But I have been ordered to gather information on the citizenry. It's benign."

"It's spying!"

"Fine, it's spying... There, it's out. We'll wear black spy gear, sunglasses, and soulless faces with diabolical intentions to conqueror the world."

Brian folded his arms.

"City officials just want to get intelligence on those who disagree with the policies of DED. What could go wrong?"

"It's unconstitutional. It grates on everybody's rights and me. I won't do it."

"What if I double your current pay?"

Brain stopped fidgeting, dropped his hands on my desk, and glared. "You're trying to bribe me. That you are. Don't deny it!"

"No, I'm offering you a promotion."

"Double my wages, you say." Brian cocked his head and chuckled.

"Yeah. This idea comes straight from our city manager."

"Jack Bellamy! The old colonel himself. Never trust the British. That's what I say."

"Well, you'll have to report to him daily. And select a large staff."

"I can see why you upped the wage. Old Fish-Eyed Jack is a sly and wily man without principles or honor. A real proper Englishman, I must say."

"And I will tell you this up front," I revealed and paused. "I am not very thrilled about this project either. But if I don't cooperate with Jack, he will hire someone else with far less integrity."

"I see."

"How about it?" I asked. I could see that Brian distrusted Jack more than I ever could. Apparently, the discord between the Irish and English was alive and well in Hemet.

"I could use the money," Brian whispered and appeared tempted, "but only if I don't have to socialize with that weasel."

"So far, they haven't made that mandatory. Not yet," I said with a sly grin.

"Fine! When do I start?"

"Today," I said with relief. "I want to be kept in the loop even if Jack wants to leave me in the dark. Remember, this is not supposed to be a witch-hunt. Everyone has a right to their own opinion."

"Agreed. I know how to handle bullies. As he keeps an eye on the public, we will keep a sharper one on him."

"And try to find staffers who, how do I say it, dislike their job."

"Oh, that won't be a problem."

We shook hands again and Brian left.

Unfortunately, I knew I was treading into unchartered territory. Everything was going to be a lot more complex. And that meant only one thing—more cooked and gooey spaghetti to gum up my life.

Chapter 14

The only good thing about nightmares is that they usually do not follow you out the front door and into the real world. I could not say the same of James Montgomery. After over two-month absence, he returned to my office with his new colleague, a young, medium-tall Texan with a slight drawl. At first, I was ecstatic: finally, we were going to get some attention from our national government! Unfortunately, it was the wrong type of attention. I was treated to a horror without an ending.

"This is Harry Tuttle," James removed his dark sunglasses and introduced his partner. "He's a special agent with us. He's new to fieldwork, so be gentle."

I shook their hands like any grateful person looking for answers and help. Little did I know that I would never be able to discover their real agenda or the exact agency they truly represented. They were almost as mysterious as the legendary Men in Black.

"We found something interesting on the outskirts of town," James said formally, "and I want you to examine it."

I was delighted to be part of their investigative team. This would give me the opportunity to report on the bizarre happenings in Hemet. Moreover, I was sure he was eager to divulge whatever he had found. This was exciting detective work. There were so many baffling questions that I started to enter them in a notebook. I was hoping that these federal agents could snap all the puzzle pieces together and view the bigger picture.

As we rode together in James's fancy black car with tinted windows, I watched them go through five checkpoints. They flashed their identification and were immediately released without the usual wait to check if they had the proper DDC—Driver Destination Clearance. They seemed neither concerned nor inquisitive about police checkpoints in the middle of the day. I would have been; it would have been my first question. When I brought up the subject, they poo-pooed it. That worried me until I realized that military roadblocks were probably a common practice in Washington D.C. and New York City. I still remembered the 1993 bombing of the Trade Towers. Six people died, but the Towers were impervious to terrorists.

My next anxiety centered on the mystery of my selection. I had no experience in investigating serious criminal cases, accidents, or unexplained phenomena. My job was boring. Who cared about a mid-level manager in a burgeoning bureaucracy? Why not the mayor or the police chief? Why was I the only one selected? My list of mysteries kept expanding by the minute.

As we reached the outskirts of the city, I had a funny feeling that these men were going to take me to a deserted spot, dig a shallow ditch, and leave me in the company of buzzards. It was a silly thought until we turned off the highway and drove down a dusty orchard road. Now I was having far more vivid premonitions of danger. I had to stop watching late-night horror films.

After traveling for eight miles down a winding road, we parked next to a small water pump station. Harry opened my door and ordered me to "get out"—not in a threatening voice, just one that carried no expression, no hint of what I might find. Once I got out, a vile, rotten smell almost knocked me over. Fifty feet ahead, I could see yellow tape surrounding a large area the size of a basketball court.

This was a mind-numbing spectacle, something right out of Steven Spielberg's science-fiction extravaganzas, laden with suspense and a cast of hundreds. Platoons of men in yellow hazmat suits were busily setting up large white tents, unloading equipment, and stacking sealed boxes. Others in white lab coats combed the area with something resembling a metal detector. An army of well-outfitted soldiers patrolled the outer perimeter premier. Teams of dog handlers combed the area with leashed dogs, perhaps sniffing for explosives or anything unusual. This was a grand popcorn blockbuster.

We walked to the edge of the crater and stopped. James held out his arms and pointed to the middle of the cordoned-off section. "What do you think?"

"Looks like a 10-foot-sinkhole." I turned to James. "Looks like nothing special," I chuckled. For all I knew, it could have been a recently-dug pond for irrigation. "It's just a hole. I suspect a farmer dug it to make an irrigation pond."

James smiled. "We asked the owner and he said he knows nothing about it. We suspect it came from that meteorite."

"Okay, I'll bite. What did you find at the bottom?"

"Nothing," Harry said in his down-home-country twang. "It's just a dry hole."

"So why are we here and why the hazmat suits?" I replied.

"It's what we found next to the crater." James raised his hand and gestured me to follow him. Like an obedient child, I moseyed over to the other side of the crater, following slightly behind him. This all seemed so pointless and meaningless, but at least this gloomy cloud had a silver lining; the longer I stayed, the shorter my workday.

We soon came to a large black tarp and stopped. James grabbed one side and lifted it up, dragging most of the plastic groundsheet away. Immediately I could see where the horrible smell was coming from. Right before us was a fleshy mound of dead animal parts. Not just dead, but mangled and hideously deformed. Amidst the mass of bloody flesh was a confusing blob of barely distinguishable bits of yellow fur, a deer's antlered head, and strips of rattlesnake skin. The gooey pile was so intertwined with animal parts that it seemed almost fused together. I stepped back. That was when I noticed millions of black flies buzzing around the rotten flesh. James had disturbed the hordes of flies when he had removed the tarp.

"What the hell?" I shuddered.

"That's what we want to know, too," James said as he kept swatting at the annoying insects. He put on a clear plastic medical mask and slipped on plastic gloves. He next grabbed a stick, moved closer, and pointed at the mass of decaying flesh, muscle, and bone. "If you look closely, you can see that there are at least fifteen distinct animals entangled. They appeared to have attacked each other. Notice the squirrel biting the deer's leg."

"But why?" I asked.

"It could take days to uncover the answer. I suspect some type of degenerative or infectious disease. Both the OEP and the Center for Disease Control should arrive within a few hours."

"So, the crater has something to do with this?"

Naturally, I got no response. I could see that James and Harry did not want to provide further details.

After a few beats of silence, I asked, "Why are you showing this to me?"

"Frankly, you're the only city official that agreed to come out. Mayor Quinn said he was not interested in examining dead animals. We went over to the health department and animal control, but they had no extra crews to investigate. And besides, they told us that your department had the bulk of city workers. What do you have now, over 100 operators?"

"More like 200. And growing."

"Hey," Harry said with a beaming smile, "I bet you get a fat paycheck."

I could see that this was perhaps the perfect time to discuss recent incidents in Hemet. "Could this strange animal behavior have something to do with what's happening in our city?"

James looked down and refused to make eye contact. "We're not here to deal with local issues. Against our rules."

"It's just your typical local politics," Harry interrupted James. "I've seen stranger. I remember when one town outlawed all guns. A week later another town protested and made it illegal not to own a gun."

"But this is different," I explained. "Our city officials are going crazy."

"So, what you're saying is that the locals have gone loco," James grinned.

"Well, not everybody. Just those who were in town during the meteorite explosion. They're the ones who have changed."

"Changed?" James stared at me.

"I mean everyone's trying to control everybody."

"Isn't that just human nature? You know, control the other person before he can control you," Harry said. "We've been doing that in Washington for decades."

"Putting up roadblocks all over the city just to check on peoples' driving destinations isn't human nature, it's insane!"

"They did that in the former Soviet Union. Did that for decades," James said. "Everyone had to take pre-determined routes. Nobody could leave for another city without proper authorizations. Even road maps were banned. Nothing new."

"But we're not in a police state." I was getting frustrated. "I mean, we're not supposed to be."

"You know what I think," Harry said. "You're just having what they call an 'experiment in democracy.'

Hey, nobody said it would be perfect. Is the general public complaining?"

"Well, no, not really," I hated to confess.

"There you have it." Harry cocked his head to one side. "Why fix something if it ain't broke?"

"You know something you're not telling," I shot back. I knew they were playing cat-and-mouse games with me. I just could not understand why.

James eyed his partner. "Well," he drawled. "We wouldn't be in our position if we did not know something more than you. Believe me, we just don't get involved in local squabbles. We're only investigators, not politicians."

"But you're investigators with some authority."

"Not really," James explained. "We're just regular grunts who write reports that nobody reads. Don't take this stuff too seriously. Government is always banning silly little things. Get over it."

"This is different," I said.

"How?" Harry asked. "I mean in my hometown, it's illegal to ride an ugly horse. And we have some really dirty-ass-looking horses. And I once got a ticket for driving a black car on Sunday."

I stood there feeling lost.

"You think that's crazy," James became animated. "Why, in Oklahoma it's illegal to shoot a whale. Yeah, you heard me right. In land-locked Oklahoma. But down the road in Tennessee, a whale is the only animal hunters can shoot from a speeding car. Don't that beat all."

"You're making this up," I said.

Harry put up his swearing hand. "All true. So help me."

James looked at his wristwatch. "I think it's time to get back."

"Wait!" I stretched out my arms. "You know something odd is happening here. How many other fireballs have there been?"

James frowned slightly. "We cannot talk about other investigations. Against policy."

Harry guided me back to their vehicle and drove me back to my office just before the lunch hour. They had told me so little that I could have found out more by reading one of the supermarket tabloids. So much for the information-gathering services of the U.S. Government.

* * * * *

I decided to stay at the office and forget lunch. I only wanted to sulk and stew in my own anxiety juices. I had expected much more assistance from a federal agency. I was begging for help, and they were more interested in showing off their mangled animal carcasses.

Before I could resume my office work, Sarah greeted me at my office doorway. She waved with the tips of her fingers and displayed a timid but heartwarming smile. I thought I heard her giggle.

She never visited me at work. I slid out of my chair, stood, and ventured a short distance. "What are you doing here?"

"Should I go?" She glanced down at the floor, appearing sheepish.

"No, I'm glad you're here," I said eagerly, "but why now?"

"It was slow at the store. Not too many customers of late. And I had a doctor's appointment downtown, so I took the day off. How about lunch?"

"How did you get here?"

"The bus. You know I'm taking the city bus until I get my car back. If the authorities ever return it."

I understood the problem. So far, the city had refused to return the vehicles of DED violators. They were even talking about confiscating them and selling them at public auction. That was completely unfair, but fairness seemed to have currently lost its sparkling attraction. "Yeah, lunch sounds fine."

We walked some distance to the new Nick's Casablanca Café. Nick had been a fanatical fan of Humphrey Bogart's *Casablanca* and had spent lavishly to recreate Bogart's famous French colonial casino and bar in Hemet. He had done such a wonderful job that I expected a piano player to start singing "As Time Goes By."

I had known Nick Gillis, Jr. since my college days and enjoyed our little chats during my lunch hour. His father, who had fought against General Rommel's Afrika Korps in Libya, had established the business years ago. When Nick took over ownership, he remodeled it with a large dining hallway, high arched ceilings, and reddish Spanish tile. The place was scattered with tall feather palms potted in stone Moroccan jars. It was perfect, right down to its dim table lamps adorned with metal shades and hanging beads. It was a movie fantasy worthy of worship. Although fabulous and extraordinary, the place was almost completely empty.

I turned my attention to Sarah and could see that she had something on her mind. She seemed pensive and moody—not a good sign. "I have something important to say," she said breaking the silence. "I think we should terminate it. I mean break off our divorce proceeding. We're getting along much better. Don't you agree?"

"Yeah, that's plausible." Before I could continue, Nick rushed up to our table.

"*Bon Jour*, Spencer!" Nick was sharply dressed in a black tuxedo and bow tie. "And who is this charming mademoiselle?" He gently raised Sarah's hand and kissed it. I had a sudden tinge of jealousy.

Nick was half-French and half snake charmer. He was handsome, suave, fully loaded with charisma and had a romantic magnetism that most romantics would envy, especially his slight French accent. At our local college, my old gang of bachelors quipped that Nick could charm the panties off the most discreet woman within five minutes of his initial impassioned flirt. It must have been his pencil-thin mustache and meticulously styled dark hair.

"I heard you're in charge of the DED," Nick murmured as he nervously wiped his hands with a small white towel.

"I'm one of the big cheeses," I bragged.

"Then you're responsible for all of this disarray." Nick's eyes swelled with anger.

"I'm only second-in-charge," I pleaded.

"You're ruining my business. People are afraid to go out since you made it a crime to drive. We're being locked down and locked out as if we were the epicenter of the Bubonic plague. Nobody books parties. It's too odious to get city permission for everyone to attend. Your *imbéciles* are bankrupting me."

I leaned straight up in my chair. "It's not my fault. I just work for the city."

"That's what everybody says. I talked to the Mayor, and he blames the City Council. City Council blames DED. And now who do you blame?" Nick threw his towel on the table. "Nobody wants to take responsibility."

"Honestly, we were only trying to help people. That's all."

"You should be more careful with the lives of others," Nick said. "We're not yours to play with. I feel that war is coming. Be prepared. It's going to be us against them!"

I cocked my head to one side, surprised by Nick's intensity. It was not one group against another. We were all the same. At least that was what most people believed. But something had changed. People were getting into combative disagreements. Tempers flared. Hostility had replaced hospitality; malice had crushed harmony. Hate reigned supreme. Maybe Nick was right. Maybe we had diverged into a violent us-versus-them society. I shook my head in disbelief. That could not be. We were all the same people. *We are them; they are us.*

"Can't we all just get along?" Sarah insisted.

"*Non!*" Nick's face soured even more. "It's too late to reconcile. Gone too far."

"I could mediate," I said. "I could make it all better," I lied.

"We must fight or flee. That is our only remaining choice."

"The city is not your enemy," I said without thinking. I hated the thought of defending the offenders. I was just as trapped as Nick. I was making excuses for the forces of injustice. I supposed it had something to do with some unconscious instinct, some defense mechanism to protect my livelihood. Besides, nobody wanted to be a traitor to his co-workers or boss. I had to fight my natural sense of self-preservation.

Sarah looked up at Nick imploring, "We're not too thrilled with what the city is doing. In fact, I hate it."

Nick sat next to her. "Bravo. At last someone willing to stand defiant and assault the Bastille."

I looked around the room to see if anyone was listening. The only occupied table was on the other side of the room. I motioned Nick to inch closer to me. "We're trying to do something. We have held secret meetings to discuss what to do. You can come to the next one," I proposed.

Nick stopped and looked around his eating establishment. "Maybe."

"It's just a little informal discussion group," I said.

"I've got to be careful. Someone is watching me." Nick eyed the darker corners of the room.

I sighed. The people spying on him were probably mine, except that I should have known about any surveillance of Nick's restaurant. Brian was supposed to inform me about everything that Jack commanded, unless, of course, our illustrious city manager instructed Brian to tell nobody of his plans. I got the feeling that Brian was working only for Old Fish-Eyes. I could feel an instant headache rippling across my forehead.

Nick leaned over and whispered, "They think I'm a terrorist."

"What?" I almost shouted.

"I only called City Hall to complain a little. That's all. And now strangers in black suits follow me day and night."

"What are you going to do?" I asked. I felt sheepish and conflicted. I did not have the heart to tell him that my department was probably responsible for his distress.

"I should flee," Nick said. "You know, fly with the wild geese before our wings are broken or clipped. Might just fly out one of these days. I have a beautiful Piper Navajo at the airport. If things get too rough, I will take to the airways. I will not put up with this *insensé* nonsense forever. You should come with me. Both of you."

"We can't forsake our friends," Sarah said. "We're not going to surrender. We're not jellyfish. We have backbones. This is our home, not some banana republic."

Sarah was right. I did not think it was time to lower the lifeboats and abandon the *RMS Titanic*. I was sure the situation would balance itself out eventually. Enraged citizens would demand a recall election and vote the bastards out of office, and then our lives would return to some state of normalcy.

"The offer remains. You can be my co-pilot. I know you can fly." Nick looked up and saw an older couple enter the restaurant. He quickly followed the couple to their table.

"It's a nice offer," Sarah said. "You have good friends."

"I know." I had a feeling that all my decent friends would be put to the test or the chopping block. Only then would I discover how good they really were.

I watched Nick help the older couple with their menu and felt responsible for his dying business. I should have done something long ago. But what? I racked my brain to figure out how I could have stopped this madness. Feeling a sense of shame, I pushed my guilt over to my mental back burner and turned to Sarah. As we chatted, I mentioned my trip out to the orchard and the dead animals. Sarah looked uneasy.

"I saw it two days ago," she said.

"You saw what?"

"Hundreds of dead birds."

"Hundreds?" Sarah always exaggerated.

"I saw the bloody carnage. They were attacking each other as if they were mortal enemies." Sarah paused. "Well, maybe it was only 60 or 70 of them. Hard to tell. Mostly black crows, scrub jays, and several turkey vultures.

I slowly swiveled my head closer to Sarah. "You saw them attacking each other?"

"Near my workplace. Feathers and body parts were flying everywhere. When I got there, they were all dead in a mushy ball of bloody feathers and broken bones."

"That's what must have happened in the orchard. The animals were twisted and disfigured beyond recognition."

"What animals?" Sarah asked, inching closer to hear my gory details.

"I don't want to talk about it," I said, trying to keep my stomach from churning and knotting up. "I mean... it was just awful. It was a big red ball of animal bodies that looked as if it came out of a meat grinder."

"What does it mean?" Sarah began to shiver with fear.

"I wish I knew."

"My God!" Sarah put her hand over her mouth. "Maybe it's a disease, some new pathogen. It could be affecting both us and the animals."

I assured her not to worry, that a federal agency was investigating that same possibility—although my faith in their capabilities had diminished.

"There is something bigger happening here," Sarah said. "A much bigger picture."

"Yeah," I agreed. "But the pieces of the puzzle refuse to match up."

"Do you know that the city wants to prosecute me?" Sarah reached for my hand. "They want me to serve jail time. It's becoming a nightmare."

"Don't worry. I will get you off. I have some pull at City Hall. They owe me bigtime. I've done so much for them."

"Oh, you mean," Sarah's voice dripped with sarcasm, "helping the crazies turn our lives into a living hell?"

I begrudgingly shrugged my shoulders. "Somebody was going to do it anyway."

Chapter 15

I entered my office the next morning, dragged my carcass to my desk, dropped into my chair, and closed my eyes. I sat there waiting for misery to find me, abuse me, and take away any last hope of surviving life. Instead, a parade of misery walked up right next to me. It was Tommy with eyes like stars and a grin made of sunshine. I was feeling sick.

Tommy was usually the first to greet me at the office. I had promoted him to my assistant. I had to do that. It was the only way to keep an eye on Tommy's extracurricular activities. However, today he was keeping an eye on me. I knew that mild look of alarm. It reeked of bad news, especially since I was without my morning caffeine.

Tommy hovered over me and watched.

"What is it?"

"Well, I hate to ruin your day so early in the morning," Tommy said as he handed me a cup of coffee so sugary it tasted like a warm, flat soda. "But I think we're being seriously watched."

I dropped my cup on the desk, spilling it. "Tell me you're just goofing off."

Tommy shook his head.

I stood. "How in the hell do you know?"

"I saw several men on rooftops with huge black telephoto lenses. You know, the kind that can see if your pants fly is open two miles away. I saw them right outside our window yesterday."

I slowly drifted over to the window and peeked outside, trying to hide my face without being too noticeable. I saw nothing, and slowly closed the blinds.

"I can't believe Big Al or anyone from City Hall would spy on us. I mean, we have Brian in the loop. He is supposed to keep that from happening." I began to panic. What if they had spotted me talking with Nick, or had taken snapshots of our secret meeting at my home? I had to think fast. I had to come up with foolproof excuses to prove my innocence.

"Hey, man, chill out," Tommy said. "What could they do to us?"

"Oh...are you serious? Almost anything!"

"This is America."

"Are you sure?" I huffed. There must be a way to defuse the situation; some way to fight back. "I think the SEIU labor people should know about this travesty. Get Lenny in here." I was no longer a union member, but the city might also be spying on Lenny's union members. That should get most union members hot under the collar.

Tommy grabbed my desk phone and told the secretary to locate Lenny and send him running to my office. It did not take long for the message to reach him. Lenny spent most of his time in our building anyway since the bulk of city workers had transferred to my department.

As Tommy hung up the phone, he dropped another bombshell. "There's something else I should tell you, man. And boy, you won't like this one either."

"Quick wasting time. Just tell me."

"Well," Tommy took his time to build up the suspense. "This might put you the emergency room."

"Just spill it," I ordered.

"Okay, okay. I've discovered that some expensive audio and photo equipment is targeting us."

"You're saying that we're being spied upon?"

Tommy nodded.

"How do you know that for certain? You better not be pulling a prank on me. This is not funny, not one iota."

"See, I knew this news would put you into intensive care."

"How do you know we're being monitored?" I cringed.

"I saw them on the rooftop. You know, from the bank building across the street. From what I could see, they have professional eavesdropping and telephoto spy cameras. Real expensive crazy shit."

"No, No. This cannot be happening." I buried my head in my hands, and closed my eyes.

"You should see it, man. They could pick up the heartbeat of a mosquito or snap a photo from Los Angeles."

This was getting better all the time. I bet they could listen to our conspiracy nonsense right through solid walls. Maybe I should just end it all and stick my head into wood chipper. As the seriousness of this news began to sink in, Lenny entered and plopped into a chair next to my desk.

"What you want? Came as soon as I could."

I did not feel like saying anything aloud, not even if someone asked me to start reading from the phone book. I realized that if someone was listening, we could not continue to talk in such subversive lingo. It was probably too late anyway, but maybe they were not recording every damn minute of the day. Even surveillance teams took bathroom breaks.

"Well?" Lenny was becoming impatient.

I grabbed a pen and notepad and wrote down a few words—"the room may be bugged," and handed it to him.

"The room is bugged!" Lenny yelled and jumped up. "You shitting the bull."

I dropped my head as if I were leading a funeral march. Tommy began to bang his head against the wall. What was it with these Russian immigrants? You would think they had no experience with secret police and eavesdropping equipment.

"That's the rumor going around," I moaned. "We're not sure. Probably just a joke." I tried to say as little as possible. I was not sure how Lenny would take this. Russians were suspicious of almost everything. They had lost their appetite for the truth long ago.

"No problem. I understand much," Lenny said. "That's why I leave Russia. Hate people spying on me. KGB no good. Those guys real *mudak*! Real jerks!"

"Wait," Tommy said. "I thought you were a Communist?"

Lenny rolled his eyes. "No, whatever gave you stupid impression? Nobody belongs to CP anymore. That's so pasty."

"Passé," I corrected him.

"That what I meant," Lenny huffed.

"Listen," I said. "We can talk about this later. You know, over beer and pizza. Right?" I wanted to misdirect our talk to confuse any possible listener.

"Sure," Tommy said. "No rush. There's not much to talk about anyway."

I went back to my notebook and wrote another note. It read, "Don't say anything more. Meeting tonight at my place at 8:00 PM." I held it up to everyone's face.

Tommy nodded.

Lenny stared at the note with a bored look.

"Hey," I said. "How about those Dodgers? Great game the other day!" I tried to change the subject. "Maybe this year they won't be an embarrassment."

"Never watch big football," Lenny said and stood up. "See you tonight, Spencer."

I leaned against the wall and wished I had a loaded gun in the drawer. I could just end it all now in a big display of smoke and hot lead. No need to shoot me in front of a firing squad. I could do it myself.

"Must go," Lenny said. "See you all later."

Just as Lenny retreated, Big Al invaded my space in a whirlwind. I could see that he was angry and distraught. He rudely ordered Tommy out of the room and slammed the door.

I was a goner. He must have found out every little detail about me and my subversive activities. Every traitorous plot, every mutinous thought. I was cooked, sealed, and all wrapped up in a tight bundle, ready to discard in the nearest dumpster. So long Caribbean cruises with tropical beaches and warm sandy water. Goodbye to my bloated bank account. Hello, unemployment line or confined room.

"Spencer!" Huffed Big Al, looking ill with distress. "We have serious problems."

I took a long, deep breath. I closed my eyes and expected the worst.

"They caught my mother."

"What?" I shouted as my eyes shot wide open.

"The damn police arrested my mother." Big Al started to whine like a baby with a bad case of diaper rash.

"Can they do that?"

"Get serious," Big Al huffed. "She flew in from Florida today. They stopped her at the checkpoint on State Street and arrested her. She could get ten years in prison. What can we do?"

"But she is not a resident of Hemet," I countered, trying to show some sympathy without displaying a silly grin of delight. If anyone in the world should get stung by his own stinging hive of busybodies, it was Big Al. He was the one who cracked open Pandora's Box, and now he was suffering like the rest of us peons. Bully for the impartial law. Of course, I expected the mayor to make an exception in Big Al's case. It was only human to protect your own people, even if it were unfair to everyone else.

"Doesn't matter," Big Al cried. "The city council doesn't care where a violator comes from. You are supposed to obey the laws of the land. Period. Don't you know anything?" Big Al turned a deep color of beet red. "I guess I forgot to tell her the finer details of our laws. I'm at fault, not her. I should be the one sent to prison."

I gritted my teeth and nodded slightly. I wanted to jump up, pop a bottle of Champagne and lead a parade of screaming cheerleaders around the office. Instead, I felt compelled to ask calmly, "What are you going to do?"

Big Al shallowed and looked at his hands. "I'm not sure. I have already talked with Mayor Quinn and he is adamant. He said there are no exceptions. No exceptions! What kind of law is that?"

"Well, it's a law without exceptions," I said to make my point as clear as possible. "Laws must be equally enforced; otherwise, it would be favoritism."

"My mother is 81 years old and in poor health."

"I would hire a good attorney."

"I would, but my attorney left town. Said he was never coming back. Can you imagine that? What's with some of our town's people?"

"Find another one. I'm sure he can find some loophole in the law."

"You don't understand. We took great pains to prevent any possible loopholes. We wanted to make our laws airtight."

I began to feel a little pinch of pity for this wrecked soul, but he deserved every bit of misery that he could suffer. "You caused this disaster, Al. Why didn't you foresee the danger signs ahead? You know that there are always unintended consequences to any course of action! Christ. You're in upper management. You're supposed to know these things."

"I guess I got carried away." Big Al continued to sniffle with his head hung low. "How could I know? Jack and Joe asserted that everything would work out well. Anyway, I was just following orders."

That is when it hit me like a sack of bricks falling from the sky. This had gotten to the point where even the insiders were no longer getting preferential treatment. Without some safety valve—loopholes, bribery, favoritism, call it what you will—the steam cooker would explode. When the politically savvy fall, the whole system would soon follow.

I patted Big Al on the back. This was the exact lesson learned from the Reign of Terror in France. Many of France's leaders who were more competent turned against each other. They had forged an extremist society where laws were more important than people. They had become righteous and rigid, making laws that held the public to a higher standard than those who concocted the laws. The outcome had to result in tragedy. Robespierre had condemned many of his politically skillful friends to death. In return, Robespierre found himself facing the guillotine. Terror was the only winner.

"They will not imprison my mother," Big Al said. "It's preposterous to jail an old woman."

"They're just obeying the city council's ordinances."

"Not on my watch!" And with that bold statement, Big Al rushed out of my office.

I actually wished him well. I hoped he could get his mother released. Sure, I detested him, but now that he had become one of the suffering masses, he seemed more human.

* * * * *

Arriving home early, I decided to watch parts of a particular war film. Ever since I witnessed the meteorite over Hemet, I had barely turned on my large flat screen TV. I had lost my taste for movie entertainment, except for one remarkable film, John Wayne's *Alamo*. I could watch that film until the end of time. It was a silly obsession, but it was like watching real history in the making, even better than some documentaries purporting to have the latest historical Alamo facts.

Even Sarah, the ultimate bookworm, came over to cuddle next to me on the couch. Oddly, she had the same fascination with this classic Western film. She asked me if I had some secret desire to be like Davy Crockett. I was not sure. My parents were born in Texas and they idolized Crockett and Bowie. As a young boy, I did not find it very appealing to die in a hopeless battle for a decrepit, abandoned Spanish mission. Now I was beginning to understand the reason why some people were willing to fight as underdogs in a losing cause.

"They should have just surrendered," Sarah blurted out as we watched the last big battle scene of the film. "They didn't really have a chance."

"They knew their chances were nil to nothing," I said. "They were making a stand no matter what. It was win or die trying."

Sarah still held to her guns and argued that the Texans could have retreated and fought another day. "It was such a waste of men."

I tried to put it into perspective. "They refused to run away from their bad situations. Most people scattered in fear. They would run away from their problems and hide. But these courageous men drew a fixed line in the sand. I mean, somebody has to stand up to the bullies. We cannot just walk away from them. They won't let us. Right?"

"All I meant was that they could have retreated and fought another day, she said."

"The Texans refused to do that," I said. "Of course, I often don't follow my own advice."

"You think?" Sarah taunted in a sarcastic tone. "When trouble comes knocking at your door, you're the first one out."

"Faster than a startled jackrabbit," I joked.

"Seriously," Sarah blinked her eyes in disbelief. She moved closer and gently put her hand on my forearm. "You talk of bravery, but what have you done to stop the bullies at City Hall?"

I lowered my head. "I know. But we're just talking about a movie."

"But it happened. It's history."

"You mean your master?"

"Well,… no. Maybe." This was so typical of Sarah. She would try to end an argument by passing judgement on my flimsy excuses. I knew she thought I always ran away from my responsibilities; that I found it easier to barricade myself in an easy chair than to take command of my life. But this time she did not attack my crumbling fortress. Instead, she comforted me, held my hand tighter and stared at me with her beautiful black eyes.

"Oh, I know you will do what is right."

My eyes flashed with surprise at her strong response. I was taken aback by her confidence in my abilities. "You're right, we should do more to fight back this danger. Because…"

"Because if we don't, we will lose the world we know," Sarah said. "It will not be a world worth living in."

"Exactly," I immediately grabbed her and planted a big kiss on her red lips. I felt if I was sitting next to Mrs. Davy Crockett, hopefully, a fervent fighter just as dedicated as her husband.

"I truly understand," Sarah said. She turned away and pointed to the television screen. "This is the best part." We both watched the Mexican soldiers swarm like locusts through a blasted hole in the Alamo's mud-brick wall. It seemed so futile. There were just too many of them. Nobody could survive such an onslaught. Tears came to Sarah's eyes.

She turned to me and whispered. "They gave so much for future generations. It's hard to believe. They refused to give up."

I nodded in silence.

As we continued to watch Davy Crockett blown apart in the exploding powder magazine, I reminisced about my youth. My father had eagerly given me an old beaver-skin hat on my eighth birthday. It was a poor present. The Davy Crockett fever had swept the nation long before, so my father's gift embarrassed me. I wore it once, then set it aside. I knew he was disappointed, but I had no idea that it meant something more to him than killing bears and living alone on the frontier.

As the movie credits rolled, I continued to think about the film. A small group of men had fought against overwhelming odds. They gave their lives in a dusty wasteland in the middle of nowhere, so that others could be free. They did not fight for higher pay raises, promotions, or the TV remote. They had banded together to fight an oppressive authority when they could easily have retreated. It put a lump in my throat. I only wished I had their resolve.

* * * * *

After turning off the DVD player, I began to search my house for my elusive cat. Natasha had not eaten her food from the previous day, and that was peculiar. Nocturnal and shy, she spent most of her time hiding under furniture, my bed or the bushes in the backyard. But eventually, hunger would drive her out into the open.

Even Sarah assisted in my quest for Natasha's whereabouts. This was another first, since she was the proverbial cat avoider. I could not believe that she would risk a minor allergic attack by getting close to Natasha. She got on her knees and reached down behind a big clump of bushes. Her bravery was commendable, but foolish. Why was she willing to risk an allergic outbreak over a cat?

"Over here!" Sarah shouted from our backyard. She pointed to something in the dense bushes.

I moved closer and peered down. At first, it resembled something out of Steve McQueen's 1958 *Blob* film. The storyline was also a favorite of mine. A growing blob of the red gooey Jell-O had turned a small town into a smorgasbord of swirling human flesh. The blob had dissolved and consumed half of the town's folks and swelled to the size of a building. Curiously, the monster had supposedly come from a meteorite. Great movie classic, but I had no desire ever to see it again.

I looked down at the red clump and decided that it was not my cat. The gooey mess was just too large. I stood and stared at Sarah, gasping, "It looks just like what we found at the orchard!" I stepped back and felt assaulted by a maze of unanswerable questions. Something was happening beyond our awareness, and way beyond our ability to understand.

We eyed each other in surprise, mouths open. I spoke first. "It seems we're faced with 'unknown unknowns.'"

"What?" Sarah groaned. "What are you talking about?"

"You know,.. the things we don't know we don't know."

"This is getting serious," Sarah held her hand over her mouth. "We have to do something."

I moved closer to the object. I could see some fur, but mostly bones, muscles, and a few internal organs. I kicked it. It was large, but not moving. It had to be larger than 10 or 20 dead creatures, all fused together into one fleshy ball of pulp. What a horrific sight. This could not be a natural phenomenon. "Unnatural" was written all over it.

Sarah backed away, silent, and wearing the look of horror on her face.

I took out a shovel, dug a large hole, and attempted to bury the bloody remains. I keep thinking that this thing was not part of my cat. Natasha was a little chicken-shit coward who never showed any signs of bravery. She might hiss and snarl when unhappy, but would usually back away. I figured she was still prowling the neighborhood and would return when hunger struck again.

When I had finished my grave-burying duty, I just stood and stared at the burial mound. Sarah took me inside, sat me down, and poured some wine. We both sipped a little and talked about other things, the kind of trivial conversation that makes people feel better. She was a real trooper. She knew I was down in the dumps and needed some cheering up, something that only a good wife or an expensive therapist could do.

"Something bad is going down," I said. "Whatever happened to those animals could happen to us. We could be breathing it, touching it, or even eating it. It could be anything or anywhere."

"How about those Dodgers?" Sarah put a hand on my shoulder. "They pitched a no-hitter the other day. Made some news."

"Yeah, I know." I felt like their opposing ball team. We were also batting a no-hitter.

Chapter 16

It was almost time for the meeting to start. I peeked outside from behind my closed blinds and curtains. I scanned the street for unmarked and windowless vans, hovering black helicopters or cloaked strangers loitering around my neighborhood. Seeing nothing suspicious, I locked the doors, turned off several lamps, and prayed that nobody would notice that I was holding a secret meeting.

My covert activities made me feel emboldened. I was not cowering in fear in a locked closet or hiding under my bed. I was remaining calm and clear. I had decided to dig a deeper trench in the sand; I was going to fight back, stand my ground, and not back down. One day I might be heralded as a visionary who dared to resist or spend eternity as a bullet-riddled body in an unmarked grave. Whatever the cost might be, I only hoped that my adobe would not resemble the Alamo on its final day.

As the hour neared to meet, I began to feel like the most unlikely leader of a dissenter movement. I had never considered running for any student offices at school or participated in after school sports or outside activities. I rarely had joined any social or service clubs, and freely joked that I would not belong to an organization that would accept me as a member. I was a homebody, a fly on the wall, nobody of importance. Now, I was thrust into a leadership position that took some fatalistic nerve.

Tommy was first to arrive on his bicycle, since he could not get permits from the DED to drive his vans from one parking space to another. Besides, most of his fleet of junk cars were impounded for parking violations. His last remaining unseized van was sitting inoperable in a vacant, weed-infested lot, the engine in one heap and transmission in another. It had been lounging there for years.

Tommy rushed inside, breathless, and faced me with a frantic look in his eyes. "There are armed soldiers everywhere. Man, I mean everywhere."

"Did they try to stop you?"

"They never got close enough. I outfoxed them."

"Good to hear."

"Yea, but the crackass' tards won't release my vans. They're planning to sell them for storage charges. What the shit is happening? Everything is just too trippy."

"They've got to be desperate to want your vans," I joked.

Tommy scowled at me with his shiny, glazed eyes. "It's the stuff inside they want, man. I mean they've got most of my saws, wrenches, air compressors, drills, generators, microscopes, computers, chemicals, books, paintball guns, golf clubs, rock collection…"

"All right!" I hollered as more people filed into the room. I did not have the heart to tell him it was destined to end up in a landfill.

By this time, the room exploded with people, mostly newcomers, neighbors, and friends of friends. Our meeting was a hit. The whole living room, kitchen, and hallway were crammed with incensed citizens, upset over the latest law that sentenced violators to five years of hard labor for the first violation. Tommy counted over 50 people.

"We should hang the lot of them," Grandma Smothers from next door shrilled. "Who do they think they are?"

"I've got a loose noose and a wobbly chair," another old woman cackled. "I'll hang them from my ceiling fan and kick over the chair myself. That will show the bastards."

The crowd was getting out of control. I had to bring some order before they rushed outside and carried out what they were threatening.

"There is more to this than bad laws, hefty fines, and long prison terms," I said, standing on a chair to get their attention. "Something in the air or in the water has caused this control frenzy. There must be a logical reason for their obsessive-compulsive behavior."

"They're all anal-retentive butt-heads," Grandma Smothers shouted to the delight of the agitated crowd.

"They were just trying to help," I raised my voice.

"Yeah! And we'll help them to an early grave," someone yelled from the kitchen.

"What are you going to do?" A young woman stepped forward and pointed a wagging finger at me. "You're the one in charge of this cursed DED."

"I'm the Assistant Director, to be precise. I'm in charge of operations, but I don't make policy. I risk more than you do by hosting this meeting. And I only want to end this insanity and return to some kind of normalcy."

Before anyone could comment on my statement, half-a-dozen police cars with blaring sirens roared down the street. I held my breath. Everyone turned deadly silent and stared at my front door. The wait seemed to last for hours. Were we the intended targets of their urgency? What if they caught us plotting against THEM? What would they do? The fleet of police vehicles screamed past my house and into the night. There was a collective sigh as the last siren faded.

"Listen," I said to break the tension. "We need constructive solutions to our problems. Any ideas?"

"I think some sort of peaceful civil disobedience is appropriate," a voice echoed from the back of the room. It was Sarah. I was overjoyed. She had drawn a line in the sand, or at least in our living room.

"Turn the other cheek in front of City Hall? Huh?" Someone belittled her suggestion. "You know they have armed guards and soldiers now. You'd think we lived in North Korea!"

I turned to that person, a professional-looking man in his thirties. "You want us to attack City Hall with guns? Is that what you want?" He backed down.

Before I could entertain a motion to support a protest rally, Rant, Candy, and some of their friends made a grand entrance, all dressed in black "gothic" garb. Rant's eyes were glazed and misty. "They shot Rudy!"

"Oh, no!" I groaned as the crowd clamored. "Rudy never harmed anybody."

"He ran the checkpoint near State Street." Rant moved to the center of the room as all eyes turned to her. "Who's next?"

"By God, not me," someone roared.

"And..." Rant spoke deliberately and slowly, waiting for everyone to calm down, "and now he's dead."

Rant and her cohorts were taking the tragedy personally, believing as if they must strike back before the Gestapo-like police returned for another round of street violence. I could feel the paranoia and fear choking the room. Their friend was dead, and they were demanding revenge.

"Don't get excited!" I shouted out a warning. "It could have been an accident."

Rant cut me off shamelessly. "Talk is cheap! They shot Rudy like a dog! We cannot allow this travesty to continue."

That is when I noticed the bulge in Rant's pocket. Others had similar bulges. They were hiding guns. It seemed that almost everyone was armed. My mind flashed on an image of a mosquito attacking an elephant. It was suicidal. They thought they could conquer a heavily armed force with their little band of crackpots.

I made a desperate plea. "You know what Mahatma Gandhi said!"

"No! I don't want to know," Candy spoke up. "You pacifists make me sick. Rudy never harmed anyone. It is time to take matters into..."

I interrupted her and yelled, "There is no cause for which I am prepared to kill!" The crowd turned silent. "That's what Gandhi said. He would die for a cause, but never kill for one." I was not sure if that impressed anybody.

"That's utter stupidity," someone yelled out. "We want revenge!"

Rant climbed up on a chair, screaming, "The Rubicon has been crossed! We must do something now. The Fascists from City Hall must pay the price for their atrocities. Today it is Rudy. Tomorrow it will be you!"

Rant had seized control of the center stage and refused to surrender it. I waved my hands to get the crowds attention, but Rant had soared as the new showman in the ring. Everybody was ignoring me. She had turned Rudy into a martyr, but revenge was their only thought.

"Have you heard what the city bigwigs plan to do now?" Rant yelled.

The crowd turned silent.

I made one last attempt to grab their attention. "We have to discuss this rationally," I pleaded. I was afraid to find out what Rant meant. Every time the city had upped the bar, my head would spin for hours. Still, I was almost certain that they could not raise it higher because few could vault over it now.

Rant slapped her hand over her concealed handgun. "Anyone caught violating the law is to be summarily shot. No trial, no jury, no due process, no justice."

That did it. The fuse was now lit. The whole room exploded into shouts of catcalls, hisses, and profanity. They were livid. The discussion was over. Almost everyone had jumped to their feet and were headed for the door. It was Lexington and Concord all over again. They were out for blood, and I was sure they would find it sooner than later.

"We must remain calm," I continued to shout as the room instantly emptied. I stepped in front of Grandma Smothers and blocked her path, hoping to prevent her from leaving. Urban warfare was no place for an old woman. She disagreed. With a swift flex of her foot, she kicked me in the knee, and then pushed me aside.

"Out of my way, Sonny," Grandma Smothers howled. "It's either US or THEM. No sissy talk will help now. This granny is going to get her gun!"

I stepped back. I wanted no part of this madness. As the room turned silent, only five of us remained. Surprisingly, Rant was one of them.

"We must do something," Rant demanded.

"But it's suicidal!" I said.

"I know. I know." Rant's face lowered. She slowly turned away and walked out.

Tommy scratched his head. "Like, what a rush! Wow, far livelier than a Deadhead concert."

"Is this what you call veggie-auntie?" Lenny asked. "Everybody goes crazy cowboy!"

"Shouldn't we follow them?" Sarah asked as she started to head for the door.

I grabbed hold of her arm and pulled her back. "Are you crazy? There are trigger-itchy soldiers down there with machine guns and bayonets. How can they tell the sensible people from the crazies?"

"Screw them!" Sarah struggled to break free of my hold.

"What's wrong with you?" I shook her.

"Don't you see? The enemy is trashing our lives, our families, and our way of life. We must defeat them at all costs." Sarah broke free of my grip and grabbed a flower vase, threatening to throw it at me.

Dumbfounded, I watched her dogged eyes and belligerent attitude. She was irrational. "Just slow down, Sarah. We can work this out."

"Man… Sarah is torqued!" Tommy mouthed the obvious.

"So, what are you going to do, Tommy?" Sarah's wrath had expanded to others. "Eat more wheatgrass and vegetate? They're shooting and killing us. They're not taking prisoners. Nobody is being arrested, no trial and no jury! Just instant death!"

"We're not sure that is true," I spoke slowly and softly.

Sarah lowered the vase. "I just cannot take it. Everything is spinning out of control."

I walked up to Sarah and took her weapon away. "You were always the peacemaker. Remember?"

"Yes, I know," Sarah said lowering her voice. "I don't feel well."

I helped Sarah sit down and brought her a glass of water. "Maybe we can find out what is happening." I switched on the television in an effort to confirm Rant's statement, although her information was generally accurate. All of the stations were off the air. Next, I tried the radio. I could not get any local stations, only distant ones from far away. In desperation, I considered calling Big Al at home. I hated to disturb him, but I needed to know the latest scoop. Strangely, his number had been disconnected. Suddenly, a sense of isolation engulfed me. It seemed as if we were behind enemy lines and would have to fight our way back to friendly territory. I shrugged off that silly notion. I knew it was due to my steady diet of war films.

"Maybe it's time to think about leaving," I said in a whispery voice.

"What?" Sarah grabbed my hands. "You mean leave Hemet? I thought you want to stand up to the city bullies."

"Well…" I fumbled for the right words. Before I could answer her question, gunfire echoed in the distance.

"Fireworks, no?" Lenny stole a peek from out the window.

Tommy had a better line. "Someone must be driving my van. It's always backfiring."

"We cannot leave," Sarah implored. "This is our home."

"What do you suggest?"

"I'm not sure. Wouldn't Davey sandbag his house, get out his musket, and die in a hail of bullets?"

"You mean like they did at the Alamo?" This is what I got for showing epic war films too many times. Nobody survived that horrific battle. It was a lost cause. I guess they should have left when they had a chance. "We're not fighting a foreign army. These are our own people."

"But they are killing us!" Sarah shrilled.

"Yeah, but they are Americans."

"The British were once our own people," Tommy broke in to muddy up the waters. "And look what we did. Like we were traitors to the British crown. That was some serious crapola."

I turned to Tommy. "Let's keep this to one war at a time."

Lenny tugged on my shoulder. "I cannot go also." He grinned stupidly. "Union seminar tomorrow. I prepaid. No refund."

I stared at Lenny. "There're people out there spying on us. Remember. If they have half the equipment Tommy said they have, they know all about us. In fact, they will blame us for arranging a subversive meeting. Even worse, if the people from our meeting do something illegal, we will likely be arrested for inciting a riot. If they are willing to kill poor Rudy over a moving violation, what do you think they will do to us?"

"Okay! Enough!" Lenny's eyes widened. "Hey, is only money."

Sarah grabbed my hand again. "Spencer, we're deserting our ship."

"I'm not really the captain. It's not our duty to go down with a sinking vessel. I moved closer and could see that her eyes were becoming watery. "Besides, that's why they have lifeboats."

"But must we abandon everything?" Sarah asked tearfully.

"No. We're not surrendering. We are leaving to bring back reinforcements. We need to tell the world what is happening here. We shall return and fight. That's what General MacArthur promised to do in the Philippines. He kept his promise."

"I know."

"Okay. Are you coming or not?" I asked point-blank, reaching out my hand.

"I don't know." Sarah backed away.

"There's nothing left here," I said. "We must retreat before we are trapped. I am no William Travis or Jim Bowie. I have no command to obey, no honor to defend, no courage to shed. We're just ordinary citizens."

Both Tommy and Lenny looked away.

"I know how feels." Lenny looked down. "I lost a country. I know how it hurts."

Sarah nodded and then shook her head. "I need to get a few things first."

I turned to Tommy. "Start packing."

As Tommy rushed to another room, I followed Sarah. She was lying on the bed face down, crying. I sat down next to her and wondered what to do. I put my hand on her shoulder. Like an idiot, I started to talk. "We must leave soon."

"Isn't that what you do best?" Sarah snapped. "Don't you? Always escaping from something. Usually, it's me. Now it's the whole damn town."

"What?"

Sarah turned around and faced me. "You heard me. You always take the path of least resistance."

"No, you're wrong."

"When did you ever take a stand?"

I thought about that question for some time. There was that time when… No, I just ignored the person. Well, when I faced that bully on the bus, I… No, somebody came by and stopped him.

"Can't think of one." She stared at me. "Can you?"

I got up and walked out. She had made up her mind and that was final. I had a backbone. I had courage. I just never had a good reason to display it. If she did not want to come along, well, then that was fine with me. We had nearly divorced anyway.

Back in the living room, Tommy had amassed a dozen banana boxes.

"What are you doing?" I asked.

"You said to pack."

"You cannot take all of the banana boxes from the garage."

"These are not from the garage."

I stood there in silence and made a quick calculation. If these boxes were not from the garage, and if all of his vehicles had been impounded, then…

"Okay, I'll bite. Where are they from?"

Tommy looked up. "The attic. They won't take up much space," he pleaded.

I looked up too and noticed some cracks and bulging in the ceiling. Not again.

"They won't take up much space," Tommy pleaded.

"You cannot take these boxes along. We don't have room."

"Then I'll stay here." Tommy folded his arms and sat down.

"Fine! We can make room for five boxes." I wondered if this was what most parents would do to disobeying children.

Tommy stood up and turned his back to me. "You realize, you're forcing me to leave behind my most precious belongings. I've collected these things all my life. They're my dearest of old friends. Very good friends."

He cried a little as he tried to determine which boxes to leave behind. Poor Tommy, trapped by his belongings. I wanted to label him a materialist, but that would have been an injustice. He really treated his tools and junk as treasured friends. I supposed everyone did that to a certain degree. Nobody wanted to leave behind the things they loved, their families, and their comfortable surroundings.

* * * * *

It was past midnight before we started out. Sarah carried out a few suitcases and threw them into my truck. Tommy had already filled up most of the vehicle's back section, and struggled to squeeze in more. The rest of us traveled light. Lenny brought a coat and a handful of candy bars. I brought nothing except a backpack, certain that our exodus would be short-lived.

As we drove near Lenny's apartment, I could hear more sirens, gunfire, and screams. Several large explosions lit up the skyline in blue and white flashes. It sounded like a low-budget science-fiction film with poor sound quality. Still, it gave us the shivers, knowing that it was real and that most likely friends of ours were dying.

I took a route north away from the downtown section, where I knew there would only be one or two checkpoints. As we neared the flashing roadblock, I could see a line of cars filled with boxes, suitcases, and piles of clothes. Everyone was running. What puzzled me most was why they were ordering every car back to town. I just assumed they had no permits. When I reached the front of the line, I showed the half-a-dozen police and highway patrol officials my city identification, along with my exemption card. I was one of them, and I should get preferential treatment.

"Why are you leaving, sir?" a tall and heavily armed police officer asked.

"A little vacation," I said.

"This late at night?"

What was this to him? "Well, I had to work late."

"Sorry, but nobody is allowed to leave town. All vacations and leave time have been canceled."

"On whose orders? I'm the Assistant Director of the DED."

The police officer stared at me with a funny look.

"Big deal. You can't go anywhere."

My face froze. Had they caught me red-handed? Was the word

out already? Was I just a sitting duck in a carload of subversive renegades? If only we had abandoned the ship long before it sank.

"Why not?" My voice crackled.

"Haven't you heard? Big Al took a pot shot at Joe Maffini. He missed him in his first attempt, but not his second one. Got him right through the heart. Great marksmanship."

"Good God, they're now eating their own," I screeched in a high pitched shrill. "What else can happen today?"

"Sir, you need to turn around and head back to town."

"Where is Big Al now?" I asked.

"That's the problem. He escaped our dragnet. We have issued an arrest warrant. We have mounted a 200-person strong manhunt for his capture. We'll find the perp."

"But that doesn't involve us," I said.

"It might. We believe Big Al is the leader of a secret army of die-hard conspirators. Nobody can leave town until we apprehend Big Al and his many accomplices. We're officially under a war alert."

Sarah leaned next to me and shouted at the police officer. "So, if you catch Big Al, are you going to immediately shoot him?"

"No, ma'am," the police officer faced Sarah. "We must first make a positive identification before we can execute him on the spot."

"You're joking?" I asked.

"No. Orders are shoot to kill, no questions asked. Big Al is on our Ten Most Wanted Traitors List. He's a dangerous defector."

"So, you just going to gun him down?" I asked. "No due process, no trial, no conviction?"

"Yeah, isn't that great? Almost like hunting season for wild boar. And boy, he's a big one!"

"You can search my car all you want," I said. "No search warrant needed. Then we can go?"

"I must follow orders. Just back up and turn around like everyone else. Besides, we don't need search warrants anymore."

"No warrants for anything?"

"Hey, don't you just love it?" The guard laughed, moved back, and waved us to turn around.

I had half a mind to crash through the checkpoint, but they would chase after me in their high-speed squad cars and helicopters. Bullets would fly along with bigger projectiles. Not a good scenario.

"What do we do now?" Sarah asked.

"Go home." I shrugged. "But at least we learned something important."

"Oh?" Tommy asked, looking somewhat surprised.

"Yeah. I should have taken all of my vacation time long ago."

Chapter 17

Six hours later, the sun rose above the horizon to welcome a Friday morning. A warm breeze scented the air with the sweet aroma of orange blossoms from distant orchards. It was almost the perfect day, except for one minor distraction: Hemet was under siege. Dark, billowing smoke choked the downtown section; roaring fires and gunfire were still breaking out across the city. Police sirens blared in the distance, sounding their alarm across a large swath of the city. Then again, it could just be the usual July 4th celebrations.

I walked out to the edge of my front porch and tried to ignore last night›s exodus as a dreadful omen. I instead trained my thoughts on surviving one more day. I had to figure out a way to escape our hellhole without serious injuries.

For a split second, the thought of staying home and ignoring reality seemed appealing. Obviously, that was an awful choice. I knew that reality would soon come knocking at my door, and it was not going to be a congenial Avon Lady. What really jolted me back to reality was that I was probably the new boss of DED, at least temporarily. Maybe I should go to the office. Maybe it was not too late to stop this civil war.

"Where are you going?" Sarah asked. She inched closer to me, holding a cup of hot tea.

"To work."

"Have you gone ding-bat crazy?"

I turned to her. "Probably."

"No. You can't."

I placed my hand on her shoulder and assured her I would be okay. Of course, I lied. "They won't harm me. I mean I might now be the acting director of the DED. This time I might be able to accomplish something."

"That's a laugh," said Sarah, rolling her eyes. "You won't be able to do jack shit. You'll be crushed by the chain of command. It will squash you like a bug. You don't call the shots at all. Actually, you never really did."

"I know, but I need to give it a shot," I said. "I feel a duty to try something."

"I know you would like to be a hero like Davy Crockett. I also know you can be that man." Sarah moved closer and ran her fingers through my hair, "You're not a failure. Losers never try. They just complain and blame others. You are better than that. You have tried to resist THEM in your sort of quiet way."

Sarah smiled, pulled me even closer, and planted a little peck of a kiss on my cheek. "I understand."

I believe this was the exact moment I fell back in love with Sarah. She must have changed or perhaps it was actually me. It did not matter. I gave her a big, long hug, said my goodbyes, and walked to my car. I climbed into my truck and drove off. As I backed out of the driveway, I waved to Sarah. I had a feeling I would never see her again. I knew I was taking a big risk. I had stepped across the battle line, and would soon stand in the Alamo's blood-soaked soil. I was now committed. I was staying to fight the good fight. I had to do this for myself. I had to prove that I could be a better person, someone worthy of Sarah's respect.

As I drove to the office, I fiddled with the radio dial, trying to locate a station that was not jammed, hoping for a news update about what was happening in Hemet. I finally picked up a distant station from some far-away state, but I was hearing more static than music. I kept fine-tuning my radio, figuring something had to be on the national wire services about last night's disturbances. Instead, it blared the Bad Boys' song, "Whatcha gonna do when they come for you?" I switched off the radio. Something about that song now gave me the creeps.

The road blockade near my office was the first hint that our city's late-night melees were more widespread than I had imagined. At first, I was most concerned about access to the DED parking lot. I informed the armed police that I was the acting Director of the DED and that they should let me through. They seemed unimpressed, but said I could park in a weed-infested dirt lot next to a former bank. I supposed I could live with a small change in my daily routine. Once in the parking area, I could see the police and soldiers herding everybody to a secured area for the thrilling game of identity checks and frisking by blunt hands and cold fingers.

After recovering from a bit of manhandling, I could sense that most of the city plebs felt violated. Others were in shock and struggled to grasp the magnitude of the situation. Everyone wore a fearful face. My response was different; I had better instincts. I could keep my mind clear and calmer. As more people started to follow me, I began to see myself as a steadfast shepherd, and not a skittish sheep. Although my radar was on high alert, I was no dummy who fell off a sugar-beet truck from Arkansas! I held the position of middle manager for the City of Hemet! I even had a special parking space with my name stenciled on the curb in black letters. If they could not trust me, whom could they trust? This explanation of my self-importance amused the security guards to no end. One even saluted me, but that did not stop them from frisking me.

When released, I hiked to the civic center and soon realized the gravity of the situation. The whole area displayed the raw reality of a war zone. It still had the vivid images of the burned-out city of Beirut in the 1980s. I slowed down my pace. Everywhere I looked, the storefronts were pock-marked with bullet holes, plate glass windows shattered and broken. I had to dodge large craters in the ground. I stopped at one and glanced down. It was 20 feet wide and eight-feet deep. It looked like it came from artillery shellfire. I silently mouthed to myself: what artillery and who would do that? Something was wrong. I continued my trek and approached mounds of rubble, mostly chunks of asphalt and concrete. I looked at up at several buildings. They were nothing but metal remains, blackened and twisted.

I finally reached a cluster of National Guard soldiers with M16's strung across their arms. They were jittery, probably expecting another attack at any moment. I swallowed, slowed my pace, and inhaled a whiff of oily smoke. Many of the people following me were DED workers. Tommy was among them. Everybody appeared terrified, slowed down their pace and turned dead silent.

As I entered the civic center through a small opening in a chain-link fence, I witnessed additional destruction. Walls of dirty-white sandbags, topped with barbed wire, surrounded most of the buildings. Itchy-fingered soldiers in a machine gun nest kept a hawk's eye on my DED workers and me.

As I moved closer to the DED entrance, I watched a crew of firefighters and rescue workers rushing around like busy bees, shoving stretchers into flashing ambulances. From what I could gather, the authorities had surrounded our civic center with a defensive fortress, along with a column of tanks and armored vehicles. It was like something out of an old-World War II film. I was half-expecting to see General Patton climb out of a tank and bark orders to his subordinates.

Even here, most walls and buildings stood pitted by hundreds of rounds of ammunition. Most unnerving were the chalk outlines of bodies on red-stained walkways. As I almost arrived at the DED building, I had to maneuver around another series of machine-gun nests, manned with weary soldiers. Behind them stood rows of barbed wire fences supported by a short wall of sandbags.

I stepped into line and finally showed my ID at the DED gate. It took almost 15 minutes to verify my credentials. I kept scanning for an exit routes just in case I was denied access and faced impending arrest. Luckily, they granted me access and handed me over to two military men. They silently escorted me upstairs. Within a few moments, they dumped me on the third floor and disappeared. As I entered my office, a solemn-faced appeared out of almost nowhere. It was Jack Bellamy. I never felt comfortable around Hemet's city manager. His round bug eyes were unnerving anyway, but when he became agitated, they popped out and he looked right down spooky. I tried to look away. It was a difficult task. Besides his abnormal eyes,

Old Fish-Eyed Jack appeared exhausted and worn-out. An oversized handgun protruded from his pocket, and I wondered if he had a bullet with my name imprinted on it. To my surprise, Jack had come from the mayor's office to congratulate me. They had officially promoted me to Director of the DED.

"It's only temporary until we can hire a permanent DED Director," Jack explained as he shook my hand. "I know you will do a splendid job in the meantime."

"What happened to Big Al?" I asked sheepishly.

"He's not here anymore."

"But where is he?"

"Let's just say he took an extended vacation," Jack replied, staring at me unblinkingly.

"Well, I did all the work anyway," I argued, trying to smoke out some more information from Old Fish Eyes.

"Don't worry about the big guy. He never worked a day in his life. He only looked out for himself and his long lunch hours."

"Well, I hope he's happy now," I said, still trying to glean more than what was actually being insinuated.

"I'm sure he is pleasantly resting in peace. We made sure of that," Jack laughed with a short burst of disjointed, staccato tones.

This strange encounter reminded me of the Hollywood gangster films from the 1930s. Jack spoke like a tough-talking James Cagney or Humphrey Bogart, willing to rub out leaders from rival gangs. It gave me a chilling sensation. It was as if the government had a direct relationship with the gangsters of yesteryear. There were too many frightening similarities to overlook. After all, the government had the habit of escorting taxpayers to small, confined rooms if they failed to pay protection money. And what about those little conflicts often referred to as wars? It seemed that many of these nasty disputes focused on territorial claims. Of course, Americans were free to vote for either party—Al Capone or Machine Gun Kelly.

"Stay in touch," Jack said, trying to smile. He turned and retreated to the elevator.

"Wait!" I called to him. I had to ask. "Any truth to the rumor that we now execute violators on the spot? I should be privy to official city policy."

"Sure." Jack turned around for a split moment, still walking. "It's no rumor." Before I could follow up with another question, he was gone, trailed by two of his armed bodyguards.

Tommy scurried into my room like a frightened rabbit. He slammed the door and ran for me. I jumped out of the way. His body crashed so hard against my wall that his image left permanent marks. He inched away from the wall, and then scanned the room for any movement or any sign of activity.

I pointed at the wall: "You're paying for that."

"Time-out, man! Time-out!" Tommy lifted his hands up like a football coach stopping the clock. "This is getting freakily out of control! Someone has to stop the world. I need to get off."

"You can't; it's spinning too fast," I tried to provoke some laughter or something to lessen the tension.

Tommy leaned over my desk and grabbed my hand. "Here, slap me. Wake me up! Has Armageddon arrived?"

"Quit panicking."

"I know what's going on." Tommy grabbed both of my arms and looked straight into my eyes. "It's the Y2K bug! It's the Y2K bug! They knew we were trying to stop its fiendish plans for world domination. So, they launched a preemptive strike. The computers are coming for us."

I pushed Tommy away. "Come on. Be serious."

Tommy backed away and looked down. "I'm somewhat serious," he said in a soft, weak tone.

"We have more problems than rebellious computers."

"We do?"

"Did you overhear Jack's pithy comment? Did you?"

"Well,... sort of."

"That's serious. Violators shot on sight! Seems rather harsh for a TRAFFIC VIOLATION! I thought Big Al was making that up."

"Oh, that thing," Tommy started to calm down.

"That thing! Their minds must be pickled," I said, feeling a little dizzy. I shook my head in disgust.

"Wow! We're cooked." Tommy leaned back and closed his eyes. "Man, this is a real bummer. We've got to bug out."

"Ahhh… Earth to Tommy. We tried that already."

"I know. But put on your thinking sombrero. There is must be a better alternative."

"Well, there might be another way," I said, knowing that it should be easy to leave the city now. After all, I was one of the big boys now, an insider, and a distinguished comrade of the cause. All I had to do was flex my political biceps and bark orders. "That might work," I said with a slight hint of confidence.

"Why not sneak out on bicycles?" Tommy suggested. "We can save our lives and energy too."

I was about to nix that nutty idea when I noticed that Lenny had entered my office room. He never knocked.

"No good!" Lenny rushed up to me. He was huffing and puffing, almost out of breath. "I heard the news. National Guard patrol city. Sky full of whirligigs. Nowhere to go."

"You mean whirlybirds. Helicopters," I corrected him.

"Yeah, that too. Got attack dogs. Boy, almost makes me homesick."

"Listen," I said. "I will talk to the mayor and get permission to leave town. On business, of course."

"We could use more computers and other equipment," Tommy said. "Not to mention food."

"Tommy's sure got that right good," Lenny confirmed what the rumor mills had been alleging all morning. "No food anywhere. All stores closed. They're *idioty!*" He slowly slapped his face. "This is worse than back in mother Russia. You Americans, you know how to do things up big."

Lenny was correct. It was unreal. There was a lockdown on everything. He informed us that almost every business and industry had been shut down—except for a selected few.

"Only few politicians can get stuff," Lenny said. "What you expect?"

For over a week, the city promised to solve our lack of food. The new Department of Rationing, the DOF, was set up to print and distribute food ration coupons to help the poor, but that seemed doubtful. Sarah had gone to the grocery store and the shelves were bare. What was the point of printing up food coupons when little or no food was available?

"Okay, that settles it," I said. "I must procure a pass to leave our little slice of heaven behind. I just need to finagle the proper paperwork from Mayor Quinn. After I do that, we can pack up and forget about our jobs and work." The word "work" stuck in my throat. As I caught a glance of my team of almost 300 public employees, I saw a disturbing pattern. Nobody was actually working. Most of them were just playing cards, gossiping, or reading paperback books. Something was wrong.

"Tommy, look." I pointed my finger at the masses of idle workers. "Find out why?" I assumed that our citizens had stopped calling because they had discovered an escape route, were too scared to call, or were loitering in the mortuary.

It did not take Tommy long to unearth the problem. He came running back, huffing and puffing, almost completely out of breath. He took a gulp of air and screamed, "They're being trucked out!"

"What?"

"Rumors are flying that hordes of citizens are being loaded into military trucks, and then driven to special camps."

"Special camps?" I asked with a sudden burst of alarm.

"A good friend referred to them as re-education camps."

"Come on!" I said with fear lacing my voice. "Nobody does that anymore."

Tommy shook his head. "We're screwed, man."

"That's it. We have no other choice. I have to finagle a get-out-of-Hemet pass from the Mayor Quinn."

"Boy, I don't envy you, Tommy said. "I heard he is three fries short of a Happy Meal." Tommy made circular motions around his ear. "He's loonier than a loon."

"Do you want to come along?" I asked, hoping to share the unpleasant experience.

Tommy violently shook his head. "Are you crazy? That's like strolling through a grizzly bear den. Unarmed. No can do."

Of course, I knew that was going to be his answer.

* * * * *

After I got approval to see the mayor, I flew down the stairs, and stood in front of the DED building. In a flash, I found myself surrounded by five oversized guards. Apparently, it was a fashion statement to wear a Kevlar bulletproof vest and old combat metal helmet while being escorted to City Hall. I soon discovered why. There were reports that enemy snipers had targeted several people of importance. I felt relatively safe since I was a medium-sized cog in an overwhelmingly massive machine. Who would shoot someone with such a small political footprint? Then again, I might be mistaken.

Passing through a narrow entrance between two long rolls of barbed wire, I found myself inside the belly of the headless beast, or as some called it—"Borg-Central." It resembled Hitler's subterranean bunker during World War II. The city hall building had been remodeled, and for some reason, it conveyed a prison-like, featureless style. The walls were thick gray, concrete blocks streaked with rust stains. Every window was bricked up and troweled over with a cement wash. Most doors were forged with heavy metal plates, giving the feeling of an old battleship. Military officers rushed in and out, as workers patched walls or repaired damaged equipment. A coffin would be more inviting.

"I need to talk with Mayor Quinn," I informed a stern-faced sentry. "I'm the new director of the DED."

The man nodded and opened a door into another room guarded by another sentry. Past that door, I found the inner headquarters buzzing with activity. A huge map of the city and surrounding areas was nailed to the wall. The smoke-filled room was chaotic, people calling out locations and troop strengths. A number of expletive-spewing staff officers pulled out or replaced a rainbow of colored pushpins. They had encircled the war map, all google-eyed, worshipping it like a god with the power of foresight. The other side of the room was more modern, stuffed with rows and rows of consoles with monitors, radar screens, and GPS tracking systems. I surmised that this must be their main war room.

"Spencer, is that you?" Mayor Quinn appeared in an old army coat, his arm in a sling. Jack Fish Eyes stood next to the mayor. "Good to see you. We need to talk about upgrading the equipment at DED. I fear that all of these distractions have slowed down your operations."

"Well, a little," I fibbed.

"That's horrible. I cannot believe that the good people of this city are disobeying my direct orders."

"We must boil the frog, Sir," Jack whispered cryptically in the mayor's ear.

"Not yet, Jack." The mayor turned back to me. "If people refuse to call us, then I suppose the next step is to tell them where to go. They need good judgment."

"We're already doing that," I reminded him.

"No. I mean we initiate the process. We determine where and when they go. They have no choice. We know better. They will simply flitter away their time and resources anyway. The plebs always abuse their gifts. We must take the high ground, the commanding heights. You know, show them we mean it. Squeeze them. Break them. Tell them what the score is."

"Do you mean we should not ask them where they want to go?"

"That's the point. You are a faster learner, Spencer. We cannot allow people to make their own decisions anymore. That is why we are in this horrible mess. We were elected to solve our city's problems. Every single one of them. And that is exactly what we're going to do."

"What about a spontaneous walk down the street to visit a relative?" I asked, trying to subtly argue my case.

"If they're in such a hurry, they can just walk or bike," the Mayor said, but then paused to reconsider. "Although, they might take an inefficient bike or pedestrian route."

Not this crap all over again. I eyed a gray-haired major nearby. He carried a revolver in his hip holster. I could grab it, pull it out and blow out my brains or simply blast the Mayor to Kingdom Come. Now they want to exercise control over people's biking and walking habits. When will this all end? These sociopaths were determined to oversee every strain of hair on our heads until we all went bald.

"You're very important to my operations." The mayor turned back to me and smiled with a sick glint in his eye.

"I appreciate your confidence in me, but I need more equipment to increase my department's efficiency."

"Very good. And you shall have it. I will see that you get what you need."

"Well, I need the supplies and equipment now. I'm familiar with what we need, so I could fetch them from Riverside."

"Nobody leaves Hemet. Nobody! You will get them later."

"It would not take long."

"I said nobody leaves my command! Stop badgering me! It will happen," the mayor snarled. And with that sadistic grin still glued to his face, he pulled out an old German Lugar. "Everyone stays at their post, no matter what. No retreating! You understand me?"

"Yes!" I always said "yes" to any wacko holding a gun near my face. I had developed that nervous habit not long ago.

"Now go!" The Mayor commanded, waving his weapon at me.

I found it intolerable to be treated like a serf by an elected official, especially one I voted for in the last election. I started to inch my way towards the door. It was time to give the Mayor all the space he wanted. Instead, he moved closer into my personal space zone.

"I'm not the villain here." Mayor Quinn slowly holstered his pistol. "In fact, I'm the victim. My opponents are abusing me. They're the ones who refuse to pay attention to our laws. No matter how well we construct our ordinances, somebody always disobeys. We have no choice but to weed out the bad apples before they taint the entire barrel. Our mission is to create a noble and equable society. One devoid of hunger, sickness, or want of any kind. Remember, we are the professionals. We know what is best. And we will bring order and peace, no matter if we have to obliterate the universe."

"Obliterate?" I swallowed hard and braced myself for more bad news.

"That is right. We have to defeat the other army," the Mayor said with eyes gorged with hate. "Our enemies must be defeated at all cost; they are evil incarnated."

"What other army?" I asked innocently.

"Boy, you're out of the loop."

"I didn't know there was a loop."

The Mayor stared at me as if I were the crazy one.

"Ahh…" I said trying to think of what to say to placate him. "I'm not getting much sleep. I've been putting in long hours at the DED."

The Mayor eased up. "I see. Very commendable. But we are facing a formidable enemy, an adversary with a powerful army. We have to fight them with everything we have. Every man and woman must fight to the death. If we fail, I will shoot myself before surrendering. Everyone should prepare to do the same. You should too. That is why we must win."

I felt obligated to agree. As I nodded with a forced smile, I searched around for the nearest escape exit. I had enough political speeches for a lifetime. I wanted no part of a Mad-Hatter mayor who learned his polemic skills from Mussolini and his logic from *Alice in Wonderland*. This little tinhorn tyrant needed a reality check, or a tongue-lashing, or both. If only I had something more than the truth for self-defense.

"That's why you cannot leave. Nobody can until we have crushed them," the Mayor began frothing at the mouth.

"Wow," I mouthed silently. I could see that hate was now the default reaction against those who took a different view. The mayor and his cohorts had mutated into righteous lovers of hate. They appeared embittered and hell-bent on revenge, seething with a wild, uncontrollable rage to make people suffer. It made no sense. And far worse, it seemed that the mayor and his cronies were deriving pleasure from destroying all unbelievers. I had to get out.

As I slowly backed up, the hairs on the back of my neck were bristling. I was not sure whether Mayor Quinn was just attempting to advance his political career or if something more sinister was afoot. That was what really scared me. Was this something new, something beyond the typical power play that had plagued mankind since recorded history? That question haunted me and kept my nightmares from fading away.

"Jack, see him out!" The Mayor pointed his shaking finger at me. "I think I've heard enough."

I finally left with Jack Fish Eyes, trailed by pair of armed men.

As we walked out of City Hall, I slowed down and tried to talk with Jack about his curious statement concerning boiled frogs. Jack simply shrugged. "It's an old adage, nothing more."

"I see." I knew there was more to it. They were planning something big. A frog would jump out of boiling water if suddenly dropped into a hot pot. But if the water was slowly heated up, the frog would not sense the danger until it was too late. Meaning that something was nearing the boiling point. Apparently, they had at least one more notch to go before they reached the hot final solution— whatever that was.

"If I were you, I would refrain from arguing with the Mayor," Jack said quietly. "He is not as understanding as I am."

I felt a real urge to click my boot heels and shout *Sieg Heil!* But the humor would have been lost at my expense.

After a nice walk through the war zone, my armed escort left me at the door of the DED building. I tried to use the elevator, but either it was broken or the electricity was off again. A few seconds after I reached my office, Tommy barged inside. I sat in my chair and waited for him to explode again.

"What did the tards say?"

"It's a no-go."

"Man, total bummer!" Tommy looked away.

"Yeah, that's about the gist of it." I sat and fumed. I had failed to get a pass. I did not know what to say. There seemed to be no correct answer, no winning outcome. The mayor was brandishing a gun to force his people to obey his commands. Talk about a bad way to motivate people. I knew all about incentives and encouragement. I had taken dozens of motivation classes, courtesy of the taxpayer. Bullying and threats never solved the problem.

"Who's bummed?" Brian entered my office room without knocking. Tommy stood straight up. "Nobody can get out of the city."

"Oh, that. Yes, I know."

"You do?" I asked.

"We need to talk, sir." Brian faced me and eyed Tommy. "Alone."

I waved Tommy out.

"I just thought you should know," Brian hesitated for a moment, then lowered his voice. "We have a number of problems."

"Which ones?" I chuckled. "They're growing like pesky weeds."

"I should not reveal this, but you and your wife are both on my list of possible opponents of the DED. Sort of strange, since you now head the department."

"So Borg Central called you?" I said sarcastically. There was little point in hiding my strong opinions. "Is anyone NOT on your list?"

"But sir, you cannot be against your own department."

"I just don't like the way it's being controlled from upstairs. You know, from City Hall."

"Yes, I completely understand. But Jack has asked me to do things I would never have imagined."

I sat up in my chair. "Like what?"

"You see, that's part of the problem. I cannot discuss it with anyone but Jack."

"Oh, so you've made a pinky-swear with Jack?"

Brian's eyes narrowed. "It's not like that."

"What is it like?"

"You don't understand what they will do if you get caught. They have, ah… persuasive ways."

"I'm the one who put you in your position. And now you won't discuss it with me?"

"I'm under orders. Sorry. I would… well… If I did spill the beans, it would not just jeopardize my life, but my entire family. I cannot do that."

I slumped in my chair. "Well, I hope you will at least warn me about an impending arrest warrant."

"Fair enough," Brian said. "But only if you promise me the same courtesy."

"Sure." I stood up and shook Brian's hand. "I appreciate that. Truly I do. Things are getting a might dicey. Are you trying to get out?"

"Not really. I guess I enjoy my job too much. I've always wanted to work undercover."

"Yeah, I suppose that could be exciting and dangerous."

"Anyway, good luck, Sir." Brian turned around and walked out.

I was not sure what he meant by the "good luck" part. I quickly closed my door and took a deep breath. How long before one of Brian's staff personnel disclosed my disloyalty? It would take only one minor remark by a disgruntled worker to get me into serious trouble. I was sure I had been already identified as a possible dissenter. Sooner or later, they would come for me. I began humming the tune I had heard earlier on the radio: "Whatcha gonna do when they come for you?" I could not afford to wait to find out.

Chapter 18

There was only one conceivable way to escape our predicament. We had to soar out of town like a bat strapped to a Trident missile. I knew how to fly small personal airplanes. The main problem was locating an aircraft that could carry a band of deserting misfits to safety. Earlier, Nick had generously offered us a ride, but that deal was only redeemable if he was still in town. I attempted to phone him, but his line was disconnected. Not good.

That evening, Sarah and I took a trip to Nick's restaurant, expecting a pad-locked door with boarded-up windows. Instead, we found the parking lot jammed with expensive cars. Inside, the waiting list was long and overwhelmed with droves of hungry patrons eager to get inside.

Sarah stood next to me as we waited behind a wall of patrons in the foyer, trying to get the attention of Nick or the maître d'. She appeared confused by the crowded conditions. We could barely breathe. She turned to me with a puzzled look. "You said everything would be closed. What's going on?"

"Well, it should be," I shrugged with a slight smile on my lips. I was often amused when confronted by exceptions to conventional rules. In this case, my wrong hunch led to a long wait before an open booth became available. That was perfectly fine with me. Great entertainment soon came our way. A black man in a white tuxedo sang up a storm to *Casablanca's* classic "Knock on Wood"—one of my favorites. The packed crowd went wild, singing along as if they did not have a care in the world. Even the more grim-faced military officers, all dressed up in their formal uniforms, joined the merriment. It was great fun, especially since Nick had done such a wonderful job re-creating the early 1940's atmosphere of the Vichy cafe in Morocco. It was so authentic that I almost expected to see Nazi officers drag away some of the shadier characters.

Sarah had always accused me of making snap judgments with little evidence. After scanning the large room, I found much to pre-sume. The café was overflowing with THEM—government officials, civil servants, and black-shirted officers. Two young city attorneys were cooing in one booth; three high-ranking Battalion Chiefs were drunk and loud; a cluster of Senior Civil Engineers chomped down on thick steaks as if the food shortage was nothing but a myth. A cadre of army captains clustered together and sang *Garyowens* Irish tune in the corner, toasting to General Custer. I spotted someone from the Recorder's office writing a note on the wall—very tacky. The Director of Parks and Recreation hid his dog under the table while a pool of city secretaries ogled a cluster of muscular Deputy Fire Marshals who took delight in showing off their physical fitness. Several assistants to the City Treasurer were counting piles of green-backs, while a Human Resources officer and a Planning Manager were lip-locked outside the restroom.

As I stretched my neck and looked around, I finally located the elusive Nick. He was having a grand old time conversing with Mayor Quinn, accompanied by three well-armed bodyguards. I figured that Jack must be lurking around somewhere in the crowd, but I failed to spot him.

I saw Nick leave the mayor and pushed through the crowds in my direction. This was my chance. I had to capture more than his attention. I grabbed Nick's arm as he sailed past our table. I reeled him in like a fish on a hook. He landed next to me and seemed pleasantly surprised.

"Spencer!" Nick's face brightened. "Good to see you."

"What's happen here?"

"Oh, you mean my scores of guests?"

I nodded.

"Well, I've made an agreement with important people. Now I'm the only legal joint in town." Nick's face beamed as he smiled with a wry twist of his lips.

"Great for you."

"I just hope I don't run out of supplies."

"A little low?"

"I had to make certain arrangements to prevent the unthinkable."

"So, you don't need to abandon ship?"

"Why would I? I'm doing so well right here. It's a gold mine and I tripled my prices."

"Well, Sarah and I are thinking about taking a little trip. Maybe Riverside. However, the mayor thinks he cannot spare my absence. But my department also requires additional supplies. I was wondering if I could borrow your Piper."

Nick mulled over the idea for a moment. He glanced around to see who might be listening to our conversation. He leaned over and planted his hands planted firmly on our table. He whispered, "I use the Piper to bring in my food and liquor supplies. I cannot afford to have it out of operation. You understand?"

"You could just take us out on the next run," I almost pleaded.

"I don't think the mayor would want me to help someone escape, especially a man of your distinguished position. He's very sensitive about defectors."

"We're not defecting. Just doing some business," Sarah lied. "We won't cause any trouble."

"It's not like I'm flush with options," Nick said.

"Funny. We have the same dilemma," I said.

"I'm sorry, Spence, and Madame. We did not have this conversation." Nick bowed. "*Adieu*."

I should have expected Nick's sudden change of heart. He had always been a wheeler-dealer; boasting that if he was stuck with a lemon, he would find a way to sell it as a prune.

"What now?" Sarah asked.

"I'm not sure. We could just steal it," I whispered and moved closer to her. "I mean *borrow* it."

"That's unethical and it might ruin Nick," Sarah fired back. "It's not that bad here."

"How bad does it have to get?"

Sarah shrugged with a sidelong grin. "You know... bad bad."

I paused to think. I had studied history, and I could recognize the going-off-the-deep-end warning signs. The Jews in Nazi Germany had years to escape the authorities before the hammer slammed down on their heads. Most Jews decided that things could not get any worse. Therefore, they stayed, and indeed things went from worse to unthinkable. They paid the ultimate price. I am sure Rant would agree with my little synopsis. I believed we had now reached that tipping point. For me, I figured that our Final Solution moment was only days away. I was sure that Jack Fish Eyes was ready to go after any real or imaginary enemies. He had something special in store besides flaunting a dead boiled frog. I knew that worse could easily slip into much worse, maybe deadly.

"But you can't know what will happen. Nobody does," Sarah insisted with a slight shudder.

"But we do," I insisted. "There's nothing to prevent our city leaders from getting completely out of control. They have dismantled the brakes. They can now speed ahead without any impediments. That's because they believe they are infallible."

"We could start a recall petition," Sarah suggested.

"But nobody is willing to do anything to stop this madness. Most people are either too scared to dissent or too loyal to Mayor Quinn to consider him a threat. There is no middle ground. There is no handbrake, no balance between extremes. We're tumbling down a steep hill and everybody thinks it's a joy ride."

Sarah grimaced with a faint lift of the upper lip. She turned her head away, nervously fingering her amber teardrop necklace. "I suppose that's one way to look at it. But's it not the only way."

"The real kicker is that if nobody does anything, then I suppose we deserve what we get."

"I suppose we all should have done something earlier," Sarah said. "I guess we are all at fault."

I tried to put that disturbing thought out of my mind. I was not the right person to fix our problems. I had no real leadership experience. I had not signed on to fight City Hall all by myself. That was somebody else's job. My job description did not require me to rescue

Hemet or the world. My job description had narrowly defined duties, and godly savior was not one of them.

Sarah poked me in the leg under the table and whispered, "That man over there is staring at us. Over near the potted palm."

I slowly turned and sneaked a glimpse of the mystery man through the corner of my eye. He resembled Brian, my faithless spymaster who was probably instructed to spy on me. He kept peeking from behind his open menu, playing games. He gave a curious expression that suggested both disgust and pity.

Sarah kicked me again. "I think he wants to talk to you after Nick leaves the dining room."

I had no reason to parley with Brian. Since he had taken charge of DED surveillance and security, I knew that his assigned duties had gone beyond the original purpose of spying on feeble opponents. I knew he was watching me. I was already on his list of usual suspects, so why was he making eye contact with me?

After Nick departed the room, Brian made his move. He strolled over to me, glaring in one direction but walking in another. He slid into the booth next to me, acting as if I was a complete stranger. His eyes never left sight of Mayor Quinn and his guests.

"Sir," Brian spoke softly, still refusing to face me. "You should not be here."

"Why not?"

"Nick Gillis is on our list of potential agitators and subversives. You should steer clear of him."

"Nick?"

"Sorry, I forgot to mention that I'm also working with the IAD. We're investigating Nick and some of his restaurant clients."

"What's the IAD?" I snapped. The city had created so many departments, branches, and sub-agencies that I could not keep track of all of them.

"The Internal Affairs Department," Brian said. "Do you know we have almost as many employees as you do at the DED? Of course, that is a secret. Anyway, you need to depart immediately. This place might get a little too exciting for your own good."

I got the distinct feeling that someone was going to raid Nick's Café and close it down—just like in the *Casablanca* movie. Yet, Nick had neither gambling nor any other illegal activities. No stolen passports, just ordinary food, and wine, if one could find a live waiter. What could they possibly cite for the raid? Of course, in the movie, the authorities had no valid reason to shut down Rick's café either.

At this exact moment, I realized that Brian was wearing a snappy black uniform with a German Iron Cross medal pinned to his right chest. His shirt was adorned with golden collar patches of oak leaves and a sliver skull-crossbones insignia clasped to his shirt pocket. I was particularly impressed with his calf-high jackboots. The troubling part was that Brian looked like an officer from the Waffen-SS.

I pointed to his Iron Cross medal. "What is that?"

Brian looked down at his uniform. "Oh,… that silly little thing." He smiled. "Just a little black cross representing my division."

"Division?"

"Yes, we've been organized into paramilitary units."

My jaw dropped. "You're in the military?"

"No, I'm just a volunteer in an auxiliary role. Nothing impressive."

I eyed Sarah. She also gave a worried glance, tightening her lips and scrunching up her eyebrows.

After silently drawing in my breath, I leaned back. I nodded to Brian and thanked him for the tip.

Brian stood and bowed slightly and warned us not to stay too long. He turned and went back to his table.

I leaned back and sighed. Poor Nick. Poor Brian. They were all victims of treacherous circumstances. I got up, took Sarah by the hand, and slowly retreated to the door. It seemed that nobody was above suspicion, just like the trapped foreigners in French Morocco during World War II.

Outside in the dark, we ran straight into a wall of black-uniformed men impatiently waiting for a signal. They were armed to the teeth, carrying automatic rifles, handguns, grenades, and metal batons. We moved out of the way and rushed to our car. Surprisingly, they let us through. It was obvious they were trolling for bigger fish, not small-fries like us. At least not yet.

* * * * *

On the way home that evening, I noticed throngs of people hiding behind bushes, parked cars, and turned-over trash containers lying in the middle of the street. Some were peeking from behind mountains of trash that stretched almost across the entire street, blocking traffic. Other streets were lit up with flaming trash dumpsters, roaring out of control and flaring up like rockets.

What got my attention was the creepy shadow people. They were slipping out of the dark alleys and vacant lots like vampires on the prowl. Most appeared to be carrying an assortment of weapons and gas masks. At first, I thought they were commando squads of young military men or SWAT teams planning to raid the home of suspected agitators. Upon closer examination, I could make out figures of old men in outdated military uniforms, young women in slacks, and black-garbed teenagers with nail-studded baseball bats. Many were swinging pipes or poles into the air. Some had rifles.

One firebrand was dragging a small cannon behind him on a child's red wagon. Many of the older women toted hatchets, knives, and shovels while the children clutched BB guns, squirrel rifles, and gasoline bombs, all with the determination of an invading U.S. Marine assault force. They were everywhere; hundreds of them, all heading straight to City Hall. The shadow people were both out-matched and outgunned. It would be a massacre.

Arriving back home, I noticed that most of the lights had been left on throughout the house. I was a first-class miser when it came to saving electricity, so this meant only one possibility: an uninvited guest. I suspected Tommy or Rant. It turned out to be another visitor even less savory.

"You've got to help me," Big Al rushed up to me and whined. "I have nowhere to go."

"But I heard that you shot Joe Maffini. Right through the heart."

"He threatened me. It was self-defense."

"You're now a fugitive!" I shouted as a horrible expression assaulted my face. The gravity of my situation was just beginning to sink in with a frightening conclusion. I would now be regarded as an accomplice to murder.

I had to sit down. Why do demonic douchebags always follow me home like stray dogs? Here was a man wanted for the assassination of our most prominent city councilmember. If Big Al stayed in my house, I would be cooked, served, and consumed by the politically famished. Housing a fugitive was surely a double capital offense—that is where they execute you twice. I had only a few sensible words for my former boss: "Are you out of your fucking mind? You cannot stay here!"

"Spencer," Sarah said, moving next to me. "He needs our help."

"He's a wanted assassin!" I exploded. "Christ! They'll bust a gut to find him."

"They're also looking for me." Rant stepped into the light. She must have been the sneaky culprit who allowed Big Al into my house. She was also uninvited, but unfortunately, she had a key.

"I was so worried," Sarah hugged her half-sister. "What happened?"

"I went for redress, not revenge." Rant explained how she and her posse had entered the civic center and were threatened with gunfire. "I departed as ordered."

"But what about the others?" I asked, impressed that she had the self-restraint to avoid violence.

"The looney fringe went ballast. They charged the police barricade," Rant's voice broke tearfully. I had never seen her so emotional. "They're all dead, even Candy. It was senseless. Brutal. It was as if they had a revengeful death wish. They swarmed over the barricade, blinded with rage. They fought hand-to-hand with steak knives, ice picks, and broken bottles. It was so stupid!"

"No, it's crazy," I said. "They're acting like brainless animals. Like zombies on an adrenaline rush."

"We have to get out!" Rant paused for a moment to regain her composure. "There is an evil out there. An acidity of hate and fear.

Something unseen and unnatural. Something that has infected almost everyone." She stared at me. "And you must be one of THEM."

"No!" Sarah came to my defense. "How can you say that? We're both trying to get escape Hemet."

Rant had always considered me a repugnant bureaucrat with no opinion, backbone, or moral conviction. I was just an inanimate object that happened to be in close proximity to her older half-sister.

"So even our high and mighty government employees want to flee?" Rant said cruelly.

"If you shoot us, don't us civil servants also bleed," I paraphrased Shakespeare. It fell flat.

"Don't know; I never tried shooting one," Rant poked me in the chest with her boney finger. "I always thought bureaucrats were bloodless and gutless. You know, dead on arrival."

"Spencer has been trying to stop this," Sarah argued. "He's against THEM just as much as you are."

"So, what has he done to deserve such praise?" Rant folded her arms, looking as if she might spit at me at any moment.

Rant cut me to the quick. Her remark stung like a thistle, and that was because she was correct. If future historians ever mentioned my role, they would reveal a pathetic story of a small man with hollow dreams. The chroniclers of history would depict me as the man who did nothing to prevent a catastrophe from racing to the point of no return. Nobody would ever listen to my side or know that I had acted in accordance with good bureaucratic skin-saving traditions. I had avoided conflict at all costs. Bureaucrats understood that whoever won a power struggle, the victor would still need paper-pushers to run their ill-gotten operations. We were the invincible ones. In the pecking order of life, dictators and kings were impotent and expendable. They did not rule society; the hordes of civil servants did. We were the permanent flesh of society that never died.

"I am trying my best," I said. "At least I am trying."

Rant released a flippant grunt and stormed away. "Well, try harder."

I gravitated over to the kitchen and searched for an old can of beer. Tommy had drunk the last six-pack a few days ago and the stores were fresh out of any liquid substance to dull the senses.

Tommy might have missed one, I mumbled to myself. Unlikely, but the hope for beer suds springs eternal. While I searched and practiced the blame game on myself, Big Al turned impatient. He stepped in front of me and wrung his hands, expecting help. Like a lowbrow caveman, he glared at me with an arrogant twitch of his right eyebrow. He demanded answers. "What about me?"

"Haven't you already made your own bed?" I said.

Big Al stared at me with a perplexed look on his face. "My maid makes my bed. Who else would?"

I do not know what I might have done to Big Al if Sarah had not intervened. She wedged herself between us and faced me. "Play nice. We must help those who can't help themselves."

"Why should we help you?" I looked straight at my wretched former boss and wondered if I should forgive and forget. I knew I would, but I wanted to let him squirm for a while.

"Because at least I tried to stop this insanity," Big Al said.

"By shooting a city councilmember?"

"You have a better plan?"

Big Al was simply trying to free his 81-year-old mother. But he had done more than I had. I vaguely thought about shooting Joe Maffini myself, but Big Al had beaten me to the draw. That was something.

"Fine. We'll take everyone," I finally said, trying to avoid thinking about where to store Big Al's massive ballast. "I suppose we can accomplish more if we all stick together."

"I can come?" Big Al seemed surprised.

"Yeah. I'm sure you will help out somehow."

Although the phone lines were only working sporadically, we finally got hold of Tommy and Lenny and, in cryptic double-speak, told them that tomorrow night would be our last one in Hemet.

Chapter 19

It was Saturday morning and our little extended family had settled down to discuss Operation Goodby Hemet. I disliked planning intricate events when there was more than one person involved. It was a question of complex mathematics. As more people sign on to a project, the more the "stupidity effect" reared its brainless head. With so many people involved in our group, I knew that nothing would turn out correctly. There were simply too many fingers stirring too many sticky pots. That was how I felt about my hastily- drawn proposal to escape. There were too many possible bad outcomes and not enough good ones to make it work. We had a better chance of landing on Mars blindfolded.

"The only way to escape is to fly out," I declared with a false ring of confidence. I found it difficult to sound truthful when lying. Only a professional silver-tongued politician could do that like no other. I was not a superstar in that extraordinary league of institutional liars, but my lack of double-dealing skills was not going to prevent me from trying.

"We have a plane?" Tommy straightened his shoulders and gave a dazed look of bewilderment. He rubbed his face, soon entranced in a thoughtful look of disbelief and wonderment. That reflective guise was short lived. He soon chuckled, "Yeah, that's rich."

I knew that Tommy had figured it out. He was first to puncture a gaping hole in my brilliant plan. Great for him. If only he can manage to kept it to himself.

"Hey, man," Tommy huffed, "don't you know? The airport is under lockdown. Nobody's going to trip anywhere."

I smiled. "Well, Nick Gillis has generously offered us a ride." Of course, I failed to reveal that not only had Gillis rescinded his offer, but that I was unsure which hangar housed his aircraft. Years ago, he had mentioned Hangar 12 near the outskirts of the airport. Or was it Hangar 13?

Only Sarah understood the full extent of my deception. She let me know of her disapproval and cast a dark, foreboding stare. I wanted to return the favor, but I was sure the others might suspect something wrong.

Everyone else gathered around me as if I were going to recite a beloved fairy tale. I told them we could hitch a ride in Nick's empty plane the next time he flew out for supplies. I did not mention was that if Nick were unwilling to comply, I would have to resort to cruder measures. I slipped my hand into my pocket and fingered my arsenal of last resort. Yes, I was desperate enough to shoot big wads of hard cash at Nick's face. I was willing to take him down with bribery. I could play a slick, fast-talking gangster with a fetish to use money-clip knuckles.

My major worry was that greed would get the better of Nick; he might want more. That would be a big problem. The local banks were running low on cash reserves since our economy had nose-dived into a deep recession. Our banks had little cash on hand, and nobody could make withdrawals over $200 per week. Most of my DED employees complained so bitterly that the city decided to establish its own city bank. That was a monumental, piss-poor decision. When my workers tried to cash their government checks, the city-owned bank was unable to perform. They had no upfront cash, just book ledgers of recorded liens on bankrupted real estate that nobody wanted. Without cash, the city wrote IOUs that were worthless. Some workers turned the IOUs into wallpaper or *origami* paper flowers. The upshot was that the local church mice probably had more cash reserves than our city bank.

I decided I had to take desperate action. I was resolved to borrow the plane before Nick had a chance to give me explicit approval. I was sure he would understand. I could present him the rental money afterwards by mailing him a hefty cashier's check. Then again, Nick might be detained. He might be sitting inside of a re-education camp with little need for cash, and if that was the case, he would surely want me to get away.

As I was trying to justify my dishonest actions, Tommy suddenly revealed a big problem with my plan. "You know that we cannot use Hemet's Airport. It's closed to the public."

"Are you sure?" I asked.

"I rode past it the other day. I mean the dickheads even electrified the chain-link fence—all the way around it. We're locked out, man."

"That's nothing," Lenny said as he pulled out a candy bar and unwrapped it. "I heard airport was barbed wired and mined. Many machine guns nests. Nobody leaves paradise."

"We're going to be stowaways?" Sarah could not hold her tongue.

I shook my head disapprovingly.

"Sorry." Sarah looked away.

"What?" Rant stood up and fumed. "We're not going to steal anything or I'm out!"

"No! We're renting the airplane." I whipped out the wad of hundred-dollar bills. "I think this will get Nick's undivided attention. Money has this funny habit of getting instant respect, no matter who you are."

"Hey. What if airplane's not there?" Lenny folded his arms. "Short trip to nowhere, hah?"

"That's the risk. We will have to remain there until it makes another run," I said.

"You won't get inside the hangar," Big Al glared with a smug smirk. "I know what the city leaders are up to."

I turned to Big Al in undiluted amazement. I had completely forgotten that he might have inside information. "Okay, what are they up to?"

"Security and more security. They seem to fear everyone and everybody."

"And?" I asked.

"That's all."

I could see why even Jack Fish Eyes had so little respect for Big Al. He spent most of his time out to lunch.

"But how we get in airport?" Lenny scratched his head. "Cannot stay there too longer." He held up the half-eaten candy bar and frowned. "Almost out."

Getting inside was the crux of the problem. Everything hinged on successfully sneaking past the armed guard without alarming anyone, especially the men in the airport tower.

"How about counterfeiting a pass?" Big Al suggested. "Why, that would solve all of our problems."

"But we have no idea what a pass looks like," I snapped back.

"I know," Big Al's face brightened. "How about taking a few of the city councilmen hostage. Boy, that would scare the crap out of them."

Now he was talking in the fluent language of "loonese." I was not going to hold a gun to someone's head and force him to the airport. Not my style. "We're not going to kidnap people. It's against the law."

"Why not? They would do it to us," Lenny interrupted.

"We're not like THEM." Rant squinted her disapproving eyes at Big Al. "I don't care about their silly laws or what they do, but we are not thieves or thugs of the night."

"Against the law, huh!" Lenny became more agitated. "What does it matter? Everything against law. Wait until tomorrow. Breathing will be death penalty."

Lenny had a point. The city council and mayor had voted to make almost everything illegal just to improve driving habits. It seemed ironic, but the mass production of new laws seemed to have inflated and cheapened all laws. Apparently, kidnapping, murder, rape, and burglary were now considered minor offenses.

"Make no mistake, some laws will be broken." I stared at Rant. "We don't have the luxury to sit around and argue legalities. We're on our own."

"A rat will fight back if cornered," Rant challenged me. "But that's a wild animal's response. I think we are a little higher on the evolutionary scale."

"The laws are bogus," Tommy came to my defense. "Besides, they break their own laws all the time. How come if we break them, we're the criminals, when they break them, they get promoted?"

"Fine!" Rant threw up her hands. "Break some laws! But let's not injure anyone for any reason, except in strict self-defense."

I recoiled with a gasp. Was something wrong with me or with the universe? I stuck my finger into my ear deep and twisted hard. I was not hearing that straight. Rant actually agreed with me on something. That was impossible. It was like dogs and cats getting along together in perfect harmony. Never going to happen. Maybe I had just entered another dimension of the Twilight Zone. Then again, there was the first time for everything, I suppose.

"How about drugging the guard?" Tommy suggested. "Gag him with ether."

Tommy's pre-med courses finally found some practical use after all. I suggested someone get behind the guard and immobilize him with a rag drenched in ether. The guard would pass out, and we would be on our way. It was perfect. No permanent damage would befall the sentry.

"I want to do gig," Lenny said enthusiastically.

"You mean gag," I corrected him.

"Would be like old times," Lenny laughed quietly.

"You must hold the rag until the subject passes out," Tommy spoke like a doctor. "It should take just a few seconds. Tightly hold the rag against the nose, until he stops struggling, but not enough to stop him from breathing. We do not want to kill him, man. Just incapacitate him."

"I've done it before," Lenny freely confessed. "Really enjoyed it."

There was a long moment of awkward silence.

Lenny stared back, confused. "What?"

"You've done this before?" Sarah asked as she slowly backed away towards another room.

"Sure. No big deal."

"Kill anybody?" Rant asked in an interrogating tone.

Lenny leaned back and stroked his chin, noticing the stunned faces.

"Well?!" Rant demanded.

"No!" Lenny said. "Was just military exercise. Nobody hurt. Honest."

Before more questions could be hurled at Lenny, Sarah rushed back into the room and began talking quickly about something she just heard on her bedroom television. "Come! Come see for yourself." Sarah ran to her bedroom.

Everybody followed her and soon we were crammed inside her small room. She pointed to the television set, but the TV screen was blank, flashing a snowy screen and hearing static noise. That was not usual. Only one local TV station had received city approval to broadcast during evening hours, and even that was rather sporadic. Unfortunately, there was no competition. The signals from other stations in bordering cities had been jammed.

"I saw it!" Sarah almost shouted.

"Saw what?" I asked as I banged the TV set with my clenched fist.

Immediately, television came back to life. A TV announcer holding a piece of paper stated to speak calmly, announcing that a special investigation team had arrested Mayor Quinn. An hour after the trial convened, the court found the mayor guilty as charged. He received the death penalty and was sentenced to death. Within one hour of the guilty verdict, the mayor was sent before a firing squad and shot. The accusations levied against him were far too numerous to count, but mainly entailed treason, corruption, and bribery. Next, the TV station displayed dozens of faces of so-called traitorous scum, mug shots of executed citizens. One was Nick Gillis.

"Poor Nick!" I began to hyperventilate. I leaned back against the bedroom wall and closed my eyes. I found one of my hands starting to quiver and wondered if Sarah and I would ever make it out alive. They had truly gone bat-crazy mad. I opened my eyes and saw everyone staring at each other in dead silence. There was now a greater urgency to move ahead with our escape plan and abandon the gloom and doom of Hemet. We were running out of time. One slip-up, and we would find ourselves on reality TV for the viewing pleasure of slavish TV ghouls.

It was time to put foot to pavement. I sent Tommy to find a bottle of ether. He was positive that he had one or two bottles in storage. That was a comforting thought until he started to question himself as to its exact location, which storage unit and which banana box. Luckily, Tommy had a good memory.

Lenny's duty was to locate some extra fuel for the aircraft, just in case the aircraft was empty, and parachutes—at Sarah's insistence. The others were to lay low and wait for the evening hours.

* * * * *

I had one more duty to perform before saying "sayonara" to Hemet forever. I was low on money. I could not forgo my last big paycheck. The city treasurer promised that my payroll check would be gigantic. Although my gas tank was near empty and most service stations closed, I decided to jaunt down to my office and pick up my last paycheck. That was risky. I was not sure the check would be any good. Rumors were flying that the city was bankrupt and had to issue IOUs. Still, a number of businesses and banks had offered to redeem all the city IOU checks. That tidbit of news was reassuring.

For some strange reason, the distribution of our paychecks had been postponed until Saturday, forcing everyone to stop by during the weekend. Most workers grumbled, except for the smaller weekend crew that operated the system on Saturday and Sunday. About half way to the office, I began to worry again. I began to see fire-damaged buildings, closed streets and armed military units patrolling most streets. I was expecting much more damage from the previous night's escapades. What I was not expecting was unattended fires raging out of control. I stood and gawked in silence as three commercial buildings across from the DED were burning uncontrollably. There were no crews of dedicated firefighters risking life and limb to extinguish the engulfing flames. No fire trucks, no emergency equipment, not even a firedog. It seemed like someone was allowing the structures to burn to the ground, providing only minimal security to keep away onlookers. What was going on?

"Keep moving!" a soldier shoved me forward.

I glared at the blue-eyed soldier with a helmet strapped snugly under his chin. He treated me like dirt, but I was still Director of DED, at least until I could get my paycheck.

As before, I had to go through several security checks and bouts of frisking before I could enter the heavily fortified DED building. We were informed that all paychecks were to be delivered by noon. I was late, and the line was long. Hordes of impatient employees were already waiting in line, looking worried or bad tempered.

"This is bull!" Brian came up from behind with several of his staff members in tow, still wearing a snappy black shirt. "Why couldn't we get our checks on Friday?"

I shrugged. "They're inefficient. Just like everything else in this city."

"They will hear from me Monday morning," Brian said with a threatening tone. "We work hard here."

The thought of Monday morning was both liberating and exhilarating. While everybody would be slaving away, I should be sound asleep in some comfortable bed with Sarah in a city free of neurotic busybodies and firing squads. Heaven.

All of a sudden, I heard someone shouting angrily at the front of the line. They had just started the process of handing out the paycheck envelopes. I could see people shoving other people ahead as more obscenities rattled the air. The ruckus grew stronger as I approached the pay window. The man ahead of me flashed his middle finger at the girl passing out the envelopes. He puffed up and rewarded her with a barrage of spitballs, mostly hitting her face. Something about the paychecks was agitating all of my co-workers. I finally came to the pay window, showed identification for Tommy and myself, and picked up two envelopes. I was almost afraid to peek inside the envelope.

I pulled out my paycheck. Now I understood the reason for the ruckus. The city treasurer had slashed my salary by deducting money for a new tax of epic proportions, gutting it so severely I had barely enough to buy a bag of French fries and a half-eaten Big Mac. This would not do.

"They cannot do this to me!" Brian snarled. "It's unprofessional. We'll make them pay!"

Others mirrored his outrage and shouted more vulgarities. One person jumped on top of a desk and started to kick off the monitors and computers.

I looked inside the envelope for a letter of explanation, something that might express sincere regret for shortchanging the city's hardest workers. At the very least, they should have promised to pay back wages in the near future. That would have been a decent way to do it. Naturally, the envelope was devoid of any explanation.

One of my young code monkeys kicked over a filing cabinet to get everyone's attention. He jumped up on a chair and exploded with primordial screams. "We're not fucking slaves! We have rights! We won't work for free! We won't let this injustice stand!" A sea of agitated workers surrounded the fervent ringleader and hailed him as a savior. Immediately, the mob thrust their clenched fists in the air to the rhythm of hostile voices and angry rhetoric. They lashed out at Jack Fish Eyes and city hall politicians. Their chant was concise and succinct: "Kill Jack! Kill Jack!" Demands to do just that roared down the line. Several lines of rowdies rushed downstairs to accomplish their war-mongering task.

I hated Jack, too, but I wasn't going to stay here and try to fix things. Let Jack sack the city; I was now an unemployed observer.

As I readied myself to depart, I witnessed gangs of men lifting up heavy desks and running towards the big office windows, using cheap furniture as battering rams to break thick-paned windows. Crashing through the glass, the falling desks became makeshift weapons intended to crush advancing soldiers on the ground. One participant became so carried away that he hopped on top of one desk and rode it down to his untimely demise. Now that was dedication to a falling cause.

I backed up against a wall, trying to avoid being caught up in the frenzied commotion. All I could think was that the madness was spreading with the super-speed of a flaming virus.

Meanwhile, others somehow found sledgehammers and pounded sheetrock walls as if such wounds would collapse the building. Next to the hammerheads stood a firebug who set a stack of cardboard boxes on fire. She magically transformed a hairspray can into a flamethrower. She began to chase after the staff woman who had distributed the bad checks. In a puff of smoke, the targeted woman burst into flames, stumbled, and writhed in pain. I grabbed a fire extinguisher off the wall, pulled the pin, pointed the nozzle, and sprayed her with cooling foam. I dropped the canister and directed Brian to help the woman. Brian and another man dutifully followed my instructions. At this point, I decided it was the right time to retreat to a safer loony bin. I was out of here.

As I quickly reached the stairwell's handrail, several explosions violently rocked the building. It felt like a magnitude 9.0 earthquake. I bolted back to the open window frame. Peering down three stories, I could see thongs of National Guardsmen troops attacking yellow-garbed firefighters, hazmat-clad first responders, and our building. Backed by a column of tanks and artillery, the guardsmen fired several cannon rounds at us. Next, they turned their firepower on the firefighters, who quickly retaliated with high-powered water hoses. Dozens of local police officers arrived and took up positions behind red fire trucks and squad cars, firing shotguns and pistols at the advancing military. They were attacking each other like fanatical lunatics who must have been drenched with barrels of testosterone and LSD. I surmised that the firefighters and police had also discovered a few missing zeros in their paychecks.

"We can escape out the back door!" I shouted to my remaining people. They stared back at me with a vacant expression. I suddenly realized they were wondering if I was behind their salary cuts.

"Forget him," somebody shouted. "Old Fish Eyes signed these puny checks. Let's get him!"

"He's a dead man!" Brian growled.

Again, like a caring Moses, I gestured with my waving hand to go down the back stairwell. "Everybody, this way out to safety! We must leave now!"

Naturally, everybody ignored me. I felt like an impotent bystander without any skills to command respect in the workplace.

"Let's join the firemen and fight for our rights!" one disheveled woman hollered as the others cheered her on.

I confronted the woman. "Fight with what?"

The lady pulled out a pair of rusty scissors from the front of her dress. "I'm going to carve up those sons of bitches! I will gouge their eyes out! Every single one."

And I would have thought that my people were mild-manner professionals with bright futures. Now they had converted into ragtag anarchists willing to become cannon fodder for a dead-end mission.

"I'm going to get Old Fish-Eyes," a muscular Samoan woman shrieked with delight. She whipped out a long letter opener and shoved it in front of my face. "When I'm done with him, they'll call him One-Eye Jack."

I watched in disbelief as everyone searched for the best and most deadly weapons among office supplies and equipment. It was nuts. Were they going to combat tanks with rulers, telephone books, mousepads, and floppy disks?

In the search for heavier weapons, several men grabbed computers, ripped the wires out of the wall, and heaved them through the breezy window frames at the invading troops below. One suddenly leaped out, holding a large computer monitor as if he was going to do a cannonball belly flop in a pool. He was aiming for a group of soldiers below and dropped like a human bomb. I had to congratulate him. He actually hit the target. Wow.

Understandably, the troops and tanks below were unamused by my people's antics. They turned their turret sights and gun barrels at our building and prepared another round of gunfire.

"Get out!" I shouted. "They're going to shoot!" Again, nobody listened. They acted like mindless zombies. If they did not evacuate the premises soon, they would be zombies. Of course, I suppose that was redundant since zombies were already dead. Anyway, I was not going to wait around to see it. I fled down the back stairwell.

Chapter 20

We arrived at the airport just before midnight and parked a short distance from the main entrance. We sat in our vehicle and waited for the right moment. Tommy discovered that the graveyard shift would kick in at midnight, and from then until dawn, only one guard would be on duty. Meanwhile, Sarah prepared for an acting job that could easily terminate her brief thespian career. Although the only patron to see her dramatic talent would be a young National Guard grunt.

"Don't be overly melodramatic," I instructed her. "Just be natural." I thought Rant would have done a better job, but she said it was demeaning.

"Relax. I once acted in a high school play."

"A play?" I was flabbergasted. "You were in a play?"

"Don't act so surprised," Sarah gloated as she applied a generous glob of ruby lipstick over her lips. "I was one of the leading characters in *It's a Bird... It's a Plane... It's Superman.*"

"Do you mean you played Lois Lane?" I almost choked on the thought.

Sarah nodded. "Good guess. I enjoyed the part, but it was too much work. I hated remembering all of the lines. But some people gave me kudos for my singing."

"I always wanted to be on stage," I confessed. "Except I was simply too shy. I once attended an audition for *Lion of the West.* I had practiced the part of Davy Crockett hundreds of times. Just before they called me up, I sneaked out of the dressing room. Not real smart."

"No." Sarah took hold of my hand. "Nothing worse than sabotaging one›s own dreams."

"I just wanted to play Davy."

"You still might have a chance," Sarah grinned.

I moved closer to her passenger seat. "You know, if we get out of this quagmire, we should…"

"Let's not start making promises," Sarah stopped me in mid-sentence. "Because if we don't get out, we'll be pretty disappointed. Right?"

I moved back and nodded. "Sure."

"Listen," Sarah said softly, noticing my disappointment. "When this nightmare is over, we should do something more with our lives."

"I know. Breathing and eating don't constitute real living."

"Yeah. Zombies don't have much of a life either, do they?" Sarah pulled a bottle of whiskey from a bag on the floor and twisted it open.

"True," I agreed and glanced at my wristwatch. It was almost midnight. I looked her in the eyes and felt an intimacy that I had not felt in a long time. It was like being part of a secret shared only with one's closest friend.

Sarah dropped her lipstick back into her small purse, reached over, and held my hand. She fluttered her long eyelashes and flung her arm around my neck. She spoke in a steady voice, "We do this together. You and me until the end."

I swallowed, trying to keep my head clear. I knew what could happen. I was taking this danger more lightly than she was. I was the schmuck who was letting her risk her life. I kept seeing a haunting image of Sarah's lifeless body staring up at me, eyed wide open and half her brain gone. It should be me. I finally turned away and glanced down at my watch. "I believe it's showtime."

Sarah nodded with a slight frown. "I'm ready."

I opened my Chevy truck door, slid out of the driver's seat, and landed on the dark pavement. Sarah moved over and took control of the steering wheel.

I gave her the thumbs-up signal. "Break a leg."

She radiated a confident smile. "Hey, I'll knock his socks off."

As I softly closed the vehicle's door, Sarah took a deep swig of whiskey, tore strips down the front of her sexy outfit, and ruffed up her hair. Next, she splashed whiskey generously across the front of my cab, drenching my nice upholstery. Normally, I would have gone ballistic, except I knew my precious truck had to be sacrificed to our urgent needs. Naturally, I was going to abandon my work vehicle just after I mailed in my last payment. Nothing was ever fair in this world.

I faced Lenny. He wore a generic military camouflage outfit that probably came from West Germany. In quick fashion, he slathered his face with black greasepaint. He resembled a US combat soldier except that he had a red star pinned on his black beret, something probably leftover from the old Soviet days. I pointed to a bus bench and kiosk on the sidewalk. "That's your spot over there."

Lenny nodded and quickly jumped out of the truck. He scurried across the road, landed in some dead landscaping, and crawled toward the entrance. He made a mad dash for the bus bench and scuttled under it. I could see that he definitely had extensive military training.

I ordered everyone else out of the truck. We hit the ground and crawled alongside the road. Tommy pulled a pair of black binoculars from his knapsack, but the right lens was cracked. Another piece of junk from the dumpster.

We watched closely as one replacement arrived at the gatehouse, and two guards departed. That improved our odds. There was now only one inexperienced sentry with an M16 guarding the entrance. He was no match for my Sarah.

I tapped Tommy's shoulder and pointed to a spot close to the front gate. He gestured with approval, dashed across the road, and blended in with surroundings. Rant stared at me while keeping her hand on her hidden Glock. She was backup, just in case things went wrong. As for Big Al, he spent his time moaning about crawling in the gravel and dirt. Apparently, our nocturnal activities were ruining his Neiman Marcus designer pants. What a total schmuck.

I lifted my head up a little and waved to Sarah. She started the engine, turned on the headlights, and roared off in my truck. She drove erratically, swerving back and forth across the double yellow line, almost striking a fire hydrant. Near the entrance, she stopped, revved up the engine, and with screeching wheels took off at the guard booth as if that were her intended target. Almost sideswiping the booth, she jammed on the brakes and honked the horn wildly.

"Service!" She slurred. "I want shervish!"

The guard responded slowly. He looked over his wire-frame glasses with a sour expression. He opened his glass door and peered at the shouting woman.

"I'll take two cheesy burgers and some French. Fries I mean." She giggled.

"The airport is closed, madam," the young guard shouted, cautiously approaching the vehicle, gripping the handle of his sidearm.

"Aren't you going to take my order?" She took a hearty gulp from her whiskey bottle.

"No, madam."

"Boy, this is lousy service! I'm going to report you to the manager."

The guard gave a wry smile and shook his head. He shined his flashlight inside the vehicle and searched for anyone in the back. "You need to turn around, lady. The airport is closed to the public."

"Good! Add a coke to it. But hold the ice. You always put too much ice in and cheat me on the drink."

"You know that I could arrest you for drinking and driving."

"I bet you won't, honey. You know why?"

The guard grinned.

"Because I'm so damn good-looking. Right?" With a seductive glint in her eyes, Sarah flaunted her body in slutty position, as if she was going to lift her skirt.

The guard started to open the driver's door. "I think you need to come with me. You'll thank me in the morning."

"Yeah, I bet I will, Cutie!" Sarah leaned toward the guard; her breast barely contained by her torn blouse. "How about right now?" She grabbed his hand and did something very ingenious with her fingers. She placed the guard's hand on her naked breast. His face exploded in a sea of immense pleasure, eager to try out the other one. Sarah was going to get the top grade for seducing a stranger in less than a minute.

Actually, as I watched her kinky foreplay turn hotter and wetter, a sense of envy surged through my veins. She was definitely overacting her part. She was only supposed to distract him for a few moments, not indulge in gutter sex. I felt more than a trace of jealousy. None of this was in her script. She was improvising, coming up with her own material. If only she had been this spontaneous when it came to sexual adventures in my bed.

"She's really enjoying the part," Rant chuckled.

I turned to Rant. "She's just doing her job."

Rant grinned, "Yeah, more like a blow job."

"It's just a little impromptu skit," I said, trying to ignore Rant's innuendo and hold my emotions in check.

"If you say so," Rant teased.

I turned my attention back to Sarah. As the guard prepared to lower his pants zipper, Lenny rushed in for the kill. He looped a rope around the sentry's neck and stuffed a rag into the man's face. Within a few seconds, the struggling sentry collapsed to the ground.

"Let's go!" I yelled at everyone. We ran across the street to Lenny and his prized captive. Tommy was already standing next to Lenny ready to assist him.

"Tape him," I ordered. Actually, I wanted first to kick him in the nuts and rip out his eyeballs, but Tommy prevented me from doing that. He immediately knelt next to the fallen guard and pulled out an old roll of psychedelic colored tape from his pocket. He slapped a strip across the guard's mouth. Next, he taped his hands together and dragged him behind the booth. Rant followed along and checked to see if he was still breathing. She looked up and gave the thumbs-up.

Within seconds, everybody leaped into my truck and raced to Hangar 12. It was on the far side of the main runway, separated by several dilapidated warehouses. We found the hangar locked, as expected. I turned to Tommy. He was our tool man and boasted that he had every manufactured implement known to mankind. The only problem was he could never find an unbroken tool at the appropriate time.

"I hope this works," Tommy said as he whipped out a large rusty bolt cutter. "Like, man I have a stack of these. Most of them work. Found this one in a dumpster."

"In the dumpster?" I glared at Tommy.

"Yeah, all the good stuff comes from my dumpster diving."

"Don't tell me about this crap, just cut it," I almost shouted.

Tommy clamped the jaws of the cutters around lock's shackle and squeezed as hard as he could. Nothing happened. He repeated it and bore down on the steel lock with my assistance.

"What's taking so long?" Rant butted in. "My grandmother could have done it by now."

"Just wait," I said. "Everything takes time."

"We don't have much of that," Lenny said, trying to get some attention from our little band of stymied burglars.

Tommy squeezed and squeezed the red handles and finally snapped off the lock. "See, it was the right one."

I shook my head in disgust. There were just too many variables to go wrong. We had no idea if we had the right hangar. Nick had a habit of forgetting numbers, turning them around or reversing them.

We swung the door wide open, hoping that our luck would hold. Shining our flashlights into the gloomy darkness, we saw our prize. There, in the middle of our hazy beams of light, among tightly packed crates and boxes, stood an older twin-engine Piper PA-31 Navajo in almost-mint condition. It was beautiful, painted in bright blue and red, just waiting to be taken for a short jaunt to another land far, far away. I almost wanted to kiss the oil-stained cement and sing Hallelujah.

"I hope it has fuel." I glanced at Lenny. He had been unable to locate any extra aviation fuel.

"Can't we find a better way?" Lenny asked, looking apprehensive.

It was rumored that Lenny had a fear of flying. Well, it was too late to back out now.

"Our Russian planes not too…" Lenny's lip trembled slightly. Not good. Often *suka*. How you say? 'bitch?'"

"This is good quality—American-made." I tried to comfort him. "It will work fine unless someone shoots us down," I joked.

"That could happen, no?"

"Not likely," I tried to assure Lenny. "Now help Rant load the parachutes and suitcases." It was an empty order. Rant had almost completed her task to load up the plane. I could always count on her.

As for Tommy, he was not only unreliable, but also almost paralyzed with sorrow. He had to leave behind many of his dearest friends. There was only room for three banana boxes, and he was forced to leave many behind. His pain was excruciating. In a mad rush, he started to sort through the boxes. With loving care, he cradled an oily VW piston like a newborn baby while throwing away a handful of nuts and bolts with his other hand. Tears flowed from his red, swollen eyes.

Jumping into the pilot seat, I switched on the electrical system and inspected a few of the gages and indicators to see if we had enough fuel remaining. I tapped the fuel gauge and the needle jumped up. We had plenty of fuel, but since we were going to nearby Riverside we did not need much. As I examined the other gages, I heard a noise in the front of the hangar. I looked out and saw someone approaching us.

Out of the darkness, the image of Old Fish Eyes materialized out of nowhere. A bloodstained patch covered his left eye. Several deep scratches raked across his face, some wide and purple. It seemed that someone with sharp fingernails had clawed him like a wild cat. Blood trickled down from his mangled right ear, as if he had been bitten by a rabid dog. He was a mess.

In the background stood two armed soldiers decked out in stylish black uniforms. They barely moved a muscle, their bodies resembling marble statues in a museum. They aimed their assault rifles at me.

I climbed out of the plane and faced my nemesis, wishing I had taken Rant's advice. Yes, she was right again. I was in desperate need of a strong defensive weapon.

"Going for supplies this late hour?" Jack gleamed with the delight of a father catching his child stealing from a forbidden cookie jar.

"I'm going for a quick cappuccino. Starbucks is fresh out."

"Well, we cannot let that happen." Jack moved closer, walking with a limb. "You know what I think? I think you're planning to abandon ship."

"First, there has to be a ship to abandon," I retorted.

"Cute! But it doesn't matter what you think. We need you here and..." Jack stopped in mid-sentence. He had spotted Big Al hiding behind the others.

The crowd parted as Jack sauntered through and stood in front of his former DED Director. "I see we have caught a much larger big-mouth traitor. My trophy wall will be complete. Believe me, the taxidermist will be hard put to fill my order."

"They kidnapped me," Big Al lied through his teeth as sweat beaded across his pale forehead.

"Odd! You're not handcuffed." Jack lifted Big Al's sweaty, white shaking hands.

"I just broke free. And yes, you're right. All of these miscreants are deserters. They plan to escape and never return. They're turncoats."

"One turncoat to another. Well, I see that my suspicions have been confirmed." Jack turned around and walked back to me. "So, what is it? We didn't pay you enough? Or is it the climate? Just too hot in Hemet?"

"Definitely, too hot. And a little too erratic," I said.

"I've been watching you," Jack said, as he fished around in his pocket. "Very closely. I understand that you're a good friend of Nick Gillis."

"So, you're the one who's been spying on us with cameras and sophisticated listening equipment."

"You're not that important. That's why I enlisted the services of Brian. You picked an excellent supervisor. He has been very helpful."

"Brian?" I felt betrayed.

"I know you had secret talks with Nick Gillis. I am sure it was delightful chitchat about literature and poetry. But now I find you with his plane and his ill-gotten supplies. By the way, smuggling is a crime punishable by death. I believe that is ordnance 21395."

"It's our stuff, man," Tommy blurted out as he still held his bolt cutter. "We haven't done anything criminal."

"Really?" Jack paused and eyed the stacks of banana boxes next to the plane. "I may have only one good eye left, but I know incriminating evidence when I see it."

"You have no right to tell us what to do," I said. "Besides, I believe the vice mayor should be in charge. You know, what's-his-name?" My real motive was to stall and distract Jack, giving someone time to pursue some harebrained scheme that might actually work. From the corner of my eye, I noticed Tommy inching closer to Jack. It seemed out of character. Tommy probably did not have the nerve to smack our city manager with his bolt cutter. Or did he?

"Poor Gene Holiday," Jack replied. "Unfortunately, he was also caught up in Mayor's Quinn's elaborate conspiracy. Too bad. I still have him marked on my calendar to play poker next Tuesday night. Boy, Gene was a lousy card player. It's too bad his cheating cards got revoked."

"So... You're now in charged?" I asked.

"Heavens no! The Committee for Homeland Security is in charge. I'm just the chairman."

"So, you have not been spying on us?" I asked.

"Ever since Quinn's demise, you've been on my minor shit list as a possible co-conspirator. Sure, we monitored your pathetic and meaningless activities. They did not warrant much attention. We only assigned a handful of undercover agents and installed six tapped phone lines. It was mostly a big waste of money, except for recapturing Big Al."

For some reason, I believed in Jack's assessment. He had always been stingy with the city budget and would never spend lavishly for something he could get on the cheap. Still, that begged the question—who was also spying on Tommy and me?

"You need to come with us," Jack smiled and pulled out his pistol. "Nobody is allowed to leave. Especially conspirators and smugglers."

"We're not guilty of any conspiracy," I said.

"The tribunal council will decide that. They love a challenge."

Then Sarah made her move. She sashayed up to Jack and pleaded with him. "Spencer is ill. He needs to see a specialist in Riverside. That's why we're leaving."

"We have doctors here," Jack said peering down Sarah's revealing décolletage.

Sarah made no effort to cover up her almost naked bosom. "But Jack…" Her sweet voice conveyed sensual warmth that would have put Marilyn Monroe to shame. "Most of the doctors here are unfamiliar with my husband's disease." She moved in front of Jack and fingered his blood-stained tie with her graceful left hand. "He might not recover if he remains in Hemet."

"What's the disease?" Jack leaned toward Sarah, fascinated by her advancing erotic prowess.

"Why, it's an ancient disorder—Tyrantitis!" Sarah whipped out a handgun and shoved it at Jack's chest. "Now, hand over your weapon you little tyrannical shithead!"

Jack looked down at Sarah's small pistol. He laughed with a wide sarcastic grin. "Why my dear, a little lower and you will be directly over my heart. That's a much better target."

"I know," Sarah said with a serious face, "but since you don't have one, there's no reason to aim there."

"Touché, my dear Madame." Jack appeared delighted by her response. He slightly bowed his head slightly as if to pay reverence. "Sadly, a little slug of humor will not save you."

"Oh… We'll see." Rand cocked her pistol and instantly rushed closer, right next to Sarah. With a quick snap, she slammed her barrel against Jack's forehead. "Is this better? Two bullets for the price of one."

"Immensely. I do appreciate a bargain, but you will still never escape. We have you targeted. Believe me when I say there are no places where you can escape. And I mean nowhere."

"I don't care," Sarah huffed. "Disarm and tell your goons to drop their weapons.

With a stupid smile, Jack lifted his gun up high in the air, dangling it like a cat's toy. He appeared cool and calm, but soon affirmed his surrender with a nodding gesture to the two gunmen. The two soldiers immediately came to life and dropped their weapons. They raised their arms and backed away a few feet. It was too easy. It almost appeared that his surrender had been rehearsed. I motioned for Lenny and Rant to gather the soldiers' weapons.

I stepped forward and relieved Jack of his pistol. I backed away and prepared to leave, but something caught my eye. Upon closer study of the weapon, a silly grin rippled across my face. The handgun had a distinct similarity to the Mayor's German Lugar. I suspected that Jack had to pry it from Quinn's cold, dead fingers. There is justice in the world, in a sort of twisted and bizarre way.

This was what I was trying to avoid. Our plan was to secretly escape during the dead of night and avoid complications. We were not revolting; we were retreating, but that had all changed. We were actively involved in an unplanned political coup. We had disarmed and captured Hemet's supreme authority. We had arrested the tyrant-in-chief. What were we thinking?

I turned my attention to Sarah and stared at her with a gaze of endless incredulity. Apparently, I was wrong about her meek and timid personality. Right before my eyes, she had changed into a female Rambo with an arsenal of trickery and pretense, not unlike her audacious sister.

"Where did you get the gun?" I asked Sarah as the shock started to fade.

Sarah just smiled with a look of extreme satisfaction.

"I gave it to her!" Rant stepped forward and admitted her assistance. "Self-defense is a right. Even an obligation. Besides, a gun is a girl's best friend. I've been training her. I was happy to. Rather odd though. She has always hated guns."

Sarah moved next to me. She put her hand on my shoulder and stared straight into my eyes. "I sought out Rant's help. I didn't want to feel defenseless anymore. Understand?"

I nodded.

"I'm over here," Jack uttered with a deep rumbling in his throat. "I'm supposed to be the center of attraction here. You simply can't leave me out of the conversation. I'm more important than any of you."

Tommy faced Jack and aimed the bolt cutter at his chest. "Hey, man, we've just dimmed your limelight. So, stop yakking like a big loser. You're the preening cocks who keep stepping all over us. We just want out. We don't want to remain behind enemy lines. We're done!"

Tommy was correct. We were trapped behind enemy lines, in a foreign-like land we still did not fully understand. The worst part was that the borderline to the other side was undefined. We had no idea how far we had to flee to escape its firm grip.

I searched the hangar for rope or something to tie our captives' hands but could not find anything. The hangar was crammed with boxes of produce and packaged food, and not much else. It was designed as a storage unit, not an aircraft hangar. The ceiling was rather low. I called for more of Tommy's duct tape, but he informed me that he had used the last piece of tape on the gate guard.

"You know, we will get you in the end," Jack said haughtily. "We will never give up. We will track you down wherever you go. I have special operatives on the outside. You cannot hide. Someone will find you one morning swimming in your own pool of blood."

"We should just shoot them," Big Al said matter-of-factly, displaying a sour, miserable frown on his face.

That horrible thought had crossed my mind. But we were not killers. We were not like them. We had principles. I did not have to confer with the others. They knew that Big Al's sentiments were off the table discussions.

"We've got to go," Tommy tugged my arm. "Someone will discover the gagged sentry. And boy, will the crapola really hit the fan!"

"Listen up!" I shouted. "We need to drag the plane clear of the hangar."

"Not me!" Big Al boomed and folded his arms.

"You can come along if you help us." I offered amnesty to Big Al despite my distrust.

"You're mad!" Rant pulled her Glock and aimed it at Big Al's big head. "He's one of THEM."

I had to think fast. "Big Al might be useful to people on the other side. You know, intelligence about the Hemet's ruling hierarchy and future plans."

"Give me a break!" Jack almost laughed. "Big Al is brain dead. Any neurologist could prove that in two seconds."

Rant lowered her gun. "Maybe the fat man could be helpful. Just maybe."

"I will behave," Big Al said. "You would have done what I did to save your skins."

"No! I wouldn't!" Rant walked up to Big Al and sneered. "I don't wrestle in the mud with pigs."

"We need him," I argued with the others. "He can help us to move the plane outside. Like I said before, we can hand him over to authorities on the other side." I stepped in front of Big Al and tried to get his undivided attention. "I am sure you will provide useful information to policing agencies. Correct?"

Big Al hesitated at first, mumbled something inaudible, and then grunted out an affirmation: "Sure."

Rant slowly lowered her gun, a skeptical look on her face.

Along with Big Al's minor help, everyone started to move the aircraft out of the low-ceilinged hangar. I remained as the lone guard, with my gun sight focused on our uninvited guests. I realized that if I could not constrain them, I would have to stay behind. Tommy knew how to fly a plane. Somewhat. I had taken him on many airborne excursions and allowed him to occasionally take off and fly to Palmdale and back. He was quite good. Of course, neither of us had much training for night flying. Still, anything was better than living in this hostile terrain.

I walked slowly behind the plane as everyone pushed and pulled. I noticed Jack eyeing the telephone on the wall. Finally, outside the hangar, I ordered everyone inside the airplane. I did not want Sarah to know what I intended to do. She would never leave me behind. I told everyone to get inside.

Before Tommy could climbed inside, I grabbed his arm and pulled him closer to me. "Take control of the cockpit! You must be our pilot."

Tommy looked confused. "What?"

I lowered my voice, whispering. "I cannot come."

"Hey, man, you're not going all suicidal on me?"

"Of course not. I'll explain later." I turned and walked back to the hangar.

Unfortunately, Sarah saw me heading back to the hangar.

Sarah ran back to the plane's rear door and shouted, "What are you doing?"

I could not lie. I stopped, turned and stared back at Sarah. "Listen, Tommy must take off if I can't find a way to keep these mad dogs leashed. They will call the tower and who knows what will happen next?"

"I won't go!" Sarah cried out.

"Lenny, keep her inside. That's an order."

"This is all very touching," Jack said from a distance. "Sacrificing yourself for the common good. Why, that's my duty."

"Yeah, but you sacrifice citizens' lives instead."

"Well, that's expected. We all know our expected duties. The authorities don't protect citizens, citizens protect us. It has always been that way. Nothing earthshattering." Jack walked to the phone leisurely as if he was out for his morning walk.

"Tommy, start up the engine!" I ordered.

Tommy cranked the starter. The engine roared to life.

I turned back to Jack, still pointing my pistol at him, "Move away from the phone!"

"How come I get the feeling you were never one of us?" Jack stood in front of the phone.

"You're right, I never wanted to be one of THEM."

"But you never did anything to stop us. Not only were you a traitor, but you also couldn't even do it right!" Jack smirked.

That was a hard pill to swallow. I could not help but feel guilty as charged.

"You're worse than a traitor," Jack said. "You're a coward."

I just shook my head. Few people liked Jack's caustic sense of humor or anything else about him. He had lived in bad sections of Chicago and now wanted to transplant that misery to our little city. I was sure he was going to get an award for his extraordinary misconduct. These people always did.

Jack turned and grabbed the phone.

I lifted my gun as Jack reached for the phone. It was a scene right out of *Casablanca*. Rick shot and killed the arrogant Nazi officer. Like Rick, I could not allow Jack to alarm the airport tower; otherwise, we risked imminent capture. I was on the horns of a dilemma. Was I willing to kill a man over a phone call? And yet Jack and his coterie were doing the same, injuring and shooting innocent citizens over silly moving violations. In fact, this whole travesty was all about the ends justifying the means. They believed that they could do anything so long as it might produce good results. Of course, they were the ones who defined goodness.

As Jack started to dial, his other hand reached towards his back. "And don't give me any of your crap about liberty. Most of those fallacies were taken away years ago. Remember, driving is a privilege, not a right. All your so-called 'rights' originate from us, not from some nebulous Almighty. We have the right to determine where and when people will drive. We own the roads. In fact, we own you."

"Put down the phone," I ordered as I walked closer to Jack, tightly gripping my gun in my hand. My hand was shaking, my heart beating fast. It seemed that everything around me had stopped.

"You won't shoot me, Spencer. The meek never do. So why object to the loss of a few more antiquated privileges? They have no meaning anymore. You know that. You're smarter than that."

But if he was so smart, then why was I the one holding the handgun?

Jack began to slowly dial the tower number.

I released the safety, aimed, and fired one shot near his face.

Jack jerked away to one side. He touched his ear with his thumb, studied it. He smiled when he noticed a few drops of blood. "Just a minor graze. I'll consider it a miss. You know what your problem is, Spencer?"

I shook my head.

"You're not a cold-blooded killer. Well, bully for you. But you cannot have significant change without breaking a few eggs. In fact, I bet you voted for me in the last election. I won by a landslide."

Of course, I had, but I was not going to tell him that. "Well, we can always recall a bad egg."

"So, you think society can thrive without us?"

"No. Nothing so grandiose. Just you."

Jack ignored me and put the phone up to his ear. "Hello, this is Jack Bellamy and..."

"Stop!" I fired again, hitting the wall just above his pointy little head. He must really thought he was dealing with as a spineless wuss. I just wish I could convince myself that shooting an unarmed man was self-defense.

Old Fish Eyes turned away and continued to talk at a leisurely pace. I had to stop him without killing him. It had to be now. In a split second, Jack pulled out a small-caliber gun from behind his waistband, turned, aimed, and fired. In a flash, I did the same. We both fired at the same moment. We must have apparently missed each other.

"You can do better than that, Spencer," Jack laughed. He winced with a sharp intake of breath and faced me directly. He slowly re-targeted the barrel of his gun in my general direction. He dropped the phone, trudged towards me with the innate feeling of superiority. "You lost again. You people never learn."

A small rivulet of blood began spilling out of Jack's mouth. Tilting to one side, he mumbled that I was a miserable piece of vermin. His gun barrel drifted towards the ground, finally dropping from his twitching fingers. He tumbled and landed on his back.

I rushed to Jack, knelt next to him, leaned over, and felt a terrible feeling of remorse.

Jack had no such regrets. He glared up at me with a glassy look of hate. He could not give up. He reached up with his right hand and tried to pull me down, attempting to choke me. "You meddling idiot. You had to stir up a hornet's nest. You will…"

Jack stopped breathing.

I slowly stood up and peered down at my nemesis. He did not seem so dangerous now. I looked at my gun. I was not a murderer. I was not his kind of man.

Stepping back, I glanced around. The two soldiers were long gone. That is when I saw Rant jumping out of the roaring plane. She ran towards me. They had never left. She grabbed my aimless arm and pulled with all her might. I could barely move. I stumbled as she dragged me to the airplane. I was feeling dizzy. I was still not sure of anything, except that the two soldiers had alerted the tower of our unscheduled takeoff. I sure we would soon be caught.

Tommy moved out of the pilot's seat and let me to take control of the plane. I still struggled with the instruments on the control panel, not sure where to begin. As my haziness began to subside, I reached for the throttle and pulled back. In no time, we were taxiing down the tarmac and away from all of our troubles. I wanted to go faster than normal, but that might tip off the tower that something was wrong. Tommy radioed the tower that we had authorization from Jack Bellamy to depart. I knew they would demand proof, but by the time they searched their pile of paperwork for our authorization, we would be landing in Riverside.

Tommy kept trying to reach the tower without success. I suspected that they knew we were trying to escape and refused to acknowledge our request. But then again, maybe they were asleep, or off duty.

"How's the oil pressure?" I asked Tommy.

"Way up there."

I reworked the mixture to a richer blend and performed a few of the more important cockpit checks. The main runway was ahead, and I applied more pressure on the yokes and pedals. What made my take-off more difficult than normal was that only a handful of runway lights were operational. Fortunately, the runway was very long, and I only needed a few markers to make my way. Just as I revved up the engines, blaring emergency sirens shook the air.

"Intruder alert! Intruder alert!"

Suddenly, bright lights tore through the darkness of the tarmac. Men poured out of barracks and ran to sandbagged bunkers on both sides of the airfield. Jack was right. They did have ways to stop us. I pulled back the throttle and speed down the main runway, finally nosing skyward. I was afraid to look at my RPM gauge, certain I had exceeded its capacity. I wanted to go higher and faster than possible. Unfortunately, that is when they switched on the colossal, high-powered spotlights.

I was over 4,000 feet before we ran into the anti-aircraft flak. Shells were exploding all over the sky as the spotlights struggled to pinpoint our position. I could see a line of white tracers passing to the left, and then the right. I had to get higher or find some cloud cover. Before I could roll eastward, our left wing was hit in an explosion of fire and smoke. The damage was extensive.

"We're going down!" Tommy screamed.

The aircraft jumped up and rolled to one side as I tried to control it.

"Stay tight!" I shouted. I had lost the flap controls for that wing and found it difficult to maneuver.

Smoke began filling the cabin. An electrical short knocked out most of the instruments, but I did not need an altimeter to know we were in trouble. By this time, we were out of range of the anti-aircraft guns, and likely beyond the boundary of Hemet. Still, we were still going down.

Chapter 21

We were losing altitude faster than the stock market crash of 1987. The smoke was choking us inside the cabin. It was growing denser as our battle-scarred aircraft started to vibrate. Military strategists had a term for this: a problem-rich environment. That was so true. We were plunging in a world plush with death.

I stared out the window for a flat and smooth surface of ground. Ahead was a narrow pathway in the middle of an orchard, but it was too dangerous; let the farmer prune his own trees with his own equipment. Squinting, I saw a wide paved road to the left, flanked by telephone and electrical poles. That was out of the question. Every pilot wanted to avoid entangling wires.

Suddenly, a layer of high clouds blocked the bright moonlight. Our luck had expired. An approaching wall of misty fog began to block our view. Trying to find a good landing spot was the least of my worries. We were not going to land; we were going to crash. I reached for the radio mic, pressed the button, and shouted "Mayday" three times. I tried to give them my position, but the smoke made that task impossible. It did not matter. The radio crackled with static and distant interference. I could not reach anybody.

"Oh, shit!" Tommy shouted as he desperately tapped the oil pressure gauge. "The pressure is dropping!"

"We're dropping dead!" Lenny yelled from behind. "Do something!"

"Hold on! We're going down!" I yelled as the plane began to stall. If I could only keep the aircraft from rolling and spiraling out of control, then we might have a chance to survive a crash landing. Soon that option became moot. Flames were licking the edge of our left wing and spreading. If they reached our fuel tank, we would explode into a fireball of flames.

"Brace yourself!" I shouted.

I pulled back on the yoke controls, but I was unable to pull out of our wild dive. Our chances were slim to nothing. Few pilots and passengers ever survived an emergency landing in the dark, especially when they were on fire.

But I had to keep looking down through the fuzzy clouds. I had to find a safe place to land. Luckily, the fog began to thin. Stretches of openness started to appear. Visibility improved. Gazing down between the gaps of clouds, I could see hilly terrain, rocky overhangs, and acres of orchards. That was not my best choice of landing sites. One area resembled an oil depot with a scattering of tall, rusty fuel tanks. Also not a good option.

Before I could make any decision, the clouds miraculously parted, clearing away just in time to see where we were going. I pointed to a possible level spot. Perhaps four miles away, a shaft of silvery moonlight highlighted a field at the edge of a lake. It sparkled with a sort of heavenly haze. We were blessed with a second chance to enjoy another day.

"Over there!" I pointed to Tommy.

"We're too low," Tommy had a death grip on his seat. "We'll never make it across the lake, man."

"I will jump!" Lenny pushed against my seat stood and started to rush to the rear door.

"No!" I yelled, turned, and grabbed his shirt. It was pure suicide to parachute this low to the ground. Of course, our odds of surviving a landing were not much better.

"We going die!" Lenny pulled away and made another run for the door. Rant intercepted, grabbed his arm, and slugged Lenny across the face, knocking him against the window. Not one to be subdued, especially by a woman, Lenny jumped up and tackled Rant headfirst. They rolled back and forth on the floor until Sarah pulled out her pistol and jabbed the barrel into his face.

"So help me God!" Sarah shrilled. "Don't make me!"

Lenny remained motionless on the floor, uttering a slight whimpering sound. A slight shiver shook his bulky frame. He appeared confused over the sheer fortitude of the women.

I turned and looked back, noticing Sarah's reddish and determined face. Her eyes were aglow with determination. That was my gal.

Big Al eyed Sarah with lifted eyebrows and a tight mouth, wearing a hawkish expression. He had fallen to the airplane's floor, his seat belt too small to accommodate his girth. Suddenly, he kicked Sarah in the stomach, batted the gun out of her hand, and seized the weapon. He slowly stood and pointed the handgun first at Sarah, and then swing it back and forth to include everyone.

This was my fault. I kept forgetting that Big Al was one of THEM and prone to lunacy. I was not sure why he had turned on us at that movement. His few jumbled words alluded to something about the weak being "meat for the strong." Made little sense.

Rant quickly confronted the big man. She stomped up to Big Al and demanded Sarah's gun back. Without hesitation, Big Al raised the gun, targeted Rant, and squeezed the trigger. It failed to fire.

"I was just joking." Big Al grinned with a stupid, sheepish smile.

Big Al had forgotten to switch off the safety lock

"You obese son of a shit!" Rant ripped the gun from Big Al's hand. She gritted her teeth and raised her hand, preparing to slap him back to the day of his birth. She paused at the last moment, "You're not worth the effort." Rant turned, climbed back into her seat, and snapped her seat belt. She stared at Big Al, raking him with her menacing eyes.

Tommy still sat tense and motionless, his eyes riveted on the darkness, outside, and the moon-bright field ahead. "We're dropping too fast!" his voice crackled.

He was correct. Our rate of descent was steep, actually too steep. I could do little. I had lost all control of the plane. Our nosedive was hurtling us toward a dark watery grave. If the sudden impact failed to kill us, sinking in the black water would. I slammed the throttle full power and gave full flaps just to reach level flight. It worked! I was now leveled, but very low. I backed off on the power and tried to keep the nose up and reduced the speed. As I lowered the landing gear, I could feel the water splashing against our front wheel.

At that very moment, I heard something structural on the airplane snap. I looked out and saw the burning wing breaking apart. Worse, the vertical fin of the tail was twisted and flapped loosely. We would never make it beyond our soggy grave. Feeling nauseated, I closed my eyes and wished I could hold Sarah one last time before we were smashed to pieces. Just one last time.

Suddenly, we sailed past the shoreline and over a cattle pasture.

"Hang on!"

I prepared to slam into rocky earth and said a little prayer. This was it. We would either be celebrated as lucky daredevils or appear somewhere on the back page of the obituaries. In a flash, we bounced and skipped over a low fence and swerved on our left side until we slid into a mountain of bundled hay.

"Get out!" I screamed as the hay exploded into flames. The engine and fuel tank were going to blow at any moment. We could only beat the odds so many times in one day. Everyone scrambled out in seconds. Even Big Al tumbled out the back door and landed heavily on his backside.

As I predicted, the Piper exploded like a gasoline truck in the middle of a forest fire. Pieces of the fuselage and aluminum parts rained down on us, with one large piece barely missing Tommy's head.

We watched the inferno climb across tall bales of hay. The heat was intense. It reminded me of a bonfire during homecoming at high school. So much heat. Without realizing it, I noticed that I had scratched my forearms almost raw. They were bleeding along deep fingernail marks. I had to sit somewhere. My head was still spinning. My knees were wobbly and felt like they had turned to jelly. I collapsed to the ground.

Sarah rushed to me and helped me to sit up straight. She gave me a hug and kissed my forehead. The lips would have been better, but someone said they had turned icky blue.

I smiled, enjoying the attention.

"You did it!" Sarah hugged me again. The others gathered around to congratulate me, even Lenny, although his ghastly white skin color still blemished his face.

"I never had any doubts," I mumbled in a weak, monotone. I was obviously lying to myself. Anybody could crash land an airplane.

"Good job," Lenny said, trying to distract from his earlier panic attack. "I knew you would do it." He looked down with a dopey grin of embarrassment. "I thought this was Russian plane. When things go bad, we just jump out."

Before I could reply to Lenny's asinine response, Rant tugged on my arm and pointed to car headlights traveling fast in our direction. "I'm afraid we have visitors."

Our fireworks display had apparently startled the local inhabitants out of their slumber. An old Ford truck rolled up next to the burning aircraft and stopped. A grey-haired farmer in grungy blue overalls jumped out. His long unkempt beard and straggly hair resembled that of a wild mountain man. With an eye-bulging, nostril-flaring face, the man pointed a shiny shotgun at us as if we were alien intruders from another planet.

"This here is private property. I'm Henry."

"I'm Spencer Crane," I stood my ground in front of the farmer. "We had a little accident."

"Are you all from Hemet?"

I really did not want to answer that question. I was not even sure if we had flown past the affected area. In fact, I did not know where we were.

"Well?" the farmer demanded.

"I guess you could say that."

The farmer raised his gun higher and aimed. "Well, git back where you came from. I don't want anyone here. You people are zombies-wombies."

Tommy moved up from the back, clarifying, "We're the normal ones."

"Well... yeah, ah... most of the time." Tommy smiled at me with silly coyness.

"I don't care who ya are!" the farmer exploded, eyeing us with a look of silent contempt. "I cannot take a chance with the deranged."

I moved closer. "Well, we're not like the others."

"Ohhh…?" I struggled to find the words to prove our innocence without tarnishing our few remaining scraps of dignity. I was never going to make that impossible task possible.

"For what I've seen, all of you Hemet folks is crazy. You've been trumping down my crops and attacking my steers. Why I've seen a grown man attack one of my prized bulls with his bare hands. After he injured my bull, he lunged at me. I popped that loony back to Loonyville."

"We'll be happy to depart if you show us the way," I said pointing my finger down past the dirt road.

"What about your aircraft?" the farmer asked.

"Well, you can have it all," I said with a slight dash of sarcasm.

"What do I want with a burned-out plane?" The farmer cleared his throat. "Just git out and don't start attacking each other or my stock."

I understood the farmer's concerns. In his mind, we might turn on him at any moment.

"I've found over twenty hacked-up bodies in my field over the last several weeks." The farmer lowed his gun slightly. "Goshdarnit, it was really gruesome. A bloodbath without a damn shower curtain. Horrible. Have ya ever tried to blucher something without a blood-proof curtain? Have you!?"

We all too stunned to do anything, but stared at him with wide, moon-shaped eyes. What was the farmer talking about? Blood-proof curtains? It was as if we were unwary extras in a low-budget horror flick.

I stepped forward, just slightly and said in my best movie trailer voice: "We're not like any of them. We were not in Hemet when the meteorite hit."

"What meteorite?" the farmer asked in a suspicious tone.

I glanced at Sarah. She stared back at me. Tommy inched back a little and looked around for a weapon. Rant pulled out her handgun and hid it behind her.

"You didn't see it?" I asked. Nobody could have missed the meteorite, even if sitting in a dark room watching television. It was just too bright. "You must remember it. It was like an exploding sun. It turned night into day."

"Not really," the farmer said.

That was not a good answer. If this redneck hayseed had failed to see it, then that we might still be in the danger zone. That would mean that the affected area must be enormous—way past the city limits of Hemet. Maybe all the way to Riverside.

"I did hear about the fireball and 'em other ones," the farmer confessed. "I'm no dummy."

"Them?" I blinked in disbelief. I glanced back at the others. Everyone looked dismayed.

"Yeah, the authorities reported two or three of 'em falling stars that night," the farmer said then paused. He raised his gun. "By George, why haven't ya scattered yet? I get riled easily. We had nothing but problems today. I had to shoot my dear wife this morning. She was getting too soft in the head. The bitch overcooked my eggs. Do you know how terrible burnt eggs taste? She was no good to me anymore."

The farmer moved closer to size up Big Al. "You look mighty familiar."

"I'm really nobody," Big Al pleaded.

"No. You're the head honcho of the DED. I saw your mug on the news."

"Not me." Big Al denied the accusation. "That was my twin brother."

The farmer stepped forward. "Yup. It was you all right. My son works in your department. Haven't seen him for months."

"Who?" I asked, fearing the worst.

"Brian McNally."

"I know your son," I said. "Very good worker."

"Sure, he is. But is he okay?"

"The last time I saw him, he was alive and kicking," I felt compelled to come up with my best possible evasive answer. Considering all of the hand-to-hand encounters, he was surely laying in the morgue or buried in a mass grave.

"That's my boy."

"Well," I said, trying to change the subject. "We must go. We have business in Riverside. Need to get there by nightfall."

"Won't do you any good."

"Why?" Sarah spoke up.

"They've got a blockade ten miles yonder, near the outskirts of Riverside. Don't go there. Those damn soldiers are drugged out, strung tighter than a string on a Texas hambone. They ain't allowing nobody beyond the barricades, minefields, and barbed-wire fences. They shoot first and then rob you."

"Just like home," Lenny displayed a warm smile.

"Welcome to the New World Order," Henry McNally said. "We've all been quarantined. Hearsay is they shoot anyone trying to escape. Fancy that."

"You're stranded here, too?" Tommy said.

"Yeah. But not so bad. Though I'm starting to run out of supplies." The farmer sighed. "My pappy could survive without toilet paper, but I'm having a harder time. I only wish I knew what was going on. My neighbor John said he heard that terrorists had set off biological weapons. Poor John. I found his body dismembered by one of his disgruntled hired hands. Somebody has got to hunt those dirty dogs down and slit their throats."

"I think we should be moving along," I stated emphatically.

"Suit yourself."

I was not going to hang around to be shot, carved into pieces, or gored by a bull. It was time to put some distance between the danger zone and ourselves. Before I could explain this to my group, I heard booming in the distance. At first, I thought it came from a thunderstorm, something that can occur in the summer months. Yet, this was more like a powerful, sharp crack, without much echoing.

"The booming gets closer every day," the farmer said with a glint in his eye. "Exciting as all get out. A shell almost hit my barn yesterday."

"Shelling of your farm?" I began scratching my arms again.

"No way!" Tommy's jaw almost became unhinged. "You don't mean..."

"Yup, sure do. I just love listening to artillery hammer the ground. Why it puts me right to sleep."

Lenny and Sarah stood motionless. Rant shoved her gun back into her side holster.

"You should see 'em tanks, bigger than some two-story farmhouses. Stink up the air like a herd of farting cows. Saw them on the horizon; a whole goddamn army, with armored trucks and artillery. I reckon they'll overrun my fields one of these days. But I'll be damned before I run like a scared jackrabbit. I'll stop them. I'll pop them with my pea shooter."

Tommy swallowed. "There's a war going on?"

"Hell, where have you boys been? Yeah, it's a war and they fight like blue dog devils."

"Okay," I said, nervous. I secretly motioned for the others to grab any gear they managed to rescue from the burning aircraft. Only Tommy had extracted something of value: his brown knapsack. Otherwise, we had almost nothing to carry. We soon took off on a dirt road we thought might lead us to Riverside.

"Hey," the farmer yelled, lowering his shotgun. "If you all come back this way, bring me some TP. I just hate 'em dried corn husks. Just too rough on the backside."

Ignoring the old fool, I turned and joined my friends on the narrow dirt road that likely meandered to the North. It was time to make tracks and discover if the military had actually closed the road to traffic. I had the feeling that there was some truth to the farmer's fanciful yarns.

"And don't forget," the farmer shouted with glee. "Shoot your wife if she overcooks your eggs. That will teach her. She'll never do that again."

Lenny bumped into me, looking back at the gun-toting farmer. "Boy, what crock-pot!"

"You mean crackpot," I said.

"Isn't that what I said? A cracked-crock!" Lenny laughed uproariously.

I was in no mood to correct Lenny's butchery of the English language.

Chapter 22

As the sun peeked over the horizon, we woke up and prepared for another exhilarating day of uncertainty. Our makeshift beds were uncomfortable—smelly and oily cardboard and old newspapers, right next to a burnt-out school bus—but the view from our sleeping quarters was of a peaceful countryside valley. As for breakfast, it was a delightful reprieve from normal everyday life. We feasted on four sticks of Slim Jims from Tommy's backpack and a few outdated vanilla pudding cups courtesy of Lenny's pocket.

As the temperature increased, we gathered in the middle of a forsaken two-lane highway that Tommy swore would take us into Riverside and then to Los Angeles. The roadway was empty, completely deserted of any traffic, which made us cautious. We figured that someone had to be patrolling the road. Whoever that might be, we did not want to interrupt their daily routine.

Rant was the first to react to the unrelenting sunlight and heat. Contending that the sun was too bright, she pulled out a pair of dark sunglasses from her pocket. She slipped them on and shone with the bad girl glamor. I had to keep reminding myself she was still the same old obstinate Rant. Nothing special about that.

After four hours of knee-pounding hiking, we came upon a large mangled heap of black and green metal blocking the road. From a distance, it resembled a fleet of trucks jumbled together to create a massive roadblock. Crawling along an irrigation ditch, we inched closer and discovered instead a graveyard of burned-out military vehicles that covered the highway and swept into the adjacent countryside.

"Wow!" Tommy scrambled out of the ditch and rushed up to a pile of twisted wreckage, leaped up, and crawled to the top of a bullet-riddled tank. "Wow, man, it's an M1 Abrams tank. Fricking cool!"

I followed Tommy and soon reached the top of the tank and scanned the immense battlefield. We could easily identify dozens of blackened hulks of destroyed equipment—mobile ballistic missile launchers, rocket artillery systems and armored personnel carriers. It appeared that someone had dropped incendiary bombs. Most of the tires on the transport trucks had melted, leaving the steel rims exposed.

"Look over there," Tommy instructed. He pointed to the assorted wreckage and identified particular pieces of military equipment. "At least a dozen M104 full-tracked armored Howitzers over there." He swung around and found himself blinking rapidly in amazement. "And over there are some M270 Launchers. Wow, this is a big killing field. So wicked!"

I just nodded. I had no interest in cataloging pulverized war equipment. Just not my hobby.

"It doesn't get much better than this," Tommy burst with joy. "We have a front-row seat. Look at it all."

That was not how I would have put it. It might be a sweet moment of excitement for Tommy, but I smelled the sour stench of sulfur. It quickly insulted my nostrils and restricted my breathing. The smelly gas was not the only strange thing that I had noticed. An eerie and faintly visible purplish haze hung over the low-lying area. It crept along the ground as if it had a purpose, slithering like a wide column of marching soldier ants. Must be my imagination.

A moment later, I was overcome by another odd sensation. I felt antsy and restless. A feeling of agitation swept over me. I began to question myself. Why was I here? Why was I leading a ragtag band of misfits? I deserved better. It all seemed unfair. I should head out on my own and leave everyone behind. I slapped my head. It had to be the effects of the purple gas.

I sat there thinking and thinking that I was losing my mind. I turned away and watched Rant. She had found something more productive to do. She wandered through piles of dead corpses as if she held exclusive rights to their belongings. Along the way, she bent over and scooped up a dozen or more canteens, taking only the heavy ones laden with water. I wondered if she was on a humanitarian mission or was it more nefarious?

Rant walked back to the others, entering a flat patch of weeds surrounded by twisted, burned hulks of damaged tanks. After dropping the canteens on the ground, she sat and made sure each container was completely full. When her task was completed, she handed a canteen to everyone, except Big Al.

"What about me?" Big Al bellyached.

"You don't deserve anything," Rant huffed.

His hands now firmly tied with shoelaces. Big Al sat in the shade complaining that he was being tortured. He kept insisting that we were obligated to treat him with respect, citing the Geneva War Conventions for humane treatment war prisoners. He shook his tied hands and stared at Rant. "I forbid you to treat me like this. It's inhumane!"

Rant was beside herself. She showed no intention of catering to any of his asinine whims. Shaking her head, Rant finally turned to Lenny and instructed him to dispense some discipline. "Talk to our captive. Do something useful for once. Give him a tongue-lashing."

Lenny's face turned red, his eyes flaming with rage. "I'm no schoolmarm!"

"Just do it!"

Lenny stood up and faced Rant, "No, I will not, you bitch!"

"What did you say?"

"No way, bitch! How many ways you want me say it. Bitch. Bitchy bitch!"

Rant pulled out her handgun, stretched her arm out, and planted the barrel firmly against Lenny's forehead.

"Okay," Lenny raised his hands. "I talk nice now."

"Fine," Rant said. "Now give Big Al a drink when he needs it. If he needs to be shot, give him that, too."

Big Al gulped.

"Oh, you give me gun!?" Lenny became excited. "I can shoot bastard. Nooo problem."

Big Al started to struggle and desperately tried to loosen the shoelaces around his hands. In frustration, he shrieked, "You cannot do that. You can't trust a Russkie."

"So, I can trust you instead?" Rant asked, scrunching up her nose, and lowered her gun.

"You can't just kill me," Big Al scoffed in a stranded voice. He quickly fell down on his knees, sandwiching his bound hands together as if to pray. Eyeing Rant with a look of disdain, Big Al whined a sad ballad of remorse: "Pretty please. I will be good." He smiled with a creepy glint in his eyes.

"We can do what we want. We should have lined you up against a wall long ago." Rant swung her gun towards Big Al's frightened face. "What say you?"

Sarah sprang up and marched over to Rant. She stomped her foot to get her sister's attention. When Rant refused to turn around, Sarah elbowed her in the side. "You're not going to shoot him. Not now, not ever. If anyone takes him down, it will be me."

Rant took a small step away from Big Al, still keeping her face and gun glued on her intended target. From the corner of her eye, she watched Sarah pull out her handgun. "I make the rules here, Sis! This is none of your business. I get the pleasure to put this rat out of his misery."

"Not this time," Sarah snarled. In a flash, the two of them faced each other with narrowing eyes. They pointed their weapons at each other, behaving like two gunslingers circling the other, anxious to see who would draw first. They circled each other for a solid thirty seconds.

I had to do something. I jumped down from the tank, rushed into the small firing circle, and waved my arms frantically. I had to distract them. I had to stop this madness. Everybody had turned against each other, ready to tear flesh like a horde of mad dogs. Even I had started to fall prey to this insanity. The thought of joining Sarah and Rant in a game of Russian roulette had entered my mind. I started to feel around in my pocket for Jack's small pistol. What a rush! We could have a threesome and find out who had the fastest draw.

I shook my head. I had to fight the desire to slaughter others with self-righteous zeal. I was reacting and not leading. I must have breathed in the purple mist. That toxic chemical was robbing us of our ability to think clearly. I could almost sense a malignant presence that was propelling me towards the darkness of hate and alienation. The trouble was, I found the thought of beating up someone to a gooey pulp both arousing and disturbing. My moods kept swinging between the extremes of brutality and gentleness. We had to flee this place before we found ourselves re-enacting a cheesy horror film with real deadly weapons.

I finally grabbed Sarah and tried to shake some sense into her. I thought I was being gentle, but she mistook my concerns for aggression. Now she aimed her gun at me. I quickly snatched her weapon from her hand. That set off a no- mercy, knockdown, drag-out wrestling match. We landed on the ground and rolled around in the dirt until I was on top of her, holding down her hands.

"Fight it," I said.

"I am," Sarah screamed. "Get off me, you fucking bastard."

"No, I mean the sickness from the hate gas."

"What hate gas?" Sarah blared out.

"The purple gas in the tank's deep tracks."

"You're lying."

"Just look."

"No. I should have killed you the day I married you."

"That's so sweet of you. I knew that there was always a romantic side to you."

Sarah stopped struggling. A thin smile erupted across her face. She turned on her side to get a better look at the shallow trench. She peered at the track ditches behind one of the tanks. "You mean that purplish gas?"

I nodded

"Why didn't you say that earlier?"

I simply shrugged. I had no idea if that was the cause of our infighting and bickering. In the past, it only took a tiny spark to light Sarah's fuse. But at least the scuffle had stopped, and I now had full control of her gun. I stood, lifted up Sarah, and gave her a big hug. Her mood instantly changed.

"You're right," Sarah said. "We have to get out now."

I looked around. Only Tommy was missing. I took a cursory glance from the top of one tank and saw no living soul. We now had to search for him. As we walked through the battlefield, we noticed a flock of blackbirds pecking at a half-burned corpse. They were particularly interested in the dead soldier's eye. Lenny ran ahead and shoed them away. According to Lenny, the birds were being disrespectful towards the soldiers. It was an eerier sight. The whole field was littered with unburied dead soldiers.

We finally found Tommy near the edge of a deep, round crater. Tommy sat on the crater's lip, dangling his feet, looking rather downcast.

I sat next to him. "So, what are you doing?"

Tommy turned to me. "Nothing much."

"We have things to do. Places to go."

"But I want to stay here and find out when the battle took place."

I was not an expert, but the pungent smell of burned flesh and the stench of decaying flesh meant that it might have been recent.

"Must have been days," Tommy said. "Nothing is hot or burning."

"We need to go," I tried to get Tommy out of his funk.

"Not sure what to do."

Before I could add my two-cents worth, Lenny sat down next to me.

"Boy," Lenny started to brag again. "This reminds me of...."

We all surrounded Lenny and stared at him with a fixed gaze. I had enough of his quaint Russian fairytales. He stopped talking and retreated into silence.

"Something moving to the northeast," Rant poked me and pointed. "We're not alone."

In the far distance, we could see a massive column of tanks advancing down a hillside, gun turrets blazing. We heard the rumble of cannons and the crashing of shells. The sounds of war had resumed. The sky suddenly exploded with rocket fire and aerial dogfights with blazing machine gunfire. Within moments, flaming shards of burning warplanes hailed down like hot-red rivets. We hid under the wreckage of a half-track until we heard the approach of vibrating heavy equipment.

"Let's go!" I ordered. We had to get away from the area, especially the blacktop roads. The military loved hanging around roads during times of war. They would engulf roadways with troop carriers, tanks, and an uncontrollable urge to shoot something. We ran toward a hilly area and hid inside of a narrow canyon carpeted with clusters of oak trees. There was no reason to make contact with either warring side. For all I knew, both sides might have suffered a dusting of the dangerous purple chemicals.

* * * * *

We followed the canyon for a mile or two and discovered a wide treeless valley that had miraculously escaped the fighting. As we walked down through the bushy hillside, I noticed something strange about the valley floor. A thin ground fog obstructed our view. It had enveloped the bottom portion of the valley. The color was white, not purple. Not until we had reached the valley floor did we see half-a-dozen craters dotting the landscape. "I've seen something like this before," I turned to Tommy and Rant. "Not good."

"What did you find?" Rant peered at me.

"Nothing much." I did not want to mention the bloody blob I had seen in several locales. It would only spook everyone more and force me to relive those awful moments.

"Cool crater!" Tommy ran ahead and slid down its embankment. "There's something big in the middle."

"Don't get too close!" I yelled out to him. "It might be dangerous." That was an understatement. The object protruding from the sand at the center of the round crater, appeared whitish-brown, and gave me a bad feeling. Incredibly, it had an eerie resemblance to patches of eggs in James Cameron's *Aliens*.

"Don't touch it, Tommy!" I shouted again. Of course, he ignored me and began fingering it like a child with a brand-new toy truck.

"It's really smooth, but scorched," Tommy said as he tried pushing the egg-shaped object. Naturally, it was too heavy to tumble to one side.

"Will you please stay away from it!"

"It's just a rock," Tommy responded. "Not to worry."

I was beyond worry. "Don't you have any sense?"

Tommy grinned, pulled out a dollar, and waved it in the air. "No, just a dollar."

Rant pulled off her sunglasses and faced me. "He's really something, isn't he?"

"He's just reliving his childhood," I said.

"Do you think he'll ever pass puberty?" Rant said callously.

"No, he keeps flunking that class."

"It feels really hot," Tommy shouted. He knelt closer and ran the palm of his hand over the shiny surface. "It feels like there's something moving inside."

"Damn it! Get away from it!" I yelled.

"Ouch!" Tommy lurched up, tripped, and fell forward, landing on his face.

"Noooooo!" I screamed. I climbed down the crater's wall and ran, but I had to slow my pace. Clusters of mostly buried egg-shaped objects blocked my direct path. I had to zigzag through the deepening and widening crater.

Rant reached him first, flipped him over on his backside, and knelt next to him. "Where are you injured?"

"Something bit me." He held up his bleeding finger. It was a minor puncture wound.

"Well, you deserved it," Big Al shouted, sulking under a lone tree apart from the rest of us.

"Let's get out of here!" I pulled Tommy to his feet and attempted to drag him out of the crater.

"Man. Get off my back!" Tommy yelled. "You're not my father. You don't control me."

"Something is controlling all of us," I responded.

"Leave me alone or I will..."

"Or you will what?"

Tommy pulled out a pair of scissors from his back pocket and lunged at me. I quickly dodged the first jab from his rusty blade and jumped back. I wanted to do something but I did not have the heart to injure Tommy, even if my life depended on it. I felt trapped.

"You're the cause of all of my troubles. You're the biggest fucking twat in the world."

Tommy grew angrier and started to chase me. He swung his small weapon like a fencing sword. I pulled out my pistol and aimed it at his chest. I began to feel a strong impulse to blast him to kingdom come and be done with it. At first, I was scared, but now I was growing enraged by his combative actions. I had built up a reserve of grudges against him and his stupid antics. My sudden display of a gun surprised Tommy. He froze in mid-air. He did not blink his eyes for what seemed like an eternity.

"Go on! Shoot me! Like you did to Jack." Tommy's face contorted into a rage of fury. He sneered with contempt and shouted, "Go ahead! Shoot me! You're just a stinking murderer!"

As Tommy came closer, I began to lower my gun. I could not kill my best friend. Instead, I reached out with my right arm for protection. I could not believe he would harm me. With a wide slash of his arm, Tommy thrust his scissors into my forearm. I stumbled backward and fell, bleeding like a stuck pig. I sat there in a daze. How could he do this to me? I guess I deserved it. I was too trusting. I was always looking for the goodness in people. In return, I was being paid back with insults and savagery.

As Tommy approached me, I could see his eyes widening with a half-crazed glare of pleasure. He moved closer, arching his weapon above his head, ready to swoop in for the kill. I was toast.

Suddenly, Rant snuck up from behind and coldcocked Tommy in the back of the head. He went down and out. Holding my bleeding arm, I crawled next to him. This was my fault. I should have never gotten him involved. I knelt over my old pal to see how seriously he was injured. Tommy was not responding. I shook him. Nothing.

Meanwhile, Rant turned and approached the strange object with a flurry of uncertainty. She tilted her head to one side and half-arched her eyebrow. She appeared to be on the verge of expressing a frown mingled with doubt and fear. Walking haltingly, she held her gun next to her right side and reached out with her other hand. She moved cautiously closer. Her fingertips were inches away from the egg-shaped rock surface. Suddenly, she hesitated, swallowed with a deep breath, and slowly backed away. "It's just a rock. There's no such thing as little green monsters," Rant mouthed softly, trying to reassure herself.

She slowly circled the mysterious object, squinting at it with a contemptuous grimace. Then she leaned over and spied a lizard scampering across the object's smooth surface. "But I do believe in little green reptiles... Maybe."

As Rant continued to study the strange object amidst the chaos, Sarah rushed over and jerked out the scissors protruding from my arm. The blood spewed out like a geyser. My arm throbbed with intensity, feeling as if the blade had lodged deep into my bone. Sarah wrapped my arm with a white piece of cloth. After a few moments, she took my hand, lightly squeezing it. She was in no hurry to release her grip. Without a single word, she leaned over and planted a long kiss on my cheek.

As she kept fussing with my bandage, I noticed that the white bandage had grown dark red. It was amazing how much blood could gush from such a small, deep wound. I wondered if it would ever stop gushing.

"You'll need a tetanus shot," Sarah advised as she tightened the dressing. "Tommy's cutting tool was extremely rusty."

I nodded.

"We must go," Sarah insisted.

With Sarah's help, I attempted to stand. That little rise in elevation caused an immediately dizzy spell and disorientation. I fumbled about, drowsy to the point of almost passing out, not positive what was happening. I had a faint idea that we had to flee the area as soon as possible. "Every man to his lifeboat," I shouted. "Fire the flares. Sound the sirens."

"Honey," Sarah said gently with a faint smile. "We need to settle down and rescue our friend." She pointed to Tommy's listless body, lying flat in the dirt, face down.

With a clearer mind and steadier arms, I helped Sarah lift Tommy's body up and dragged him to the base of the crater wall. With Lenny's assistance, we pulled him up and deposited his lifeless body several feet higher on the flat land, assuming it was safe. At least we hoped we had escaped from the danger zone.

Rant remained in the crater, momentary. Like a rooster guarding his paltry hens, our female Rambo protected our rear guard, making sure that danger would not overtake us. Gun pressed against her cheek, her watchful eyes and loaded Glock concentrated on anything reeking of strangeness. After a while, everything appeared safe. Adopting a more relaxed manner, she causally slipped on her dark sunglasses, beaming with confidence. She climbed out of the crater.

"Well, what did you find?" I asked Rant.

"From what I could see, nothing. There was no devilish xenomorph or any type of alien predator. Just a little green lizard. A cute one at that."

Tommy finally stirred and opened up his eyes. He was not particularly happy to hear Rant's all-clear assessment.

"But the thing lunged at me, man! Not cool! Not cool at all!"

"Maybe you should keep distance," Lenny said. "Little playthings can kill. I should know."

"I know how to handle a lizard," Tommy said as he sat up and shook his head.

"Maybe it just couldn't handle *you*," Rant chuckled. "We should not let our fears control us."

I agreed with Rant, but I knew there was something out there. We just couldn't see it.

* * * * *

We followed a cow path for hours, sneaking across meadows, around barns, and down dry washes in weather too hot to breathe. The heat was sapping my strength and taking away my desire to escape to Riverside. But at least my arm wound had stopped bleeding through my cloth bandage.

When the land became flatter, we moved farther away from the rocky cliff hills. We passed through fields of brown oats and reached an overhanging bluff. Columns of smoke dotted the horizon as far as the eye could see. That was probably the front line with all its chaos and murderous spectacle. Thousands of men, perhaps several divisions of infantry, were advancing north to Riverside, while an equal number attacked from the east. We were definitely in the wrong place at the wrong time.

"We better wait for dark," Sarah suggested.

"Yeah." I looped my arm around her waistline and drew her closer as we watched the battlefield. This was better than any late-night John Wayne war flick. Now, if only I could find some buttered popcorn.

"We're not getting through," Rant interrupted us with her stern assessment of our situation. "We're trapped."

"Maybe," I nodded and told everyone to find a place to hide out until nightfall. We fanned out, and Tommy was the first to discover rows of freshly dug trenches and foxholes. They were perfect for our circumstances, except dozens of Army Rangers already occupied them.

We waited to proceed any further. When darkness hid our movements, we crept on hands and knees between two widely spaced foxholes. We heard no sounds and saw no human movement.

"Don't move!" shouted one black soldier hiding in a foxhole. He popped up and swung his rifle at Tommy's head. With a quick hand motioned, I signaled Rant to circle behind our armed adversary. She immediately followed my orders.

In a moment's time, Rant had sneaked up behind the soldier. She crawled next to him and nudged her cold barrel against his head. "Boo!"

The soldier raised his shaking hands and threw down his rifle. He turned around and faced Rant, pleading in a soft whisper, "Don't shoot me! Don't eat me! I surrender."

I glanced around to see the reaction of Sarah and Tommy. They both wore stunned and bewildered faces. What was our captive ranting about, I mouthed silently? Who eats people?

"I have Hepatitis C. My liver would kill you."

I leaned back completely dumbstruck. Our captive must be afflicted with some craziness pathogen. As I tried to decipher the soldier's message, Rant silently checked out the adjacent foxhole. She crept to the nearest one and spied a row of military men occupying the trench-like pit. I could see the tops of their heads peeking above the ground. As she prowled nearer to the edge of the foxhole, the enemies appeared asleep or incapacitated. She was plainly visible to the enemy combatants, yet they failed to shout out an alarm.

"Are they asleep?" I questioned the soldier in a low voice.

"Are you for real?" the man laughed nervously.

I found nothing funny about my question. It was almost past twilight, but the air was still sizzling with heat. They might be suffering from heatstroke or hyperthermia.

"They'll stay put," the soldier chuckled more loudly. "Yeah, they won't need their dancing shoes anymore."

I scrambled over to foxholes, peered down, and confirmed his story. Indeed, they were all dead, pale-faced, and missing an array of body parts. It was startling. Most of the bodies were devoid of legs and arms as if a meat-market butcher had skinned them alive. Even stranger, the ones still with legs were bootless. Their bare feet were gashed and smeared with blood.

I climbed into the trench and warily tiptoed among the mangled men. I felt nauseated. I struggled to avoid trampling over severed body parts or slogging through red pools of blood. That feat was becoming harder. There was little unspoiled ground. I could not help but crush or trip over the heaps of dismembered bodies. It almost looked like the men were sliced and diced with a meat cleaver. For some reason, the butcher left the bare bones sticking out past their fleshy parts. Who would do such a thing?

I had to get out. To make matters worse, swarms of buzzing flies were assaulting me, acting as if I was also on their menu. It was indeed the land of the dead. I clawed my way out of the trench and stumbled back to the black soldier, my head spinning in a daze. I peered down at him. "Why would anyone sever human body limbs? Why?"

"They refused to fight," the black soldier said in a pain-stricken voice. He looked away and swallowed. "That's the whole terrible truth. I'm alive because I obeyed. By God, I wanted to resist. But I also wanted to live. I turned pragmatic. I shot at my fellow man out of fear. I killed my brothers to save my skin. God will never forgive me. I'm an untouchable."

I glanced at Rant and Tommy. They were just as shocked and disgusted as I was. No decent words could adequately describe my feelings. He was a man chained to a life of repentance, sorrow, and deep misery. He cradled his sadness with a heavy sadness of guilt. All I could do was offer our condolences and find out the quickest route away from this hell. I tried to show my kindest smile and most sympathetic eyes. "Well, can you show us the way to Riverside?"

"You won't get through," the black soldier snapped back. "Don't you know? "

"Know what?" I was almost afraid to hear the answer.

"That's World War III erupting out there. Your timing's impeccable."

At that moment, I decided to be more understanding. I introduced my wandering troupe of ragtag survivors to him. The soldier capitulated and told us he was Sergeant Cliff Jones. He was under the command of the 8th Army Rangers. He said he was a reservist who never expected to do actual duty again.

"Our position was raked by aircraft this morning. Everybody wanted to retreat. I stayed."

"Why didn't you retreat?" Rant asked.

"I knew our commander would take drastic measures to stop any deserter," Cliff divulged. "I could see it Captain Manuel's eyes. He had this nervous tick when people disagreed with him. He would start pulling out the hairs from his eyebrows. At other times, he would cut notches in his arm, slices out little strips of flesh, and eat them. We called him 'Manuel the Cannibal.'"

"Are you from Hemet?" I asked.

"Sun City."

"Which side are you on?" Tommy asked, sitting down next to Cliff, ears fixated on his every word. Rant moved closer to hear what our captive had to say. Like always, she fiddled with her gun. Sarah

244

squatted and listened with curious attention. Big Al sat under a tree, looking miserable. Other things had distracted Lenny. He spent his time munching on a cache of recently uncovered candy bars. In fact, Lenny had rifled through most of the dead men's pockets and backpacks. Who could eat at a time like this?

I faced the soldier and asked him the same question. I needed to know. I needed to know now. "Where do your loyalties lie?"

Cliff looked away uncomfortably. I decided to break the ice and tell him about our position. Someone had to make the first move.

"We're escaping from Hemet on our own," I said. "We're just trying to get away."

Cliff looked relieved. "You're not one of THEM?"

I shook my head.

"Me neither. I should not even be here. I was visiting my mother in Sun City. A bunch of jackboot thugs marched into town, set up checkpoints, and took over. They rounded up all the young men and women and forced them to join the military." Cliff lowered his face. "We had to fight. They told us they would kill our families if we refused. What kind of people live in Hemet anyway?"

"Did you see the shooting star several months ago?" I asked.

"Who cares what I saw?"

"Answer the question." Rant towered over him like perched buzzard with a bad attitude.

"Sure. I saw it. Everyone did. So what?"

Sarah knelt next to Cliff. "They said they would kill your whole family if you refused to join them?" She asked with a slight tremble in her voice.

"Would I lie about that, sister?" Cliff took out of a pack of cigarettes and lit one up. "Never saw anything like it." He looked over his shoulder. "By the way, do you have any pain meds or antibiotics?"

We all shook our heads in unison.

I felt obligated to ask. "Why?"

"I've been injured," Cliff said as he noticed my injury. "And you?"

"It was just a stupid accident. "Friendly fire."

"Not for me," Cliff moaned in a harsh, throaty voice. "They made me suffer on purpose."

"You're welcome to come with us," I offered.

"I suppose that's a generous offer." Cliff looked uneasy again. "But I'm not going anywhere."

"All of your buddies are dead," I tried to reason with him. "Anybody who checks up the status of your unit will think you also perished. Your family will be safe. Just switch dog tags with one of the corpses."

"I can't." He glanced down at his feet. "They cut us. Our feet. So we couldn't retreat."

I leaned back. I had this nagging feeling that he was not telling me the whole truth. Perhaps he was still under a blackmailed threat. His military commander might have warned him that his family would be executed if he had any contact with the enemy.

At this point, I motioned Tommy to follow me. We slowly meandered away and took a short walk along a low ridge.

"He's lying," I said. "Nobody could be that cruel."

"Think again," Tommy disagreed. "During the Gulf War in the nineties, the Iraqi military cut the Achilles' tendon of any soldier they thought might become a deserter. Like they did not care about their men. Dictators never do."

"My God!" My injured arm began to ache in pain. I had never heard of anything so savage. Tommy was a tremendous wealth of information on every possible subject. He was more valuable to us than I had ever thought.

Cliff started to move. Using his hands, he painfully crawled out of the trench, dragging his feet behind. He sat near a pile of dirt. "They butchered all our feet. Hard to run away without an Achilles tendon." He lifted up both feet and showed us his bloody wounds.

"For added insurance," Cliff disclosed, "they stole our boots. I'm not going anywhere, no how."

"We won't leave you behind," Tommy became more sensitive to Cliff's plight. "We could carry you out."

"I'm not worth it. The infection will probably kill me. They dipped their knives with some type of slow-acting toxin. At least that is what they said they had done. Listen, you are in dangerous and occupied territory. It's at least five miles to sanity."

I sat next to Cliff and tried to soothe his worries. "My father fought in World War II as a U.S. Marine. He said the Marine Corps' sacred duty was to leave no man behind. That sounded like a good policy to me."

"I know. I know. You don't have to preach to the choir."

"So, you will come with us?"

Cliff shook his head in disgust. "Yes. Fine. But this war makes no sense. What's wrong with you people in Hemet anyway?" Cliff bit down on his lip and stared at me with his resentful eyes. "I was just heading out to seminary school. I was planning to become a minister of a Baptist church. Then wham, all of a sudden the world goes to hell."

"It should never have happened," I said.

"Then how did all of this crap start?"

"The roads," Tommy interrupted. "They wanted to control our driving habits. Tell us when and where to drive. They said it was more efficient."

"Shoot! All of this shit over roads? You're jacking me."

"Does seem silly," Sarah said with a timid sneer. "It just started with little innocent things. Nothing too important. Then it descended into a stupid slippery slope debacle."

"Sister, stupid is not the word," Cliff chided in a harsh tone. "You don't go around controlling things like that. How can you get anything done if you can't go where you want to go? That is what they did to my people once. Nobody could go anywhere without permission. We called it *slavery*, but I suppose in Hemet they call it something else."

"But we had to control where people go." Big Al walked over.

"Don't you know nothing?" Cliff looked up at Big Al. "Roads are just pathways. They remain open and free because nobody knows where it might lead them. Nobody. The future leaves no footprints. We all must choose our own highways at our own pace, and at our own time. That's why there are so many directions for mankind. I can make that decision. Only God and I know where life will take me."

I could plainly see that Cliff had a knack for rousing sermons. He had a promising career as a minister with the gift of gab.

"You don't need a road," Big Al jeered. "You can't even walk or drive. You're not going anywhere."

"Big Al is not one of us," Sarah spoke up. "He's with the other side."

"You mean the dark side?" Cliff quickly whipped out a combat knife strapped to his chest. "You better keep him away from me."

Sarah nodded.

"I will cut him, so help me."

"His hands are tied," I said.

"Then why is he with you?" Cliff asked, still holding a death grip on his knife.

"It's complicated," I said. "He used to be my boss. I could not just leave him behind. Maybe there is a medical antidote for this madness in Riverside."

"My, my," Cliff said. "You people are very forgiving. I can understand that. I think it is stupid. But it's somewhat understandable, at least to bleeding-heart preachers." Easing up, Cliff returned his blade to its sheath.

"God works in strange ways," Tommy said.

"You got that right, brother," Cliff said as he gingerly repositioned his injured body. "You know what I think? I think some motherfucker put weird shit into Hemet's drinking water. What else explains it? An entire goddamn war fought over where people can travel. You might as well as try controlling what people eat."

Lenny raised his candy bar. "Nobody ever bans sugar. That would be even worst crime."

I ignored Lenny and glanced at Cliff. "You must come with us," I said with a determined tone. I had taken an intense liking to Cliff and his no-nonsense outlook. "We won't leave you behind."

Cliff became silent and turned his head away.

"He'll slow us down," Rant complained. "You can't be serious?"

"He is one of us," I pointed out. "For all we know, we might now be in the minority. We have no idea what is happening. This might be some type of invasion and we need every man to fight back. Who knows, maybe our little action here will be the turning point in defeating THEM."

Sarah moved closer to me. "I'm willing to help in any way possible," she said.

"Sure," Lenny spoke up. "All for one and none for all. I think that's way it goes. No?"

I wanted to correct Lenny's statement, but it seemed pointless. He would merely deny the mix-up. But we knew what he meant.

* * * * *

Late that evening, I found myself sitting alone with Tommy. I had meant to talk to him about our chances, which I considered poor. Rant was right. One of the most dangerous areas during warfare is near the ever-changing battlefront line. I had seen many magazine articles about it. Over 60 million people died in World War II and two-thirds of them were civilians. I knew that as non-combatants, we were not equipped, informed, or trained to survive in such a hostile environment. We had to cross through the middle of a slaughterhouse, and hope that nobody mistook us for a hanging side of beef.

"Could you look after Sarah?" I asked Tommy as we perched ourselves on an uneven boulder. Tommy was paying more attention to his knapsack than me. After a long search, he pulled out an old can of sardines.

"Sure."

"I mean if something happens to me."

Tommy stopped fiddling with his sardines. "If something happens to you?"

"Earth to Tommy!" I paused to see if I had gotten his undivided attention. "We might not survive tomorrow's ordeals. Ever consider that?"

"Well, then I guess I won't have to look after Sarah."

Tommy was either just too logical or too slow-witted. "I mean if I should not make it. If I die. Okay?"

"Wow. Yeah, that could happen," Tommy said with a thoughtful frown. He turned and stuffed the sardine can back into his pack. "You're right. We might all end up in a landfill. Real bummer."

I could see that I had squashed his appetite. "I don't want to scare anyone. But going down there tonight will be like going through a meat grinder."

"I never eat meat," Tommy smiled.

"Yeah, I know." I decided not to press forward with my train of thought. I guess it is better to think about the future after it happens. Most people do. Why should I be any different? But Tommy soon surprised me.

"I'll look after her," Tommy said. "I wish I had someone special. You know, someone to lay a bouquet of flowers over my grave."

Now I began to feel bad. I hated to see him depressed, especially when he was usually good-natured and optimistic.

"I'll look after Sarah if anything happens to you." Tommy nodded with a heavy sigh.

"Thanks, man."

"You know this is entirely my fault."

"No!" Tommy put his hand on my shoulder. "Wrong track. Don't go there. Nobody could have stopped this. I mean we had no advanced warning of the bigger picture. These strange rocks could have exploded over the entire country. And we might be just a small island in an ocean of death."

I rolled my eyes. Now I felt even better or maybe worse.

"I mean it could be anything. We're living in the darkness of ignorance. Maybe it was a biological weapon or something that had been accidentally released from a military level 4 laboratory. Or we're just destroying ourselves. We've done that before," Tommy said with a sheepish shrug.

I stood and shook my head. "You just making this sound worse. It does not matter what caused this war. What we need right now is to discover a way to escape its grasping control."

"But this might be our destiny," Tommy suggested and started to look for his can of sardines again. "This might be what is supposed to happen. Like man, there have been between 4,000 to 14,000 wars since the dawn of mankind. Maybe war is embedded in our DNA. It's in our nature because the contagions in meteorites have put it there."

"Are you sure?"

"No, nobody knows. But think about it." Tommy faced me with a serious look. "Like maybe that's what has caused all wars since the beginning of civilization. The microbial gases, dust, and viruses that meteorites carry to earth. Maybe it is some type of alien organism. You know. A syndrome that forces people to kill each other in an orgy of hate."

"You mean some type of apocalypse syndrome?"

"Wow, you hit it right on the head. You really get it."

I leaned back and rubbed my aching head. It was a macabre and frightening thought. "Well, that would explain why large groups of people periodically go crazy and start to murder everybody. Maybe the politically adept take advantage of this mass psychosis. Maybe they use social upheavals to control and conquer people." I started to rub my forehead again. I was not feeling well enough to dig deeper over what was happening to us, but that did not stop Tommy.

"The microbes from meteorites might magnify our inherent craziness. And then it results in a sort of psychotic rage. Like when we lose touch with reality. Right? I mean they say that since 3,500 B.C., only 300 years were times of peace."

"Okay, maybe." I started to feel dizzy.

"Psychosis can lead to paranoid delusions. Boy, that's heavy stuff." Tommy stopped in deep thought, stroked his shorthaired goatee, and carefully prepared his next words. I could see that a host of flashbulbs had gone off all at once. "Okay, it boils down to this. Paranoia causes intense feelings of distrust, and this creates us versus them mindset. You are either with us or against us. Friend or foe, black or white. I guess you could say it is in all of us. We are them. They are us." Tommy shuddered at the thought.

I stretched my hands out to stop his psycho-babbling gabfest. "I can't believe our biggest moments of history are due to exploding rocks from space. There is more to history than warfare. Why, that would mean that we went to war at every drop of a meteorite."

"What?" Tommy asked. "Not enough falling meteorites to account for all of our wars?"

I smiled. "No. It's just, I think economic, social, and political turmoil precede many armed conflicts."

"But the turmoil might have resulted from these rocks in the first place."

I sat back down and reconsidered Tommy's assertion. "I suppose. Well, then Hitler and Stalin must have almost been struck by one of them."

"Too bad they missed," Tommy laughed.

I stood. Enough was enough. Peering to my left, I saw Sarah sitting with Cliff in the moonlight. I was worried about Cliff's wounds. I glanced at Tommy. "If only you had some antibiotics in your knapsack. You know, for Cliff's feet."

"The cut was deep," Tommy said, appearing worried. "I washed it out as much as I could. Tetanus is always a bad boy. We'll have to watch to see if his muscles stiffen. That means lockjaw might develop. Yet, I wouldn't know what to do. I should have finished my pre-med classes. I could have been a doctor."

"You only took a few courses."

"Okay, a caregiver?"

"No, you would make a fine doctor," I said, trying to make him feel better.

"For sure," Tommy's face brightened. "There are so many people trying to tear people apart. It's dreadful, man. Death stalks us like a bounty hunter. We need more dedicated people to treat injuries. Make them whole again."

"So they can go out and kill again?" It was a poor attempt at humor, but really, it was no time for joking. Tommy's quest to help the suffering was noble. I must be turning into a bitter, pathetic middle-aged man.

"I was too young," Tommy confessed. "I could have gone into the medical field. I just went off half-cocked. No real direction," Tommy confessed with a regretful sigh.

I stood there quietly and gazed up at the dark skyline and hazy moonlight overhead. Why did crises make people reflect so much about their pitiful and shallow lives? I began to wonder if I myself had chosen the right path. Maybe I should have done more with my life, something that would have given meaning or importance to my life. I had simply followed the flow of least resistance and drifted into a dead-end job that might be responsible for the death of thousands. I should have taken a better-traveled road.

Chapter 23

Darkness had swallowed the land. It was so black that I could barely see where to put my next footstep. The moon had surrendered itself to the dense clouds of smoke and fog, leaving us in the dark.

At least nobody could see us. I took the lead and we continued to trek up the side of a small mountain, trudging along an abandoned dirt road more useful as a deer path. From down below, I could hear intense fighting and gunfire. Not only that, but I swore I could hear the steady trampling of marching boots. Not good.

In a flash, I found myself engulfed in an artillery barrage. I was near its outer edge, but its ghostly flashes of light continued to creep closer to me. I turned and directed our group to disperse, but was too late. The shelling was spreading terror to neighboring areas. Everyone scattered to hiding places around large boulders and clumps of sagebrush. I dropped to the ground while hot pieces of shrapnel flew from overhead. Within seconds, circles of small brush fires burst into flames across the hilly slope. Sarah rushed over to me and tightly clung to my arm. Tommy gathered the others around him like a mother hen. There was almost nowhere to hide or escape.

I could barely breathe. The smoke burned our throats and reddened our eyes. The blazing fireballs began to sear our skin. It was as if we had set foot into the fire pits of Hades. I leaped up and told everyone to follow me down the hill, and away from the wildfires and shelling. Luckily, the shelling started to overshoot us, targeting some other nearby area.

I thought we had finally maneuvered away from the combat zone. I was wrong. A steady stream of machine gun fire racked our position. The worst part was trying to dodge the red tracers that streaked overhead. We all had to jump back to the ground and found ourselves crawling on our bellies. The crawling seemed to be a safe movement until we realized that we were not alone. The region was infamous for its rattlesnakes, patches of spiky cactus, and roving herds of tarantulas, and I dreaded any such encounters.

As I dragged my body through a small, shallow ravine, I took particular notice of the artillery bombardment pounding the land that skirted our planned escape route. I had a feeling that someone knew we were out here, trying to escape, but had temporarily lost our exact location.

Tommy moved next to me and suggested we sneak through an area that had been recently destroyed by heavy artillery.

"Are you sure?" I asked.

"It's unlikely they will waste more ammunition on an already devastated landscape," Tommy insisted.

He was convinced that it might provide us a narrow path of uncontested land. I was not so sure. I assumed the artillery shelling had concentrated all its firepower on important military objectives. However, as Tommy pointed out, the men and equipment would either have retreated or been destroyed. Seemed plausible.

I took Tommy's suggestion. Indeed, we found no throngs of troops or war equipment, only deserted land pockmarked with burnt vegetation and crater-strewn fields. We were all alone.

As we peered down the mountain slope into a large, wide valley, we started to notice something out of place. At first, we could not put our finger on it. Something was missing. In a flash, we noticed the complete absence of city lights. From our higher vantage point, we should be witnessing a bright blanket of twinkling urban lights stretching from as far as the eye could see. Riverside and its nearby cities were a vast inland empire. Instead, it revealed only a black canvas, reminiscent of the night sky in the remote Mojave Desert. Did the civil authorities impose a blackout policy to avoid nighttime bombing raid? Was that even a possibility?

We had to figure out that mystery later. We needed to move faster. Our nighttime cover was almost ready to expire. We lifted ourselves off the ground and prepared to rush down the mountain slope, towards the city's outskirts.

But before we could run down the hill, we had to consider Cliff's travel arrangements. We had given Big Al another chance to redeem himself by helping to carry Cliff. He refused to comply and continued to behave erratically, huffing with an air of indignation. He immediately whined that he was not a beast of burden. Then he pronounced our whole plan reckless, ridiculous, and doomed to failure.

Lenny had volunteered to be one of the two carriers for Cliff. Without the assistance of Big Al, the chore would return to Tommy, who was running low on energy and strength. Lenny did not take Big Al's checklist of excuses well. Every time my old boss looked away or became distracted, Lenny would secretly kick him in the pants. Next, he badgered Big Al with odd Russian proverbs: "To teach a fool is same as treat a dead man. Reap the same chickens you hatched." I was not sure of the exact meaning. I guess Lenny's adages did not translate well to English.

Tommy and Lenny were again burdened with carrying Cliff, who had nearly passed out from his infected wounds. The climb was difficult because of the steep terrain. We tumbling down the slope through rocky outcrops and stands of manzanita. Nearer the bottom, we could hear the clash of hand-to-hand combat not far to the west.

A little past the flatland, the region looked empty. This area was probably close to the line of demarcation, where the two armies had converged, clashed, and retreated. I only hoped that the battle borderline would remain steady until we had crossed it.

It now became imperative that we move at a faster pace. Luckily, the moon started to play "peekaboo" with the clouds and allow us to see her fuzzy light shine on our pathway.

Rant came up from behind and walked next to me. I could see the worry lines rippling across her forehead. She was not going to compliment me on my actions. Her skeptical eyes fixated on my pale skin and worried frown. She knew I was playing it by ear. I had no real game plan. It was all improvised with a little luck.

"You know that our chances are slim to none," Rant said, stating the obvious.

I faced Rant. "You have a better alternative? I'm all ears."

Rant floundered helplessly to come up with some reasonable option. "There are always no-win scenarios."

"Well, then I guess it is simply in the hands of God."

"I don't believe in God."

"So, you're saying that we have nobody on our side? Not even God?"

"We could turn back."

"So, you want to return to crazyville and drink their tasteless Kool-Aid?"

"Well..." Rant's eyes blinked rapidly.

I had apparently caught Rant off guard. She slowed down her pace to rethink through her argument. I had said nothing earth-shattering. We were simply on our own. We were like rats, scurrying around in the dark before death took hold of us. We had no safety net, no rescue line. God pity us.

As we approached midway through the open flat field, we found ourselves in a grassy cow pasture pockmarked with a scattering of smoking craters, burning vehicles, and lifeless bodies. We slowed, and I took the forefront in order to ascertain the enemy's position. It was perhaps the most dangerous duty I had ever taken, and it was solely my decision. I had chosen this path. It was my turn to actually take charge and stand tall.

After 20 minutes of carefully advancing, we entered the mother of all killing fields, a vast graveyard of dead and dying soldiers. So much carnage covered the ground that it looked like a red carpet.

Tommy refused to look down. Rant gazed up. Sarah softly apologized to each dead body. Lenny pulled out a candy bar and acted as if it was a walk in the park. Big Al hummed a silly tune and plowed through like a king. I felt queasy and extremely disgusted. I had this distinct feeling that the fallen men were now much happier than I was.

I looked up. The early morning twilight had arrived, display-ing ribbons of pink and blue. Everything was fuzzy and dim but the soon to rise sun provided some visibility. I stopped and squinted at a barbed wire fence 500 yards ahead. It was guarded by a horde of rifle-men and a row of impressive tanks. Apparently, we had reached the picket line for our side, the first perimeter of what I hoped would be a refuge of sanity and stability. If only we could surrender peacefully without a mistaken shot to the head. That was an awfully big "if."

"I'll go first," Big Al pushed me out of the way. "I know how to handle grunts." He ran towards the fence, impervious to our dangerous surroundings.

"Sure, be my guest," I whispered under my breath. Let him rush in front of them like a proverbial Sherman tank, completely unaware of the consequences. Who cares if he is the first one to cross the finish line? Who was I to block his ambitions? I never did that at work.

"Why is he volunteering?" Sarah slid next to me and blurted aloud. "He's up to something."

"I think I know what he's doing." Rant put her cold logic into gear. "He will betray us." The annoying problem with Rant's hunches was that they were usually spot-on.

I smiled at Rant. "Let's see if they shoot first and ask questions later. I bet he will get shot before he gets to the fence."

"It's not worth consideration," Rant shook her head, with no patience for chitchat. "He will not get far in life or on the battlefield. The foolish never grasp the truth."

Actually, Rant's little proverb was far more prophetic than I could ever have imagined.

Meanwhile, Big Al dragged himself closer to the fence. He stopped, exhausted and sweating all over. He held up his bound hands and begged for help. That only caught the attention of the border guards. When he started to move again, a group of soldiers started shouting, warning him to stop advancing. He lifted his head and yelled that he was trying to escape from us, that he was a hostage.

"Shoot the people behind me," Big Al shouted. "They're crazy assassins. They're the enemy."

Rant turned to me with a broad grin and a buoyant expression. "See, I never bet against nature. And I'm never disappointed."

The soldiers continued to yell and ordered him to stop advancing. They acted peculiarly. They wanted Big Al to stop, but were unwilling to run out and help him. What were they trying to do?

Suddenly, the ground exploded right under Big Al's big feet. He flew into the air and dropped like a wounded bison, but only some of him fell in the same spot. It was a terrible sight. His legs had been blown off. It had to be a landmine.

I faced away. Poor bastard. In reality, Big Al did not get very far in life. I wanted to think that he could have been an amazing person, but that would be a lie. I supposed I always look on the bright side of life, even if that brightness could be my undoing.

Rant glared at me. "What did you expect? Bad conduct is always rewarded with bad karma."

"We're in the middle of a minefield," Sarah screamed. She moved next to me and cringed in fear. "This means we're also trapped."

"Boy! Sucks big-time," Lenny whined. "Mines not good."

"Yeah, well it could be worse" Tommy said.

I stared at Tommy. "Could've been worse?"

Tommy shrugged his shoulders. "Well, it could have been us out there."

I glared at everyone as they started to crowd around me. "I need options, not banter." My eyes narrowed back at Tommy. I figured that he must have some wacky idea that might get us out of our predicament. He was our idea man and usually had a bag of surprising tricks for such an occasion. "Well?"

"Not to worry. We can get through," Tommy said without blinking an eye. "It's only a minefield."

"Oh, really! Just explosive devices hidden underground? An easy walk in the park?" My voice dripped with sarcasm.

"No," Lenny said, thinking that I was serious. "More like walk through valley of explosions! Right?"

"Well,..." Tommy said, taking a moment to think about our dilemma. "I believe there is a way to get through intact."

I glanced over and roared. "You're bat-crap crazy! They're landmines. Nobody can get through them," I roared. "Jeez, the explosives are underground. And it's still pretty dim out there."

"Would dawn be better?" Tommy asked innocently.

I rolled my eyes.

"Seriously, it's easy," he explained. "You've seen it done in old war movies. We crawl and poke the ground for the landmines. Then we simply go around them. You can go first, and everyone else can follow your trail. No sweat."

"You'll follow my trail?" I asked with a stunned look.

"Sure, man."

"Oh,... I see." I muddled the idea over. It was crazy, and yet it almost seemed reasonable. Our soldiers in World War II had used that technique to get out of similar tight spots. Humphrey Bogart did it in Sahara, or was it John Wayne in Sands of Iwo Jima? Not sure. Anyway, if they could crawl through landmines, so could we! Then, I slapped my face. That was Hollywood! I had discovered long ago that almost everything Hollywood portrayed in the movies was fake or inaccurate. Oh sure, there was a grain of truth, but most of that had been written out, revised, or left on the cutting room floor.

"We don't have any equipment," Rant commented and folded her arms.

Tommy pulled out a bent piece of metal from his knapsack. He grabbed it and then stretched to almost two feet long. "Will this do?"

"Maybe," I nodded. "What is it?"

"An old radio antenna from my car."

"Oh! Right!" I said with a blank stare. "A car antenna. Sure, why not? I'm surprised you don't have a metal detector."

"Well, I did," Tommy frowned, "but I had to leave it behind. Too big."

"Right," I nodded my head.

"It will lock into place and has a razor-sharp tip," Tommy said. "Real neat. Huh?"

I decided not to ask him why he was lugging around such a useless piece of metal, but then again, it turned out not to be so useless. Tommy's plan seemed half-baked but still feasible. I tested the antenna, and it appeared strong enough to probe for landmines. Of course, we were not flush with options. It was either move or die. Life expectancy was not too long in the middle of a minefield.

"It is great for free-diving spear fishing!" Tommy finally revealed the real purpose of his car antenna. "I speared several lingcod in Monterey."

"Okay," I said as I grasped the antenna and hoped that they had not improved landmine technology since Hitler's demise.

Naturally, Sarah protested and pleaded, arguing that someone else ought to volunteer for a suicide mission. She backed down when nobody else volunteered. As I told her, it was my responsibility to take risks and get us out of harm's way. I was their leader: I was their heroic Davy Crocket. I was not going to let anybody do this if I was not willing to do it.

I faced everyone and explained our elaborate plan. "We're going to crawl on our bellies like snakes until we reach the border fence."

"That's it," Lenny grumbled.

"No," I said. "You need to follow my lead and not make any detour."

"Just follow you?" Lenny huffed. "How we know you get through?"

"Because," I said with a sarcastic tone, "if I don't, I will be turned into little toothpick sizes of raw meat. Okay!"

"Oh," Lenny said, looking annoyed. "I think I will notice that."

After answering Lenny's asinine questions, I immediately dropped to my knees and slowly lowered myself on my stomach. I began to inch my way through a poorly plowed dirt field and stopped every few seconds to prod the earth. I would rather be watching a movie in my easy chair, but that pleasure was no longer available for me.

As I repeatedly poked the ground, I kept arguing to myself that the landmines were probably clustered only in a few selected areas. They were probably too costly to spread across a wide tract of land. At least that thought made me feel better.

I glanced behind me. Tommy was crawling directly behind me. Cliff, apparently feeling better, followed him, crawling with effort. Then came the women. Lenny took up the rear.

After about 50 feet, I came to a hard spot. I kept poking at the object. It could be a rock or a landmine. The morning light had increased and I believe I saw a small metal tip protruding from a round flat area. I zigzagged away to the right. I pointed to the object and gestured to everyone to move away from the hotspot. I should not have to say anything. My body left a wide, shallow trench. Anybody could follow it.

Halfway to the gated roadblock, a small band of soldiers started shooting at us, probably convinced that we were an advance guard preparing to launch an imminent attack. I held up my hands to show them we were unarmed. The sun was almost ready to peek over the hills, but they probably only saw dim outlines of crawling figures.

"We're civilians!" I shouted. "Don't fire!"

Surprisingly, they stopped, but enemy forces behind us had taken a keen interest in our situation. They opened fire on the mine-field with mortars and rocket-propelled grenades. We had to move much faster. As the mortars zeroed in on our position, I had to make a quick decision. It was drastic. We had to make a mad dash through the landmines. Talk about jumping from the frying pan into a powder keg. But since I had found only one mine, it was reasonable to believe that we were not destined to be fitted with prosthetic legs and arms.

"We have to make a run for it," I yelled and looked back at the others. "Follow my footsteps. If I am hit, Tommy, you take the initiative."

"No!" Sarah cried. "You'll be killed." Sarah quickly crawled next to my side. "Can't you send someone else?"

"Who?"

Sarah turned back and glanced at the others. She saw a wall of sour faces. Nobody appeared eager to fill the role of a trailblazer. She faced me again.

"Just pick someone," she said. "Anyone. You've done your share."

I glanced away, my mind in disarray.

"Someone has to do it," I said, my voice starting to tighten.

"I know." She closed her eyes and uttered a soft, "I love you."

I wanted to immediately grab her and hold on tight. Suddenly, a barrage of mortar shells rained closer to us, bringing down chunks of rocks and dirt.

"Get ready!" I got to my knees and watched the mortars set off several mines in the middle of the dirt road. I wanted to stand and make a frantic run but I froze. I started to scratch my forearm violently. I just could not move an inch. I was so scared that my body would not obey orders. The corpse of Big Al lay in the road ahead. I did not want to end up like that—all torn apart and bloodied like freshly ground hamburger. I looked at Sarah.

She looked up at me and said simply, "You can do it, Spencer!"

I nodded. Yeah, Davy Crockett would have considered this a cakewalk. No sweat. I gathered all of my strength and stood tall. If I were going out, it would be without fear. I hated fear. I hated cowering. I was not going to be that person again. I moved slowly at first, looking down for little mounds or metal spikes, but I realized that they would be impossible to see quickly enough to identify them. I walked faster and my people carefully followed my lead, trying to plant their footsteps inside of mine. I increased my speed a little more, but not so fast that my people could not keep up with me. As we passed Big Al, I saw a gaping hole in his side. Half of his head was missing. It was an awful sight.

As we got closer to the roadblock, the soldiers cheered us on.

We were only 40 yards away and the mortar fire became more intense. They were relentless in their determination to wipe us off the face of the earth. I would not be surprised if someone from Hemet's city hall was personally directing their firepower at just me.

I finally reached the fence and turned around. Several soldiers rushed up and patted on the back. It was a great feeling, but I could see that Lenny and Tommy were now struggling to carry Cliff. Lenny collapsed to the ground, huffing and puffing. I had to go back. Just as Sarah arrived, I swept past her, avoiding her arm stretched toward me. There was no time for sweet congratulations.

Reaching the three of them, I took Lenny's position and draped my hand across Cliff's shoulder, and lifted him up. "Get up!" I yelled back at Lenny. He was still lying on the ground looking drained. "Get your butt into gear!"

There was no way we could rescue another person. We had our hands full. Finally, Lenny got to his feet and staggered towards the gate. I was proud. We were going to make it.

But that is when it happened. As Tommy and I started picking up steam, a mortar shell rocked the ground to the left of me. We all three tumbled to the ground and landed in the middle of the road. A piece of shrapnel had torn into my thigh. Blood flowed out like a rushing water faucet. I slapped my hand over my burning wound to stop the bleeding, but it kept gushing. I struggled to get up, but my knees buckled and I fell backward on the hard ground. I looked at Tommy. He was knock-down flattened and crushed, appearing lifeless and dead. I crawled over to him and felt the blood oozing down from his head wounds.

"Noooooooo!" I cried out. I searched around for help, but the smoke had grown thicker as more explosions encircled us. Everything was turning gray. I groaned with pain and collapsed. This was my worst possible nightmare: I was going to die alone, bloodied, and defeated. Our struggle had been for naught. Our final odyssey had ended as a tragedy. But at least Davy Crockett also had his last final bad day.

Chapter 24

"Spencer Crane?" A man in a uniform hovered over me and seemed concerned about my comfort. He felt my forehead and pulled the white sheet up to my neck. Before I could say anything, he started to walk down the hallway. I soon blurted, "Yeah, what?"

He quickly turned back, leaned over me, and raised an eyebrow, saying "Welcome back."

"I'm in a...hospital?"

"Correct."

"Who are you?" I asked. My eyesight was still fuzzy, but the man looked generally familiar. I was never very good at matching faces with names. I could not count the number of times when someone greeted me by name, shook my hand, exchanged a few pleasantries, and I would draw a complete blank. But this time I had an inkling that I had met this man before. It was in Hemet and in my office.

"I'm James Montgomery. We talked several times."

"Yeah, I remember."

"You took a nasty hit. Luckily, the medics and your wife were there to help. Otherwise, you would have bled to death. But now, you're all in one piece."

I glanced around for Sarah.

"Looking for your wife? Well, she's doing fine, along with the others. Tommy had a few bad head gashes and Cliff is scheduled for foot surgery." James took out a clipboard and began to write. He sat in a wooden chair, stretched out his legs and yawned. "Heard it was rough. But you should have stayed clear of those mock military exercises."

"Exercises?"

"That's right. The military was engaged in military combat games. Nothing out of the ordinary."

My thoughts flashed back to the minefield and the mortar fire. I had to be hallucinating. "But... But.... What I saw was not ordinary. Right?"

"Well, sure it was. You're just a civilian. You cannot be expected to know what goes on during war games."

"But what about Hemet? Didn't it go crazy?"

"Just a local disturbance."

"You call bloody riots, mass executions, and vast tank battles 'just a local disturbance?'"

"Again, that was all part of the mock game. And I cannot go into very much detail. It's all classified," James smiled and shrugged his shoulders. "Nothing too extraordinary."

I stared at him. "You're hiding something. You know the meteorite had something to do with this. In fact, I bet you know about the other shooting stars."

"Other?" James straightened up in his chair.

"All throughout history there have been eras of mass madness and murder. Perhaps this was just another example."

James relaxed. "Possible. But we don't have any definitive evidence that proved any connection to the meteorites. The lab found nothing suspicious at the crater sites. Nothing."

"What about the animals near the crater? That was unnatural."

"Not really. We discovered that the animals were infected by a rare strain of rabies. So, it is just a coincidence. Nothing of importance."

"You're not disclosing everything. That's what I think."

"You can think whatever you want. It's a free country."

I paused and thought back to what Jack Bellamy had said at the airport—that we had been targeted, that there was nowhere to hide. Was that just disinformation? I was not naïve. I could add up all of these bizarre incidences and reach my own conclusion. I knew what was happening. His story did not add up, no matter what version of the new math he was employing. I had read George Orwell's novel. I knew that two plus two would never equal five.

"There was nothing important that happened in Hemet," James reiterated. "It was just a small misunderstanding."

I bit down on my lip and shut my eyes. "Okay," I came back with a different request. "So why was the city spying on me and my friends. What was so important about us?"

"You'll have to ask them."

"Come on, you were the ones spying on us. Right?" I tried to lift my arm to point an accusing finger at James, but the IV tube would not reach that far.

"We're not supposed to spy on our own citizens. It says so somewhere in one of our manuals. Maybe the city was just curious about your activities. You were having secret meetings at your house."

"How did you know that?"

"Oh, I believe that some city official mentioned it."

"Some city official?" I huffed.

James stopped, pulled in his lanky legs, and stood up. "Listen. Sure, some of your city leaders displayed few behavioral oddities. I mean, they're just normal people. They were probably playing too loose with the facts."

"You mean they were lying to us," I said.

"Well, I wouldn't go that far. Lying is such a nasty word," James replied.

"You must have some agenda here. You must know what really happened. I mean Hemet resembled the Reign of Terror during the French Revolution."

"Never liked history," he said briskly.

"Well. You might not have an interest in history, but someday history might take an interest in you," I suggested angrily.

"Okay," James quickly stood up." I think I have all the facts I need." He stopped writing, studied his wristwatch, and set down his clipboard.

With those few vague and hazy words, my initial debriefing was over. It was unsweet, short, and a waste of time. There were more debriefings in later days, but the flow of information mostly flooded one way. They continued to asked me stupid questions, which inspired me to give stupid replies. I had a distinct feeling that they did not know what had actually happened. They were just speculating on the causes, just as clueless as the next guy. Of course, I told them my theories. They nodded and appeared unimpressed, but I suspected they could not fully comprehend the bigger picture. After all, they were in positions of power, they were our leaders, and they were part of the government. Which meant that they were both out of touch with reality and powerful enough to forget any lessons learned.

I felt betrayed. This injustice forced me to write down my experiences. I did it in a diary format, trying to remember the exact timeline and all of the details. I did not want to forget what happened. I felt it was my duty to recall and record what really transpired in Hemet. My experience just might help somebody in the future. The truth of our profound experience needed to be told—even if nobody would listen.

* * * * *

The six of us, which included our newcomer Cliff, were relocated to a quiet town in Central California, far away from Hemet, battlefields, and crazy city councilmembers. The military arranged the rental of a large old house in the central part of Salinas. Along with housing came offers of high-paying jobs in the city government. I laughed. They were serious.

Actually, the house was an old two-story Victorian-style dwelling with many bedrooms, a large cellar, and a white picket fence. Every one of us decided to live in the same house for a while and later figure out what to do with our lives. I had no qualms about living with Tommy or Lenny, just not Rant. But I was trying to persuade myself to embrace a "live and let live" attitude, considering what we had gone through.

Our neighbors were friendly and hospitable. They loved to chat and pry into our past lives with hungry ears and little magnifying glasses. One such resident, a retired army officer, Earl Winston, was impressed that we had lived in Hemet. He had heard many stories about Hemet and the evacuation of its residents, as well as residents of neighboring cities. The official report in the news media blamed the incident on a massive natural gas leak from unknown origins. Apparently, the release of gas was a natural phenomenon, caused by a series of small earthquakes. Other sources, the more conspiratorial ones, reported that a nasty virus has ravaged the area with mind-altering afflictions. One report contended that military forces had successfully stopped a possible pandemic. My neighbor wanted to know the truth. I said I wanted that, too.

"I lived in Hemet most of my life," I told Earl a few days after we moved into our new house. I simply told him I was under orders by federal agents not to discuss the incident. That was not exactly true, but I did not want to relive the experience. Of course, my answer made Earl even more determined to uncover every gory detail.

"You must be able to say something about your exploits?" Earl asked.

"Nothing was very exciting." I was not going to tell him what I had witnessed. At first, Earl seemed unimpressed but soon developed a thirst for every tidbit of gossip.

"I heard you were right in the middle of the battle," Earl said, starting to badger me.

"Sure, but I saw very little," I said. I was getting better at lying. He seemed to believe me. Maybe I should run for some elected office.

"Well." Earl glared at me. "What I heard was rather disturbing and strange."

"I mean, we did run into a few difficult situations," I said, still trying to keep everything as secret at possible.

Lenny joined us in the front yard. "Yes, was very bad."

"I'm sure we will enjoy this neighborhood," Sarah said as she walked up and kissed me on the neck, a little reminder that the Dodgers game was going to start soon. She now watched baseball games with me. What a hoot.

"Newlyweds?" Earl asked.

Sarah nodded. "You might say that."

I just smiled. We were on the right track this time around. We actually had something in common. We had barely survived an ordeal that few Americans would ever experience. We cheated death together. Now that was a romantic adventure to tell our grandchildren.

"What part of Hemet did you live in?" Earl was getting rather nosy.

"Near downtown. Been there since childhood," I said, engaging in yet another falsehood.

"Heard the whole town has been quarantined because of some possible contaminants."

I nodded. The city was contaminated all right. It was full of power-hungry potentates and Machiavellian clowns with explosive tempers.

"What kind of contaminants?" Tommy asked as he joined our merry band of survivors.

"Not sure." Earl rubbed his forehead. "They didn't say much on the regular news. You have to go to alternative news sites to get the full details of the incident."

"News, all lies." Lenny unwrapped a Clark Bar and took a bite. "Like *Pravda* newspaper back home. Never told truth."

"Yeah," Earl said. "I suppose you cannot believe what they say anymore." In a flash, he trained his eyes on Lenny's candy bar. "You know that is very sugary, very unhealthy."

"Haven't eaten all day," Lenny said as he held it up. "Light snack."

"You're a Russky, aren't you? Don't they teach Russian kids that sugar is bad for your health?" Earl snatched the candy bar right out of Lenny's hand, threw it to the ground, and stomped on it. "Refined sugar is just so, so bad. It will kill you."

"You can't do that!" Lenny exploded with a burst of rage. "You owe me another one!"

Earl smiled. "You will thank me one day when sugar is banned. Everyone will be better off. You'll see."

We all froze.

"You know, I think I will see the mayor about this. You can't imagine how much our health would improve if sugar was prohibited," Earl declared with a sense of accomplishment.

I stepped back. This could not be happening again. Earl must have seen the horror in my face.

"Well, maybe that is going a little too far, but I bet refined sugar will no longer be allowed on supermarket shelves. Just a matter of time."

Earl stood there with a stern face, oblivious to what he had done. He flatly refused to reimburse Lenny or provide the tiniest of apologies. Earl began to boast about how he would one day banish sugar and save all of humanity. He said his anti-sugar campaign would rate as the next great civil rights movement.

As Earl dreamed of glory, Lenny circled around his scattered and crushed candy bar. He bent over and attempted to retrieve the flattened chunks of candy. We discreetly held him back.

"We understand the problems of white refined sugar," I said softly, "but we're not children. We have to make those decisions for ourselves, good or bad. Right?"

"People are too stupid to know what's good for them," Earl declared matter-of-factly. "That's why we must protect our citizens from engaging in bad lifestyles."

"Isn't that for us to decide?" I suggested.

With a sour face, Earl shook his head with a smirk that faded into a caustic frown.

"Well," I said politely. "I have to get to my Dodgers game."

"Hey! Wait!" Earl tapped my forearm lightly, "I almost forgot. Why don't you all come over for a block party tomorrow night? Half the neighborhood will be there. And there will be plenty of chow, desserts, and cold beer."

"Sure." I graciously accepted the invitation.

"Great." Earl seemed pleased.

We headed back to the house to watch the Dodgers game. I glanced back and saw Earl still standing on the sidewalk. He was staring down at the broken candy bar. He lifted his foot and repeatedly crushed it with his heel. I could see his face swelling with anger as he ground it down into the concrete.

From that moment on, I knew that our stay in Salinas would be temporary. I now knew that part of THEM was inside us all. We are them. They are us. But how far will it go? How far will THEY take it? Where will it end? I guessed that would never be up to me again.

--END--

www.ingramcontent.com/pod-product-compliance
Lightning Source LLC
Chambersburg PA
CBHW071249250626
47163CB00002B/398